THE WORLD'S END

THE WORLD'S END

God Stones Book 4

OTTO SCHAFER

Sound Eye Press

Published in 2022

ISBN 978-1-7341154-6-8 (hardback)
ISBN 979-8-9860760-1-0 (paperback)
ISBN 979-8-9860760-0-3 (ebook)

Cover design by Damonza
Editing by The Blue Garret

Sound Eye Press
www.ottoschafer.com

For Mandy.
You've been a good friend, always taking the time to pre-read my books and always with a level of detail that never fails to impress me. My work is better for it, and I appreciate you. Thank you.

Contents

Part I

INTO THE JUNGLE

Part II

VIE FOR THE PORTAL

PART I

INTO THE JUNGLE

1

No Trust

Wednesday, May 4 – God Stones Day 28
Northern Mexico

Lenny's foot raced toward Garrett's face. But Garrett didn't even flinch, slowing the unwelcome appendage with a single thought. He pulled the focus easily to his mind along with the fresh smell of forest floor and trail dust kicked up as he padded down a trail on the balls of his feet. This was how he dialed in focus and slowed time.

Like his foot, Lenny's whole body slowed to almost a stop as he balanced on the ball of his foot, frozen in the moment.

"Now, David!" Garrett shouted.

David stepped in and swung the staff low. The staff moved at full speed toward the back of Lenny's foot. They had been trying this maneuver over and over all morning, but every time David got within a couple feet of Lenny, he slowed too. This time, though, something different happened – something unexpected. David didn't slow, nor did the staff.

The staff hit the back of Lenny's foot, sweeping it out from under him. His foot slowly lifted from the ground as David's eyes went wide in surprise. "It worked!"

Garrett let go of the focus, returning Lenny to full speed, the force sending his feet high into the air. Lenny twisted, whipping his head back as he tucked his legs tight to his chest and completed a full backflip rotation, landing on a wide branch a few feet off the wicker deck.

The sound of Lenny's and David's excited voices rose like the volume on a stereo as time sped back up, rushing into Garrett's ears.

"Whoa! How the hell did you recover that, Len?" David asked in awe.

"Ha! It helped that I knew it was coming since it was, what, our tenth try? But, Garrett, you pulled it off! You slowed time just for me and not the surrounding area. This is huge, bro! Just think, you keep getting better at this and you'll be able to slow a whole army of giants and dragons while we kick their asses!" Lenny said, hooking a thumb back toward himself.

"I don't know about that, but it's a start," Garrett said, all motion and sound normal now as the Sentheye dissipated, ready to be called upon again when needed. All around him, trees groaned and creaked in their relentless forward march. Since the memory Governess had shown them of thousands of giants, dragons, and Jack being eaten by a giant kraken, they had traveled another full day and were now moving deep into Mexico.

This was Garrett's first time in Mexico. Hell, it was the first time for a lot of things, he guessed. Mexico, though, was somehow different from what he'd expected. But then, he was also traveling in a moving forest, which made it difficult to see very far. He knew a vast mountainous terrain lay to the west because he'd caught glimpses and Bre had said the Copper Canyons were over there somewhere. Then, sometime back, they'd passed by what was left of Torreón to their east. It had been hot out here on the edge of what he guessed were foothills.

For several days the terrain had been desert-like, with only patches of green now and again. The green got churned up by the roots of the giant sequoias, redwoods, and oaks. Garrett always knew when they were in a green patch, though, on account of the wet, earthy smell.

Now, as a decimated Mexico City lay somewhere to the southeast, they'd entered the mountains, and the smell of freshly churned dirt became constant. Garrett's ears popped from the altitude changes as El

Tule carried them up steep mountainsides only to descend into vast jungle valleys. He didn't know how the massive cypress kept their platforms so balanced; except for his popping ears or occasional glances over the side, he wouldn't know they were climbing up or down. He was sure El Tule balanced with his roots somehow, though Garrett had no idea how the bulky tree pulled it off.

Somewhere behind him, the sounds of metal striking metal clanked as Breanne and Paul sparred with knives across the platform.

"That's good, sis! Now, after that, thrust, step in close, and come around behind. If you're quick enough, I won't have time to reset for a strike before you drive your knife into my side."

"Garrett, don't you see? Now Paul's battle plan might actually work!" David said.

"What's this about my plan?" Paul shouted, stealing a glance over his shoulder.

"Like this!" Bre said, grunting.

"Ouch! Shit!" Paul said.

"Oh, Paul! I didn't mean it!"

Garrett spun toward them, frowning. "That didn't sound good. Come on!"

Lenny front-flipped off the tree branch, and the boys bolted toward Bre and Paul, jumping from one platform to another, climbing vines and dodging several wooden obstacles as well as the wooden dummies Governess had created at Garrett and Lenny's request.

"What happened?" Garrett asked when they reached the siblings.

"It's okay, we were just sparring. I heard you guys getting all excited, and I guess I lost my focus," Paul said, waving a hand. "She just grazed my side."

Breanne's eyes were tearing up.

"Stop that, sis. You didn't do anything wrong. When you're sparring with knives, you're bound to get a little nick now and again." Paul held one hand pressed against his side.

"That looks like more than a nick, Paul!" Breanne said, her face creased with worry. "I don't know what good knife fighting is going to do against giants, dragons, or Apep anyhow, and now look what I've done."

"Bullets are limited, and knives are what we have. We don't know what we'll face, but fighting skills and weapons training are always good to have. Even if knives are all… we got," Paul grunted, pressing harder on his side. "Besides, we can't only train our magical abilities. For one… one thing, it's too mentally exhausting. And for another… we need to keep up our fitness… Knives, swords, guns, they will all… come in handy… and we need to be…" He trailed off, frowning down at his side.

Garrett and Lenny glanced from Paul to each other, sharing a knowing look as crimson seeped between the man's fingers, betraying the claim of minor injury.

"David! You better take a look," Lenny shouted.

Gabi came running. *Oh! Ouch, that's a lot of blood,* she said in mind speak. Gabi almost never spoke aloud, not since they'd climbed aboard El Tule.

"Yeah, it is. Let me see it, big guy," David said, mustache scrunching over pursed lips.

"If Garrett can hone his time-manipulation skills to slow attackers as they come… we'll be able to slip in, inflict damage, and then slip out… before they know what hit them," Paul said, his face still fixed in a painful grimace as he lifted his shirt to reveal both an entry wound and an exit wound.

The long, double-edged stiletto Breanne had scavenged off a man she had been forced to shoot in southern Mexico had entered Paul's side from the front and pierced clean through. Garrett couldn't imagine what that must have been like for her and Gabi – to have to shoot real people.

Garrett looked at the girl's face, creased with this new worry. *Worry on top of worry,* he thought. Bre was carrying so much of it, and not just for Paul's knife wound. That could be fixed easily enough. But he knew what really ate at her was her concern for her brother, Ed, a prisoner of Pando the tree queen. Ed was being held hostage along with the rest of humanity. Now it was up to Garrett and the others to save them. All they had to do was get to another planet and find a magical item that would give the trees of Earth the ability to remain unbound – an item he wasn't even sure existed – and then somehow get back to Earth. *Six months to save the world.* This was Garrett's mantra now. This was all that mattered. That's how long Pando had given him – six months from the moment the portal opened. *Six months to get there and back,* though he didn't know how. But know-how simply didn't matter, did it? At least he had his friends, and somehow together they would figure it out. They had to. If they failed, Ed was dead along with every human on the planet. Garrett's stomach felt like it tipped over at the thought.

He suddenly realized Bre's worried face might mirror his own. Boy, was he feeling the god-awful weight of it all? Like a giant boulder pressing down on him and every decision he'd made up until now. He'd run off to save the girl and she'd ended up saving him, convincing the queen of trees that Garrett could help them – that if freed, he could find a way to keep them unbound. Bre's quick thinking hadn't just saved him, she'd saved them all. But it was he who'd made the promise, wasn't it? It was he and he alone who'd sworn they could do the impossible. *Six months, Garrett.*

Blood oozed faster now from Paul's wound, pulling Garrett back to the moment.

Paul quickly slapped his hand back over the wound and pulled a face.

Breanne gasped. "Oh, Paul."

"It's all good, Bre," Lenny said, slapping David on the shoulder. "You know old night bright is going to fix him right up."

"Sure. No problem." David shrugged, rubbing his hands together as though he were Mr. Miyagi.

"David. Wait. Listen to me," Garrett said. "I want you to heal him without passing out." He knew David could do it. He had healed a couple of bumps and scrapes already, and even Breanne's and Gabi's blistered feet, all without passing out. Though he had appeared to black out momentarily while healing the blisters – and then he'd yacked. But it was progress. Gross, but progress nonetheless.

"Oh, I don't know, Garrett. This is pretty bad. I haven't healed anything like this without passing out."

"We believe in you, little guy," Lenny said. "Besides, if you pass out, I'm going to use Breanne's dagger to shave off that lip brow of yours."

"That's not funny. If I pass out, you better stay good and far away, Len. You hear me? Good and far!"

"Settle down. I'm just messing… or am I?"

"Garrett, you better not let—"

"Guys, I'm bleeding over here."

From across the platform, Pete and Governess quickly approached.

Lenny nudged Garrett in the arm with his elbow. "Look, here comes old Captain Kirk and his latest love interest."

"Captain Kirk?" Garrett asked.

"You know how old Kirk was always banging every space alien chick he encountered. Well, that's our Petey," Lenny snorted.

"Oh my God, Lenny!" Breanne laughed.

"What's going on, guys… Oh shit, that doesn't look good," Pete said, wincing at Paul.

"Yeah, he'll be fine. David is about to heal him *without* passing out," Garrett said.

"Oh, cool."

"Yeah, and if he fails, I get to shave his mustache while he's out." Lenny smiled.

Governess's auburn eyebrows raised. "Shaving the little chubby one? I shall enjoy observing this human activity."

Garrett couldn't help but laugh. He wasn't sure where he stood with the tree woman and, after what she had done to Ed, he didn't know if he could ever truly trust the creature. Paul certainly wouldn't. Besides, she'd made no secret of her feelings toward humans and her desire to see them all dead. Pando's order that Governess accompany them and ensure that the tree queen's interests were served was the only thing keeping the volatile peace between them. So they were allies, for now anyway, and if they could somehow pull this off, maybe they would stay that way.

"I'm not getting shaved! Pete, tell her to stop calling me that!" David said.

"I'm getting lightheaded over here," Paul said, looking pale.

"Just focus, David. Stay awake and you won't have to worry about Lenny shaving your 'stache," Garrett said.

David's face twisted in betrayal. "I thought you were better than this, Garrett," he said, motioning to Paul to sit.

I'm praying to Mother Mary for you, David, Gabi said, squeezing his hand.

"And I am praying to Mother Druesha that you slip into unconsciousness," Governess said, her lip teasing at a grin. It was slight, but Garrett saw, and it gave him a hint of hope.

David, on the other hand, glared at the tree woman sourly but held his tongue, turning his attention to Paul.

Paul kneeled with a grunt and then sat with his back against a modified wing chun wooden dummy. Governess had grown it right from the wicker floor. A normal wooden training dummy was just that, wooden and stationary, with little stubby arms that allowed you to work elbow, forearm, and palm strikes. However, the dummy Governess had created had arms that actually moved into different configurations as the user threw strikes and blocks. It was more like practicing with a real thinking and reacting person than it was a wooden dummy.

"Move your hand, Paul," David said, reaching for Paul's bloody wounds.

Paul shot something between a smile and a grimace at David. "You know, back in the day when I was flying missions, the ones *they* don't let me talk about, I… I lost a lot of friends, David."

Garrett caught a look of surprise from Breanne. It was part disbelief and part confusion, and without her saying so, Garrett knew they were hearing something seldom spoken – maybe never spoken.

"What we… I… wouldn't have given for you back then when we were in the shit."

David nodded and tried to smile, but his lips pressed into a tight line as he placed one hand over the entry wound and the other over the exit.

Paul grabbed David's wrists, staying his hands.

David looked up, confused.

Garrett could see it. The man needed to say this, whatever it was. If he didn't, maybe he never would.

"I tried to land the Black Hawk easy, but there wasn't going to be anything easy about how we went… went down… Nothing easy about the days that followed, either. I lost two men in the crash, dead on impact. No one escaped injury… except for me. Goddammit, except for me. In the end, I couldn't save them, David. I couldn't keep them alive… I wanted to die then. I wanted to die with my men. And Samantha… Samantha was under my command… She was… well, there was something between us, but we hadn't acted on it. We were professionals, but still it was there you… you know? And in the end, her wounds were too… too much, and I couldn't save her either."

Tears spilled down Breanne's cheeks as they all listened in a sudden and somber quiet. Garrett had known that Paul served in the military and knew he'd been an army pilot, but he'd had no idea he'd been in battle or that he'd lost soldiers.

"After I was captured and… and, well… David, I just hope you understand the gift you've been given is… is truly special," he said, letting go of David's wrist.

"Here goes," David said quietly and closed his eyes.

Garrett reached for Breanne, squeezing her hand consolingly.

Paul nodded. "Now stay awake this time, kid," he said, closing his own eyes.

"A ten spot says he passes out," Lenny whispered.

Garrett elbowed him in the ribs.

David glowed.

Garrett knelt down next to him. "Open your eyes, David, but don't let go of it."

David's brows knitted as he opened his eyes, eyes that now glowed golden like sunshine. One shone dimmer than the other as he squinted, fighting for control, his mustache twitching like cat whiskers.

"Hold it loosely, David, like a fishing pole with a bite on it. Hold it like you are about to set the hook and you don't want to scare the fish."

David lifted his hands from Paul's side just a little. Golden light, thick as honey, filled the space between the boy's hands and Paul's side.

"That's it!" Garrett whispered urgently. "Focus on the fishing pole, David. Give it just enough. Don't scare the fish."

David's eyes rolled back as he listed to the side.

"I told you he was going to pass out. Bre, your dagger please," Lenny said, motioning to the stiletto strapped to her lower leg.

David reached out with one now-bloody hand and balanced himself, blinking back whatever fog had tried to consume him.

The golden glow faded.

"David? You okay?" Garrett asked, placing a hand on David's shoulder to help steady him.

David nodded. "I think so." Still blinking, he looked to Paul's side. "Are you okay, Paul?"

Paul balled up the bottom of his shirt and wiped the blood away, revealing only a light scar set into his dark skin. "Aches a little. Ghost pain I guess, but yeah… yeah, I'm good!"

"I did it, Garrett! I did what you said, and it worked! How did you know?" David asked.

But before he could answer, David bent forward and hurled onto the wicker deck.

"Humans, such vile creatures," Governess said with disdain as she rolled her eyes dramatically.

Ignoring Governess, David wiped his mouth. "I'm okay. Garrett? How did you know?"

"I didn't know. I just knew your two favorite things were video games and fishing, and I didn't have an analogy for video games," Garrett said, smiling. "Listen, your problem isn't tapping into your focus, David. It's controlling it. From what I can tell, when you tap into it, you're putting it full on like a water faucet cranked open." Garrett looked at the others. "It isn't just you either. I think this goes for all of us. I think it's like a rule or something. We can manipulate it and we can control it. We just have to learn what helps us focus, but more, once we have the focus, we have to control it – we have to learn how to make it flow."

“I really wish I could have shaved that ’stache,” Lenny said, feigning disappointment that was apparently lost on David.

“You’re a dick, Lenny! You know, I was going to give you a cool superhero name, but not now.” He pointed at Pete. “Eagle Eye!” Then Breanne. “The Oracle!” Next, he looked at Garrett. “Time Bandit!”

Garrett frowned, not so sure he wanted to be called the bandit of anything.

Hooking a thumb over his shoulder toward Gabi, David said, “Mind Meld!” He nodded at Paul next. “Flex!”

Lenny laughed. “Flex?”

“Yeah, laugh it up, Len, because I decided on your name just now! Super Dick!”

Garrett threw a hand against his forehead, noticing Bre’s eyes go wide.

Lenny drew in a deep breath, opening his mouth to speak. “Why, David, however did you—”

“Oh my god, Lenny!” Breanne shouted, clapping her hands over Gabi’s ears. “Gabi is right here!”

Pete shook his head in disgust.

David’s face flushed. “That’s not what I—”

“It’s David’s name!” Lenny said, pointing. “Besides, Bre, I’m sorry, but your innocent little Gabi is well on her way to joining the navy.”

“What are you talking about?”

“The kid cusses like a sailor! And she’s climbing the ranks fast!”

Gabi!? Breanne asked.

Gabi smiled and shrugged. *David taught me all the curse words in English… Well, the ones I didn’t already know.*

Breanne blinked.

“Listen up, superheroes,” Paul said. “I don’t mean to get serious here, but can we just talk about the major breakthrough this was today? Garrett slowed time for just Lenny, allowing David to attack him without getting caught up in the time attack.”

“Saw that, did you?” Garrett smiled.

“Like I said, I overheard.”

“Oh, that’s a sweet name for it, too! Time attack,” David said, grinning.

Paul gave David the side eye. "Anyway," he continued, "Garrett, if the battle plan David and I have been creating is going to work, you need to keep practicing. You think you can slow two people at once with one of us moving in between them at full speed?"

"No, not yet. But, hey, if David can stay awake while he heals, and if I can slow Lenny but not David – anything is possible. We just need time."

"Time is the one thing you have little of, Garrett Turek," Governess said. "We will arrive at what you humans call a fork in the road two days hence."

"Oh wow, is your boyfriend, Petey, teaching you new metaphors?"

"Lenard Wade, my intelligence requires no tutelage from humans. The breadth of my knowledge far surpasses the most intelligent of your species."

"Well, Your Shrubbiness, at least you're modest."

She cocked her head to one side like a curious cat. "Tread lightly, Lenard Wade. I find no humor in the incessant noise of your vocal folds."

"Whatever, big bush," Lenny said, waving her off and turning his attention back to Paul. "Tell me again why David is helping you create a battle plan? He's only been in one fight, and he got his ass royally kicked by Jack."

"Literally kicked, if memory serves," Pete chimed in.

"I already told you he understands battle magic better than any of you."

"Battle magic isn't a real thing!" Lenny said, shaking his head.

"It is now!" Paul growled, pointing up at Lenny as he pushed himself to his feet. "And who better to help plan how we fight in a unit with magic than a kid who lives on role-playing games?"

David was beaming. "Yeah, Lenny. Boy, I'd sure like to see you try to strategize a group attack on a level one hundred and ten dungeon mummy in the Crypt of Anguish!"

Lenny looked at David like he'd just spoken a completely different language. "I'm not even going to respond to that – other than to say you're stupid."

Garrett held up a hand. "Governess, please, finish what you were saying about two days? The fork in the road?"

"Ah, yes. In two full days we will depart El Tule so that he may carry on toward the pyramid, where he will take his place at the front of the forest."

I don't want him to go! Gabi shouted.

"Gabi De Leon, El Tule must fulfill his destiny. The burden of leading the charge to destroy the portal falls upon his canopy. In this, my queen has spoken. Thus, if we are to go to this cenote of yours, we shall have to depart on foot."

Gabi crossed her arms, and her eyes shot daggers at Governess, as if it were Governess herself sending El Tule to his death.

"This is the price owed for coming to the defense of humans," Governess said flatly.

"How close can he get us?" Breanne asked.

"We will depart El Tule at the farm you and Gabi De Leon used for shelter."

Breanne chewed at her lower lip. "That's another day on foot from there to the cenote, and since the cenote isn't on the way to the pyramid, we have to double back to the farm, which will be another day. Then from there we will have another long day of hiking to the pyramid." Her voice was laced with worry.

"Garrett, assuming this all goes to plan, we won't get to the temple for another four or five days. How do we know the portal won't open and close before we get there?" Pete asked.

He absolutely hated what he was about to say, but he knew it was right – it had to be. "Because we aren't there yet."

Pete frowned. "Because we aren't there yet?"

The portal won't open until the sages are there, Gabi said, filling all their minds with her timid voice.

"So, it's a matter of faith?" Breanne asked.

Garrett winced at the word as he watched her glance across the group until her eyes fell on him. Then, answering her own question, she said, "It's always been about faith."

Garrett supposed it had, but he didn't have to like it. "If we believe in prophecy, then the portal should open when we get there, and the

Keepers of the Light should arrive at the same time. Don't look at it as a god thing. This Turek… whatever he is must be beyond what we are, right? So, faith comes in by believing he is behind the scenes pulling some strings, that's all."

"Okay, what matters now is we continue to train our abilities like our lives depend on it. Because they do," Paul said. Then his face went stone rigid as a dark veil seemed to cloud his features. "Look, guys, I don't like to talk about this much, but I have been in places where things got… well, FUBAR, and I'm telling you there is one thing that always rings true. When the shit gets deep, it boils down to training, plain and simple. There will be no time to think. We have to have a plan, and that plan needs to be drilled into us so that when we are in the shit and everything goes to hell – and believe me, it will go to hell – we don't think, we react."

A quiet fell over the group as they nodded somberly.

"Sounds good," Pete said, turning to follow Governess, who had already begun her retreat across the platform.

"Wait, hold on a sec," Breanne said hopefully. "Governess, don't you know some ancient god language you can teach us? I heard Jurupa use a strange language to command the tree roots, and then you both used it when creating sleeping quarters and the platforms."

"That's right! Governess, you used commands at the river and when you created this training area," Lenny said.

Governess turned back to the group, but she didn't approach. "The language you speak of is protected by our kind. It is not to be shared with anyone outside of our forest, least of all flesh sac—" Governess stopped abruptly, then continued. "Least of all humans."

"Now hold on a minute. If you're fighting with us, then you need to be in this all the way. No secrets," Garrett said.

Paul sneered. "I saw what you did to Ed. When we're in the thick of it, who's to say you won't turn on us? Now you want to hold out on us. This just further proves we can't trust you!"

"I agree with Paul," Lenny said. "We can't keep secrets if we're going to be one team."

"Yeah, you put your hand in the pile, Governess," David said.

"Ah, Paul Moore, you wish to judge *me* and my allegiances? You, the one who has launched missiles into forests. You, who are responsible for killing more trees than any other here. Yes, I know about you and your flying war machine."

"But you tried to kill my brother!" Paul shot back.

"And you killed thousands of my brothers!" Governess fired back.

Paul's anger softened. "I was a helicopter pilot. I did what I had to do. War is ugly. I make no excuses."

"What you had to do?" Governess said, spitting the words, then turning to Lenny. "And you, Lenard Wade," she said, pointing a finger. "You wish to pretend you are righteous? You say we cannot keep secrets and yet you harbor the greatest secret of all, do you not?" Governess's soft features hardened to oak as her face contorted to a sneer and wood grains streaked her facial features. "Typical humans, irreproachable as long as the deed suits their cause."

The group exchanged uneasy glances; all of them knew, but none said it. Lenny's secret was his and his alone. Besides, if he did tell Governess, what would she do with the information? Would she tell Queen Pando? Would Pando use Lenny as a pawn against Apep? Lenny was half dökkálfar, son of Apep's brother Syldan and thus heir to the throne of Osonian. If Apep knew, he'd do anything to kill Lenny, maybe even give Queen Pando a way to stay unbound. If Governess had somehow found out the truth about Lenny, Pando could already know and, for all Garrett knew, they could be walking into a trap. But if she knew the truth of it and planned to betray them, why bring it up at all?

When no one spoke, Governess finally did. "This is what I suspected. You require trust, but you give none in return. Such smugness for a species of inferior intellect is to be expected, I suppose." The petite tree woman with fair skin and auburn hair spun on her heels and walked away.

Pete leaned into the group and whispered, "Before you accuse me, no, I didn't tell her. I would never do that. But if we want her to trust us and teach us what she knows, you might think about what she said." He pulled back, turning toward Governess.

"I'll think about it," Lenny said, frowning. "Hey, where do you think you're going? You should be training too, Pete."

"Oh, I am. I've been practicing on the upper level with an ancient tree lady who apparently has an intellect far superior to yours, Len." He shrugged. "But then, who doesn't?"

Garrett tipped his head up toward the uppermost platform. El Tule no longer contained one, but now three levels, thanks to Governess's modifications. Each level was offset from the main one in different sections of the canopy, allowing room to spread out and train.

"I got news for you! You're human too, dumbass!" Lenny said.

"Yeah, but she was definitely talking about you, bro!" Pete laughed.

"Okay, Petey, show us what you learned!" Lenny said, spinning his staff.

"Not yet, Len. Let me keep practicing. But trust me, it's going to blow your mind."

"Well, just remember, I have a clear view of the platform from here, so when you leave, I am going to make it a point to keep my eye on you."

Pete's eyes narrowed toward Lenny as if squinting into the sun.

Lenny's staff flew from his hands as if yanked by an invisible force. "Hey!" he shouted.

"Really, Len, you're going to eavesdrop?" Pete said, his *r* sounds distorting excessively – a clear sign he was getting all wound up.

Lenny spun, chasing his staff to the edge of the platform, snatching it just before it rolled off. "Dick!" he shouted back over his shoulder.

"Nice, Pete!" Breanne said, as Garrett gave him a fist bump.

"Alright, I'm off to learn so that next time I can toss Lenny off the platform along with his staff." Pete smiled.

"Later, Eagle Eye!" David grinned.

Paul unfolded a piece of paper and made a note. "Better control of his telekinesis. This is good. This is very good."

Then why, Garrett wondered, why did something deep in the pit of his stomach feel so horribly wrong?

2

A Crimson Breeze

Tuesday, May 3 – God Stones Day 27
Panama Bay

Jack steeled himself for the insanity of what he was about to do. He could stop. He didn't have to do this. There were, after all, other options. Cerberus, Jack's three-headed dragon, had survived the attack from the elders. He was okay and airborne. If Jack continued to disease the rotten pocket of flesh he was sheltering in, he could work his way through the kraken's throat, or mouth, or whatever the hell this long tube of teeth was. Like a cancer, he could use the Sentheye to eat through until he penetrated the outer wall. Then he could jump into the ocean and swim for it until Cerb found him. And maybe, just maybe, they could get away before one of the monster's hundred-foot-long tentacles slapped them from the sky.

Sure, he could make a run for it, but here was the thing: Jack had never been smart enough to back away from a fight, no matter how big the other guy was. No matter how bad a licking he was sure to get – Jack Nightshade didn't run. Something inside him wouldn't let him, not even when it was for his own good. Well, except once, in a tunnel back in Petersburg, when he chose to jump into the river rather than finish the fight with Garrett Turek. He regretted that, regretted it like hell, and there was no way he was ever going to feel like that again. Besides, no one was going to write songs about his fight in the tunnel with Garrett, just like no one was going to write songs about him and Cerb if he ran from this.

Far as Jack figured it, the only way out of this hell was to go through it. Careful not to slip, he peered out over the side of the rotten cavity of flesh. He still had the sword he'd found wedged up to its hilt between two spikes of the kraken's teeth. He'd stuck it back into the fleshy floor of his little rotted nook by leaning heavily on the hilt and driving the blade as deep as it would go. The handle against his hip was the only thing between Jack and slipping over the edge. Above him, nephilbock and dragons plummeted from the sky, roaring and screeching, dropped from tentacles high above the toothy opening. While only twenty yards below him, the meat-grinder of spiked-tooth death oscillated back and forth like a hungry garbage disposal, gnashing bone and shredding flesh, devouring everything and shunting it deeper into itself.

Jack nodded to himself. *That's my path.* Jack wasn't jumping away, not like he had with Garrett – not like a coward. No, he was jumping in.

Jack! Tell me where you are! I will come get you! Cerb urged, filling Jack's mind with his desperate pleas.

Stand by, Cerb!

JAAACCCKKKK! Whatever you are thinking, don't!

They're going to write songs about us, Cerb! They're going to bow before us and sing songs! Cerb was still yelling, but Jack tuned him out, focusing instead on the grinding teeth. Foot-long serrated spikes, white as dead animal bones bleached under a summer sun, spiraled downward, changing to crimson, then black before vanishing into the soup of mangled flesh. That's where he focused, that's where he took his mind and pushed. He leaned out, one hand on the hilt of the sword, the other reaching, as if his hand could somehow span the twenty yards and reach into the gore.

Another young dragon bounced off the wall of spiked teeth, squawking as it tumbled down into the kraken's throat, teeth ripping one wing from its back, then another. The dragon's eyes went wide as it screamed. Jack was sure it was staring right at him as it was pulled apart. But there was nothing he could do. Then the dragon folded in half and was gone, or at least what it had been was gone – what remained now was something else. Then the kraken swallowed and there was nothing.

Anger swelled inside Jack as disease poured into the throat of the kraken. The kaleidoscope of teeth hitched and seized as if someone had tossed a wrench into its gears. The bottom of the beast's throat constricted tight. Constricting and compressing nearly all the way up to Jack's delicate position in his nook. Blood and gore rose up through the beast's gorge, splashing over Jack, warm and rank. *Choke, you bitch! Choke to death!* Jack kept pouring it on, but the life force of the kraken was filling him to the brink. He needed to release it soon.

From below came a gurgling sound as the kraken's throat opened in a wide gasp, swallowing the new carnage, and with it chunks of its own now-rotted throat and teeth.

Somewhere beyond the electric hum of power filling Jack's mind, Cerb was there, shouting to him as if from a great distance. Jack stared down into the open pit of black, diseasing and taking, pouring and pulling. He screamed as the hum became a whole beehive of buzzing in his head.

A slimy tentacle slapped like raw meat on a cutting board against the wall of the kraken's throat to his left. Then another to his right. They groped between the spiked teeth like a finger digging for a piece of stuck food. Jack's body shook as he struggled to hold on to what little of the kraken's life he'd stolen. More tentacles and still more plunged in from above, trying to find the source of this new pain. He couldn't stay here. Any second a tentacle would find him.

Jack glanced once more, past the now-rotted grinder of teeth and into the newly opened pit below, but all he could see was void of light – a black abyss of nothing. For all he knew, there was no bottom to it. *You don't have to do this,* he told himself. *Blast a hole through the wall and get the hell out of here!* Jack's body shook uncontrollably while every fiber of his flesh pulsed, as if about to melt. Fear gripped him like a seizure, but he knew he only had seconds.

Through a clenched jaw, he shouted, "Fuck it!" and tipped over the side.

Jack dropped fast, gravity yanking him downward, twenty yards gone in a short, panicked gasp. Just before he reached the hole, a tentacle struck him in the side, slipping across his body but failing to grab on.

Once through the meat grinder, darkness swallowed him and for three long seconds he was weightless, wrapped in darkness. Whether he was in outer space, a kraken's belly, or hell itself, Jack couldn't say. When he finally found bottom, he knew it was the last.

Plunging through a layer of chunky liquid, Jack splashed down hard. Flailing, he kicked himself up and gulped rotten air. He would have gagged if not for his locked jaw. Seized too were his fist and toes, both curled into cramps as the grip of the kraken's life power swelled in him like a balloon ready to pop. Never had he pulled in so much power. Jack had pulled life from people, ancient trees, and even an elder dragon, but never something like this. He'd held the stem closed as long as he could, but no more.

He let it all go.

All the bottled-up power lit the stomach of the kraken as it poured from Jack, black but electric, dark but shining. Sentheye hit the great monster's stomach wall, ripping it open with a wet tear. Light filled the kraken's belly, revealing the horror of nephilbock chunks intermingled with dragon parts. It was all he could do to tread in the thick stew, to stay head above slop.

A moan from the kraken vibrated his very soul as the monster listed to one side, ocean pouring in like a tidal wave through the massive wound.

Jack pulled a breath as the force hit him, pushing him under and spinning him beneath the current.

He swam as hard as he could, but he couldn't be sure he was swimming up! It felt like up. If it wasn't, he was dead.

In his head, Cerb spoke: *Jack! What did you do? How did you…*

But he couldn't focus on Cerb. He couldn't breathe, and he had to breathe!

Finally, Jack pulled in a breath of coppery water as his head broke the surface. He choked and spit out bits and pieces, choked and gasped again. He spun around, trying to get his bearings, and realized with horror that he was rising.

Jack burst back through the rotted meat-grinder, rising up the throat of the kraken with the surge of water pressure. *Cerb! Cerb, help me!*

Where, Jack! Where are you?

Jack looked up. A hundred feet to the top, and he was moving fast. *I'm coming out its mouth, Cerb! I'm coming fast!*

I'm coming!

When Jack breached the mouth of the beast, an explosion of projectile kraken vomit accompanied him. For a moment, time seemed to slow as he soared higher and higher into a perfectly blue Panama Bay sky. Crimson streaked down Jack's face, but the sun was warm, and for a moment he couldn't smell the vileness around him or on him. The air was fresh, just like everything an ocean breeze should be.

As the moment played out in a surreal contrast of horror and ecstasy, gravity took hold. Jack slowed to a stop and, in an immeasurably brief moment, a lifetime seemed to pass. He didn't know if he was about to die, but he knew what he had done. He knew as he hung motionless that he had killed the kraken. Jack Nobody, from Petersburg, Illinois. Son to a shitty father and an absent mother. Brother to a murdered sibling and creator of a three-headed dragon named Cerberus the Mighty! Jack knew in that nanosecond they *would* write songs about him and, *by god,* he would never be forgotten!

After the longest, shortest second, gravity tugged at Jack, and he fell. But he wasn't scared. Even as he caught flailing tentacles in his peripheral, he wasn't scared. Even as the angered cry of a dying kraken threatened to pop his eardrums, he wasn't scared. Even though he was plummeting back toward the toothy mouth of a monster, he *was not* scared. *Danny, look at us now. Look at what we did!*

As Jack's eyes rolled back into his head, he felt the tentacle around his waist. He forced consciousness to hold and his eyes to open. What he saw next brought out the biggest smile ever. Wrapped around his waist was not a tentacle – but a talon.

Cerb. My brother!

Can you hear them, Jack? Can you hear them chanting your name? Jack Nightshade, defeater of the forest! Slayer of the ocean mother! His mind filled with laughing and he laughed too, the laughter taking him away into unconsciousness.

3

Let Them Sing

Tuesday, May 3 – God Stones Day 27
Panama Bay

King Helreginn stood on the beach, watching the yellow sun turn blood orange as it slowly dipped behind the heap of a dead kraki. Not any kraki, but the mother of all kraki, Hafgufa. The carcass of the sea mother was too large to sink. Instead, she tilted sideways, resting on the ocean floor yet still protruding high above the surface. Unmoving in death, her strange head slanted like that of a curious Great Wolf. No longer did her appendages flail for prey, nor her bottomless hunger devour all within reach. Hafgufa – the kraki of all kraki. He wondered, what was she curious about? The great king imagined her asking how a human boy could best her, the mother of the ocean, the goddess of the sea. *Hafgufa, in this we both ponder.* But if it were true, if the boy had killed Hafgufa… then there could only be one answer.

The great sea mother had followed Helreginn from the center of the world, intent on vengeance. Seeing her here, now, erased any doubt she would have followed him to the ends of this planet and the next, if that's what it took to avenge the death of her child.

Thinking back, the skull of the young kraki had once made the perfect throne and its bones the perfect armor. Enough to outfit all of his High Guard. Even now, as his High Guard warriors helped the last of his people onto the beach, they wore their distinct black bone armor.

In the distance, beyond the break of the surf, dozens of long black tentacles floated a hundred feet in every direction from the black heap. High above, dragons circled slowly, making their way toward the north – toward the mighty king's destiny.

"My king," Gato said, approaching as he slammed a fist into his breast armor.

"My son," Helreginn said, returning the gesture. He did little to hide his joy that his favorite son had survived the river crossing, the kraki, and those cursed trees. The gods continued to smile upon him. "You look well."

"Yes, Father," Gato answered.

Helreginn's choice to use "my son" was permission enough for Gato to speak less formally, using "Father" rather than "King." "Tell me, how many did we lose to the sea mother?"

"Many – more than a thousand," Gato said, tipping his head in reverence.

Helreginn gazed back out to sea. His heart panged for the loss of his people. He knew without the need for confirmation that some of the lost would be his own children. Perhaps some of his wives were lost too. No matter, every one of the more than twenty-five thousand nephilbock were his children – his family. Since returning to the surface, he had lost thousands, but their numbers were still great. Hafgufa was dead, and they were well over halfway to the pyramid – over halfway to joining their nephilbock gods and going home to fight the final battle!

"After thousands upon thousands of years, Gato, Hafgufa is no more."

"Those who saw are calling him Jack the God Killer. I have heard some singing of this day, Father."

"Then it is true?"

"I witnessed it myself. The human boy was eaten. Then sometime later, Hafgufa split open, and the boy rose from her accursed mouth as she died."

Helreginn had not seen it himself. The king had been one of the first to cross. A giant tree had fallen on a handful of his High Guard, pinning them beneath the water. He and several others took up ax and sword to free them while defending against the onslaught of trees. "Where is the human now?"

"The three-headed dragon took him away," Gato said, pointing northward.

"My son, this aberration is no mere dragon or human, for only a god could kill a god. Let our people sing of this day. I cannot say why this god has taken the form of a human and a three-headed dragon, but I have a feeling we will see it again," Helreginn said, turning his attention from the ocean to the north. "When we do, we will have songs prepared for his praise."

"Yes, Father."

"Let us move inland. The way is forward. The earth is scorched. Let us not wait for these cursed trees to fill the void the dragons have created. Send word back through the ranks. Pyramid formation, Gato! The gods are waiting!"

4

Signs of the End

Thursday, May 5 – God Stones Day 29
Rural Chiapas State, Mexico

Breanne's eyes sprang open. She had been dreaming about Times Square in New York City. It was like the dream she'd had on Oak Island, full of dragons screeching, buildings melting beneath the strange flame, and screams… horrible screams.

After blinking away the nightmare, the first thing Breanne noticed was the cold, which was odd considering the last couple of days of travel had taken them deep into southern Mexico. If anything, the climate should be even warmer than the last two days, which had been cloudless Mexican scorchers.

It was still pitch black and her exhaustion told her she'd only just fallen asleep, but the dream felt like it had been going on for hours. With no stars or moon above, the sky was an impenetrable membrane of darkness, which could only mean clouds. That's when she noticed the second thing. Accompanying the all-wrong cold were tiny flecks of ice melting against the skin of her arm as it hung exposed over the side of her cocoon. She pulled it back. Not ice, snow. Snow in southern Mexico?

"It's freaking snowing," Lenny announced from the direction of his own bunk.

Breanne dragged her pack onto her lap and rummaged through, finding her grey hoodie. She tugged it on and zipped it up. She could hear the others digging through their own packs.

Gabi, are you warm enough? Do you need my sweater? She remembered the girl had an oversized flannel but wasn't sure that would be enough.

Gabi, I have a stocking cap and some gloves, David said.

Thanks, David! I'll be fine, Bre.

We are approaching the farm. Governess's voice echoed in her mind. They were all using mind speak as much as possible now. Sometimes they would forget and speak aloud, or they would use it, but they wouldn't all hear each other, and sometimes everyone heard everything when they meant only one person to hear. It was still Paul who struggled most. Despite this, it was Paul who insisted on it. He said they would be much better in battle if they could communicate this way rather than yelling. And in theory, no one would hear what they were saying.

Governess, can you do something about the dark? Garrett asked.

I can see fine, Lenny said.

Well, good for you, kid, but I can't see my hand in front of my face, Paul said.

Such a limited species, Governess said as a small green glow grew until it lit the surrounding platform.

The tree woman was holding what Breanne thought was a green torch on the end of a crooked tree branch, but it wasn't fire, it was just light.

Come forward, Peter Ashwood.

Pete's silhouette stepped into the green glow as he reached forward and took the torch. A thought pricked Breanne's mind. Why did she choose Pete first? But the thought was short-lived as Governess whispered something and another torch grew in her hand and lit with the green liquid glow.

Governess was being guarded with the language of the gods now that she knew they wanted to learn it. Breanne wished she had taken notes all the times she had heard Jurupa, Governess, and Apep speak the strange words, but for the love of god she couldn't remember a single word now.

Breanne Moore, come forward. Breanne pushed herself from the warmth of her cocoon bunk, slung her pack over her shoulder, and stepped into the glow, taking hold of the strange wooden torch.

You can lead us to a place to shelter for the remainder of the night? Governess asked.

Breanne nodded.

David hurriedly pulled fruit from the vines and began stuffing it in his pack.

Governess held up a hand. *Halt! It will be senseless for you to carry this extra weight when I can grow more at will.*

David stood with his arms full, like a burglar caught in the act. *You sure you will make us more?*

Do not worry, chubby one. I will not let you go hungry.

David dropped his arms, dumping the fruit out onto the floor. *You're going to knock it off with that chubby crap, lady!*

Breanne noticed Garrett and Lenny whispering over by their bunks, and she wondered what or who they were whispering about. *No secrets, huh?*

She walked toward them. Shit, what if they were talking about her? The last several days hadn't been easy, and she could feel the tension growing between herself and Garrett. Who was she kidding? It was more than just tension – it was attraction intermingled with guilt for feeling attracted to a boy while the world was in chaos and everyone she loved was in danger. Over the past few days, she and Garrett had spent hours talking, telling each other their entire life stories. She felt like she had known this boy forever. Despite the guilt and the horrible timing, it was killing her not to be with him, but she couldn't let him see the truth of it. She couldn't let him see how badly she wanted him.

She had only ever kissed a boy. Well, except that one time with Jacob when his hands wandered a little. But she had stopped that when he tried to go under her shirt. The thought of Garrett going under her shirt made her suddenly flush warmly. She shook her head, scolding herself. *Focus, girl!* She couldn't let him see… she was falling in love with him.

Did she just admit that to herself? She couldn't be falling in love. She didn't even know what love was – but this sure felt like what she thought it should feel like. *Shit.* Love or not, she needed to be clear-headed, and she needed Garrett focused. If these feelings were really… were really *that*, they would have to wait.

"You two want to share what you're over here being all secret about?" she whispered.

"We don't know what you're talking about," Lenny said in an even lower whisper.

Breanne narrowed her eyes and crossed her arms. "You two are talking out loud, which tells me you're obviously afraid someone will hear your mind speak. You're also being totally obvious about it. Now what's up?"

Garrett leaned in close, his warm breath washing over her ear, eliciting instant goose bumps. "Once El Tule leaves, Lenny is going to tell Governess about his heritage."

Lenny's eyes flashed. "Garrett! What the shit?"

"Forget it, Len. She's way smarter than both of us put together. You could never keep it from her."

Breanne uncrossed her arms. "What?! Why? Lenny, how do you know Governess won't capture us right then and there and take us back to Pando? Apep may give her what she wants if he knows you're Syldan's son!" Her frown deepened as she searched for understanding.

Lenny glanced over one shoulder, then the other. "Listen, Bre, she could teach us some of the god language, but she won't tell us if she knows I have a secret and that I don't trust her to keep it. For all I know, she already knows I'm half dark elf, anyway. Why else would she have said what she said?"

"She could have overheard something, but not enough to put it together. If she knew it all, she would have told Pando by now! She holds no allegiance to humans! Besides, she tried to kill Ed! And now you want to trust her?"

Garrett took her hand, and her stomach fluttered. "Bre, I'm not sure she was trying to kill Ed. Wouldn't she have finished the job if she wanted him dead? Maybe she meant to take him alive."

Breanne shook her head. "I don't know. Are you sure a few ancient words are really worth the risk? Besides, we don't even know if they will work for us."

"I don't follow," Garrett said.

Breanne sneaked a quick glance back and leaned in closer to the two boys. "Who's to say it's just knowing the words? Sure, she says them and roots burst from the ground, fruit grows, or El Tule changes shape, but she's a tree, you guys! Maybe the words won't work at all for us – for humans."

"This is about more than just getting some ancient words. Plus it's my decision, and I'm telling her once we get off this tree," Lenny said with the firmness of a mind made up.

Breanne held Lenny's gaze for a long moment as she tried to read his face. When she found no compromise in the boy's eyes, she turned to Garrett.

Garrett shrugged. "We have to find a way to trust each other if we're going to fight what we saw in the tree memory, Bre."

The memory came back to her, dragons and giants by the thousands making their way toward Mexico this very moment. They truly needed all the help they could get. "Okay. Just please wait until tomorrow after we get a good night's sleep. If you still feel this way, tell her when the sun is up."

Garrett frowned. "Why when the sun is up?"

"So we can all see what we're fighting," Breanne said.

Lenny nodded. "Thanks, Bre."

"I just hope you're right about this, Lenny."

They made their way down and through El Tule's many trunks until they reached the ground, where they gathered at the base of the tree. A soft weeping and sniffling became a full-on watershed of tears and sobs.

Gabi? Oh, Gabi, I'm sorry, Breanne said, pulling her close and hugging her.

I don't want him to go! He's going off to die! This isn't right!

Gabi De Leon, El Tule must follow his destiny now, Governess said, displaying no emotion.

Gabi ran forward and spread her arms as far as they would go, pressing herself into the tree. *This is my fault! El Tule, you shouldn't have saved us. Now they're making you die!* Gabi's face pressed into the trunk as tears streamed from her cheeks onto the big tree's bark.

For the first time since they were on their way to meet Pando, the deep voice of El Tule boomed out loud, his voice rumbling through the night, building like growing thunder as he spoke. "Gabi De Leon, do not cry for El Tule. Do not regret the time and stories we have shared over these few days. Instead, hold these last days with El Tule in your heart as El Tule holds you in his."

"Oh no! María Purísima, no!"

"Listen to me," El Tule continued. "El Tule is very old. He has lived a full existence, and he has been blessed to spend his last days with you. Now go, little lion. Go and follow your own destiny and make this world better for us all."

Breanne had suspected, but now she was sure. These last several days, all this time, Gabi and El Tule had been talking. Her heart broke for Gabi, and for a moment everyone stood quietly waiting. Even Governess said nothing. As snowflakes gathered on their clothes, they stood and they waited. After a long moment, Gabi took a step back, wiped her flannel sleeve across her eyes, and said, "Goodbye, El Tule."

"Goodbye, little lion."

Governess waved a hand, whispered a word, and El Tule's canopy glowed green like their torches. The platforms and all they contained withered, withdrawing back into El Tule, bringing him back to his natural state. "Die well, El Tule Ahuehuete," Governess said quietly.

A moment later, El Tule vanished off the road, swallowed by the waiting forest.

Silently, the group made their way down the road toward the farm.

The next morning, Breanne woke on a bed of straw with someone's arm draped over her. She was warm, folded into the heat of another body pressed against hers. She and Garrett had lain down next to each other, eventually scooting close enough to share some warmth. Back on El Tule, the tree cocoons were only big enough for single occupancy, making this the first time they had actually slept together. When exactly the lying close had turned to spooning, she wasn't sure.

"Breanne," Garrett said hoarsely. "Do you feel that?"

Breanne's eyes narrowed, then suddenly flew wide as they both vaulted up from beneath their blanket, sharing a look. They didn't have time to let the cuddle become awkward because the ground was shaking beneath them.

"Trees?"

No, Governess answered in their minds. *This is not us.*

Earthquake! Gabi shouted.

"Hurry! Everyone outside!" Paul ordered.

Breanne and the others pushed their way outside the barn and into the morning sun. There was no sign of snow, only the muddy remains of weather that made little sense, and the temperature was already rising.

The shaking ground grew worse until finally they had to sit to keep from falling. Across from the barn, the farmhouse collapsed into a heap and trees toppled, snapping and crunching. Near the pasture, an enormous tree fell, crushing a fence.

Then, without warning, everything went still. The ground stopped shaking.

Breanne sat motionless, her heart racing as she panted for breath. She looked back toward the barn, which somehow still stood upright. Aside from the others' labored breaths and the beat of her own heart, everything was quiet.

Finally, it was Governess who broke the silence. *This results from Apep assembling the God Stones into the Sound Eye. If the Sound Eye is not disassembled or taken away from here, soon it will destroy everything. The power of the Sound Eye is simply too great for a planet this small. This is where is starts, the strange weather, the earthquakes. It will become worse, both in intensity and frequency, until the entire planet is pulled apart.*

Looks like we got lucky. I mean, that was pretty intense, but it could have been worse, Paul said.

Governess rooted to the ground and stood silent for a long moment, still as a mannequin. A moment later, her roots withdrew from the ground, and she seemed to reanimate. *We were not the epicenter, Paul Moore – California was.*

Oh no, was it bad? David asked.

Devastating. We lost many trees, but we take some solace in knowing most of our oldest had already moved inland toward our queen or toward the pyramid. Thank Mother Druesha for her mercy.

I was talking about Los Angeles, San Francisco, San Diego! David said.

Ah, your human cities… Leveled and sinking, Governess said flatly.

Oh my god, that's awful! Breanne said.

Movement caught Breanne's eye right at the same time Garrett pointed.

Look!

Coming up the driveway of the farm were six men dressed in camo with hydration packs on their backs. Breanne squinted at the men, and a horrible feeling grabbed her as she realized they were all carrying guns.

Those guys look like military, Paul said, drawing his handgun. *Bre, draw your gun but don't point it, not yet. Just be ready.*

The group was in a single-file run, heading straight toward them, and all were brandishing their own guns.

Breanne freed hers from its holster as a female began shouting.

"Brandon, the little Hispanic girl is a mind-breaker. And watch that white kid in the middle. He can slow time," she said, pointing.

"Spread out!" a man ordered. "He probably can't slow all of us. DeKeyser! Time?"

"Five seconds," a wiry bald man shouted, running off to the side.

Paul raised his gun. "That's close enough!"

Breanne's heart slammed against her chest bones like a caged animal. *What is this?!*

Lenny stood. *I don't know! Something is wrong!*

Spread out, guys! Get into fighting positions like we practiced! Garrett shouted in mind speak.

The bald man reached down and planted his palms against the ground, stood, and started running again. This time, he crossed the driveway between the two groups. "Three seconds!"

5

The Ultra Six

Friday, May 6 – God Stones Day 30
Rural Chiapas State, Mexico

Garrett guessed whatever the hell was about to happen, he needed to focus on the bald man running lengthwise across the road. It made no sense how he'd touched the ground, then taken off, crossing right between the two groups from Garrett's left to right.

"I got it," the bald man shouted, dropping into a squat and reaching for the ground once more.

Garrett thrust both hands toward the man as if he were going to grab him; he was ten yards ahead, far out of physical reach – but not mental. *No, I got you!* Garrett shouted in mind speak as he slowed time for the man.

The man's hands nearly froze a foot from the ground.

"He's slowing time!" the woman shouted, reaching for her hip.

Abruptly, eight pistols were drawn and pointing at Garrett.

"Unless you can slow all the rounds we're about to unload, you would be best advised to cease and desist!" said a man with a salt-and-pepper beard.

"You shoot! We shoot!" Paul shouted.

"Trust me when I tell you it won't matter," the man said.

Garrett could hear the distinct military tone in the man's voice, a voice that rang with absolute honesty. There was no deceit in it. If Garrett didn't stop, people were going to die. Still, he hesitated, unsure of their intentions. If he let go and this guy touched the ground, were they all dead? But what other choice did he have?

Garrett let go.

The bald guy's hands slapped the ground.

Directly in front of Garrett and the others, a thin fog rose from the ground. It stretched from where the bald guy had touched the ground for the first time, all the way across the driveway to where the man currently crouched.

The peculiar fog lifted like a flat screen, almost as if held between two panes of glass. This newly formed wall appeared to be only an inch or so thick. It stretched across the road in a curved arc, bending back toward each side, forming a 180-degree horseshoe. The man with his hands on the ground stood and hurriedly stepped through the fog to join his friends.

From behind him, Garrett caught sight of motion as Governess darted past him, leapt into the air, and struck the fog with her sword. Her weapon and body pressed into the fog wall, flexing it in like a thumb pushing into a balloon.

"DeKeyser! Will it hold?" the one with the salt-and-pepper beard shouted.

The bald guy didn't answer.

Garrett stepped back into a fighting stance, ready for whatever came next.

Everyone stood unmoving, their eyes on the petite redhead as she bent into the opaque wall.

"She isn't human!" the woman said.

"What do you mean she isn't human, Jenna?" the leader barked.

The strange fog slowed its stretch to the point Garrett was sure Governess was going to push through until finally she came to a brief stop.

The fog snapped back, flinging the tree woman backward.

Governess hit the dirt and rolled across the ground, twisting unnaturally and then shifting and ending up back on her feet.

The bald man called DeKeyser lifted his chin in triumph. "Of course it will hold!" he said, as if now that it had, the question was stupid.

Garrett's mind exploded as Breanne and the others started talking all at once. *Guys, stop!* he shouted.

"Oh wow, they're using telepathy," Jenna said, nodding toward Garrett.

"What are they saying?" asked a tall guy in an army-green boonie hat with an acoustic guitar strapped to his back.

"How in the frack should I know, Dex?" Jenna called back.

"Listen, whoever you guys are, we're lowering our weapons, so lower yours," the leader guy said, letting go of his pistol grip.

The gun fell from man's palm to dangle nonthreateningly from a single finger. But Garrett wasn't stupid. He recognized that with only a quick flick, the gun could be pointing at him, ready to fire in a heartbeat.

There were six of them. Five guys and a woman, all hazy now through the strange murky wall of swirling grey smoke. Garrett noticed they all carried lightweight packs and wore footgear similar to his own. Their clothes were breathable and loose, comfortable for moving quickly, and their bodies were lean and toned. Garrett knew this look all too well. These people were runners. "Why should we trust you?" he shouted.

"Mostly because you don't have a choice, kid," salt-and-pepper beard guy said, approaching the wall. "You won't get past this wall. Your powers can't penetrate it, and rounds won't pass through it. But that's not the case from our side. You see, from our side, rounds pass through just fine. And so will our abilities."

Guys, what's our move? Lenny asked.

I don't trust this, Garrett, Paul said.

Me either, David said, his voice shaky.

Bre, can you see anything? Garrett asked.

Nothing, she said uneasily.

Dammit, Garrett thought. "What do you want with us?"

"Start by telling us what you're doing here, kid," the man said.

Garrett hesitated, then said, "We are trying to get to a friend who was working south of here. She's hurt. We're on our way to help her."

Good, Garrett. Don't tell them any more than that, Paul said.

"And you guys? What are a bunch of American ultrarunners dressed like military doing this far into Mexico?"

Salt-and-pepper guy spit tobacco juice into the weeds, nodded, and grinned. "My name is Shawn. This big, beautiful, bald Black man to my right is Jason."

Jason, every bit of six-six, nodded, face as emotionless as rock. Garrett narrowed his eyes, peering through the smoky fog and realizing exactly who the tall man was. In fact, Garrett had a poster of him hanging on the wall of his bedroom. Well, when he'd had a bedroom. He looked at Lenny.

Lenny nodded back, his own eyes going big.

"The guy behind me in the wide-brimmed hat is Dexter."

Dexter nodded.

"The Dr. Evil–looking bald gentleman responsible for this little layer of protection between us is Mr. DeKeyser."

"You can call me Greg," he said, raising a gloved hand. "I'm not really evil… or, am I?" He grinned, pressing a pinky to the corner of his mouth.

"The little stack of dynamite standing next to Dex is Bill."

The shortest of the group, Bill, just stared through the fog, eyes assessing them dangerously.

"And this lovely lady to my left, reading all your powers – that's Jenna. Speaking of powers, you all are stacked with a ton of it, including having your own healer, a seer, a mind-breaker, and something that is not human. This tells me you are either here for some other reason you don't want to tell me about, or the injured friend you are trying to help is the president of Mexico. So why don't you tell me what's really going on here?" Shawn asked in a tone that seemed more curious than threatening.

Now that Garrett had heard the names, he recognized both Shawn and Jenna as pro ultrarunners, like Jason; he figured the others were also, but he couldn't place them. "Look, Shawn, we don't want any trouble. We just need to get to our friend," Garrett said.

Shawn nodded, lowering his hand and with it the gun, but he didn't holster it. Instead, he just left it loose at his side. "Kid, we aren't interested in engaging with our own. There's plenty of nasty shit out there to worry about without killing each other."

"So why did you come at us like this?" Lenny asked, pointing the end of his staff toward the wall.

Shawn nodded again, spitting another mouthful of dip spit into the weeds. Jason leaned down to Shawn's ear and said something Garrett couldn't make it out.

"Fair question," Shawn said. "Maybe you've all been hiding under a rock, but in case you didn't notice, the world has gone to shit. We come jogging in and Jenna here registered your abilities. You understand we can't exactly come walking up and ask if you're good guys or bad guys, right? So, you see" – Shawn motioned at the fog – "this little wall here ensures we can have a civil conversation without the concern you might attack us. Sure, it's a little intense at first, but we had the element of surprise on our side."

The shorter guy, Bill, spoke up. "And if we don't like what we hear, we can light you up."

Shawn held up a hand. "Easy, Bill."

"So, what are you doing here, Shawn?" Garrett asked again.

Shawn stole a glance at Jason.

Jason nodded.

Shawn tipped his head only slightly, arched an eyebrow, and started in. "The US government began receiving intel that trees were moving en masse toward southern Mexico – not just a few trees, but whole forests. That's about the time dragons started appearing, and now we're hearing stories of giants moving this way from Central America. Look, we don't know what the hell is going on, but we know something is pulling the trees south and the giants and dragons north. What we don't know is why."

"So, you're military?" Paul asked.

The man nodded. "We're a special unit. Organized in the event recon power is out on a massive scale and the need to move quickly becomes a foot game," Shawn said, this time spitting out the whole wad of tobacco and retrieving a small can of dip from his pocket.

"You're saying the military plans for a situation like this?" Breanne asked skeptically.

"No. Not like this. Terrorism, yes. A solar flare, hell, even an asteroid – you bet."

"I expected zombies, myself," Dexter said, clearly disappointed. Then he added, "God, I really wanted it to be zombies."

"Zombies sure as hell would have been better than this," Bill said.

"One minute left," Greg said quietly to Shawn, who nodded.

"But you're all ultrarunners. Jesus, I had a picture of you hanging on my wall," Garrett said, pointing at Jason.

The tall man's expression didn't change, but he gave a slight nod.

"Who better to do recon in a world with no electricity than a military unit of ultrarunners?" Shawn asked.

Garrett guessed that made sense. "But it's only been thirty days. How did you guys get here so fast?"

"And how long have you been in Mexico?" Paul asked.

"Yeah, and what's the plan?" David asked.

"Thirty seconds," Greg announced.

Shawn slid his pistol back into its holster. "Guys, in thirty seconds, this wall between us is going to drop. I need to know you and your people are okay. I need to know you won't attack us."

They're our military. We can't attack them unless they attack us, Paul said in mind speak.

Agreed, Lenny said.

And you are sure they are who they say they are? Breanne asked.

At least three of them are famous American ultrarunners, so yeah – I'm sure, Garrett said.

Governess, do not attack them when this fog comes down unless they attack first, Garrett said. *But everyone be ready for anything.*

"Fifteen seconds!"

"You're making Bill nervous, kid. And trust me when I say you don't want Bill nervous. Now, if you guys are done powwowing with your people, I need to know, can we trust you?"

Garrett nodded. "Yeah. You can trust us."

The shield between them dropped, and for a long, very tense moment, everyone just stared at one another.

Shawn stepped forward and extended a hand. "Shawn Brandon. Nice to meet you, kid."

Hesitantly, Garrett reached out and took the offered hand, half expecting some sort of trickery but finding none.

"You asked how we covered so much ground in only thirty days. The answer is as simple as it is badass. We had a healer by the name of Colloton. He was healing us multiple times a day."

Dexter nodded. "With Colloton's healing, we could cover a hundred miles a day."

"A hundred miles?" Lenny asked in awe.

"No way! How could he have been healing all of you multiple times a day *and* running a hundred miles?" David asked, crossing his arms.

"Didn't I just mention he was a healer?" Shawn asked, smacking a finger against the lid of his dip can a few times.

Jenna pointed at David and smiled. "Just like you, in fact."

David frowned. "Well, where's your healer now?"

Their faces dropped. Even stone-faced Jason looked suddenly grave.

"He didn't make it out," Dexter said, reaching over his shoulder and running a hand down the neck of the guitar.

David made a noise that sounded as if he were trying to swallow a cat.

"That was his guitar?" Lenny asked, looking like a starved lion staring at a gazelle.

Dexter nodded. "Affirmative. It's all that's left of him now. I can't play it, but it didn't seem right to leave it behind. He loved this guitar."

"May I?" Lenny asked.

Dexter held Lenny's gaze for a moment, then removed his pack, unstrapped the guitar, and passed it over.

Lenny closed his eyes, his expression like that of a boy who'd just tasted his first sip of water after crossing a desert. His fingers danced across the strings, working their way down the neck, and when they were only a couple inches from his other hand, they stayed there. Lenny's face twisted, his eyes squeezing shut as his fingers began to move too fast to follow. After a moment, he strummed his hand across all the strings, opened his eyes, and smiled. "Thank you for that," he said, letting out a long breath, his deep thirst for shredding chords momentarily quenched.

"That was amazing, kid. What's your name?" Dexter asked.

"Lenny D. Wade," he said, holding the guitar out by the neck and offering it back to Dexter.

Dexter reached for the guitar but stopped short. "No. You keep it, Lenny. I think Chris would want you to have it. In fact, I have this feeling you're meant to have it."

Lenny looked down at the guitar anew, a huge smile stretching across his face as he slid his hand down the neck. "Thank you! You don't know what this means to me."

Garrett laughed, wondering if Len was going to make out with the thing or what. He cleared his throat. "Anyway, guys, we have to be on our way. But the barn is a safe place to shelter if you need it, and of course you're welcome to it."

"Look, Garrett. We appreciate that, but we need something else. Like I said, we're on a mission, and we need to get back and report what's happening here. If you guys go that way," Shawn said, pointing down the dirt road, "you're as good as dead. Giants are real, and they're coming, but worse, dragons are already here in force. I'm talking hundreds. They killed our healer, and they'll kill all of you if you go south down that road."

Dragons, Bre! Gabi said, filling Garrett's mind with rage. The feeling nearly overwhelmed him.

He blinked back the red and tried to hide his sudden and inappropriate anger. "Which is why we need to be on our way, guys. I'm sure you can understand. We don't have time to waste."

"Right, your friend needs you. Well, listen, I can't make you come with us, but like I said, we need to get back. The world's survival may depend on us getting this intel back to base. We will need to mobilize everything we have on stopping the force coming from Central America."

Garrett nodded, knowing that the force of giants wouldn't be coming any further north than the pyramid. Once the portal opened, the dragons and giants would leave the planet, and that would be long before the military could mobilize. "Right, well, take care, Shawn."

Shawn held Garrett's gaze, but neither he nor his men moved. "I'm sorry. Let me just be blunt here. We're going to need your healer to come with us."

6

The Red Devil

Friday, May 6 – God Stones Day 30
A seaside village, Panama

When Jack opened his eyes, pain racked his head, and he immediately slammed them shut. It felt like someone had poked sticks into his eyes. "Je-sus!" he croaked, and fresh pain gripped his throat as if he'd swallowed razor blades. He didn't know where he was, but the pain told him he was at least alive.

This wasn't the first time he'd woken. There had been waves of this happening over and over, each time ending the same, with darkness pulling him back. Jack had dreamed then. Dreamed of his father being eaten by dragons, of the look on Pete's face when he told him he'd ordered his mother killed, of Danny, too, when Garrett had flung him into the Sangamon River – to his death. Sometime during the throes of his unconscious anguish, he'd seen the kraken – felt her power coursing through him.

He lay there now, his eyes shut up tight. This time, the darkness didn't take him back – this time, he held to consciousness by his fingernails. The kraken had spoken to him just before she died, hadn't she? What had she said? Her words were there, just beneath the pain.

He moved his head only slightly and, son-of-a-bitch, he wished he hadn't.

Jack! Jack, can you hear me? Cerberus asked.

Oh my god, Cerb. Don't speak in my head! Speak aloud or don't speak at all. Not yet.

"Alright. Just take it easy," Cerb said. "Can you open your eyes?"

Jack cracked one eye open, then squeezed it shut again. *Hurts. Just let me get my shit together.*

"Señor, por favor," a woman's voice urged as a hand gently pressed against his chest. A moment later, the same gentle hand placed a cool cloth across his forehead as another caressed his neck.

At the touch of the stranger's hands, Jack forced his eyes to open again. *Cerb! Who is this?*

"Easy, Jack, you needed care I couldn't give. So I brought you here and convinced this woman to care for you."

Here? Where is here? The light was still too painful, the scene before him too blurry to make out. But he could hear the ocean lapping on the shore. He pushed himself forward, trying to sit up, but the pain – Jesus, the pain.

"¡Acuéstate, por favor!" the woman said, pressing on his chest a little more forcefully.

Jack collapsed back into the soft bedding, the world spinning beneath him.

"We are north of the battle with the sea demon in a small coastal village. West of the army's path."

But… But why, Cerb? The nephilbock need us to clear the way. The trees! We can't let them… He moved again.

No, Jack, Cerb said, and this time, the dragon spoke in his mind.

Jack winced. It hurt less, but he stopped trying to get up.

We have done the hardest part. Your hordes are handling the trees.

His hordes? Last he knew, each horde was led by one of the Queen of Queens's asshole elders. *Cerb? What about the elders?*

Mivras the Blue and Zudrian the Old tried to kill me, but after I drowned Zudrian in the ocean, Mivras fled.

Too afraid to face you one-on-one, Jack guessed.

Not afraid, Jack. Not of Cerberus. It was the sea demon. She attacked, and he fled. I let him go. Instead, I stayed as close as I could until you finally answered me. As far as the others, Ahi the Silver is still leading his horde alongside ours. Jymas the Breaker was lost to the sea demon, but his horde also follows the orders to burn back the trees.

You called them my *hordes?*

Yes, of course they are yours! Cerberus said, his deep laugh filling Jack's mind. *After what you did, they will follow you when we return from the dead.*

Jack thought about this for a moment. He wasn't so sure any dragons would follow him and Cerb as long as the Queen of Queens lived. *Queen Azazel? She doesn't know we're alive?*

I've told her nothing, Jack, for I cannot live if you are dead. But I am listening. When she speaks to the commanders, I hear her orders. Once she learned the kraken had been killed and that you and I were lost, she ordered a small group of dragons, five hundred strong, to join her at the pyramid in Mexico.

Jack sucked in a breath, considering all this new information. A fresh pain he hadn't noticed filled his chest, and his ribs ached. Despite this, anger consumed him, followed quickly by worry. Mivras the dick was still alive somewhere. Mivras, who tried to kill his dragon after the kraken had eaten Jack. *Are you okay, Cerb? They didn't hurt you, did they?*

Cerberus laughed. *Mere weasels cannot kill Cerberus the Mighty.*

Still, Jack wanted to see – to make sure his brother was okay.

He tried once more to open his eyes. But again, the sunshine felt like sandpaper raking across his open pupils. The rag he'd already forgotten lay across his forehead; it was lifted away, replaced a moment later by a fresh, cool one. Then, moisture pressed to his lips. The woman said something in Spanish. Jack didn't understand, but he parted his lips and cool water spilled into mouth. *Cerb, why am I so messed up? And why did you bring me here instead of flying north to the Queen and Apep?*

You used too much magic, and it nearly killed you. You can't go back like this. Your hordes need to see you strong! They are singing and telling stories about us, Jack. I hear our own horde, and I'm sure the others are doing the same. They are singing about you! Nightshade the Taker, slayer of the sea demon! But they are also beginning to ask questions. Right now, we survive in rumors, but they whisper of our return, Jack, and so you must be healthy! Your return must be epic!

Nearby, the lady spoke in nervous Spanish, and then there was another voice, only slightly different. Either this other woman hadn't spoken until now, or in his agony, he'd simply missed that there were actually two of them. *How did you get these women to care for me?*

I promised not to eat them and allowed their children to flee into the woods. Cerberus barked out a laugh. *They will most certainly be eaten by nephilbock or dragons, but these humans don't know that. As for the rest of the village…* He paused to laugh again. *I have a village's worth of humans in my belly, including this older woman's mate!*

Jack swallowed dryly. He didn't know what bothered him more: the fact Cerb only thought of humans as food, or that he himself – despite the horror of learning of the slain village and likely murdered children – felt absolutely nothing. Well, that wasn't true. His head still hurt like a horse had kicked it, his body was one giant ache of raw nerves, and he still couldn't open his eyes.

These two I saved for you, Jack.

Again, a gentle hand replaced the already warm cloth with a cool one, made cooler still by a light ocean breeze. He must be burning up. He listened for a moment more, and through his own pain he could hear the soft sobbing of one woman crying as she worked. The other woman was whispering urgently. Jack didn't speak Spanish, but there was a lot that could he could read in her tone. He guessed the other woman was pleading for her to stop crying.

Jack forced his eyes open, blinking furiously. He groaned, trying to bite back the pain, and for a moment he worried he'd gone blind. But no, he wasn't blind. The women were there in his vision now – nothing more than blurry red shapes, one on either side, but they were there. He reached up to his chest and took one of the women's hands gently in his own and forced his eyes to open even more.

Jack's eyebrows rose high as a moan escaped his twisted face. *Ah, fuck me!*

The woman looked into his eyes and gasped. She tried to pull her hand away. "¡Ojos rojos! ¡Diablo rojo!"

The other woman let out a wail and screamed the first English words Jack had heard since he woke.

"¡Dios mío! Red devil!"

Jack drew her life into himself like a cold drink on a hot day. He pulled and pulled and the woman screamed until her vocal cords rotted in her throat and decay took her life. But still Jack took, greedily, insatiably – ravenous as a man starved for weeks. He pulled until there was nothing but a dried husk ancient in appearance, beyond old – beyond dead. Jack's vision cleared just in time to see the woman collapse into a pile of skin and bones jumbled inside a colorful flower-patterned blouse and matching skirt.

The other woman stood on wobbly feet at Jack's opposite side. Perhaps she was younger than the one he had just consumed, or perhaps older. Maybe this one was the mother of children she didn't know were already dead. Jack looked into her eyes and for a brief moment, he hated himself – hated that he didn't… No, scratch that, not that he didn't. He hated that he *couldn't* feel bad for any of this.

The woman steeled herself, and in a moment of bravery, she found Jack's eyes. "Red devil!" she shouted and spit in his face.

Jack lunged forward, his body no longer aching, as he grabbed the woman by the throat. "Red devil?" he growled from a throat that no longer burned. He understood it then, the red tint coating everything he saw. The other woman's brown skin – tinted red – wilted before his eyes as he drew her into himself. The blue sky speckled in white clouds tinted red, and the ocean still blue but now with a red tint. The sand of the beach, his own skin, Cerb's black scales – all tinted red.

Cerb? Why did she call me that? Jack asked, his eyes locked on the woman as a final squeak escaped her throat. Her body relaxed then, knees buckling, the sudden weight pulling her from his grasp.

The center dragon's head drew in close, Cerb's breath washing over him as saliva dripped down its jaw and onto Jack's chest.

Cerb, what is it? Jack asked, turning his attention away from the corpse.

The dragon's solid ruby-red eyes met Jack's own.

My brother! Your eyes! It's like looking into my own!

7

Shared Secrets

Friday, May 6 – God Stones Day 30
Rural Chiapas State, Mexico

At the announcement that the military was taking David, the air around Breanne became unexpectedly hard to breathe. A panic attack? She hadn't had a panic attack since her mom had forgiven her when Gabi was almost eaten by the giant snake. Sweat beaded on her forehead, and her heart beat against her chest like five hundred fans stomping on the bleachers at a homecoming game. All the shit she had been through, and this threat to take David away was going to push her over the edge? Was it because they wouldn't be able to say no? This was the military. These were adults who worked for the United States of America. This was like an order from a police officer, but worse.

Garrett! You can't let them take me! David said, his voice filling her mind. The others were talking too, but those were the only words that got through. *You can't let them take me!*

In front of her, the bigger guy, Dexter, shrugged on his pack, while Jenna took a sip from her canteen, DeKeyser seemed to assess their surroundings, and the guy they called Bill just stared at them as if at any moment he might decide to shoot them. Jason watched impassively as if this was the way it would be and that was that.

It was pin-drop quiet when she heard Garrett swallow and clear his throat. "You can't take him," he said hoarsely.

"I'm sorry, kid. Did you say I *can't* take him?" Shawn asked.

Breanne noticed the others quickly change their demeanor, coming to the same level of readiness as the Bill guy. Instantly, they were no longer passive. A switch had been thrown, as if someone called them to attention.

David, I want you to know you are one of my best friends in the world, and I'm sorry for what I'm about to say.

What? No! Garrett! Please don't change your mind! Don't let them take me! You need me! Aw, come on!

Garrett, what are you doing? Pete asked.

Garrett, he's your friend! And Sarah needs him! Bre pleaded. Jesus, if they didn't take David, Sarah would be dead for sure.

Then the others started in too.

Guys, enough! Garrett shouted in mind speak as he lifted his head to lock eyes with Shawn. "Shawn, he can't do what your healer could do."

"Explain."

"He can heal, but only one at a time, and he can't even heal himself. He hates running and wouldn't make it three blocks. But that's not the worst of it. Every time he heals someone, he passes out and has to sleep for hours. You see? He wouldn't be any good to you. He would slow you down, not speed you up."

Lenny, seeming to catch on, added, "And his feet smell god awful. He hates bathing, and he refuses to cut off that patch of lip mange infecting his face. For all we know, it could be contagious."

David opened his mouth to speak, but his words fell short as his brow scrunched. Instead, he closed his mouth, crossed his arms, and frowned.

Jason leaned in, and Shawn whispered in his ear.

"What's that?" Garrett asked.

"What's what?" Shawn countered.

"That thing you're doing. What are you whispering about?"

Um, Garrett, Gabi said shyly, *when you talk to Shawn, he is reading your mind, then reporting what he learns to the Jason guy.*

What? Are you sure? Garrett asked.

Yes, sorry. It took me a minute to figure it out, but when you are talking, you are somehow vulnerable to his mind-reading ability – it lets him in. That's why he is asking the questions even though Jason is actually the leader.

Breanne shook her head. *Great, it's hard telling what he's learned already. Can he read what we are saying to each other now?*

No. He can only know what you are thinking when you are speaking directly to him.

The two men continued to murmur to each other.

"Jason," Garrett said, directing his attention to the tall man. "You understand now why you can't have him? He will only slow you down."

"You can talk to me," Shawn said.

Garrett looked across the group. "Jenna, right?"

Jenna nodded.

"Tell Shawn I won't be talking to him any further."

Jenna smiled. "He figured you out, Shawn."

"Well, it took you guys long enough." Shawn idly opened his can of dip, grabbed a pinch, and stuffed it into his cheek. Once he poked it into place with his tongue, he pointed a finger at Garrett and smiled. "Listen, don't be all bent out of shape. I read your mind. You do have a friend to go look in on. You didn't lie about that, but I know you're not telling me the whole truth, either. Seems you're on your way to stop whatever the hell is happening in southern Mexico, and while I couldn't keep you talking long enough to determine exactly what that is, I can see you're on the right side of it." His finger moved to point straight at Governess. "But what I want to know about, Garrett, is the tree."

All eyes fell on Governess, who remained stone-faced and silent.

Garrett stared at Shawn for a long moment, tension filling the space between them. Then his gaze shifted to Jason. "Jason, here is what I am going to tell you."

Shawn smiled over at Jason and shrugged.

"All you need to know is that the attacks on the cities have stopped so we can be here right now to do what we need to do. That includes saving a friend and stopping the end of the world. But if you try to take my people, or attack any of my friends" – Garrett paused, looking directly at Governess then back to Jason – "we will be forced to activate every tree around us." He waved a hand to emphasize his point. "Guys, you're surrounded by an army you can't even fathom."

The ultrarunner soldiers looked around, seeming to take in the forest with fresh eyes. Even Bill fidgeted uncomfortably.

All eyes fell on Garrett and Jason, who seemed to be locked in some kind of macho staring contest.

For Breanne, the moment of boys staring each other down felt unnecessarily long. She wanted to scream, "Sarah needs us now!" at the top of her lungs, but when she finally opened her mouth to speak, a smile stretched across Jason's face.

"Roger that," Jason said.

Shawn nodded. "Well played, Garrett. Now, however you and yours are planning to unfuck this world – get after it, would you?" He smiled and extended a hand.

Breanne could hear Garrett exhale as he took the hand. And just like that, the standoff seemed to be over.

Dexter approached David. "So, you're having trouble staying conscious when you heal, huh?"

David nodded, the blood slowly returning to his face, though he still looked like he might faint. "Yeah, I'm trying, but it's so hard."

"I think if Chris were here, he would tell you to stop trying so hard."

"I don't know what that means," David said.

"Well, listen, you ever heard of a band called 38 Special?"

David shook his head.

Breanne hadn't heard of them either and, judging by her friends' expressions, she wasn't alone.

"Jesus, kids today. You don't know what good music is! Anyway, the next time you heal, think of these lyrics." Then, so loudly it made Breanne flinch, Dexter sang something about holding on loosely, so you don't lose control.

David blinked.

Lenny frowned. "You should stick to running, bro."

"And on that foul note, we need to move out," Shawn said.

"Dexter, you sound like a wounded animal, or was that your idea of a dragon mating call?" DeKeyser grinned.

"Shut up, Greg," Dexter said.

Jenna approached Breanne. "Hey, girl. That looks like a Smith & Wesson M&P on your hip. Nine mil?"

"Oh, uh… yeah."

"Same thing the other guy is carrying?"

Paul nodded, walking over.

She pulled off her pack. "Look, if you guys are heading further south into the shitshow, you're going to need these more than we will." Jenna rummaged through her pack and pulled out a plain, unmarked box. "Here's fifty rounds of the lightest-weight nine mil ammunition you will ever shoot." She smiled as she held it out to Paul. "No one has this stuff. We were given it specifically for light carry."

"Hooah," Paul said, taking the box and weighing it in his hand as he nodded approvingly. "Thanks for having our six."

Jenna smiled grimly. "Yeah, well, consider it a spoon, soldier."

"A spoon?" Breanne asked.

Paul returned Jenna's hard look. "For the soup sandwich we're about to walk into."

Jenna nodded. "Roger that."

Five minutes later, they were moving southward toward the trail that would take them to the cenote.

David, who was already trailing behind, jogged to catch up to the group. *When you said, "Sorry, David," I thought for sure you were going to give me away.*

When Garrett stopped and turned, the others stopped too. *David! Is that what you think of me – of this? Even if I had lost my mind, do you think your friends would have let me give you to them?* Garrett shook his head. *No way, David. They wouldn't – I wouldn't. We would have fought them if we had to.* He turned to the group, taking them all in, and Breanne could see it – the disappointment in his eyes. *And you guys should have known better. We will stick together through this no matter what, and not one of us matters any less than the others.*

Pete nodded. *Sorry, Garrett.*

The others nodded too, and Bre felt ashamed she'd even thought he was about to cave. After all they'd been through? She should have known better – they all should have.

Paul slapped his shoulder. *Well, listen. You did good back there, Garrett. They were no joke, and you were convincing.*

Yes, Governess said, *I especially like how you convinced them you could "activate" the trees surrounding us and order them to attack. I would enjoy hearing more of your command over the trees.* She raised her eyebrow in curiosity, but the slight curl of her lips betrayed the beginning of a smile.

Garrett grinned and nodded. *It was a gamble, but I figured if they attacked us, you might have some trees nearby that could help. Mostly, though, I just wanted them to believe it.*

In truth, only trees around a hundred years of age are capable of movement. My queen has given most of the older trees in this area orders to move toward the pyramid. However, there are some watching, ready should I need them.

Garrett and Lenny exchanged looks that didn't go unnoticed by Breanne – or Governess, for that matter.

What is it? Governess asked.

Lenny turned and, for whatever reason, spoke aloud. "Listen, stick chick, you're one of us now whether you like it or not, whether we like it or not. For now, anyway, and for however long it takes us to get back here with a magic thingamajig. See, I've been thinking about what you said back on El Tule, and I've decided, oh wise woody one, you were right. Trust goes both ways. Look, I… I don't want to keep secrets from you, Gov, and I hope you'll take this as a sign of trust."

Governess arched her eyebrow. "Do tell, Lenard Wade. Do tell."

"I'm not fully human. I'm something else…" Lenny started, then stopped and swallowed, like he'd made a mistake.

"Go on," Governess urged.

Breanne and the others gathered around, unsure how this would play out. Once Governess realized Lenny's value as the son of Syldan and the heir to the throne of Osonian, she could call forth whatever trees were close, order them captured, and march them right back to the tree queen. If that were the case, she knew what came next. They wouldn't be taken alive. Not this time. Not again. Maybe Lenny was right to hesitate. Maybe this was an epic mistake.

"I'm half dökkálfar," Lenny said.

For a moment no one spoke. In the silence, Breanne thought she could hear the groan of trees. Trees readying themselves to attack.

Finally, Governess said, "But that is not all, is it, Lenard Wade?"

Now Lenny arched an eyebrow. "No, it isn't. Why do I get the feeling I'm telling you something you already know?"

"You are the son of Prince Syldan Loravaris. The nephew to Apep Loravaris. The grandson of King Vulmon Loravaris. The rightful heir to the throne of Osonian. The throne to a kingdom Apep will stop at nothing to claim as his own."

Lenny's eyes went wide, his breath hitched, and then his eyebrows bunched. Glancing around the group, Breanne saw shared confusion.

"You knew?" Lenny asked.

"Of course, I knew. We have known what Apep was since the time of Turek. We learned long ago of his purpose for coming. The same is true of Syldan, the Dragon Master. He defeated the dragons long ago, and in doing so, he saved our kind."

"But you knew about me? All this time?" Lenny asked.

"No, not all this time." She looked around the group then, only one emerald eye visible, the other obscured by a dangling lock of auburn hair. "You cannot whisper your secrets while standing atop a giant tree that hears everything you say – no matter how quietly you say it."

El Tule?! Gabi said.

"Indeed."

Garrett nodded slowly, no doubt understanding, as Breanne now did, that Governess had known what Lenny was since Utah. "So you've known all this time. And Pando is still good with this? She will hold to the agreement despite what Lenny is?"

There was a long moment of hesitation, as if for the first time Governess was unsure how to respond.

Pete narrowed his eyes. "You didn't tell her, did you?"

"My queen is unaware of this piece of information," Governess said.

"But you could have told her anytime you wanted. Why haven't you?" Paul asked.

Breanne chewed at her lower lip. Why hadn't she told? What would make her keep this kind of information from her queen? Suddenly, the answer seemed obvious. "You don't want her to know, do you?"

Governess stared at Breanne with an expression of discomfort. "No. I suppose I do not."

Breanne found Governess's facial expressions interesting. Were they tied to her emotions, like those of humans? Or was she intentionally making the expressions to replicate her own emotions in a way humans would understand? Interesting – yes, and she'd love to better understand the tree woman's emotions. But did it matter right now? Not at all.

"Do you care to share with the class why it is you don't want her to know?" Lenny asked.

Governess rolled her eyes dramatically and sighed. "If my queen learns what you are, she will order me to bring you back, though every day we get closer to the portal opening, the less likely that seems. More logically, she would order me to deliver you to Apep for the trade we failed to secure before."

"Alright, but that doesn't answer my question," Lenny said.

Now Governess's expression was one of reluctance. "The course set is the course we should pursue."

"So, you disobey your queen to help us get a stone?" Lenny asked.

Breanne spoke directly into Lenny's mind as if whispering in his ear so only he could hear. *Careful, Lenny. Let's not talk her into changing her mind and telling Pando.*

Lenny gave Breanne a slight nod of acknowledgment, but he still looked confused.

"I have not disobeyed. My queen only instructed me to make sure you all go through the portal, help you obtain a means for us to remain unbound, and return. That is my mission. That is what I intend to do."

Breanne nodded like she understood, but she knew that was semantics, and she doubted Queen Pando would be very forgiving if she knew Governess had withheld this information from her. But, frankly, that wasn't their problem, and this was the preferred answer… and for god's sake, she just wanted to go. She wanted to get to Sarah and get her healed. "Okay. That's enough for me. Can we just get going?"

The others gave confused nods, forced to be satisfied with an incomplete answer. Forced to trust in something they didn't understand. The group set their eyes on the road and started to walk.

But Governess didn't move.

Breanne turned to find Governess locking eyes with Pete, seemingly struggling with a decision no one understood.

"Wait," Governess muttered.

"What is it?" Pete asked.

Governess pressed her lips into a tight line and turned from Pete back to Lenny. "I said that if you told me your secrets, perhaps I would tell you mine. Trust begets trust, Lenard Wade. You have placed trust in me despite knowing how great the cost could have been. I will now place my trust in you, also at great risk."

David rubbed his hands together. "The God Stone language? You're going to teach us?"

Governess shook her head. "No, chubby one. I will not teach you the ancient words. The ones we know are specific to forest-spell casting. If they work for you at all, you are just as likely to hurt yourselves with this knowledge."

David's face fell. "Well, that sucks."

Governess hesitated then, as if reconsidering what she was about to say.

Anticipation filled the silence, and finally she continued, "The truth is this. My queen is the oldest and wisest being on this planet, but if she chose to make a deal with Apep as I fear she would, I would find… Well, I would find fault with her logic. She would have me ask for a God Stone in trade for Lenard Wade-Loravaris. When Apep refuses to give her what she wants, and he will refuse, my queen would, in all her wisdom, settle for a promise from Apep to leave quickly and close the gate with haste. My queen would then spend whatever time remained wiping humanity from the Earth before becoming bound once more." Hesitating again, Governess looked at each of them in turn. "I do not feel this is the way, and I am not alone in my belief. Many of my kind also believe this is not the way. We want more than a peaceful world – we want our freedom! We would rather force your kind to share the Earth than be bound to it. Even if this means war – even if this means we lose everything."

A sudden realization dawned on Breanne. They were attempting to find and secure a magical item to keep trees free in exchange for a truce between humans and trees. But what if humans didn't want a truce? What if they wouldn't share the Earth with trees as equals?

"So, Lenard Wade, this is my secret. We must go through the portal. My queen must not find out who you are, lest she make a deal with Apep, close the portal, slay every remaining human on the planet, and settle for an Earth where trees are bound once more."

Breanne looked across the road at the forest, which was peaceful and still. Sentient bystanders silently watching – watching and waiting – waiting and brooding. Just beneath the façade of serenity, an anger simmered. Why she hadn't felt it before, she wasn't sure, but she was damn sure she felt it now. Damn sure that beneath the false calm, a storm brewed. Damn sure trees would be free, no matter the cost. She imagined it so clearly now… a forest ready for war. A war that might be inevitable no matter whether… Oh, dear god… whether they failed or succeeded.

8

A God among Liars

Friday, May 6 – God Stones Day 30
Rural Chiapas State, Mexico

B*zzzzz. Bzzzzz. Bzzzzz.* Incessant. Constant. It needled in the back of Apep's mind, always there, reminding him of his power, reminding him of his destiny. He laughed to himself, knowing he was one with it now. No longer did it threaten to unravel him. He could not be undone. He was omnipotent! *Bzzzzz. Bzzzzz. Bzzzzz.* He chuckled inwardly. There was no pain, no power, no other greater than he, and he could adapt to anything. *Bzzzzz. Bzzzzz. Bzzzzz.* He laughed outwardly now, full and boisterous. *Thank you. Thank you for joining me. Thank you for being here with me. Thank you for showing me.*

"Dökkálfar?"

Apep didn't answer; instead, he looked daggers at Ogliosh as if the giant were a child interrupting two adults speaking. He held the glare, daring him to speak again.

The giant was silent.

Apep turned away, Ogliosh's footsteps fading as he sank back into his hood and into himself. *Where was I? Ah, yes.* He smiled. *Omnipotent, I am.*

The valley below him stretched across ten miles of charred ground. Two days before, the Queen of Queens had sent several hundred dragons to the pyramid. Upon their arrival, he put dozens to work burning the jungle in a ten-mile radius around the pyramid. Others he sent to patrol, acting as his eyes. And the rest roamed beyond, searching for food and doing whatever it was dragons do.

As he gazed out across the still-smoldering valley from high upon the pyramid, he could feel the trees watching him through the smoky haze. The jungle beyond was restless and hateful. So much hate – hate thick enough to cut. He knew the tree queen wanted the Sound Eye, and he knew she would soon send every tree on this planet, if that was required, to take it away from him. What he didn't know was what the hell she was waiting for. Why not attack now before his army arrived in force? It didn't matter. Come now, come later, she would never take it away. No one would take it away. Even now, it rested heavily beneath his hood. The god's crown. *My crown!*

Just a few more days and his army would arrive. The valley before him would fill with nephilbock, and dragons would fill the sky and blot out the sun. A few more days were nothing after the millennia he had already waited.

From above him, a screech penetrated the electric buzz of his mind. He frowned, craning his head upward toward the sun, its shine assaulting his eyes. Apep lifted a bone-thin hand to his brow, the smell of rot assaulting his senses like smelling salts. He pulled a face. The dead finger flesh was still burnt at the tips from the heaps of Sentheye he'd poured into dragon egg after dragon egg, but it had been worth it. The dragons were clearing the way for the army, and his human puppet was leading them on a three-headed beast. Idly, he wondered if he would lose his fingers. All of his attempts to heal the burns had failed. It seemed a Sentheye burn could not be healed using more Sentheye.

A shadow eclipsed a rapidly sinking sun as the Queen of Queens descended onto the pyramid's platform high above the valley.

Apep didn't bother to address the queen as Azazel folded her wings.

"You look close to death, dökkálfar," she said in her bizarre dual voice. "And you smell worse than even an elf should."

Apep pulled a face, puckering sourly. Her voice was like two twins speaking together, but in distinctly unique tones. He had never given it much thought, but now he found the two voices grating. "Oh, shut up, dragon!"

"You dare speak—"

"Yes! Yes, I dare. Aren't we past this, Azazel? Aren't we past calling each other by species? You know my name. Speak it proper!" Apep snapped, climbing to his feet as if going from sitting to standing would somehow make him taller to a dragon. "Why are you here? Where is our army?" He almost said *his army*, which it was. "Report, dammit!"

Azazel leaned down, drawing closer to Apep's face, her forked tongue flicking in and out, tasting the air. "You're losing your mind! Oh, how lovely! I can see it in your eyes. The power you refuse to let go of is eating you from the inside out. But I need you to live, Apep. At least long enough to get us all home and free my people."

"Then worry about the battle to come. Worry about defeating the army of Osonian. Now, report!"

She drew back, delighted. "The air surrounding you tastes of death, but fine. The children who came ahead of me, they didn't tell you?"

"They said their queen ordered them to silence." Apep narrowed his sunken eyes.

Azazel smiled toothily. "The hordes are clearing the way for the nephilbock, but we have lost nearly a thousand of my children."

"A thousand?! The trees killed a thousand? But how could this be?" His mind spun. All that work, all that Sentheye – his fingers!

"No, Apep. Not the trees. The sea demon. The mother of all kraken. She attacked your nephilbock off the coast of Panama when they attempted to cross the canal at Panama Bay."

From deep inside the chamber came the sledgehammering of footsteps pounding stone. Apep turned to find thirty feet of angry one-eyed giant barreling toward Azazel.

The same spell that had once imprisoned Apep beneath the sands of Egypt had imprisoned these two creatures directly beneath the very pyramid he stood upon. Confused and angry, the two had woken simultaneously at the very moment Apep broke the spell holding Balor and Sylanth, along with the other five dragons and five giants, each paired two to a prison all across the world.

"Have you come to finish what we started below, foul creature?" Ogliosh bellowed.

Azazel hissed, turning toward the giant with her mouth open and throat aglow.

Apep stepped in between the two and raised his hands, one toward each. His hood slipped off his crown as his face fixed in a sneer. Pained fingers splayed with the cracking of burnt skin as Apep called upon the Sentheye. Despite his haggard physique, the Sentheye answered Apep's command as grey magic thick as molasses swirled around his hands. "Enough!"

Ogliosh stopped, pulling up short. His six-fingered hands curled into boulder-sized fists. His face twisted, revealing double rows of teeth more suited to a shark. But at the sight of Apep, his single eye blinked, his anger changing to shock.

Apep frowned up at him, then he looked at the dragon queen, who wore a similarly surprised expression. "What?"

"Apep, the Sound Eye!" Ogliosh said, pointing down at it.

Apep drew back, stumbling away from them both and nearly falling in his retreat. They were going to try and take it! "What? What is it?"

"Apep, you must remove the Sound Eye from your head… It's affixing itself to you!" Ogliosh said.

Apep reached up and touched the crown, running his bony, charred fingers along the edge where it contacted his forehead. He'd lost nearly all feeling in his fingers, so it was hard to say, but it appeared there was no seam between the Sound Eye and his skin.

"Look at him. He will not listen to you, giant one. It is the Sound Eye that holds him now," Azazel said.

"You must, Apep. You must remove it. Your skin is blackening around the crown – you can't heal with it on. Allow me to hold it for you, so you can heal," Ogliosh begged.

Azazel laughed. "It would be unwise to trust a nephilbock. Let me hold it for you, dökkálfar. Our arrangement to free my people will ensure we stay aligned."

"Our agreement with the dökkálfar is no less important than yours, Azazel!" Ogliosh growled.

"Your people aren't enslaved, you one-eyed oaf!" the dragon queen shot back.

"Silence! No one will take this crown from me so long as I breathe air! But be warned, should any try – it will be they who draw their last breath," Apep said, silencing both.

Ogliosh shook his head. "Suit yourself, Apep. But what you have placed atop your head is no crown. Joining the God Stones together was to be done only when the seven races came together in unity, for the purpose of opening portals to other planets. The Karelian races were never unified and never ready to travel among the stars."

"Yet here we are, Ogliosh. Here… we… are. As much thanks to you as me. But if you are having second thoughts about our agreement, you can be easily removed," Apep warned.

Queen Azazel purred.

"No, Apep. No second thoughts. But understand this. When the time comes to open the portal, that *crown* of yours must come off your head and be placed atop the pyramid altar."

"I understand what is required. Now, the two of you must ensure you keep the peace between each other and between your armies. I won't lose more dragons or nephilbock before we leave this wretched planet. We've lost too much already."

Ogliosh's single red-haired eyebrow furrowed. "I thought you said my nephilbock were safe? I thought you said the losses were minimal!" He looked accusingly at Azazel. "I thought you said the dragons were with us, protecting us!"

"We were, you fool!" Azazel said.

"It seems a sea demon attacked your nephilbock," Apep said as if tasting the words.

"A sea demon?" Ogliosh said. "The goddess of the sea? I saw her once, not long after we tried to open the portal last time, when the water receded from the great flood. My Earth children told stories of her. We know her as Hafgufa. Legends say she is the daughter of one of the seven gods – Rán, goddess of the sea! It is said Rán left her daughter here to rule the oceans of this world."

"Perhaps. But it is of no matter now. She is dead," Azazel said flatly.

"And how is that, exactly?" Apep asked.

"Mivras the Blue killed her," Azazel said.

"Really? By himself?" Apep asked skeptically.

"No, Jymas and Zudrian helped, but they are both dead. Mivras finished off the vile demon. I am told he burnt a hole through the side of the beast, flooding it with ocean water and drowning it."

"You want us to believe a few dragons killed Earth's goddess of the sea? This seems unlikely," Ogliosh said.

Azazel's lips drew back, revealing a row of menacing, bone-white teeth. "I already said what I was told."

"Told by whom, Mivras the Blue?" Apep asked.

"Yes," she hissed in irritation.

"And where is Mivras, Azazel?"

"Close. I have sent him to lead a small group on an errand to fetch humans. I wish to continue making *drac* slaves. Do not worry, Apep, I'm sure he will be along shortly."

Drac. A term Apep had not heard in over ten thousand years. They called them the lizard people in the days of old. "Continue? How many have you made?" Apep asked.

"Perhaps a thousand. I was bored, and besides, there may be very few humans on Karelia, and they make such obedient slaves."

The ritual concerned dragon blood magic. It was a disgusting process that turned humans into creatures viler than they already were. But they also became far more dangerous. A queen of Azazel's power could control hundreds, maybe thousands, of the dreadful creatures. Thousands of dracs could be useful in this war. If he remembered right, the survival rate for converting humans into dracs was less than fifty percent, as most lost their minds, went insane, and died. The dead became food, so there was really no loss per se. For the ones who survived, their minds would be enslaved to the queen forever.

"Where are the drac you have created?" Apep asked.

"I will send a small horde to retrieve them once the armies are safe here."

Apep nodded absently, wanting to ask about Jack but desperate not to seem overly eager, so he asked something else. "And what of Ahi? Is he dead too?"

"No. He was preoccupied clearing a place for the nephilbock to come ashore and didn't see what happened. Ask what you really want to ask, Apep," Azazel said, clearly seeing through his false concern for her elders.

Damn, was he really so obvious? He was brilliant, but even someone as wise as himself would do better to remember he was dealing with an ancient dragon. His plan for overthrowing Azazel once he had his kingdom might well depend on the human boy and his three-headed beast. But the trap was already sprung, and he had walked right into it. "Yes, well, of course I am curious. They are, after all, powerful assets to our cause. So, what of Jack and the three-headed dragon?"

Ogliosh's eyebrow pinched into a horseshoe shape, like a big bushy orange cat arching its back. "What is this you speak of? A three-headed dragon and a human boy?"

"It matters not. They are both dead. Killed by the sea demon," Azazel said with smug indifference.

Apep should have known a pathetic human couldn't play at this level. *Bzzzzz. Bzzzzz. Bzzzzz.* He resisted the urge to pinch the bridge of his nose as he tried to quiet his mind and think. It was just as likely Jack had been killed not by the kraken but by the dragon elders, following the orders of the queen. Still, the boy's use of the Sentheye and the three-headed dragon had been impressive. However, it was of no matter – what was done was done.

He realized Azazel's eyes were boring into him. He did his best to hold his composure and not let Azazel see his disappointment. To show too much would be to tip his hand. If he had no plans for the boy and the dragon beyond having them serve in the war on his father, he shouldn't be overly disappointed.

He lifted his chin and shrugged. "Ah, well. The boy and the dragon would have been a boon in the war to come, but such is life."

Ogliosh shook his head. "My people are the keepers of history. No one knows more about the past than us. A three-headed dragon was said to be the son of Typhon. What was his name?"

"You think I don't know my own god's lineage, nephilbock?" Azazel spat.

"Then speak the name of the three-headed one, Azazel," Ogliosh demanded.

Azazel did not speak his name.

"The human named him Cerberus," Apep said.

Ogliosh's one enormous eye went wide. "Cerberus, the son of Typhon!"

"Mere coincidence. Humans know the name from history," Azazel snapped. "Some nonsense about a three-headed canine. Likely from stories started long ago by loud-mouthed nephilbock! Besides, as I already said, it matters not. The abomination is dead!"

Ogliosh said, "There have been too many coincidences since you joined the God Stones, Apep! I fear your use of the Sound Eye to wake sea monsters, grow dragons, and bring consciousness to the trees of this world is angering the gods! You are dabbling in powers meant for gods and using them for your own gain!"

"For *our* gain. And need I remind you, it's *you* who have been cross-breeding humans with nephilbock since we arrived on this planet! Do you think you are innocent in this, great king?" Apep asked, condescension saturating his voice.

"I did what you asked… I… I…" Ogliosh straightened. "No. No, Apep, I am anything but innocent. Nevertheless, we would all be wise to make a hasty retreat from this planet."

Apep nodded. "In this we agree."

"In this we agree," Azazel echoed.

"Azazel, how many of my army were lost in the crossing?" Ogliosh asked.

"Two thousand. Maybe more. But do not fear, nephilbock king, your army is massive and, thanks to the diligent endeavors of my dragons, I estimate more than twenty thousand remain on course to this destination. They will begin arriving in force on the morrow."

Ogliosh nodded. "Since we agree a hasty departure is best for us all, I propose we remain allies until we are safe on Karelia and the war on Osonian is behind us."

"I agree," Azazel said, bowing her head.

Apep nodded sagely, putting on a face. *Are they kidding? Do they think I'm stupid?* But beneath the façade, anger rose like a swelling tide, and in his mind, the noise grew louder. *Bzzzzz. Bzzzzz. Bzzzzz.* They were talking like *they* were making the decision to form an alliance – as if they had a choice! Next, they would be plotting a way to kill him and steal the God Stones for themselves! They might even plot to destroy Osonian before he could take it back from his father. No. No. No! He couldn't let them! When would they strike? When he took the Sound Eye off his head and placed it at the top of the pyramid? Once the portal opened, the Sound Eye would exist in both places at once. But it would come back to the one who had placed it atop the pyramid. Unless… *Bzzzzz. Bzzzzz. Bzzzzz.* Unless he was dead. That was it! That was when they would strike! They would either kill him before he stepped into the portal or when he stepped out, before he could don the crown once more.

"Apep!" Azazel shouted.

"What?" He startled back to the present, reflexively throwing his hands out once more and summoning the Sentheye. He blinked in confusion. Had they been calling to him? *Bzzzzz. Bzzzzz. Bzzzzz.*

The two creatures shared unsettled looks.

Good, Apep thought. *Fear me. Fear me each and all.*

"What say you, wizard? We are allied to follow you and fight your war," Azazel said, nodding her massive head toward Ogliosh. "But you must keep your promise to free my people and then leave us to live in peace on our own lands."

"And you must maintain peace with the nephilbock. So too must you keep your promise to return our God Stones – not only ours, but the other three chosen. We will allow you to keep the humans' God

Stone, giving you two and thus more power than the rest of us," Ogliosh added.

"Swear to us, Apep," Azazel ordered. "Swear the oath as we stand witness to one another. You will keep your word, and you will have an unstoppable alliance and a kingdom soon to follow."

They thought him a fool. They believed gods to be fools. *Bzzzzz. Bzzzzz. Bzzzzz.* They believed a god like himself to be so easily killed as to plot against him to his face! They would never keep to their end. But if it were a fool they wanted, then a fool he would play. "Isn't it enough proof of my word, Azazel, that I grew you an army to take home? And you, giant king, isn't it enough that we are bound by a treaty signed in my own blood? Isn't it enough? I already told you both that I am committed to keeping my word! Still? Still, you need more and more and more!"

"You are not yourself, Apep. No. It is not enough," Ogliosh said.

"Yes. Yes, we need to hear you swear it," Azazel said.

Apep blinked tiredly and groaned out a breath. "Of course, you have my promise. I swear unto my death! You will have your freedom, your peace, and your God Stones. Isn't that what we have been working toward? A better tomorrow for all of our people?" He gauged his conspirators from behind shadowed eyes as they exchanged looks made to go unnoticed. But they should know that gods notice everything. A king of giants and a queen of dragons. Mortal enemies united in their plot against him. A fool he wasn't, but a fool he would play. For now. *Bzzzzz. Bzzzzz. Bzzzzz.*

"Good," Ogliosh said.

"Good," Azazel said. "But, Apep, show the wisdom you claim to possess and heed these words. You may find it difficult to pat yourself on the back when there is a dagger sticking out of it."

"You need not threaten me with betrayal, Azazel! I fix my eyes upon you both, and they see through your treachery."

"Apep!" the queen gasped, as if hurt. "You need not fear I am duplicitous. I only warn of where your underestimation and overconfidence can lead. Heed me or pass over my words as folly. Either way, 'tis a shame I won't be here to see how you fare."

"I tire of your riddles, Azazel." *Enough of this trite mortal company,* he thought, wishing they would all go away and leave a growing god to his thoughts. *Bzzzzz. Bzzzzz. Bzzzzz.*

Tired of the charade, Apep tipped his head back to consider the sky, and his vision halted. Far above, Apep observed another silhouette descending toward them. The setting sun cast the massive shape in a magenta glow. At first, he simply thought it another young dragon, but then he realized this one was larger than the queen, larger even than Mivras the Blue. But it was not the size that stretched a smile across Apep's dark face. No, no, no. It was its three heads.

Apep pointed to the sky. "Well now, Queen of Queens, it would seem your gossip's sour."

9

Sorrow and Rage

Friday, May 6 – God Stones Day 30
Rural Chiapas State, Mexico

Weary from the day's travel, Garrett and the others approached the opening to the cenote. So far, except for a few giant bugs and three separate times when dragons flew over high above, the trip down the trail had been safe enough. They had been walking with purpose for a few hours when Breanne stopped and said this was the spot where the men had jumped them several days back.

Garrett half expected their dead bodies to still be lying on the trail, but there was no trace of the dead men. He could tell the lack of bodies made everyone feel uneasy, but no one brought it up. Though the men were missing, the rifles the girls had stashed off the trail were still there. David and Pete each took one; Paul strapped the third one to his pack after a long argument with Gabi.

Finally, after searching the area, Paul bent and picked something up from the ground. *Gabi, take this,* he said, offering her a round stone half the size of a golf ball.

A rock? I ask for a gun, and you give me a rock? she said, crossing her arms.

Look at it. It's not just a rock, it's a perfect slingshot stone.

Like I already told Bre, you can't kill a dragon with a rock! I need a gun, Paul!

For now, you get this. Look, I promise. I will teach you how to shoot my handgun, and when I'm sure you know what you're doing, I will give you mine.

When? she asked, relenting a little but not uncrossing her arms.

Tonight, once we get settled at the caves. I will teach you all the basics, and I'll even show you proper stance, racking the slide, and loading the magazine.

Gabi stuffed the rock in her pocket, smiled, and held out her hand. *Deal!*

Not to be a party pooper here, but I'm not sure a gun will be much more effective at killing a dragon than that rock, David said.

David! Breanne scolded.

Not helpful, bro, Lenny said.

It WILL work! It has to! Gabi shouted.

David held his hands up. *Sorry, Gabi. My bad! I just don't want you to get hurt. And, honestly, I hope we don't have to fight any dragons.*

Well, maybe if they had killed your family, you would feel different, Gabi said, turning away.

Gabi! I didn't mean to—

Don't. It's fine, Gabi said, turning back to him, the pain unmistakable on her face as she tried to look apologetic.

An uncomfortable silence stretched across the afternoon. No one knew what to say, so instead they said nothing, retreating to their own thoughts. Soon, evening shadows crept along the jungle floor while, far to the south, white smoke filled an ever-darkening sky. Garrett was about to break the silence and ask about the smoke. He was sure he shouldn't be able to smell it so far away, but he definitely could. Finally, he gave in. *Do you guys smell that?*

Smells like smoke, Pete said.

There's a fire to the south, Paul said, pointing a finger. *But we shouldn't be able to smell it. That fire's dozens of miles away… and downwind.*

Governess stopped and rooted to the ground, appearing as motionless as a tree. Well, she was a tree, Garrett supposed, but her human features looked so real that it was easy to forget.

After a full minute, she spoke. *The fire to our south is coming from around the pyramid. The dragons have burned off the jungle in a ten-mile radius. But fear not, my queen has positioned General Sherman on the north side, staging for battle just outside the charred ring.*

General Sherman? Breanne asked.

That is what humans call him. Of the family you call sequoia, General Sherman is the largest single-stem organism on Earth. He is absolutely fearless and would be the first onto the battlefield if not for my queen's order that El Tule must lead the charge.

Up ahead, Garrett watched as Gabi vanished around a bend in the trail.

Governess's eyes turned from the smoke in the south to the path ahead. *The smell is not from the south. This is not the smell of my people burning… it is the smell of yours.*

A moment later, Gabi screamed.

Garrett jerked instinctively, raising his hands to defend as Governess's roots ripped from the ground, shifting back into her feet as she bolted forward.

Breanne's scream followed. "Gabi!"

They all ran.

When Garrett rounded the bend, he saw Gabi collapsed onto her knees in a large patch of ashen earth, her eyes fixed on a sheer cliff wall blackened by flame. Garrett frowned, not understanding at first. Then he saw the smoke leaking from the top of a narrow gap in the stone face. A warm breeze lifted ash from the ground, swirling it into the smoke to be carried away on a black-flecked cloud. This was the source of the smell.

"Sarah!" Breanne shouted, running past him toward the opening.

"Wait, Bre! It may not be safe!" Garrett shouted after her. But she didn't wait. She ran, pulling her shirt up over her mouth as she vanished into the void.

"Bre! Dammit, wait!" her brother shouted.

"Shit!" Garrett ran in after her, hearing the footfalls of the others on his heels. The narrow passage sloped downward. He sucked smoke thick into his lungs, burning his throat. Coughing, Garrett dropped into a squat and shuffled forward, trying to stay under the smoke. *Bre!* he tried, hoping she would at least answer in mind speak. Nothing.

An orange glow up ahead told him he was nearing the end of the dark crevice. When he reached it, he stopped, trying to get his bearings. Someone collided into him from behind, shoving him out into a larger area. Garrett sprawled forward onto his hands and knees, grunting when he hit the stone floor.

"Garrett? My bad, sorry!" Lenny said, grabbing him by the arm and pulling him up.

"It's okay." *Bre! Where are you?* Garrett said in mind speak, not wanting to yell. Fires burned to their left and right. They were only small fires now, but he could tell they had once been larger. He pushed forward through the smoke. Once clear of the overhang trapping the smoke and choking up the entrance, he found there was open sky. Through the haze and low light, Garrett could just make out water spilling from high above on the far side, forming a glassy lake that stretched out all the way across the enormous space.

The others were there now.

Paul stood next to Garrett. "Where's my sister?" he asked, scanning the chamber.

But there were plenty of areas beyond the small fires veiled in dark shadow. Plenty of areas he and Paul couldn't see into. "Lenny, do you see her?"

Lenny looked around, his eyes lighting up with energy that fractured outward from the centers of his pupils like golden spiderwebs. "Over there!" He pointed.

Garrett and the others followed as Lenny hurried across an area littered with metal cook pots, utensils, and bricks. This had been a camp and, from the looks of it, there had been several people here, but now fire had burnt everything. What had happened, and where had the people gone? Clearly it had been something awful – some kind of attack.

Bre was on her hands and knees, staring into a dark nook, sobbing. She sat back on her heels, her shoulders bouncing.

"Bre? Bre, what is it?" Garrett asked softly, a sinking feeling in the pit of stomach.

A soft moan escaped her, but no words came.

Garrett peered into the dark nook, trying to see.

"Oh, god," Lenny whispered, turning away.

"Len, what is it?"

Paul dropped to his knees and leaned into the nook. "Jesus. Oh, Jesus. Oh, no." He turned to Bre. "Is it her, Bre? Are you sure? How can you be sure?" Paul begged.

The tears ran, and Breanne couldn't speak. She could only point.

Garrett crawled next to her and followed her trembling finger. The body was burnt to the bone, with only shreds of blackened flesh still clinging to the prone skeleton. This could have been anyone, man or woman. Garrett's eyes traced the badly burnt arm that lay at the body's side. There, dangling from the skeletal wrist, was a bracelet with a single charm. He narrowed his eyes. It looked like a tiny garden trowel.

Finally, Breanne whispered, "I gave that charm to Sarah when we were on a dig site in Egypt." The sobs broke loose, and Breanne cried.

Eventually Paul stood, wiping his own eyes. "I'm sorry, Bre. I'm sorry we didn't make it, but this isn't your fault. We did the best we—"

Breanne held up a hand, silencing her brother. And then her body shook again, racked by a fresh wave of sobs.

Paul sighed, heavy and sad. He placed a hand on Garrett's shoulder and nodded. Garrett nodded back, his lips a tight line, his heart aching for Breanne. The understanding between them needed no words. Breanne cried until she became sick. She retched until there was nothing left, and then she cried more. Garrett stayed there with Bre, saying nothing as he rubbed her back.

She didn't ask him to stay, but she didn't ask him to leave her alone either and in this, he somehow knew she needed him. And he would be there – for as long as it took.

As the others explored the cenote proper, they reported what they were seeing to Garrett in mind speak. He wasn't sure if they were being careful to only speak to him, or if Bre was hearing it all too.

Garrett, we are finding more people… or what's left of them, Lenny said.

Burned? Garrett asked, rubbing at his arms. They were starting to feel all tingly and weird.

A few but… um, no. Most are just, um, pieces mostly, Lenny said.

Something fed here, guys, Pete said.

Garrett's pulse quickened.

This is the work of dragons. One or more came in from above, feeding on these humans before they could get away, Governess said evenly.

Hey, I see several caves on the other side. Maybe some of them made it to safety, Lenny said.

"How am I going to tell Dad that Sarah's… Sarah's gone?" Breanne whispered.

Garrett drew in a deep breath. The tingling was starting to burn. "I'll be there with you, right by your side. Bre, can you stand? I think we should—"

"It's going to break him, Garrett. It's going to break his heart." She threw her arms around him, and he held her for a long moment as she cried once more. But then Garrett felt an emotion so out of place it took his breath. Like a sudden rage.

Breanne pushed herself back, her hand on his chest. "Garrett, did you feel that?" she asked.

"Yeah, I think so. What was that?"

Guys, did you feel something odd? Pete asked, sounding agitated.

I just felt so pissed off I wanted to punch something in the face! David said.

Gabi! Gabi, where are you?! Breanne asked, climbing to her feet.

She never came inside! David said.

Oh, no! Breanne said, pushing past Garrett.

They all started for the entrance, but before they reached the crevasse, they heard a long, low roar from the caves across the cenote.

What the shit?! David said, scrambling for the crevasse opening.

Lenny's eyes flashed golden in the low light. "Balls!"

Crap! Lenny, you want to translate that for us! Pete said.

Dragons!

Three small dragons appeared from the caves on the other side of the cenote, instantly leaping airborne, flying toward them low across the water.

At that moment, Garrett knew two things. One, as soon as he'd felt the strange sensation in his arms, he should have acted. And two, it was obvious they weren't all going to make the crevasse and, even if they did, the dragons would likely burn them before they made it out the other side. *Guys! No! We can't make it!* Garrett said, turning to face them full on. *Pete, hit one with your eyes before it crosses,* he said, drawing his sword.

I'll try! Pete said, squinting hard at the one on the far left.

They were closing. *Paul, David, and Bre – shoot for the eyes of the one in the middle!* Garrett said.

Gunfire erupted from David's rifle and Paul's handgun, but when Garrett looked for Bre, he found her standing behind him, frozen, her eyes solid white. *Damn.* When he turned back, the dragon on the far right opened its mouth and roared. Its throat lit up, illuminating the whole chamber in a wash of warm light filtered by its brown scales. Just before fire erupted from its mouth, Garrett grabbed time and slowed the dragon to a near stop.

Only fifty paces away, the young dragon, throat charged with fire, hung in the air, suspended in time.

Garrett had it, but he wasn't sure what to do with it. He knew one thing; he'd better not take his eyes off it until he figured it out. Carefully he started walking toward it, cautious not to let the simple action of placing one foot in front of the other cause him to lose his focus.

Thirty-five paces.

The dragon had one eye pinched shut, glued that way by some viscous liquid that gave it the appearance of an old, festering wound. Despite the missing eye, its one good eye burned bright like a red star, angry and fixing all its hate on him.

Garrett continued forward, holding his fragile grip on time and with it the beast's stare, while around him the chamber erupted with yet another roar, then a massive splash. Water rained down as a green glow filled the chamber, followed by more gunshots, then several clicks. Paul grunted from somewhere to his left and the ground shook.

From the corner of his eye, roots burst from the ground. Despite the surrounding chaos, he dared not look – he dared not even blink.

Twenty-five paces.

It's coming out of the water! David called out.

It's breaking the roots! Paul shouted.

A giant version of Governess, fifteen feet tall if she were an inch, ran past him and vanished from his peripheral vision. Garrett wanted to look – god, how he wanted to! Instead, he stepped forward again and again – ten more paces.

Now! Pete shouted, as a horrific sound of breaking bone filled the chamber, reverberating off the stone walls.

A dragon shrieked.

Garrett was at the water's edge, staring into a mouth full of dragon fire the scaly creature couldn't release. The beast wasn't much larger than an elephant with a giraffe-length neck, yet despite the monster's size, he could feel it fighting his will, trying to break his hold on time.

Feeling the panic consume him, Garrett hurriedly waded the final five paces out into the water, cocking his sword back for a swing, but his hold on time slipped.

Dragon fire spilled from the one-eyed monster.

As fire consumed him, Garrett swung the sword in a high arc, slicing deep into the left side of the dragon's neck. He could never get used to this part, nor would he ever assume fire wouldn't burn him. How could he? All his human instincts screamed that fire was hot, and it burned – would burn. And of all the fire in the world, dragon fire was the worst. On a heat scale, dragon fire must rank just above molten iron and lava. He wanted to scream in anticipation of the pain, but just as before, the fire was warm and momentarily blinding, but he did not burn. And like before, the strange dragon runes glowed beneath his skin, protecting him from a terrible and absolute death. In an instant, the water around Garrett's legs boiled and evaporated into a cloud of steam.

As the inferno whooshed past, Garrett's eyes cleared and snapped wide as a new horror emerged, all teeth and scales. The dragon's forward momentum carried it into him, knocking him back onto the shore. The dragon collapsed into death, pinning Garrett's legs beneath it.

Then came something unexpected – the pain. It came in a wash of agony that nearly caused his bladder to release. Confusion blossomed, but an incomprehensible suffering overshadowed it, and for a moment, he lost all rational thinking. From just above his knees, down through his toes, Garrett burned. Desperately, he tried to push the dragon off his legs, but it was no use. Jesus, the pain! Had the dragon crushed his legs? No. This wasn't broken bone pain. His legs were literally burning! They were on fire! *Help! Please!* He tried to look past the dragon's bulk to his left, but he couldn't see over it. He couldn't see the others.

Garrett's vision blurred and his eyes rolled back.

I'm on fire! Please! he begged, but he knew that was wrong. He couldn't be on fire. The dead dragon had Garrett's legs pinned beneath it on a wet shoreline, yet still he burned.

Through the agony of his burning legs, his friends' voices were becoming distant in the chaos, like they were moving away from him.

Garrett blinked, trying to stay conscious, trying not to let the pain take him. *Please!* Then he heard her voice cut through everything – Breanne.

Guys, I had a vision! Another dragon is coming! It's a huge blue one!

10

The Sound of Dragon Fire

Friday, May 6 – God Stones Day 30
Rural Chiapas State, Mexico

Breanne crossed the chamber in a full run, dodging past Paul, who was holding one of the dragons by a wing. The dragon was trying to get into the air, but her brother yanked it down onto the ground as Lenny leapt higher than should have been possible, cracking it across its ash-colored snout with his wooden staff.

As she neared the center of the chamber, she saw Pete staring at a rust-colored dragon, his eyes fixed in focus. Next to him, Governess stood three times her normal height, her hand splayed and covered in the now-familiar green glow. The focus of the tree woman's attention was the same dragon, bound to the earth in a tangle of thick roots that, despite their girth, were snapping under the dragon's efforts to free itself. Just when Breanne was sure the dragon was going to break free, she heard a horrific crunch. The dragon shrieked, collapsing back onto the floor as the roots constricted with renewed strength.

Breanne darted past Pete as he dropped onto one knee, still staring at the dragon and at what he'd done. Something deep inside the beast had broken under the strain of Pete's glare. Perhaps the dragon's spine?

She couldn't be sure, and she had no time to understand. Garrett needed her.

She pressed forward, fixated now on a third dragon lying motionless. She didn't see the fire Garrett was screaming about, but she expected she would when she reached the other side. What she feared most was finding Garrett on fire. Her stomach tightened as she braced herself, prepared to grab him and drag him into the water. And why, if he were on fire, hadn't he just thrown himself in the water? All this ran through her mind as she slid to a stop just past the dragon and looked to her left. There! Garrett was there, but he wasn't burning. He was flat on his back with a dead dragon lying across his legs. *Shit!* How was she supposed to get him out?

Garrett! Garrett, can you hear me?! Pain twisted his face, and his eyes were rolling back in his head. She grabbed him under the arms and heaved. This wasn't going to work. There was no damn way she could do this!

"My legs… my legs are on fire, Bre. Jesus, they're burning!"

She frowned, "Garrett, your legs are pinned, but they're not burning."

A roar deep as the ocean filled the cenote and the whole place darkened.

Breanne craned her head back as a shadow passed overhead, blotting out the sky. *Paul! Help! Someone! Garrett's trapped under a dragon!*

Lenny's voice answered. *If Garrett's stuck, you better go, Paul! I'll get the others outside!*

Seconds later, Paul was there beside her.

Pull him out, Paul!

No good! That thing is too heavy, he said, pointing at the dead dragon. *If I pull him, I'll rip his legs off.*

"It's coming, Paul! Do something!" Breanne begged.

Her brother took three steps back, set his feet, and ran forward. When his shoulder hit the dragon, it sank deep into the dead beast's scales. The dragon lifted from the floor of the cave and flopped over, landing in the water with a splash.

She looked at Garrett's legs, not knowing what to expect, but they looked… fine. Even his pants looked okay. They were wet, but they hadn't been burned.

She exchanged confused looks with Paul, but the mystery would have to wait. The giant blue dragon appeared above the cenote, flapping its great wings and locking its gaze on her.

The blue dragon roared.

Run, Bre! Paul said, grabbing Garrett by an arm and pulling.

She ran.

Across the cenote, the others were nearing the entrance.

The deep roar rose like thunder in her bones as a blue glow filled the cenote. Breanne dared a glance back to find the angry dragon's scaly blue neck lit from within. They would never make it. It would burn them in the crevasse before they could get out the other side. Dear god, they were all going to die.

As Lenny, Pete, David, and Governess reached the crevasse, Gabi appeared, nearly colliding with them.

Back, Gabi! Go back! Breanne shouted.

But she didn't go back, and Breanne felt another wave of anger as the young girl darted past them toward the center of the chamber.

The blue dragon's roar became so loud the walls and even the ground shook beneath them. Breanne wanted to stop. She wanted to turn and go back to find Gabi, but there was no time. When the dragon opened its mouth, the glow was so bright even the crevasse before her disappeared in its shine. She couldn't see. She ran blindly ahead, knowing instinctively that even the crevasse wouldn't save her. Still, she ran forward, waiting for the burn to come.

Behind her, she heard Garrett find his voice. "Let me go, Paul! Let me go and get Bre inside! I can block the flame."

Paul must have complied because suddenly he was beside her as she hesitated. "But, Gabi!"

"No time!" Paul shouted, snatching her by the arm and pulling her into the crevasse. They pushed their way through the darkness, running from the inevitable flames and the certain death that would follow.

Over the past month, Breanne had learned a dragon's roar was a distinct thing. As it got closer to breathing fire, the roar climbed not only in volume but also in pitch. And when the fire came, it too had a distinct sound – its own angry roar. She'd heard it in the temple back in Petersburg when Sylanth killed Janis, and as she made her way through the crevasse, that's exactly what she heard now.

She heard the sound of dragon fire.

11

I Invoke Dragon Law

Friday, May 6 – God Stones Day 30
Rural Chiapas State, Mexico

Jack and Cerb descended onto the north side of a massive pyramid. The pyramid was a strange thing, not like the Egyptian ones Jack had seen pictures of. This pyramid had a flat top with a massive, box-shaped stone building atop it. A large doorway was cut into one wall, but despite its size, Jack didn't think Cerb could fit inside. Nor could Cerb fit on the wide ledge that wrapped the building. Especially not with a giant, the size of which Jack had never seen before, a full-grown dragon, and Apep already filling the north ledge and the opening.

Jack wanted to make an entrance, but crowding onto an overstuffed ledge and getting his dragon stuck in a too-small opening wasn't what he had in mind. The building atop the pyramid was at least half the size of a football field and flat, except for some openings in the roof and something that looked like a stone altar. Jack smiled to himself. There'd be plenty of room for Cerb up there – plenty of room at the top of everything. *Drop even with the ledge, Cerb. Once I'm off, land on top and let anyone who looks see you.*

Cerb laughed. *I like the way you think, Taker!*

Taker – this was the first time Cerb had referred to him as Taker. He liked it. He liked it a hell of a lot. Jack smiled, popped the collar on his leather jacket, and prepared to dismount the dragon.

Cerb lowered himself below the edge of the pyramid opening and onto the steep stone stairs leading to the valley floor far below. The dragon's talons bit into the stone, finding purchase as he extended a wing onto the stone floor in front of the opening.

Jack stood, careful of his foot placement, as he walked down Cerb's long wing, doing his best to act as though he hadn't a care in the world. He kept his eyes downcast. If he fell, he'd be dead before he reached the ground, hundreds of steps below. Finally, he stepped onto the stone ledge with hidden relief.

Cerb withdrew the wing and leapt into the air, flapping his great wings as he rose.

"Jack! Good to see you, my boy!" Apep said.

Slowly Jack lifted his head to find the elf wizard's dark-blue skin was now tinted in a filter of red, just as everything was tinted in a filter of red.

Apep's eyes sprang wide, but it was nothing compared to the stretch of the giant's big egg-shaped orb, and even the giant's apparent surprise was only half what Azazel showed as she hissed and drew back.

"Is it?" Jack asked, taking a hell of a lot of joy in their surprise while doing his best not to show it.

"What?" Apep breathed, doing nothing to hide his awe.

"Is it good to see me?" he asked, but his eyes weren't on Apep, they were on the Queen of Queens… his queen.

"We thought you dead, Jack. They said the sea demon ate you before Mivras could kill it," Azazel cooed.

Her fake-ass concern brought on a wave of anger radiating up Jack's spine and flushing his face. "Who's they? Who… says? The truth, my Queen." He spat the next words more harshly than he meant to. "The sea demon didn't have the stomach for Jack Nightshade!"

His words echoed down the tunnel that led deeper inside the pyramid to who the hell knew where. They all looked at him like they might shit themselves. *Good.* “The truth,” Jack said again, holding his hands palms up, “is that I killed the sea demon with these two hands! Without even the help of my brother. Why? Why do you think that is?” Before anyone could speak, Jack continued, “Because your elders attacked my brother and tried to kill him!”

“Ridiculous!” Azazel snapped.

“You said the bonding made me one of you. You said we were sworn to protect one another.”

“And I meant it, Jack,” Azazel said, both her voices soothing as a mother’s whisper. Or at least as soothing as Jack imagined a mother’s whisper would be.

Above them, Cerberus roared, shaking the whole pyramid. Apep’s surprise had now been replaced with a crazy-looking grin.

“Cerb killed Zudrian the Old, and he would have killed Mivras too, but the coward got away,” Jack said.

“That is not what Mivras reported,” Azazel said.

“Did you order them to kill us?” Jack asked.

The Queen of Queens laughed. “Do you think by asking me you will learn the truth? You speak to me as if you hold some authority, as if your words alone may compel my tongue to speak truth – you, a tiny human boy. But you compel nothing from me.”

He stood silent for a moment, puzzling out the sentence, quickly concluding that she was basically calling him a nobody. “I can already see through your lies.” Then just to the queen, he said, *I guess it’s good I’m no mere human. Dragon blood flows through these veins, same as yours. But even more, I killed a god! Look into these eyes, Mother, tell me what you see!*

Azazel hissed and bared her teeth. When a dragon, especially the mother of all dragons, bares teeth, you piss yourself right there on the spot. But Jack wasn’t afraid, not even a little. In fact, he found himself snarling and baring his own teeth.

“No one is killing anyone,” Apep said. “What really happened doesn’t matter now. You are here, the nephilbock are safe, and both them and the dragon hordes will be here soon.”

Jack turned and narrowed his red eyes at Apep.

"Need I remind you all what we are trying to do?" Apep said, his own eyes dark and sunken.

Apep had lost even more weight since Jack had seen him last. Shouldn't he be rested from all his overuse of Sentheye? He had been at pyramid for a few days now. Instead of refreshed, he looked worse than ever. Back in Peru, Jack had become used to seeing the Sound Eye sitting atop the elf's head. His crown. The one thing that made everything possible. But something was different now. The crown looked like it was becoming part of Apep's head, melting into his flesh. No, melting wasn't the right word – fusing maybe. Jesus, why hadn't he taken the thing off? Even his tall, pointed ears appeared to be stuck to the thing. Clearly Apep wasn't all there before, but now he looked batshit crazy.

"Now, Jack, I'm glad you're back, but we've much work to do," Apep said, pulling his hood back in place, as if he'd noticed Jack's eyes on the God Stones. With the Sound Eye crown concealed, the half-dead–looking elf continued, "The trees are preparing to attack, my armies have yet to arrive, and the repairs on the pyramid are not complete." He pointed across the valley.

Jack followed Apep's gaze far across the long, scorched valley toward a grove of trees that rose high above the Mexican jungle – hundreds of feet tall. Taller than any trees Jack had ever seen, and over the past several days, he'd seen a lot. He turned back to Apep. "You said what happened doesn't matter. Well, I say what really happened is all that matters." He looked up at the giant. "When your armies get here, you will know the truth of what I've done."

The giant stared at him steadily, but there was an uneasiness about it.

Jack smiled inwardly. *They're afraid of us, Cerb. They're all afraid.*

As they should be, Taker.

To see that something so big and menacing was afraid of him – afraid of Jack Nightshade from Petersburg, Illinois... Well, it felt right and proper – it felt damn good, is what it felt. "Where's Mivras? I have unfinished business with the Blue," Jack asked, turning to Azazel.

"He is on an errand collecting humans for slaves. When he returns,

I shall show you what becomes of humans I decide not to make a meal of."

Was she trying to threaten him? He looked at her. His red eyes narrowed, one twitching. "Guess it's good I ain't no human then – not anymore."

She seemed to sense he wasn't afraid. "Best you remember, Jack. I am your queen, and you will obey my wishes."

"And what is it you want?" Jack asked.

The dragon stared down at him, her forked tongue flicking in and out. Whatever she was about to say, Jack knew it would be a lie. Because he knew two simple truths in this whole mess. She wanted him dead, and she was too afraid to say it. Then again, if he were wrong about her fear, one of them would have to die right here and now. Just like the old days, Jack balled a fist, ready to throw his haymaker, but he'd be sure and pack this haymaker full of disease.

The queen glanced at Apep. "I want you to help Apep, Jack. Whatever the dökkálfar needs. We need off this planet."

His fist relaxed. "And then?" he asked.

Her voice filled his mind so only he could hear. *Then you lead my army, Jack. Just as I promised you. And then I will have my revenge on the dökkálfar.*

He thought to ask what came after, but he realized it was pointless because she would be long dead before there was ever a need to concern himself with after. Instead, he bowed his head toward the queen. "I understand. Let me know when Mivras gets back from his errand."

"Why should that concern you, Jack?" the queen asked.

"Because he must answer for what he's done," Jack said evenly, making sure his words held no question.

"I forbid this, Jack. Mivras is my most powerful dragon and my senior general. He is an essential leader in this army. The dökkálfar requires his assistance in the war to come."

"I can spare him," Apep answered quickly.

Azazel's eyes shot daggers at the elf.

"He is not the most powerful dragon in this army – Cerberus is, or do you disagree?"

"It does not matter! As your queen, I forbid revenge on Mivras!" Azazel snapped.

"Does not dragon law allow a challenge to the death when one dragon attacks another unprovoked?" Ogliosh asked, and it was the first time Jack had heard the monster actually speak. The thing sounded like it had a throat full of rocks.

"Do not quote dragon law to me, nephilbock," Azazel said. "There is no evidence in these accusations!"

"You calling me a liar?" Jack seethed, his fist balling up again.

"Mivras will face the accusations upon his return. Until then, there is no point in debating this further," Azazel warned, her tail flipping up, only to slap back down like raw meat on a countertop.

"Fine, but when he returns, I expect you to follow your own laws! Cerberus and I challenge your punk-ass dragon to a fight to the death."

"Careful, Jack," Apep warned.

Azazel peered down at Jack, a sudden brightness filling her eyes. "Do you? Do you, Jack Nightshade, invoke dragon law?"

"No, no, he doesn't. Let this go, Jack!" Apep warned again.

"Yes! Yes, I do! I invoke dragon law!" Jack shouted, pointing a finger at the queen.

"Well, Jack, you should be more careful what you wish for," Azazel said, lifting her chin. "The law in this is clear."

"Good," Jack said, straightening.

"Indeed. Now, who did you say Mivras attacked, Jack?"

"I already said – he attacked Cerb."

"Let this go, Jack. I command you to let this go!" Apep ordered, shaking his head.

Jack frowned, not understanding. There was no way he and Cerb couldn't beat Mivras in a fight. He'd disease him, and Cerb would blast the fat Smurf-looking bastard off the face of the Earth before he could even breathe fire.

Queen Azazel laughed. "Challenge accepted. Cerb and Mivras will battle to the death. However, Mivras did not attack you, and therefore you have no charge in this."

"What? What do you mean I have no charge?" Jack asked, not understanding.

"The law is clear, Jack. The law you demand!" She lowered her head to meet his eyes. "You will play no part in this, except to die should your dragon lose."

12

Gabi and the Blue

Friday, May 6 – God Stones Day 30
Rural Chiapas State, Mexico

Three seconds. That's how long it took Garrett to stand on burnt legs. That's how long it took for him to push himself up and in front of the crevasse opening. This wasn't the first or even the second time he'd stared into dragon fire, but that didn't make it any less terrifying. Especially when he didn't understand why his legs still felt like they were on fire. What if his immunity was wearing off or something? What if he couldn't stop the flame? What if this time his whole body burned?

The runes on his arms stung and glowed as the light from the dragon's mouth blinded him. All he could do now was pray his body would block enough of the dragon's fire from entering the crevasse and give the others a chance. But then he remembered Gabi was out there in the chamber, somewhere in front of him. Somewhere beyond his protection, and he couldn't see her. Maybe he could slow time and save Gabi. He grabbed for time, but he couldn't reach it. He couldn't focus through the pain of his own burning legs. It took everything for Garrett just to stand and be the shield his friends needed him to be.

Three seconds. That's how long it took for the flame to come.

Garrett held out his arms, closed his eyes, and screamed.

The roar of dragon fire filled the chamber, washing him in warmth. But right away, he knew something was different. Garrett cracked one eye. The dragon's flame didn't hit him.

Instead, far to his right where he had fought the small dragon, fire lit the floor and walls of the cenote. The dragon had turned its head. The rumbling roar trailed off as the blinding light faded, replaced with an ignition of firelight fueled by pooled dragon blood – blood spilled by Garrett's own sword.

In front of him, the massive blue dragon landed at the water's edge, its wings stretched across the cenote. *How big did these things get?* Garrett craned his head back as if to look at the moon high above, hoping to steal a glance at the beast's face. Its head was bigger than an SUV, and it had vertical rows of smaller spikes that stretched from the tip of its nose all the way up its head. Massive horns – Garrett could see at least four – protruded above its serpent eyes, pointing back behind its head. The size of this dragon was twice that of the two-headed dragon he'd fought in Petersburg and way larger than even the biggest one that had attacked them on the ferry.

Garrett didn't need to strain for a look. The big blue dragon lowered its head and blasted an angry roar, but this time, there was no fire in it. Instead, teeth as big as shovel blades dripped with drool as a long, forked tongue extended, trembling in the wave of bellowing breath. Garrett realized it wasn't even roaring at him. When he followed its gaze, he saw the focus of the dragon's attention.

Gabi, run!

But Gabi didn't run. She didn't move. She just stared up at the big blue dragon. *Gabi! Gabi, what are you doing? Get out of there!* She didn't answer. Instead, Gabi pulled Garrett into a conversation taking place between her and the dragon. Gabi had opened the door of her mind to let him in – to let him hear.

You dare to interfere with Mivras the Blue! You dare to meddle in my mind!

Tell me where the one they call Azazel is, Mivras! Tell me, and I will allow you to die quickly!

The dragon's creepy cackle filled the cenote, echoing off the walls. *You seek the Queen of Queens!*

Tell me where she is! Gabi shouted again.

Garrett could feel her anger, but also something else. He could feel her power.

What came next was a battle of wills as Gabi engaged in a struggle for the giant dragon's mind.

Mivras opened his mouth again, a prelude to fire, and this time his neck glowed.

Garrett blinked furiously, the pain in his legs threatening to take his consciousness. They needed to get out.

Leave him to me, Garrett. You… should… leave. Gabi's voice strained to reach him, even in mind speak.

In that moment, Garrett realized Gabi didn't need him to save her – the tiny girl was trying to save him.

Garrett Turek! The one the dökkálfar seeks! The one they say is blood-marked! Mivras swung his monstrous head to the right, then to the left toward Garrett, its blue throat growing brighter. Before its serpent eyes could settle on him, its colossal head froze, as if it hit an invisible wall. The dragon's head began to shake, writhing against Gabi's control.

Gabi's own head shook too, as she fought to insert her will and force the blue dragon's eyes to meet her own.

She was clearly struggling, but as Garrett looked back at the giant dragon, his neck went cold once again. Was she winning?

The dragon groaned out a desperate roar.

Garrett's burnt legs threatened to give out.

Gabi's whole body trembled. She was battling in a war of the minds, and Garrett didn't know what to do – how to help. She couldn't maintain this. Garrett feared she would slip. She would lose control, and if that happened, even for a second – she would be dead!

The dragon's head jerked forward like a striking cobra, snapping its mouth shut just short of Gabi's face. The tiny girl didn't so much as flinch. Concentration fixed her face in an awful grimace. *Where is your queen?!* she shouted. *I command you! Tell… me… now!*

The blue dragon's lips curled up, revealing its yellowed teeth once more. *She is at the pyramid preparing to open the gate back to our—*

The dragon's voice cut off.

Garrett felt the dragon's frustration. A frustration rooted in confusion. A rage was building, but so too was its focus. The dragon was pushing the frustration down, taking back control of its own mind. Gabi was going to lose control.

She is there now?! Gabi pressed, her voice suffused with excitement.

Garrett could feel her energy rising and her concentration falter. *Gabi, please. Run!* Garrett begged.

But she didn't run. The blue dragon lifted from the ground with one flap of its wings. *Perhaps you would like to meet her!* The dragon's long taloned foot reached forward, wrapping the tiny girl and jerking her from the ground.

Garrett tried to run forward but collapsed to his knees on the first step, the pain too much as his burnt skin stretched. *Focus, Garrett!* he told himself. *Jesus, please! Ignore the pain and focus!* He reached forward, grabbing the trails of his mind, and slowed the giant dragon as it tried to rise.

Voices exploded from behind him.

"Oh god, no!" Lenny shouted.

"Gabi!" Breanne screamed. "Please, Garrett, don't let go! Don't let go!"

The others were piling back through the crevasse now. If he could just hold on to it a little longer, Pete could use his eyes, Governess could root it, or maybe Paul could grab it.

But it was Lenny who came bolting past him, flipping through flames still fueled by spilled dragon blood. Lenny passed through the fire and landed on the dead rust-colored dragon. Taking two hurried steps, he leapt into the air. As Lenny's body came close to the dragon, the boy slowed, as if he'd launched himself airborne in slow motion.

Slowly, the dragon rose, twisting toward the sky.

Garrett couldn't slow it all the way. He couldn't make it stop completely. He tried to keep his desperate grasp on time – desperate and slipping.

Lenny reached out, his own body matching the dragon's speed as he tried for a grab.

Garrett turned his extended hands into fists and cried out.

Lenny's hands clasped two fistfuls of the dragon's tail.

Finally, the dragon roared and pulled with a final force of effort.

Garrett tried to hold on – god, how he tried. But he couldn't keep his grip. The dragon was so big. So powerful. It ripped itself free of time and, with another flap of its great wings, it launched skyward, as if slung upward by a catapult.

Then the big blue dragon was above the rim, with Gabi locked in its talons and Lenny clinging desperately to its tail.

Jesus, Lenny! Pete shouted, narrowing his eyes to focus.

But the blue dragon twisted and snapped his long tail like a bullwhip.

Lenny's hold slipped, and he dropped, arms flailing to right himself.

Pete's eyes went wide, his own focus apparently lost.

Garrett tried to grab the Sentheye, hoping to lasso the beast with it like he had to the dragon back on the river, but it rose so fast. Before Garrett could even call to the Sentheye again, the dragon was out of reach, disappearing beyond the rim of the cenote's cliffs.

Lenny shouted as he splashed down into the cenote. Any chance of saving Gabi vanished with him as he slipped beneath the water's surface.

"No!" Breanne screamed. But the blue dragon was gone, and so was Gabi.

13

Little Speck

Friday, May 6 – God Stones Day 30
Rural Chiapas State, Mexico

Jack had stepped in it, and he knew it. *Sons-a-bitches, why do I have to go off and run my big fat mouth like that?*

What is it? Cerb asked.

I screwed up big time, Cerb. I challenged Mivras to a fight to the death for trying to kill you, Jack said.

Taker, worry not, my brother! You have just slain a kraken! We will make quick work of this fat blue bastard!

Jack liked Cerb more and more with each passing day. That last comment could just as easily have come from Danny's mouth as Cerb's. *Cerb, there's a problem. After I made the challenge, Azazel said that since it was you Mivras attacked, you have to fight him by yourself. I can't help you!*

There was a long silence. *It's okay, Taker. I will defeat him.*

But Cerb didn't sound confident. *I'm sorry, Cerb. I thought we could both fight!*

Stop. You have done nothing wrong. This is our way. This is how it must be.

Instinctively, as if from somewhere deep in Jack's core, he knew Cerb was right. It was their way. The dragon way. *But he's way bigger, Cerb, and he's been in a lot of battles. How are you going to beat him?* Jack asked, feeling his throat constricting.

You need not worry. I am Cerberus, the Mighty God Son, birthed from the fires of Typhon! No dragon can kill me! Let him come! Let him come and face my judgment!

Actually, Cerberus had hatched from an egg Jack doused in a powerful release of Sentheye, but he wasn't going to ruin the moment. Personally, Jack didn't believe in real gods, even after killing the sea demon, but if he ever met an actual god, he would do his best to kill it, just like he'd done with that overgrown octopus. What good were gods anyway if they let a kid get beat on by a drunk? What good were gods if they let a kid's mom abandon him? And what the hell good were gods if all they did was sit around while good people like Danny died. No, Jack had no use for gods, even if they existed. What Jack knew about Cerb was this: Cerb was real, and together they were unstoppable. But Cerb was young, only weeks old. He had three heads, sure, but he was smaller than Mivras. Maybe only slightly and size wasn't everything, but still. The giant blue dragon had been alive for thousands of years and been in countless battles.

Do you doubt me, Taker? Cerb asked.

No. No, I believe in you, Cerb, Jack said, but the way the words came out, even he didn't believe them. *Damn.* Why shouldn't he believe? He had been the underdog plenty, and plenty of bigger kids had underestimated him and ended up on their backs. Jack nodded slowly, clenching his jaw, and latched on to a new conviction. Cerb could do it. He had to do it! *You can do it, Cerb. I know you can!*

The dragon belted out a laugh. *Ha! Good! Now I believe you! And you better be right, Taker… or we're both dead!* Cerberus laughed again.

Jack laughed too. Not in his mind, but out loud.

"What is wrong with you?" Azazel asked.

"Yes, tell us, Jack. What do you find funny at this moment?" Apep asked.

Jack looked up, only just remembering himself. He was still

standing before the queen, Apep, and Ogliosh. "I… I was just laughing at what a mistake you've made, my queen," Jack said, dropping the laughter but not the wicked grin.

Apep snorted, and this elicited a sneer from Azazel in his direction.

Azazel swung her head back toward Jack, meeting his gaze, her mouth stretching into a delighted smile, all teeth and gums. "A mistake?" she hissed. "Oh, Jack, I know you are human and young, yet despite the former, perhaps your stupidity and ignorance could be improved if only you had time. But sadly, I see your life clearly now. It burns hot, though not like a sun. No. Yours is like the exhaling of dragon breath set aflame. Fire pure, brilliant, and beautiful, but oh, so fleeting. You pull the attention of those greater than you, and we look, Jack. And we glimpse your shine – but then what? I will tell you what, little human. Then you are gone – gone and forgotten. A flash. An exhale. A brief moment, barely significant, and then… and then nothing. You stand here and speak to me of mistakes, but you will learn soon enough, little one. I do not make mistakes." Azazel narrowed her eyes as if daring Jack to say anything.

Jack gave a bored sigh. "Well, first time for everything," he said coolly.

"Have care who you speak to like that, Jack Nightshade – have care," said the queen, in a quiet voice that sounded like a whisper in a nightmare.

Jack opened his mouth to say something he knew he shouldn't when his mind filled with the voice of Cerb. *Taker, it seems we will find out soon enough who will be victorious. Mivras the Blue approaches from the west!*

Jack's eyes blurred, and he staggered back momentarily, losing his balance. Since waking from his overuse of the Sentheye in that little village in Panama, this was the first time Cerberus had been out of Jack's sight. He was only just above him, sitting atop the pyramid, but still Jack couldn't see him.

Apep glared at him with that sickly curious look. "What's wrong with you?"

Jack held out his hands, steadying himself. He could see Mivras coming, but there were no other dragons with him. In his right talons, he held a human. Beyond, or maybe through this tableau, he could see Apep, Azazel, and the enormous giant, Ogliosh, staring at him. It was so strange, one view overlaying the other, both of them semitransparent. "I... I see... Mivras. He's coming, but he is alone. Wait. Except... except he has a small girl with him."

"What do you mean, you see him?" Azazel asked, looking out the north-facing opening to the sky above the valley. "I see nothing."

"He's coming from the west," Jack said.

Ogliosh started toward the opening but drew up short as Mivras appeared, flying into view just as Jack said, from the west. The blue dragon settled onto the pyramid's stone steps.

"My queen," Mivras said, bowing awkwardly and, Jack thought, nervously.

"What is this?" Azazel asked, looking at the young girl now standing on the steps next to Mivras. "I ask for slaves to make into dracs, and you bring me one tiny girl! Where are those who accompanied you?"

"We gathered many, fed on some, imprisoned others in a cave. I left the young ones guarding them while I went to find more. When I came back, the young dragons were dead. This one and a few more killed them."

"What? This... this human slayed my children?" Azazel hissed, dipping her head low to appraise the girl.

Ogliosh stepped forward and looked down at the girl. "Gabi!"

Jack frowned. The giant knew her name?

"You know her?" Azazel asked.

"This is the girl? The one who escaped with the Moore girl?" Apep asked with more excitement than Jack had seen from the walking corpse since he'd landed on the pyramid.

"This is she!" Ogliosh said.

"She was with another she called Garrett. I believe he is the one you seek, dökkálfar," Mivras said.

"Why did you not bring me Garrett Turek?" Apep shouted. "Instead, you bring me some insignificant girl!"

"This one was trying to control my mind. She asked for you specifically, my queen. I broke her mind control and grabbed her before the one called Garrett could attack."

Jack looked at the girl and frowned. She was small, thin, and weak-looking. Mind control? She didn't look like much. "Where is Garrett now?" Jack asked.

Mivras's annoyed look turned to surprise when he noticed Jack's red eyes. But he composed himself quickly, turning his gaze back to Queen Azazel.

Jack looked at the girl. "You're a friend of Garrett? Tell me where he is, and I might be able to keep you from being eaten." But the little girl ignored him! Instead, she just stared ahead at Azazel like she wanted to kill her. Shit, maybe she couldn't speak English? There was something else about her, though... Something strange. And why would Mivras bring her here if that's what she wanted? Why would...

"Where is Garrett now, Mivras?" Apep snapped.

"I believe the human you seek is hiding near here in a cenote that is open from the top. The humans had cooking fires burning, and the smoke led us right to them. We ambushed them easily—"

"Shut up!" Apep snapped, turning to Jack.

The little girl pointed at Azazel. "You're her. You're Azazel. I remember you."

Jack looked at her and frowned. Guess she spoke English after all. But still, there was something off.

"Forget her, Jack. Pay attention. This is your moment – *your* true purpose. This is what you want, yes? To kill Garrett Turek? To take your revenge? Take Cerberus and seize your moment, Jack," Apep said, wrapping an arm around him.

Behind them, the giant said, "Apep, we should deal with this human."

As Jack allowed Apep to steer him away, he glanced over his shoulder at the little girl again.

"You killed my mamá y papá," the girl was saying. "You killed Fredy, Manuel, and María, and because of you, Sarah is dead! Because of you, Azazel!"

"Go, Jack – go, and when it is done, you can close this chapter and begin your new purpose," Apep urged.

"I've come back here to kill you, Azazel," the little girl said.

At the girl's words, a sudden silence filled the stone mouth of the temple.

Jack saw Apep's expression change as some realization struck him. Apep spun back toward Mivras and pointed at the girl. "Mivras, why did you bring her here? Why would you leave a wounded Turek and bring this girl? Why, when you know how much I want the boy?"

"I… I don't know? I think… I broke the mind hold… And then I decided. I… I took her… She wanted to come and I… I…" Mivras struggled, his eyes darting back and forth.

"You didn't break her mind hold, you fool! You did her bidding!" Ogliosh said.

Azazel's eyes flashed as she lowered her head and hissed at the girl. "Little speck! If you survive the blood ritual, you shall be my next drac! Do you know what dracs are, speck? They are mindless, obedient creatures who do what they are told until they die! I shall be extra careful not to let you die. Not even when you beg! Not even when you plead! Not even when you wail for mercy and promise to do anything I ask. No, not even then. Oh, speck, I will ensure you serve me well beyond your years. Well beyond your insanity. This will be your fate! This will be your—"

The queen stopped speaking abruptly as her face suddenly twisted in confusion.

Jack frowned, but he didn't move.

The girl smiled.

Ogliosh started forward. "I told you to deal with her!"

Apep shouted, "Ogliosh, kill her!"

The little girl pushed a hand outward, and Ogliosh stopped as if stuck fast, statue-still, unable to move.

"You should have closed your door, Ogi!" the girl said.

Mivras was babbling and talking to himself like a blubbering idiot. Like he didn't know where he was or even who he was.

"Kill her, Azazel!" Apep shouted.

Azazel's mouth stretched open, but as it did, her jowls shook. Jack knew dragons well enough to understand instantly what was wrong.

Azazel wasn't fighting to open her mouth – she was fighting to keep it closed.

"Kill me, Azazel! Go on! Kill the little speck!" the girl screamed, and the dragon roared. No one else dared step toward the little girl now lest they step in the path of the Queen of Queens's dragon breath.

The queen's roar filled the chamber.

Jack clapped his hands over his ears.

Apep screamed something, backpedaling.

A glow built in the throat of the Queen of Queens's neck, like heating elements on a stove but so much faster. And instead of red, the glow was a blinding white behind the scales of black – as if a star were being born.

Jack stopped, hands still covering his ears as he watched. In those fleeting seconds, he knew Apep and Ogliosh weren't going to see what they thought they were going to see. No. This was something else.

The little girl reached behind her back and pulled something out of her waistband. At first, Jack thought it was a gun, but it didn't look like a gun. Then she reached into her pocket and pulled out something else – something small.

As Azazel's roar reached a deafening pinnacle, the girl drew back, and only then Jack did know what he was seeing. *It's a slingshot! A freaking slingshot!* He almost laughed. *You can't kill a dragon with a slingshot!*

Beyond the roar piercing Jack's ears, even through his hands, he heard something else – something from deep within his own mind. Two tiny words blossomed in a thick Spanish accent. They were as small as the little girl who spoke them, but they were certain.

Goodbye, Azazel.

A white-hot flame ignited in the back of the dragon's throat as the little girl let fly a small stone.

14

You're the Key to All of This

Friday, May 6 – God Stones Day 30
Rural Chiapas State, Mexico

For the second time that day, Breanne collapsed into a heap of sobs. *No. No. No! Gabi!* She screamed her name and then she screamed it again and again, but Gabi didn't answer. She was gone, and she either couldn't hear Breanne in mind speak or wouldn't answer.

Near the shore, Lenny appeared, finally able to get his feet under him. He waded forward and slapped his palms against the water in frustration. "I thought I had her!"

"Bre, I'm sorry. I tried. I tried to get her to stop, but she wouldn't listen to me," Garrett said.

She could see he was clearly in pain. He wasn't even trying to use mind speak. "But I don't understand! Why didn't it take you? Why her?"

Garrett's twisted face fell.

She hadn't meant it to sound like that. "I'm sorry, but I just don't know why it would take her when you were right there and wounded."

David knelt next to Garrett, tears threatening to spill down his face as he struggled to find words. He and Gabi had become close. Breanne could see he was almost as panicked as she was.

David motioned to Garrett. "Where does it hurt?" he asked, his voice cracking.

Garrett pointed at his lower legs. "I think they caught fire, but I didn't burn when the flame hit me and I… I don't understand." He looked up, finding Bre and the others. "I'm sorry, David. All you guys, I'm sorry, but the truth is, I think Gabi did something to the dragon's mind. I think she made it take her."

"What?" David blinked in confusion, gesturing to Garrett to take off his pants. "But that's suicide! Why? Why would she do it?"

"She was talking to the dragon about Queen Azazel. The dragon told her Azazel was at the pyramid and then it… it said something like, maybe you want to meet her, and that's when you guys came in."

"Oh, my god! Garrett, that has to be it!" Breanne said.

"You're telling me Gabi went with the dragon on purpose?" Paul asked.

"That's exactly what she did, and that's exactly why she isn't answering me!" Breanne snapped as she moved toward the opening. She couldn't stay here! Panic seized her chest, compelling her to go – she had to go, and go now! She had to get to the pyramid.

Breanne Moore, you cannot go to the pyramid now, Governess said.

If we don't go now, she'll be… she'll be dead, Breanne argued, her eyes filling with tears.

She's right, Bre – we need to rest. It's over a day's… day's hike from here, right? Garrett winced as he stood and unfastened his cargo pants, letting them drop to his ankles with a hiss.

Can you even get us there in the dark? Pete asked.

Are you guys even hearing me? Gabi will be dead if we don't go get her!

Sis, we hear you, but it's almost dark, Paul said. *You can't go charging off into the night!*

Actually, it was more than a day's hike. They would have to shelter at the farm yet again, then head out early to the pyramid. Two full days of hard hiking. Even then, Breanne could only get them close; she had been counting on Gabi to get them through the jungle to the pyramid. But Governess knew the way. She could lead them. *What are we supposed to do?! The dragon will kill her! Governess? Can't you get us there by cutting through the jungle?*

Breanne Moore, we will not save time that way. The trail and subsequent dirt road are our most efficient route. We would not be wise to travel by night when most of the creatures Apep altered are nocturnal and dragons can see in the dark quite well.

Garrett! Your legs, your skin! David said, pulling a face as he averted his eyes.

Breanne looked and instantly wished she hadn't. *Oh, Garrett!* Giant blisters filled with pink fluid had formed, and some of them had split. White skin sloughed off his legs like a shedding snake; blood and pus seeped from open wounds. Strangely, though, the burns stopped in precisely the same spot on each leg, just above his knees.

How on Earth did you get those burns? I thought dragon fire couldn't hurt you, Breanne said.

Me too, Garrett answered, face draining of color.

Paul rubbed his whiskered chin. *I've seen burns like this before. This isn't from fire. Garrett? Where were you standing when the dragon breathed fire?*

Garrett swallowed dryly, peering toward the dead dragon, some realization lighting his face. *I was standing right over there… in the water.*

Her brother nodded. "You're immune to dragon fire, Garrett, but not boiling water."

Jesus, Garrett, you boiled your legs, Pete said, looking like he might be sick.

Lobster, anyone? Lenny said, but no one laughed. *Sorry, David… can you do your thing please?*

Sure, but you guys know I'm going to pass out, right?

Garrett frowned and winced again. *Look, David, if you start off thinking that way, then you will for sure…* He sucked in a breath as if struck by a new wave of pain. *Remember that Dexter guy and… and that god-awful song? You… you remember? Just hold on loosely. If you cling to it too tight, you'll lose control of it. Like the fishing pole, David! Remember… remember the fishing pole.*

Thanks for not singing that, Pete said, his face still sour.

Carefully, Garrett laid his pants across his hips and thighs, being careful not to let the cloth touch his burns. Breanne wasn't sure if his shivering was from being cold or if he was going into shock.

Right, hold on loosely. Okay, but I'm putting my pack right here just in case. Please put something under my head. Oh! And cover me up, would you? Last time I woke up freezing. And don't let me sleep too long! I mean, I know I won't wake up until I'm ready, but try, huh? We need to go after Gabi. Oh! and don't do anything stupid like go after her without me. You might need me, you know. I might be scared, but we're talking about Gabi! And there is no—

Hey, Yosemite Sam! Start twitching that little trash 'stache of yours and get to glowing, Lenny said, glaring as he pointed down at Garrett's legs. *Can't you see the kid's in pain?* Then he changed his voice to mimic David's. *Oh! And if you pass out, you're going to wake up with your head resting on that dead dragon's nutsack!*

Whatever, Lenny! You don't even know if they have nutsacks!

Pass out and we'll find out, Lenny said, motioning impatiently.

Breanne knelt next to Garrett, trying, at least for the moment, to push the worry for Gabi away. "Take my hand," she said.

Garrett smiled weakly. "It's nice to hear your real voice," he said, taking her hand. "Oh, I mean not that it isn't… nice when you are in my head… I mean… you know…"

"I know," she said, forcing a smile.

"Thank you," he said, smiling back.

David's mustache twitched, and he glowed, lighting the quickly darkening chamber.

Garrett pulled a pained face as his legs began to heal. The blisters burst as the skin stretched and grew anew. "God!" he roared through a clenched jaw. "I don't remember it hurting so much before!"

"It's okay, Garrett. It's almost over," Breanne said, her reassuring smile fading as something caught her eye from a across the cenote. A human shape from one of the caves the dragons had come from was clearly visible in David's golden glow. Immediately, she recognized the silhouette. *Juan?*

The glow faded, and David wobbled.

Lenny knelt, holding on to David's shoulders to steady him and keep from hitting his head.

Is he okay? Pete asked.

Oh yeah, I'm good, David said weakly, as his eyes rolled back into his head. His body went suddenly slack as he tipped into Lenny's arms.

Shit, I really thought he had it, Lenny said, laying him down carefully on the cave floor. *Anyone want to help me drag him over to the dragon?*

Guys, we have company, Pete said, pointing across the cenote.

Paul racked the slide on his handgun.

Wait, you guys, that's Juan. He helped Gabi and me, before. The farmhouse is his place, and he was on the dig site when Gabi's parents were killed. "Juan! Juan, it's Bre! Are you okay?"

"Sí, we are okay," came the man's voice from across the cenote. "You killed the dragons! But how?"

"I'll explain later! Stay there, we'll come to you," Breanne said.

Garrett stood and pulled on his cargo pants and boots. *What about David?*

I'll stay here and keep an eye on him, Lenny offered. *Someone should guard the entryway and watch for dragons.*

Peter and I will stay as well, Governess said. *I do not like caves. I would prefer to be outside, but at least the sky is open here.*

Pete glanced at her in surprise, trying and failing to hide a smile. *You want me to stay with you?*

Governess stared at Pete for a moment that stretched on awkwardly, then she said, *Did you not understand when I said we would both stay here?*

Pete's face glowed a bright red and his smile stretched impossibly large.

Breanne shook her head and turned to Garrett. *Feeling better?*

So much better. They just ache a little, he said, shaking out his legs as if he were preparing to go for a run.

Maybe stay here and rest for a bit. We shouldn't be long, Breanne said, motioning to her brother.

Garrett nodded. *Probably best I stay anyway. Someone needs to keep Lenny from rubbing dragon nuts on David's face.*

Breanne and her brother circled the cenote on a narrow pathway between the water and wall. When she had been here before, Juan had mentioned the caves as a place to hide if they needed to.

Juan met them halfway, leading them the rest of the way around while explaining what had happened. She soon learned the dragons had entered from above. The dragons killed and ate those who tried to flee. The rest they herded into a dead-end cave, plenty large enough to hold dozens of people with no way out.

"Please prepare yourself. What you will see is not pleasant. Some are injured. Some have died. Those who passed, the dragons consumed right in front of us, leaving a mess," Juan said, his voice breaking.

Even bracing for the worst did nothing to prepare Breanne for what she saw. The smell hit her first, a combination of feces and death. Then she saw the people silhouetted in the green glow of Paul's torch. Those who could walk came forward tentatively. "Is it true? Are the demons dead?"

Breanne's eyes brimmed with tears, and for fear of her voice betraying her, she simply nodded.

"Not the big one, though," Paul said.

The people just looked at Paul, frowning.

"Not the big one," Juan said, most likely in Spanish, but for Breanne it was all English as her mind translated the words unconsciously.

Chatter broke out as the people panicked.

"We can't stay here. The large blue one may return. We have to get these people out of here," Juan said.

"I understand. Everyone stay calm!" Breanne said, holding her hands out. "Juan, let's start by getting them out of this cave. We have more friends on the other side. One of them is a healer."

"A healer?" Juan asked, his thick brows creasing.

"We have wounded who can't walk!" an older man said.

"Okay, Juan, tell him my brother and I will help carry the

wounded. We can make multiple trips if we have to, but we need to get over near the exit and make our plans from there."

Bre, what the hell is going on? How are you understanding these people? Juan's English is broken at best and you seem like you're understanding every word from everyone? I know your Spanish isn't THAT good.

I don't hear Spanish, Paul. I hear everything in English, Breanne said, taking a woman's hand and guiding her past them. She was looking for someone specific. She could just ask Juan, but she feared the answer.

But how? Do you have the Eyra of Tunga? I thought David had it?

No, it's something Gabi taught me how to do with my mind.

She taught you how to speak Spanish? her brother asked as three children passed between them single file.

The children were somber. Very unchildlike. The poor kids couldn't have been older than eight or nine. *They must be terrified,* she thought. She looked at Paul. *I don't speak it, Paul. Like I said, I just hear English.*

Can you show me?

Gabi could. I don't know how it works. But the artifact, the Tunga thing. I almost forgot about it. When we get back to the others, let's have David pass it around, so we all learn the language.

Good idea, Paul said.

Breanne's heart sank as the last of the able-bodied people passed by them. Violeta, whose husband had died from a centipede bite on the trail to the cenote, was not among them. Her skin crawled as she recalled fighting the centipede, probably coming close to death herself. Last she had seen, the kind woman was caring for Sarah. Violeta had pointed them toward life-saving medicine. Until this very moment, she had thought their going for the medicine was an epic fail. But it hadn't been a failure. If they hadn't gone, she and Gabi might both be dead. And Garrett and the others most certainly wouldn't have made it away from Pando. Breanne understood now. The trip for the medicine had saved lives. It was just that no matter which decision she had made, there was no avoiding tragic loss.

"Back here. Help, please," Juan said.

Breanne pulled her shirt up over her nose and followed Juan toward the back of the cave. There were a dozen people injured bad enough they couldn't walk. Some injuries were obvious burns. Four people had severely injured legs – a folded knee, a broken ankle, and a broken leg. Then she heard someone call her name.

"Breanne?" the woman with her grandmother's eyes groaned.

"Violeta!" she shouted, running to her.

Violeta reached out, and the two embraced. The woman gave a soft moan of pain. Breanne pushed herself back to look. *Paul, bring the torch closer so I can see.*

He did, and Breanne gasped. The woman's cheeks were blistered and the eyes that had reminded her of her grandmother were now squinting, bloodshot, and watering. Breanne felt sick.

"I'm sorry, child. I tried. Truly, I tried to save your Sarah, but the demon punished me. In the end, Juan pulled me away. But I'm afraid it was not soon enough to save your Sarah."

"It's not your fault," Breanne whispered, but the woman didn't understand her words. "Juan, tell her it isn't her fault!"

"She knows this. She does not blame you," Juan said.

Breanne took the woman's hand in her own. "Por favor, déjame ayudarte," she said in her limited Spanish as she guided Violeta out of the cave and back around the cenote.

Governess made Juan his own torch. They didn't want to make any fires at all, but they needed to at least see well enough to get the wounded around the cenote. After that, Garrett, Lenny, and the others went back and forth, bringing all the severely wounded back to the area near the entrance while Breanne did her best to make Violeta and the others comfortable. Governess grew a wall of fruit-covered vines. All thirty-four of the able-bodied refugees, including children, filled their bellies with the fresh fruit and drank from the cenote. But there were still another thirteen badly wounded, including Violeta.

Forty-seven people total. What were the dragons going to do with them? Why had they taken them prisoner? Breanne couldn't worry about that now. Right now, she needed to at least try to wake David.

After a few attempts, David gasped, blinked, and sat up with a start, shoving his backpack away.

David, it's okay.

Where's Lenny? How long was I out? he asked, looking toward the dead dragon and taking in a relieved breath.

Forty-five minutes, she said. *You know he only does that to mess with you, right? That's how I can tell you're such good friends. He cares about you, David. You should have seen how gentle he was when you passed out. He laid you down and put that pack under your head. Then he sat with you, making sure you were safe.*

David frowned, then stretched and yawned. *Really, Bre? He has a funny way of showing it.*

Really. Listen, I have brothers, remember? This is what brothers do. That's how close you guys are – like brothers.

Well, where is he? David asked, looking around. *What the... who are all these people?*

The dragons were holding them prisoner in one of those caves, she said, pointing.

David nodded. *Sheesh, glad they're okay.*

That's just it. They're not all okay. In fact, many of them are hurt. Some are hurt really, really, bad. That's where Lenny and the others went. They are getting them back over here. Back to you.

To me?

You were only out forty-five minutes, David – maybe less. You're getting better, but tonight, you're going to become a pro at healing people.

David looked around again, this time with fresh eyes. *Bre, I don't know if I can. And what about Gabi? Shouldn't we start making our way back to the farm?*

You can, David. Breanne said, handing him a piece of fruit. *I know you can. These people need you. You have to heal them, David, before the dragon comes back. You have to heal all of them. I want to go after Gabi right now! But we can't leave them like this. We can't. But the sooner you fix them, the sooner we can save her.*

David looked around, taking in all the people. *I'll try, Bre,* he said doubtfully.

Breanne smiled. It was forced, but she knew David needed to see it. He needed to see her confidence in him. David was a good kid. It was funny – she thought of him as a kid when he was only a couple of years younger than her. But being fifteen seemed like a lifetime ago now.

David tried to return her smile, but it faltered and fell away, his expression unsure. *What if I can't?*

David, you know you're the key to all of this, right? she asked.

Huh? What are you talking about? I can't fight worth a crap, and I'm always passing out when the guys need me the most. David looked down at his hands. *Plus, I'm scared of everything, Bre. Like majorly scared.*

David, how many times would Garrett be dead if it weren't for you? Two? Three? And you saved Ed. And Paul. And gosh, let's not forget Pete! David, without you, there is no journey. Without you, we can't save the world. Jesus, David, without you there's no do-overs, no second chances. When Garrett fights a dragon in the water and it boils his skin off, without you… he dies. Without you, we probably all die. Without you… The words caught in her throat, as the memory of a vision came rushing back. The memory of Gabi standing before a black dragon as it roared, its mouth filling with fire brighter than any she had ever seen. She squeezed her eyes shut, wishing the memory away. *Without you, Gabi might die, and for sure these people – some of whom can't see, can't walk, have infections – without you, they all die.* Tears dripped from her eyes. *None of us can do what you can do, David. So yes, you ARE the key. Now I need you to believe it and get to work, okay?*

David's eyes glistened in the low firelight. She heard him swallow. "Thank you, Bre." He spoke the words quietly aloud, looking back toward the somber crowd as they sat absently eating fruit and drinking water. Nodding, David pressed his lips tight with determination. *We're wasting time. Where do I start?*

Breanne smiled again, and this time it wasn't forced. It was real and full of hope. *Wait here,* she said, standing and returning only a moment later with an elderly woman in tow. *David, this is Violeta.*

15

Supernova

Friday, May 6 – God Stones Day 30
Rural Chiapas State, Mexico

From within the belly of the Queen of Queens shone the light of a thousand stars. Like an infant protostar blanketed in a vessel of dragon skin, light traced every scale and somehow continued to grow brighter still – impossibly bright.

The Queen of Queens and the murderer of Gabi's parents belched forth a roar that threatened to draw blood from Gabi's ears. The roar stretched out, pained and angry, twisted and wrong. Gabi could feel the queen's panic as she tried to make this stop – tried to close her mouth.

Gabi did not flinch as her eyes widened, but not from fear. Hers were wide with hunger, starved for revenge. With swelling hate, she stared into the back of the roaring dragon's throat. No one would rob her of this moment – of her destiny. She could see a sinus open far, far in the back of the dragon's throat as liquid fuel gushed out like water from a hose.

Fire ignited, building instantly into a growing, roiling ball of hell.

Still, Gabi refused to look away. She stared into the dragon fire as it filled the back of Azazel's throat. Even in death, she would not look away. But it wasn't the fire she watched, it was the open sinus and the small stone in flight – the stone that sailed arrow-true.

Ogliosh shouted, struggling to make his feet move.

The big blue dragon screamed gibberish as it fought to unscramble its mind.

But Gabi held them with all her will. She only needed the time of a stone's throw.

Apep was shouting now, ancient words – words of the God Stones.

Someone charged her from her left.

Still, Gabi did not look away.

The stone shot into Azazel's mouth, lodging in the gushing sinus.

Azazel's roar abruptly cut off.

The chamber went suddenly quiet as all eyes locked on the dragon queen's open mouth stretched wide in horror. The queen's eyes blinked rapidly as her jaw worked side to side uselessly – hopelessly.

As Gabi watched unblinking, the dragon's throat became so bright it swallowed Azazel in its shine. The light was as blinding as a supernova – like seeing a star being born, aging, and dying before her very eyes.

Goodbye, Azazel! Gabi turned to her right, took three running steps, and leapt over the side of the pyramid.

One-one thousand. Two-one thou—

Above Gabi's head, an explosion of fire and scales shot out from the pyramid's opening, lighting the late evening sky in a brilliant silvery glow.

Gabi missed the stairs, landing instead on steep, polished stone. Below her was a long slide to the ground. She was still wearing the oversized flannel shirt Breanne had given her the very day they met. As she slid, she did her best to keep her feet pointed down and her back and bottom on the oversized flannel. The material offered little resistance in the way of friction against the smooth stone. She was sliding fast – maybe too fast. Carefully, she craned her head back to glance at the opening and realized someone was sliding down the pyramid with her.

It was a boy! A boy with curly hair and red eyes. Luckily, she must have been sliding way faster than him because she was pulling away! If she could get to the ground first and run, maybe… maybe she could get to the trees. But the trees were so far. She wasn't sure. Until this very moment, her every thought had been focused on killing Azazel, not what happened after.

Burning scales and guts rained down around her. Black scales. Azazel's scales. Tears came to her eyes. She had done it! She had killed the queen of all dragons! Just like in the story Bre told her – the story of David and Goliath. Like David, she used a rock from a slingshot and, like David, it was the rock that made it possible. But the rock hadn't actually killed the dragon. The rock was only the catalyst. The fuel must have ignited before she plugged the hole, turning the dragon into a bomb. Or maybe obstructing the sinus caused the fuel to burst from somewhere else – somewhere it shouldn't have. But it didn't matter! She didn't need to understand how it had worked, only that it had. Gabriel De Leon had slain her dragon! Her parents were avenged!

Cerb! Help! a voice shouted in her mind. But the shout wasn't meant for her to hear. It was the boy with the curly hair. It had to be.

Far above her, a dragon flapped its wings. She expected Mivras, the big blue dragon. But even though she could see it only with the faint light of a new moon, it was clear this dragon was unlike any she had seen before – at least in real life. But this dragon had three heads, just like the one from the memory Governess had shown them. That meant the pursuing boy had to be Jack. But wasn't he supposed to be dead?

As Gabi neared the end of her slide, bits and pieces continued to click and splat against the surrounding stone. Far behind her, she heard an *umph* and grunts, followed by a new slapping sound. She bent her knees, planting the soles of her feet down hard against the stone in an effort to slow herself before she reached the ground. It seemed to help a little, but she was still moving fast. Behind her, the grunts and smacking continued, and then she heard a sharp yelp. She turned her head again to find the boy was no longer sliding. He was tumbling out of control. The recklessness had him quickly gaining and, worse, the strange dragon was descending fast.

She wasn't going to escape. She was going to die. The foot of the pyramid would be her grave, but it didn't matter. This was her fate, and she would do it again and again. *Maria Purísima! I will be with you soon, Mamá y Papa!* But before she died, she wanted to tell Bre she'd done it. *Bre, I don't know if you can hear me, but I did it! I've slain the Queen of Queens! I killed her, Bre! I killed her! My parents are avenged!*

As the shadowed ground drew close, Gabi launched herself off the stone with all she had. The small girl went airborne, her momentum carrying her forward much too fast to stay on her feet. She shoved her arms out to the sides and flailed for balance, trying desperately to keep her body upright so she wouldn't face-plant when gravity finally pulled her to the ground.

Somehow, Gabi kept her feet under her until she landed. She tried to hit the ground running, but momentum carried her faster than even she'd expected, faster than her feet could keep up with. She shoved her arms out as her body crashed into the rocky soil. Her arms gave way as her face bit painfully into the ground, tearing her shirt, then her skin. Flesh scraped from her hands, face, and arms. A sharp crack split her head, everything blurred, and darkness took her – then there was nothing.

When Jack realized the little Mexican girl had a slingshot, his first instinct had been to laugh. But when the giant started screaming that he couldn't move, Mivras started babbling stupidly, and Apep started chanting, Jack knew something bad was going to happen. As soon as that small rock vanished into Azazel's mouth, Jack ran for the girl. But the little shit took off and jumped over the side – actually jumped.

Jack never hesitated as he set his jaw and followed. Now he was sliding out of control.

Cerberus, help! Jack shouted just before hitting a patch of mushy Azazel goo. The sudden change from smooth to sticky stone flung him into a tumble. He was rolling out of control and every bounce against the unforgiving stone hurt. When he finally hit the ground, he must've rolled twenty times, feeling every sharp rock stab into his ribs, arms, and legs. For a long moment, he lay there, staring up at the darkening sky as he watched Cerberus growing larger and larger in his fuzzy vision.

Jack pushed himself up onto unsteady feet, sure he'd broken at least one rib and possibly his wrist. He must have bitten his tongue too, because as he looked around for the girl, the taste of copper filled his mouth.

Cerb landed behind him.

Jack spat into the dirt. *Where the hell did she go, Cerb?!* He spun, holding his side.

They stood on a mound of dirt, the remnants of which had once hidden the pyramid. Jack shuffled forward to look over the edge of the piled dirt where it fell steeply away to the valley floor. Looking over the side, he didn't see her anywhere. *What the shit!* He needed her. He needed to drain her life to take away his pain.

She's right there, Taker. Heal yourself quickly, Cerb said, staring past him.

Jack turned and saw nothing. *Where? What are you talking about?*

You can't see her? She is lying right there behind you.

I don't see nothing but rocks… and dirt, he grunted, ribs on fire.

She's messing with your head. Quickly look through my eyes, Jack – do it now!

I'm not sure how to do it. I… I… But then he saw… himself, and it was weird. He was staring down at himself from Cerb's center head and, just as Cerb had said, there was the girl. She was lying right behind him, impossible to miss. Jack watched through Cerb's eyes as she pushed herself up and bolted in a running limp toward the slope. *I see her now!*

Drain her and heal. We need to—

A dragon roared, and for a second, Jack thought it was Cerberus. His vision blurred and his balance shifted, like a carpet being pulled from beneath him. Jack staggered forward, the shared vision broken as he found himself staring at Cerb once again. But Cerb was in motion, rolling toward him. Jack leapt out of the way. The sudden jerking to his ribs felt like someone stuck him with a knife and twisted it, stealing the air from his lungs. *Ce-rb,* he grunted, as not one but two beasts tumbled over the side of the mound, right where the small girl had vanished. Cerb was caught in a tangle of blue wings, dripping teeth, and razor-sharp talons – *Mivras!*

Cerb! Jack shouted. Finding his breath, he ran forward, but they were already on the floor of the valley. Mivras was on top of Cerb, pinning him down. Cerb's three heads snapped like the jaws of angry Doberman pinschers.

Why was Mivras attacking now? What the hell was he thinking? Jack looked for the girl, but she was gone… or invisible… or, more likely, crushed to death. It didn't matter now. Cerb needed him! *I'm coming, Cerb!* Not trusting himself to stay upright, Jack sat down on his ass and slid over the edge of the slope. It was steep, but not as steep as the pyramid had been. The torrential rains had already eroded deep fissures into the slope and, as he slid, Jack had to be careful not to fall into the deep gouges on either side of him.

When he made it to the valley floor, Mivras was still on top of Cerb, his massive jaws locked around Cerb's bleeding middle neck while his taloned claws pinned his other heads to the ground. Jack didn't hesitate as he sent disease into Mivras's back. Fire shot from Mivras in an angry roar, dousing the valley floor all around Cerberus, whose scales began blistering.

"No!" Jack screamed, drawing in the life of Mivras. The giant dragon's magnificent blue scales fell away from rotted skin, along with horned back spikes and flesh.

Mivras released Cerb and spun on Jack. "You are no dragon. You are cattle, and this one is an abomination. I should have killed you when you attacked Goch the Red. You and this abomination will never be dragonkind!" Mivras stomped forward, closing the distance between him and Jack. "She told me, human! My queen told me two moons ago that Cerberus would return and challenge me to a fight to the death. She told me you would try to interfere! She told me you would both die!"

"Well, I guess she lied, you gigantic piece of shit!" Jack said, holding out his hands and smiling. Sentheye drawn from Mivras the Blue flowed through Jack, mending bone and renewing flesh, leaving him whole and loaded for bear.

Mivras glanced back at Cerb, who was now on his feet and circling. "You do not respect our ways, Cerberus. This is why you will never be dragonkind!"

"Jack, don't! He's right! You have already done enough. This is my challenge!"

Mivras smiled. "I am going to enjoy killing you. And when you are dead, I will lead the dragon hordes until a new Queen of Queens is named! I will be the king of my people!"

Cerb, I am really getting sick of hearing this guy talk shit.

Pass me the power you are holding, Jack! Hurry, before you explode! Cerb urged.

He could do that? Pass the power? He had passed it through Cerb before, but he'd been touching him. What if he hurt him? What if he—

Do it now, Jack! Cerb shouted.

Mivras was still going on about how awesome he was as Jack shifted all his focus to Cerb.

"Yes! The king of dragons. Perhaps I will call myself the King of Kings!"

Please, don't let this be a bad idea! Jack released a powerful burst of Sentheye, striking Cerberus right where his three thick necks came together, knocking the dragon off his feet.

16

The Savior

Friday, May 6 – God Stones Day 30
Rural Chiapas State, Mexico

By the time David had healed the last of the cenote survivors, the sun's molten glow had pooled into the Pacific Ocean, quenched by the cold sea, replaced by a soft, white, moonlit sky.

It amazed Garrett that somehow, after Bre's talk with David, the kid was able to heal practically nonstop until he'd made every single person healthy and whole. He healed burns, rashes, cuts, infections, disease, and broken bones, and he did it all without passing out once.

They think he was sent from heaven to save them, Breanne said.

Can you blame them? Look at him. Look at what he has done, Pete said, shaking his head.

Whatever you said to him, it worked. Garrett smiled at her.

Yeah, whatever you said must have been a whole lot better than Garrett's fishing pole analogy, Lenny joked, nudging him with his elbow.

Or your threat of rubbing dragon balls on his face, Garrett shot back.

Pete laughed.

That doesn't even make sense. I said I was going to put his face on dragon balls, not the other way around.

Either way... either way...

When David's glow faded away one last time, Garrett watched as a woman who appeared to be in her early thirties stood and carefully eased her weight down onto a foot that had been broken and gangrenous only seconds ago. She tested it gingerly at first, flexing her toes. She lifted her opposite foot, letting her bad foot support her full weight as she smiled in wonder and hopped once, twice, then a third time. The wide-eyed woman made the sign of the cross. She held out her arms and spun on her new foot, laughing with joy. "Thank you, David! Oh, Mother Mary, thank you. I was sure I would lose my foot. Oh! Oh, you *are* a blessing from heaven," the woman said, as she dropped onto her hands and knees. She grabbed David's hand and kissed it, tears of joy spilling down her cheeks.

The woman was speaking Spanish, but Garrett understood. After each of them had taken a turn with the Eyra of Tunga, they all understood. It was weird. Just a few minutes holding the item while those around him spoke Spanish, and he just knew. It was like with the tree language, but with the tree language, he couldn't speak it. Human vocal cords weren't capable of making the sounds. With Spanish, though, it might as well be his native language now. *Thank you, mysterious magic language item from another world.*

The woman continued kissing David, who was gently trying to pull his hand away. "Oh, gosh. Um... no. No, please! Don't do that. I'm not Jesus or nothing."

Garrett felt for him, knowing exactly how uncomfortable it was to have people bow before you. Still, better David than him.

I don't know what your deal is, bro. That's the most action you've had since your mom kissed you goodnight. Lenny laughed.

That was YOUR mom, Len, David said, finally freeing his hand.

David, how are you feeling? Pete asked.

Tired. I need to lie down. Just for a little bit.

No-can-do. We got to move and move now. I know we said we didn't want to go in the dark, but honestly, we are gambling every minute we stay here. That dragon saw you, Garrett – it could be back any minute, Paul warned.

David nodded and tried to stand. He wobbled and blinked.

Lenny lunged forward, steadying him while Garrett grabbed his other arm. *David, I think it's time.*

For a nap?

No, David. For you to try and heal yourself, Garrett said.

Oh, I don't know. I'm so tired, and what if it doesn't work?

But what if it does? How badass would that be, bro? Lenny smiled, slapping him on the shoulder.

David nodded slowly. *You're right. I'm going for it!*

Attaboy, Garrett said.

Just be careful, Breanne said.

Don't worry, guys. I feel good about this. Stand back! David said, taking a deep breath as he stretched his arms out for space.

Garrett nodded at Lenny, and they backed up.

As David began to glow, the chamber fell silent. Everyone turned their attention to the golden boy. By the time David stopped glowing, the survivors of the cenote had all dropped to their hands and knees, bowing in worship.

Then David's legs buckled, and he dropped like a wet towel, landing hard on his knees as he tipped backward.

"Shit!" Garrett blurted, trying to catch him before he smacked his head on the stone floor. Between him and Lenny, they managed to ease him safely to the ground.

Can we please lay him on the dragon's nutsack now? Lenny asked in a voice that seemed as irritated as it was serious.

You guys, in all seriousness, we need to go. We can't wait for him to wake up, Paul said.

We need a way to carry him, Garrett said.

I believe I can provide a transport device, Governess said.

Five minutes later, David lay across a makeshift stretcher grown out of woven wicker with wooden handles on each end. What took longer was the heated debate among the cenote survivors over who would get to carry him.

Guys, David's famous, Lenny said.

The others chuckled, but it was cut short when Breanne gasped. *Did you guys hear her!*

Hear who? Pete asked.

Gabi! It was Gabi! Breanne said, tears coming to her eyes.

Oh, thank god! Garrett said. *Well, what did she say? Is she okay? Did she get away?*

Breanne's smile was wider than Garrett had ever seen it. *She said she killed Azazel! She said her parents are avenged!*

No way! Garrett cheered.

How? How did she do it? Paul asked.

Breanne stood silent, her eyes darting back and forth as a crease formed on her brow. *She isn't talking. I don't know if it's because she can't hear me or… or because she can't answer. Dammit, Gabi!*

Just try to focus, Bre, Garrett offered.

Breanne slammed her eyes shut for a moment more, then they opened. *It's no use. She isn't answering.*

But she did it, Bre! She killed a dragon! THE dragon! The Queen of Queens, Garrett said.

Breanne smiled and threw her arms around him. *She killed a dragon!*

For a moment, Garrett felt something strange, and it took him a second to realize what it was. Something he hadn't felt in a long, long time replaced the knot in his stomach. He smiled at Bre and then the others, and he could see they felt it too – hope. Now, more than ever, Garrett felt energized to make haste. Now more than ever, he felt an urgency to get to the pyramid, and the look the others returned told him he wasn't alone. They all felt it. *Come on, guys. Let's get moving!*

They made their way through the crevasse, into the humid night air, and back onto the trail. Finally, free of the sadness of the cenote, Garrett felt better already.

Once on the trail, Pete said, *It would be nice if we could hide this trail. When you think about it, if the dragon comes back, it won't be that hard to figure where we went. I mean, there's only one trail leading in and out of this place.*

Your point is valid, Peter Ashwood, Governess said, waving a hand that glowed green. Behind them, the forest seemed to come alive, as the foliage shook, grew, and adjusted itself.

Garrett watched as Governess rooted to the ground, then quickly uprooted. *I have nearby trees capable of movement and have ordered them to position themselves on the trail. This trail will vanish in our wake.*

Pete leaned in close to Garrett and whispered, "I love it when she calls me by my whole name."

Garrett drew back and shook his head. "She calls everyone by their full name, Pete."

"What are two whispering about?" Lenny asked.

Crap, if Lenny heard this, Garrett would have to listen to him give Pete a hard time all the way back to the farm. "Never mind." Garrett chuckled, shaking his head at Pete.

Garrett Turek, we need to have a word. There is something you must know, Governess said.

As Juan led the survivors forward, Garrett and the sages stopped, gathering around. Garrett elbowed Pete. "See – what'd I tell you, Pete? She does that with everyone."

"Sure, but she doesn't say yours like she says mine." Pete smiled and winked.

Garrett chuckled and shook his head. *Okay, Gov, what's up?*

At the sound of her abbreviated name, Governess cocked her head like a curious puppy. *If you will recall, prior to the fiasco at the cenote, I rooted to see where the smoke was coming from. During this time, I looked at the pyramid and the destruction of the forest surrounding it.*

Right? Garrett said, uneasiness grabbing him.

I saw something else. Something I did not have a chance to share at the time, but it is of great importance, Governess said.

Well, out with it then, Lenny said.

Abruptly the unease twisted up tight in Garrett's stomach, a precursor to doom to come.

Lenard Wade, she started, then stopped, shifting her gaze across all of them before settling on Garrett with an expression that was too serious, even for her.

Garrett's mouth went dry as he tried to swallow. Part of him wanted her to keep it to herself, whatever it was, just for a little while longer. Just to let them laugh a little. Didn't they deserve that? Didn't they deserve this moment of hope? Gabi slayed a dragon! David did the impossible, and they all escaped the cenote. For shit's sake, they deserved a moment to believe that somehow everything was going to work out! But then there was another part of him – a darker part, the part that knew better. The part that twisted his guts and stole his breath. That was the part he couldn't hide from – not even for a moment. That was the part that wanted her to just get on with it, whatever *it* was, to just say it already and get it out. Come on, Governess! Just get it—

Jack Nightshade lives.

17

El Cucuy

Friday, May 6 – God Stones Day 30
Rural Chiapas State, Mexico

Gabi blinked and squinted her eyes. Pain shot through her head and something warm ran into her eyes. She must have blacked out when she hit the ground. The boy was pushing himself up and brushing himself off. Another gigantic dragon landed on the other side of Jack. María Purísima, the dragon was looking right at her. She pushed herself into the boy's mind; she had no idea what she was doing, but his mind was wide open. *Don't see me, oh please don't see me.* She thought the words more to herself than to Jack. But then she heard him talking to the dragon.

Where the hell did she go, Cerb?! The boy spun, holding his side.

Only a few paces ahead, the ground fell away. Gabi understood it then. She hadn't landed on the valley floor; she'd landed on a pile of dirt that once hid the pyramid.

The boy hobbled forward, looking for her over the edge.

She's right there, Taker. Heal yourself quickly, the dragon said, staring right at her.

Jack spun toward her. *Where? What are you talking about?*

They continued to argue back and forth, Gabi hearing it all in her own mind, just like she had with Apep and Ogliosh. It was easy to listen in on creatures that didn't know how to guard themselves. But now something else was happening!

Quickly, look through my eyes!

She needed to move and move now, but her whole body shook, frozen in fear. Gabi willed herself up and hurried to where the ground fell away. She jumped over the side and into an eroded fissure, the result of loose dirt washing away. The fissure was narrow, deep, and pitch-black. She pressed herself as deep as she could go – plenty deep enough to hide her whole body. She had no intention of staying here. To stay would be to die. But before she could even move, she heard and felt a loud crash as something massive rolled over the top of her and down toward the valley below. Dirt rained down into the gap, burying her in a thin layer of soil.

She heard grunting and scuffing, distant at first, but then closer as loose dirt sprinkled into her hair and face. Suddenly, Jack was right above her. Even in the dark, Gabi could make out the boy's hand in the moonlight as it slid along the edge of the fissure, close enough to reach out and touch. Death was close enough to touch. She held her breath and tried to hold perfectly still, pressing her feet into the sides, willing herself not to slip. Was she still invisible to him? If Jack looked down, would he see her? If she was visible now, would the combination of dirt and darkness be enough to hide her?

Jack didn't look. At least she didn't think he did. Whatever was happening on the valley floor had his full attention now. But she was sure when it was over, they would come back and search for her. If she wanted to live, she needed to be gone when they did. And she did want to live. Maybe she hadn't known until the moment she killed Azazel, but she knew it now. She felt it. A pulling to survive. A desire to be in this all the way. To help Breanne, Garrett, and the others save the world. She blinked, wiping away the blood and dirt from her brow. Her head was killing her, and she wanted to cry, but she wouldn't let herself – not now. Right now, she wanted to live.

Beyond the pain in her head, she heard voices now. Jack, Cerberus, and Mivras the Blue. She shimmied several meters down the eroded fissure, being careful not to slip. On the valley floor, the two dragons were fighting. Mivras was on top of the three-headed dragon.

Dragons had burned the valley of all vegetation, but as Gabi looked around, the moonlight revealed a few rock outcroppings in the distance to her east, and in the other direction she could make out the outlines of a few burnt-out cars. She was on the north side of the pyramid. Base camp had been on the north side, which meant these were the vehicles left over from the archaeologist's team. If she stayed close to the mound, she could work her way toward the abandoned vehicles. From there… Well, from there, she didn't know what. But she knew the vehicles were to the west and when Breanne and the others came, it would be from that direction.

From above, she heard more grunting and looked up, but she couldn't see who was coming. She would have to step away from the wall of dirt to see. But she didn't need to. She could feel it. The ground was shaking beneath her. She needed to go. She needed to make a run for it, before Ogliosh and Santa María only knew who else came sliding down from above.

Wait, there was something. Gabi's breath caught as a shape materialized not fifteen yards in front of her. Tall and lean, with strange lights atop its head… Apep! Gabi shoved herself back against the dirt, pressing herself into another fissure, but this one was much smaller and she couldn't fit completely inside. If he turned around, he was going to see her. She just knew he was!

Another dozen yards past Apep, a burst of… of something shot from Jack's hands into Cerberus, and the dragon went tumbling backward.

"No! Jack, wait!" Apep shouted.

Why would he do that? she wondered. Why would he try to kill his own dragon?

But Cerberus didn't die. Instead, the dragon rolled onto its feet, his eyes glowing brighter than volcanic lava! He pushed his chest out, and to Gabi, he seemed even bigger now… or maybe he was just making himself look bigger? Gabi didn't know, and she didn't care. She needed to move now, while there was a distraction. She eased forward out of the fissure.

"Stop this, Jack! Don't be a fool! He is the only one who knows where Garrett is!" Apep said.

Then she heard Jack yelling back toward Apep, back toward her, "I don't know what you mean, Apep. I'm not doing shit."

"Order your dragon to stop!"

Gabi moved quicker now. She needed distance – she needed to get far enough away to make for the burnt-out cars without being seen!

Firelight lit up the ground in front of her in strange colors. When she looked back, she saw dragon fire coming from Cerberus's left and right heads. The color reminded her of the time her father had placed a small piece of copper pipe in their campfire, changing the color first to green, then to blue. But this flame poured from the dragon and directly into the face of Mivras. Gabi paused to watch, though she knew she shouldn't. She knew better than to stay put one second longer, but she couldn't help it. Colorless flame came from Cerberus's center head. No. That wasn't right. Not colorless. Wrong. It was wrong. Her mind struggled to understand what she was seeing. It… it was black… black flame. As Mivras struggled to climb off the three-headed dragon, it was Cerberus who held on, unrelenting.

The giant blue dragon screamed in terror and pain. And when it fell limp and lifeless to the ground, thick smoke trickled up from its hollowed-out eyes.

"What have you done?" Apep shouted.

Gabi gasped and turned away. She didn't run. As bad as she wanted to, she didn't do it. She forced herself to move slowly and methodically, placing distance between herself and Apep's back one careful step at a time.

"What did we do? We replaced the Queen of Queens, Apep," Jack said, his voice getting closer to Apep – closer to her. Gabi knew without looking that Jack was facing her.

Please, please, please. Oh, please don't see me!

"With Mivras dead, there is no one left to challenge me and Cerb. We will lead your dragon army now, Apep."

"What makes you think they will follow you? You may have ruined everything, you pathetic little—"

"You may not want to finish that sentence, Apep," Jack said.

Still following the wall of dirt, Gabi had doubled the distance between herself and Apep. Now for the hard part. She had to leave the safety of the dirt wall and make her way to the closest of the three vehicles. The distance was a good fifty yards. She took in a deep breath and readied herself, but just as she was about to bolt, a giant slid to the ground. Then came another, and still another. They were standing only a few meters away, in the area she had left only moments ago. Gabi pressed herself back into the wall of dirt, wishing there was a fissure large enough to hide in, but there was nothing significant.

Stop, Apep. Don't kill the boy!

She knew the voice. It was Ogliosh. He was using telepathy. Shit, what if he sensed her? She couldn't run. Not now! Not with so many, so close.

My mind is strong. She only needed to keep hidden. *I can do this.* She wasn't the helpless girl she had been when Ogliosh found her. She had come full circle – she had slain her dragon!

If you kill him, you are sure to lose the dragons, Ogliosh said.

Jack shouted savagely, "I don't back down from fights, Apep! I don't care if you have the God Stones or not! I don't back down."

Gabi watched as something dark swirled around Apep's hands. She couldn't see it clearly, but she could see his hands disappearing, then reappearing, only to disappear again.

"You will obey me, Jack. You will obey me, or I will kill your dragon and watch you die. Do you think because you slayed a kraken that you can kill a god? I only need think a thought and you will be no more. A simple thought to wreck you, Jack. Do you understand?"

The boy's voice lowered to a fierce whisper. "I understand."

"And you will obey?" Apep asked, but it wasn't really a question. It was a dare that carried with it a murderous edge.

"Yes… Of course," Jack said, his voice steady now. "But I can lead them, Apep! I can lead them for you! You don't need Mivras."

Screeches sounded from the sky as smaller dragons descended.

"We needed Mivras to find the cenote! We needed him to find Garrett!" Apep seethed.

"No, we don't. We only need the girl," Jack said.

Gabi gasped, slapping a hand to her mouth.

"Well," Apep said, holding out his hands, "where is she?"

From what Gabi could see at this distance, Jack appeared to be pointing. But he wasn't pointing at her. He was facing in the opposite direction.

"Judging from where I last saw her, she must have gone that way. Or she is hiding in one of those washed-out cracks on the side of the dirt pile."

The giant and Apep turned away from her, following Jack's gaze.

It was now or never. Gabi ran, Apep's voice trailing behind her: "Well, find her!"

A feeling overwhelmed her. A strange déjà vu, but then it was more. It was a memory of a younger self. A little girl running through a dark room, leaping toward her bed, afraid of El Cucuy. Oh Santa María, so afraid! Afraid the monster would appear from the darkness, from her closet or under her bed. A monster ready to give chase – to grab her and take her! Now, like when she was a little girl, she ran alone through the dark. Only this darkness wasn't filled with her childhood monster, El Cucuy, or any other monster conjured from the mind of a little girl. These monsters were real. And that feeling, oh, that horrible feeling! The feeling that right as your feet leave the ground to jump for the bed, the monster will get you! It will get you, and when it does, it's going to pull you away into the darkness.

Gabi ran. The silver moon lit her way just enough for her not to trip over loose stones. The monsters were there! She could feel them reaching, about to grab hold, and she leapt. And she dove. And when she landed behind the closest vehicle, a utility truck, she wished she had a blanket to yank over her, to hide under, because monsters couldn't get you under a blanket.

She scrambled back onto her knees and spun to look, knowing the monster would be there, reaching for her. And when she turned, it was all she could do not to scream.

Ten meters away, a small, dark-scaled dragon, no larger than an elephant, was coming right toward her. *Don't see me! Don't see me!*

Gabi could hear it breathing and hissing. Its tongue tasted the air. It was looking right at her. *Don't see me!* Her pleading changed to something else. Now she was ordering it not to see. She pushed herself into its mind. *Do… Not… See… Me.* Tears streamed down her face, and she wanted to move, needed to move, but her feet wouldn't listen.

The dragon walked closer and closer until its breath washed over her face and its forked tongue threatened to touch her cheek. She was going to die.

The utility truck had toolboxes mounted on three sides of the truck's bed. With the truck upside down, this left a gap between the top of the tailgate and the ground, big enough for Gabi to squirm through. *Go!* she told herself, and finally, freeing her gum-glued feet, she went, pushing herself headfirst into the gap. As she dragged herself underneath the truck, she held in a scream, sure that any second the dragon would bite down on her legs. She kicked and squirmed as fast and furiously as she could. Only when her whole body was under the truck did she allow a sob to slip from her, no louder than a mouse's squeak. But her breath was coming rapidly – too rapidly. Her eyes flashed with panic. She couldn't breathe. *Oh, please no!* She was hyperventilating.

The dragon sniffed around, hissing. Then what must have been its head whacked into the side of the truck with a loud crunch, spinning it, the truck bed slamming into her and pushing her across the rocky ground.

Gabi yelped as the rocks raked her side. When the truck stopped, she slammed a hand over her mouth to keep from screaming. *Go away! She is hidden by the pyramid in the dirt mound. Go! Go find her!* She heard wings unfold and flap. Fine dirt and ash gushed through the opening, filling her eyes and mouth.

Blinking the soot from her eyes, Gabi pulled her shirt over her face and tried to stifle a cough. Her breath hitched, but she managed one deep breath, then another and another. A moment later, everything was still. The dragon had listened!

For the moment, she was safe. But she knew they would come back, and if she hadn't figured out a plan by sunup, she'd either be discovered or cooked alive inside this metal box under Mexico's full sun.

18

Find the Girl

Saturday, May 7 – God Stones Day 31
Rural Chiapas State, Mexico

Back atop the pyramid, at the mouth of the temple opening, Jack surveyed the surrounding area. Chunks of Azazel still littered the opening, and if not dealt with by the time the sun came up, they were going to really stink. The mess was already drawing flies.

"How did you and Ogliosh avoid being injured when she exploded?" Jack asked.

Apep didn't look at him, but finally, after a long moment, he answered, "It takes more than a mere scuffle to kill a god, Jack."

Such a prick, Jack thought.

I grabbed the Sentheye, and faster than you can draw a breath, I put up a shield, Jack. Now why are you up here and not out there finding the girl you allowed to escape? Apep asked.

He asked in Jack's mind, which meant… Shit, could he have heard what Jack had just thought? Come to think of it, this wasn't the first time he had cursed the elf in his mind. Had Apep always been able to do that? Was he reading his mind now? No, surely not. If that were the case, all the bad shit he'd thought… Apep probably would have killed him by now. No. He must have heard him because Jack spoke to him with his mind. Even though he didn't mean to. *So, we can talk like this now? You can hear me?*

I can hear you. You have been talking to your dragon this way?

Yes.

You leave your mind open, Jack. This is very dangerous. You said earlier the girl was near you, but you couldn't see her. Then, when you looked through Cerberus's eyes, you could see her?

Yep.

Apep closed his sunken eyes and sighed, then opened them again to gaze back over the valley. *So, all the time you were down there looking for her, she could have been right under your nose.*

Jack cocked his head in thought. *I guess so, but it's been two hours, and I've been mostly looking through Cerb's eyes. I don't think she can hide from him, and we've looked everywhere.* Cerb was flying over the valley even now as Jack scanned the valley floor through his dragon's eyes. Connecting with Cerb's vision was as easy as speaking to his mind now.

Not everywhere, or you would have her! She is out there somewhere, cowering behind a rock or in a hole!

Jack turned away from the valley below and looked up at the elf. Speaking aloud, he said, "The cenote can't be far. Let me take a group of dragons and search the surrounding area. I'm sure we can find it."

"In a valley where everything is burnt to ash, you can't find a single girl! No, we will stay this course. Search, Jack! Search until the sun rises and find that girl. She can't have gotten to the tree line. Have you searched all the fissures?"

"Fissures?"

"The washed-out cracks in the dirt mounds, Jack! Have you searched them all? She may have covered herself with dirt," Apep said in a voice that made Jack feel stupid.

Jack didn't like it when adults made him feel stupid. "Yes, we checked them all! Why can't you use that Sentheye of yours to find her?"

Apep's eyes flashed angrily, reminding Jack of a look worn too often by his father after a night at the bar. "The look" usually accompanied shouting, a wash of boozy breath, and the stench of cigarettes – a sure sign that a stiff backhand was in his future. But Apep didn't strike him. Instead, the look fell away as he retreated into the shadows of his hood. "I don't know. I tried *feeling* for her, but I find nothing."

"Maybe she's farther away than we think," Jack offered.

"No. I suspect something else is at play here. For an inferior human, this girl is powerful, Jack."

"She didn't look powerful to me. She looked like a weak little girl who got lucky with a rock."

Foolish human! Apep's voice boomed in Jack's head, causing him to flinch at the abruptness of the crazy elf. *Azazel reigned over the dragon kingdom for twenty-five thousand years. She was the most powerful dragon on Earth, perhaps even on Karelia. A lucky shot? A lucky shot does not kill the Queen of Queens.*

Then what? Jack asked, equally annoyed.

Fate, destiny, Turek at work? Yes, perhaps there is something to this prophecy. Perhaps that girl you can't find is more powerful than you can fathom. Maybe she is tapping into the God Stones' power in a way you can't. We must find her! We must extract the location of the cenote and kill her! You want to rule the dragons? Apep pointed a long, blackened finger at Jack. *Then you must avenge the murderer of your queen!*

Jack's eyes narrowed in thought. Son of a bitch. The crazy elf was right. He'd just wanted to go look for Garrett and get his revenge for Danny, but now he realized, as much as he hated to admit it, Apep was right. This was bigger now, and he had to be smarter. His dragons would expect blood for Azazel's death. He needed to be the one to give it to them. *I will find her,* Jack said, turning away.

Wait.

Jack turned back to Apep, frowning.

Not like this, Jack. Not with your mind open. No, no, no. Best you send your dog to sniff her out – send Cerberus to find the girl, Apep said, his thin lips twisting into something like a smile.

"I don't understand."

Apep's face dropped, and he sighed. *No. I suppose you don't. Imagine your mind is a house. You don't want people to come in, so you close the doors and windows. However, someone could open the door or lift the window, so what do we do?*

Still frowning, Jack shrugged and said, "Lock the doors and windows."

Apep nodded. *Lock the doors and windows, set an alarm, get a guard dog. There are many things we can do to secure our homes. Your mind, Jack. Your mind is wide open. The doors and windows full agape. You didn't even see, did you? When the girl killed Azazel with the "lucky shot"? No, of course you didn't see. Azazel did not want to breathe fire at the girl, Jack. The girl made her open her mouth – made her breathe fire! For a moment, Ogliosh couldn't move, Mivras couldn't think. Power, Jack. The girl is full of power, and your mind isn't secure enough to face her.*

For a moment, Jack didn't speak. He hadn't thought about it until now, but Apep was right. He had seen the others freeze up. But Jack hadn't frozen up. He had run for the girl. If the girl could have stopped him, why didn't she? The answer was clear. She didn't need to. He was too late. He didn't pose a threat. *Why didn't you stop her, Apep?*

Ah, that is your first good question. I didn't stop her because I am always two steps ahead. For all of Mivras's faults, he would have obeyed me with Azazel out of the way.

But Azazel was obeying you.

Azazel was planning to turn her army against me the first chance she had. She would have made a play for the Sound Eye once I opened the portal home. Apep walked toward Jack, speaking aloud in a low voice. "Ogliosh and his nephilbock may try the same thing, but with you leading the dragons and loyal to me, I believe he will stay in line and see this through."

Jack nodded slowly. It made sense enough.

"You *are* loyal to me, aren't you, Jack? After all, if it were not for speaking my name, the dragons would have killed you along the banks of the Sangamon River."

Jack knew Apep was right. God, that seemed like a lifetime ago now. Goch the Red finding him along the river, him convincing the giant dragon he knew Apep. *Of course I am. One hundred percent I am.* Okay, that was bullshit. He was only one hundred percent loyal to one person. That person used to be Danny, but Danny was gone. No, not gone… dead. Danny was dead. But he had Cerb now and as he thought of loyalty, he answered Apep with honest assurance, but in his mind, he thought only of his new brother, Cerberus.

"Good. And when you speak to me with your mind open, like now, expect others to hear what you are saying. If you want to speak to me in confidence, speak aloud."

Jack shoved his hands deep into the pockets of his leather jacket and nodded again. "The others? You mean like the nephilbock? They could be hearing everything I say?"

Apep lifted his brows, but they dropped right back down as if he were too exhausted to fake interest. *Indeed. Telepathy is a specialty of the nephilbock. On our world, they are known for their use of telepathy, but only gifted dökkálfar and few other species can speak with their minds. Among one another, the nephilbock almost never speak aloud. They are masters of the mind.*

Why can we use it so easily here?

Because of the God Stones, Jack. Because the Earth is twenty-five times smaller than Karelia. The concentration of Sentheye is therefore twenty-five-fold what it should be. Now couple that with the fact I assembled the stones into the Sound Eye, increasing the concentration even more. The saturation on this world is allowing even weak-minded humans to touch its greatness. It's like giving a baboon a loaded machine gun. Thankfully, the Sentheye will soon destroy this planet, but we will be gone before that happens. Regardless, the point is this. The concentration of Sentheye is having profound effects on the creatures of this planet.

The ground began to shake beneath Jack's feet.

Ah, Ogliosh is climbing the steps now. I asked him to show you how to protect your mind. Until then, send out the hounds, Jack. Let them continue the search.

Should I worry about Cerb? Jack asked.

No, he saw her when you couldn't. Dragons have stronger minds than humans, and I suspect Cerberus's mind is unnaturally strong. Additionally, five other nephilbock are searching and several dozen small dragons. The sun will be up soon. She can't hide for long, Apep said.

Jack nodded.

Apep looked suddenly bored, seeming to sink deeper into his hood and maybe, Jack thought, into himself. *By tomorrow, thousands of nephilbock and dragons will fill this valley. Once they arrive, there will be nothing that can stop me from opening the portal and claiming my destiny.* The old elf laughed then, and it was a low laugh, strange and unwell. The kind of laugh that just goes on and on, not making sense. Jack had seen some of the old coots at nursing home where his grandpa died laughing like that, and he knew then that at least for now he and Apep's talk was over.

Cerb? Can you hear me? Jack asked.

The gnarly voice of the dragon filled his mind. *Yes, I hear you, brother.*

I need to stay up here for a while. Keep searching the valley. I don't think she's gone far, or we would have found her. She's got to be hunkered down somewhere close. Jack looked down, not far past the mounds of dirt. He didn't think she could still be in one of those washed-out cracks. Beyond the dirt were several rock outcroppings; those were spotty throughout the valley. Maybe she crawled into a den under a boulder or something. Only fifty yards from the dirt mounds were some burnt-out vehicles, leftovers from when this place was a dig site. One was a utility truck like his dad used to drive. The others were Jeeps. All were upside down or on their sides. He had seen several dragons around the vehicles, sniffing and smacking them with their heads. If the girl had been hiding in one, they should have smelled her.

The sun will be up soon, and she won't be able to hide. Start turning over boulders and, just in case, have a dragon search those vehicles again. She's here, Cerb. I can feel it.

We will find her, Taker.

19

James the Keeper

Saturday, May 7 – God Stones Day 31
Central Mexico

The road from Illinois had been long and hard, though despite the challenges, they had moved with superlative haste. Faster than even James had thought possible during their preparations after the departure of Garrett and the others. When Garrett had decided to follow his heart and set out for Mexico with his sages, James agreed he would lead the Keepers of the Light in his brother's stead. No, not agreed – promised. James promised, come hell or high water, he would get Turek's chosen to the portal safely so that Garrett could fulfill the prophecy and lead them to the other side – lead them home.

The constraint should have been the horses, limiting them to forty miles a day – less because many of them were pulling wagons. Even if they hit forty, the trip into Mexico should have taken fifty days. But at only eighteen days into their journey, James and his Keepers of the Light, just over one thousand of them, were already deep into Mexico and nearing the portal.

As it turned out, the constraint was the solution, after all. The Keepers' horses had been raised by Emily, a young Keeper who'd been recently widowed. Emily and her now-deceased husband, Petersburg police officer Mike McMullan, owned a large horse ranch on the outskirts of Petersburg. The night Apep assembled the God Stones, he'd also killed both Mike and his partner Dan in Glen Patterson's basement after they responded to a house fire at the Tureks'. Other Keepers had died at the hands of Apep that night too, including James's own father, Phillip.

Mike and Emily's ranch had been in her family for decades, funded by the Keepers all the way back to the founding of Petersburg, allowing her family to raise horses for the sole purpose of outfitting this journey when called upon. But even James couldn't have predicted her steeds would perform like this anymore than he could have predicted how the Sentheye would affect Emily's mind.

Emily's love for horses went beyond her love for people, and this hadn't gone unnoticed by James or the other Keepers. Since the untimely passing of her husband, Emily preferred the company of her horses to the company of humans. Maybe it shouldn't have been a surprise to anyone, least of all James, when late on the first day, Emily discovered that through her focused concern and a loving caress, she could bring an instant calm to her steeds. But that wasn't all. To everyone's astonishment, her touch not only relaxed them, but it also energized them, and each time, with no more than a simple stroke of their mane or pat on their muzzle, the horses became vibrant once more and ready to run anew.

Of course, James asked her to try her newfound ability on one of the exhausted Keepers. And the raven-haired woman tried, but after several failed attempts it became clear her incredible gift only worked on the horses. Maybe it was her special bond with the animals. Perhaps a deeper love formed through the grief of her tragic loss. Whatever the reason, even if given a choice, James knew this magic was better spent serving the horses than those they carried.

Besides, with just over a thousand Keepers moving en masse, horses alone would never have been enough. James knew this. The Keepers had always known this. They'd needed something else independent of electrical or combustion power. The solution was twofold. Construct lightweight supply wagons and augment horseback transportation with pedal power. The latter resulted in the purchase of hundreds of high-end bicycles over the last several years.

But then came Emily's surprise, blessing the Keepers with over three hundred horses that never tired. With the advantage of their modern wagons, cyclists could trade off for a few hours of incremental rest, resulting in the Keepers' ability to move twenty hours a day, rotating to allow those who needed rest to rest.

James had said it then. "Let all who hear listen! Listen and believe. We are not alone! Turek journeys with us! Behold Keeper Emily! Witness the power bestowed upon her! A gift to ensure we are where we need to be when we need to be!"

The second boon bestowed by Turek came early on the second day after James had woken from a short nap. He hadn't wanted to lie down, but Elaine was persistent, and he had been awake for nearly forty hours. "We need you sharp, James – sharp and rested." James had obeyed. Besides, Elaine, descendant of Turek himself and mother of Garrett Turek, had played the part of James's mother for the last dozen years. James hadn't known his own mother, and Elaine felt more like his mother than anyone ever had. He knew – despite his over nine hundred years of age, despite his lack of biological connection to her, despite it all – Elaine looked upon him as her son too.

James had found sleep quickly, only to be jostled back into consciousness by knobby wagon tires bouncing over road debris. They were deep into southern Illinois, and he had been dreaming of a wiry greying man with a full beard. Turek, his friend, his leader, his lord, and now the Templar Knight, had come to him in his dream just as he'd been in life.

"Find the Sentheye, James," Turek said.

Confused, he'd said, *"I don't understand. Apep has the Sound Eye and we are on our way to the portal, my lord."*

"Your lord?" Turek had asked, smiling. *"You think me a god, but have I ever claimed to be one?"*

"What? I mean you are… Of course you are."

"Touch the Sentheye, James. Find it in yourself. For to fail in this is to fail my people."

"Me?! But I… I don't know how!" James said pleadingly.

"Of course you do. Mother has given all the ability to touch her."

"To touch... her?" James asked, his brows bunched in clouds of confusion.

"Hurry, my child, gather your flock – they're coming," Turek had said, pointing to the sky.

James woke, threw back his blanket, and hurried to the front of the wagon. "Elaine, they're coming!"

"Who?" she'd asked.

"I don't know! I mean, I think... I feel... I don't know. Jack, I think! Jack and the dragons!" His eyes flashed to the sky. "Stop! Full stop!" he shouted, stepping over the back and onto the old Ford Bronco bench seat of the wagon.

"Whoa! Easy. Easy, fellas," Dr. Moore said, pulling back on the reins.

Standing in between a seated Dr. Moore and Elaine, he waved a desperate arm and made a fist – the signal to stop.

The rest of the Keepers stopped – no one understanding why.

Gather your flock. James cupped hands over his mouth and shouted, "Pull the horses, wagons, and everything as close together as possible!" he ordered.

"Are you sure we shouldn't try to find cover, James? Perhaps we should shelter in the woods!" Elaine said, fear filling her voice as she searched the sky.

"No! No time!" And he had been right. In the distance from some unseen place, a screech crossed the sky. But this hadn't been the shriek of a hawk or the call of an eagle. This sound had been wrong and out of place.

"James, what's the plan?" Dr. Charles Moore had asked.

"I don't know! I... I just need to focus."

"James! This is crazy. We're sitting ducks on this road," Elaine had said, her voice pleading now.

Dr. Moore held out a hand. "Please, Elaine... wait. I see it, James. Do it. Find your focus."

Elaine had frowned, not seeing anything.

James shook his head. "Ahh! I... I need to be in the middle!" he shouted, jumping from the wagon.

Beyond the trees, the dragons' screams multiplied, drawing ever closer.

James had made his way to the middle of the group. "Silence!" he commanded, closing his eyes as he touched a horse to his left and to his right. The terrified Keepers quieted, and following James's lead, they joined hands, each touching another on either side.

The dragons appeared from the north, flying directly toward them. There had been no way they could be missed and nowhere to hide. Not a thousand people, over three hundred horses, dozens of wagons, and hundreds of bicycles. Nowhere to hide. That ship had sailed.

The moment seemed to stretch on forever, but James focused, and he reached, and he prayed, "Please, Turek! Please save us!" He felt it then, a warmth filling him, like hot chocolate on the coldest day. Then came a prickling through his mind, down his spine, and out through his hands and feet. And suddenly he felt the horses and the people and the road. He felt it all, and all he didn't want the dragons to see. *Oh god,* he'd thought, squeezing his eyes tight. *Don't let them see.*

From the crowd, someone moaned, "They're going to see!"

"Silence!" someone else urged in a harsh whisper.

But the moaner spoke again. "No. No. No! This isn't right! We should have made for the woods."

Suddenly, there was a commotion. The gears of a bicycle clicked as the moaner mashed down on the pedals. "Follow me if you want to live!"

James couldn't see from his position in the center of his people, but he understood well enough what was happening from the rattle of a bike chain and clicking gears. A bicycle was breaking from their ranks. In the moment, he hadn't been sure if others broke rank or if it was only the one.

Lord Turek, save these people, James had prayed, then he opened his eyes to the sky to find that one dragon from the approaching group was diving low overhead. He heard the gasps as the dragon flashed past their west flank.

Not far from their group, he heard the man scream.

James had been in enough battles to know the sound a man can make when he knows death is closing, and that was the sound he'd heard. It was the sound he would continue to hear echoing in his mind for god only knew how long. But in life, the screams only lasted a few more seconds. Then came the roar, and the man screamed no more.

The rest of the Keepers stayed quiet as the dragons passed overhead.

As James had looked to the sky, one very large dragon accompanied by several smaller ones moved past them. As he watched, the missing dragon rejoined the group with what was left of a Keeper of the Light clenched in its jaws. More disturbing still, he saw a human riding atop the smallest dragon – Jack Nightshade.

Even though Jack and his dragons had looked and should have seen – they saw nothing. Or perhaps they saw the road, the scattered broken cars, and an otherwise empty street. Whatever they saw, they passed over, moving west toward the Mississippi, screeching and screaming and roaring, blind to the bounty before them.

Thank you, Turek.

And so it went. Six more times, James would need to gather his flock of Keepers under his wings, like a mother bird shielding her young from a harsh rain. Each time he would feel the Sentheye wash through him, and each time the dragons would fly over, oblivious to their presence.

Each time, when James called his Keepers to come together, they obeyed, and never again did a Keeper falter in their duty. Turek had given them all the reason they needed to believe. He had given them more than faith! It hadn't stopped with Emily and her horses, or James and his ability to hide his Keepers at will. The world too was different. The trees had nearly destroyed all the cities, at least the ones James and his Keepers had passed near. But then, as suddenly as the attack had started, it stopped, and the trees went quiet once more.

Now sitting upon Shadow, a beautiful black mare, James led the Keepers forward in a generally southward direction, deep into the Mexican jungle. After traversing some challenging mountain roads, they were passing through more manageable foothills.

Despite how well their journey had gone, something was pulling at James. It was a niggling at the back of his mind that wouldn't go away, and despite their haste, the threat of dragons, roving gangs, trees, and all they had faced and would face in the days to come – despite the road to Mexico and the journey that awaited them beyond the portal – that damn niggle festered like a splinter beneath the skin, becoming more than annoyance. Now it was consuming him. Why had Turek said, *You think me a god, but have I ever claimed to be one?* What did that mean? Why had he said that? And what the hell did he mean when he said, *Mother has given all the ability to touch her.* Mother?

James had told no one about the dream, not even Elaine. It was, after all, just a dream. He'd known Turek in life. He'd lived for over nine hundred years because Turek had opened his third eye so long ago. The prophecy was coming to pass, albeit with a few surprises, but in a couple of days, they would be at the portal and soon enough, they would be on Karelia! But still, he knew better. It hadn't been just a dream, and he hadn't mistaken what he heard, nor what he'd done after he'd woke. So, what then? Was this a test of his faith? Surely not. Not now. Not after all this.

The night stretched as he pondered his thoughts through the midnight watch and nearing the cockcrowing of a new day. But no matter the hours that slipped away, lost in this strange riddle, James simply couldn't understand. Sighing to himself, he realized he was no closer to figuring out the strange dream now than he had been yesterday or the day before that. *Turek, I know when you're ready, you will show me the answers.*

The sun would be up soon, and dragons were flying over with more frequency. Once they descended into the next valley, they'd need to stop and take rest. His Keepers were tired, and a small reprieve was well earned.

A pained wail broke the quiet of the night, startling James from his thoughts. He pulled back on the reins, spinning Shadow in a one-eighty to face the wagon behind him. The source of the cry had been Elaine's wagon, but the scream hadn't belonged to Elaine.

James drew the arming sword from the scabbard at his hip.

Charles Moore cried out again.

20

There's Something I Have to Do

Saturday, May 7 – God Stones Day 31
Rural Chiapas State, Mexico

The news that Jack lived stole Garrett's breath. He would rather have heard that Apep was waiting for him around the next corner than that Jack still drew breath. His mom had raised him better than to wish someone dead, but god how he wished it for Jack. He'd be lying to himself and everyone else if he tried to pretend otherwise. The news brought with it a sick feeling in his stomach that hung with him all the way back to Juan's farm.

"Now that we've stopped, can you please check and see if you can find Gabi?" Breanne asked.

Governess nodded, rooted, and closed her eyes.

For a long, nail-biting moment, as Juan led the cenote survivors into his barn, Garrett, Breanne, and the others stood in silence as Governess searched. Garrett figured she must be searching through the memories of trees to try and determine Gabi's last location. Meanwhile, Garrett focused on Breanne. She looked like she was going to lose it. He took her hand and squeezed. *It's going to be okay, Bre. We will find her.*

Breanne squeezed his in return and forced an uncertain smile. *Thank you.*

Governess opened her eyes. *The last sighting of Gabi De Leon revealed she was in the talons of Mivras the Blue. The dragon landed atop the pyramid at the entry to the temple. We cannot see where the girl was taken from there. It is still too dark, and the area around the pyramid has been burned. However, the girl states she killed Azazel, and we can corroborate a bright explosion soon after the blue dragon landed.*

So, she did it, Pete said, shaking his head in awe. *Somehow Gabi killed the Queen of Queens.*

And with no gun? How the hell is it even possible? Paul asked.

There appears to have been a battle on the valley floor right after the explosion in the pyramid. I could see what appeared to be dragons breathing fire. Though I am not sure who was the target of their foul fire, Governess said.

So, she could have made it to the valley floor? Maybe she got away! David said, hope filling his voice.

I'm sure she did, Garrett said, turning back to Breanne. *Bre, maybe you should try to reach her.*

Garrett, you know I have been trying to reach her since we left! She doesn't answer.

No, I mean reach her like you tried to do with me when you had the vision of the future. When you saw Pando put me under the ground before it ever happened.

Breanne nodded. *I can try, but what if I can't? What's our plan?*

Garrett knew what she wanted to hear. *We aren't staying here. We are moving straight on to the pyramid.*

Garrett, we haven't slept in… in, Jesus… I don't even know how long, Lenny said.

The sun will be up soon. We can't wait, not while Gabi is out there, he said, glancing at Bre. *She's a sage, guys – we have to go get her.*

Breanne smiled, and this time it was honest. She squeezed his hand again.

I slept for at least a couple hours, David said.

Well, that's great for you, David, but I'm smoked, Lenny said.

Pete rubbed his face, pushing his fingers into his eyes. *Yeah, honestly, guys, I will go even if it means I have to crawl, but I'm just saying, I'm dead on my feet.*

No, listen, David said. *That wasn't what I meant. I meant I am rested enough to heal all of you. I want to try an area-of-effect spell.*

Paul nodded. *That's good, David. Do you think you can do it without passing out?*

Hold on? Area of effect? You mentioned that before. What is it exactly? Lenny asked.

In gaming, it's a spell that affects everyone within an area, David said.

You're casting spells now? Lenny asked incredulously.

Well, no. And it isn't really an area of effect either, but it sounds cooler than saying hey, I want to try a group healing, or everyone hold hands while I try to heal us.

Lenny smiled. *Fair enough, but what do we do if you pass out?*

Well, fortunately for me, there are no dead dragon balls for my so-called friend to rub my face on.

Lenny placed a hand on his chest as if aghast. *David, I was actually being serious. What do we do with you if you fall out while you're healing us? It kind of defeats the purpose, right?*

I will carry him until he wakes, Governess said simply.

You can do that? Breanne asked.

I am quite powerful, Breanne Moore.

That's my boo, Pete said with a grin.

Lenny slapped a palm to his face.

I am not familiar with "boo," Peter Ashwood. What does it mean?

I'll tell you later. Let's get on with this – my everything is sore, Pete said, rubbing his hands together as if he were about to perform the healing himself.

Wait, before I try to reach Gabi, there is something I have to do. It can't wait any longer, Breanne said.

Garrett didn't need the explanation, and he could tell Paul didn't either.

Paul looked at Garrett. *We'll be with you, sis. We'll tell Pops together.*

He is going to be devastated. I've been putting it off since Gabi disappeared, but I can't keep what happened to Sarah from him any longer. He is going to want to know that I'm safe. He won't want us to do what we're about to do. But I don't want to lie to him.

Do what you think is best, Bre. If you must tell him the truth, then do it. The pyramid is our destination anyway, and it will be good to check in and see how close the Keepers are getting, Garrett said.

I know, you're right. Let's just get this over with, then we can do the healing, okay? she asked.

Garrett wondered if secretly Bre hoped that when David healed her fatigue, it would somehow heal her heart too. Of course it wouldn't, but it didn't hurt to hope. Garrett pressed his lips into a serious line and nodded. *Okay.*

Wearing the necklace Breanne's father had given Sarah around her neck, Breanne reached out and took both Paul's and Garrett's hands. The physical connection allowed Garrett to hear her father's voice when he finally answered.

What… Baby girl? The man sounded as if he'd been sleeping, but he quickly pulled himself together. *Baby girl! Jesus, it's been days! I've been worried sick! Tell me, are you okay? Did you make it back to the cenote? Tell me everything!* her father said, practically frantic.

We made it back, Daddy.

Oh, thank god!

But…

But what? Bre, what's happened?

Daddy, are you okay? Did I wake you? How is it going for you and the Keepers? Where are you?

We are okay. We are finally moving through Mexico. The terrain is challenging, but James is… Well, the man is amazing. His abilities and leadership saved us more than once! He is quite… Bre, you're stalling! What is it? What's happened?

Oh Daddy! I don't how to tell you! Bre said, and Garrett could feel the knot swelling in his throat.

Is it Paul? Has something happened to your brother?

No, Pops, I'm here. Can he hear me, Bre? Please tell him I'm here.

Paul is here, Dad. He's holding my hand. He can hear you and he is fine.

Then what is it? I don't…

There was a silence that seemed to stretch out for eternity. As long and horrible as it was, worse still were the words that came next. The words that brought tears to Garrett's eyes.

Is it Sarah? her father croaked, his voice breaking.

Breanne began to sob.

Garrett wasn't sure if her father could hear her crying or if it was more of the horrible silence on his end.

But then Dr. Moore spoke again, desperation in his voice. *Please. Tell me she isn't…*

I'm sorry, Daddy. We were too late. Dragons attacked the cenote while we were gone. Sarah… she…

Dr. Moore wailed in a gut-wrenching moan. Finally, he spoke. *Did… did she… suffer?*

In truth, Sarah had already suffered greatly, but in death, her end was quick. Dragon fire had seen to that.

No, it was quick.

Another painful wail, then silence.

Garrett wiped the sleeve of his free hand across his eyes. With the other hand, he squeezed Bre's.

I'm so sorry, Daddy, Breanne said, her telepathic words broken by sobs.

It isn't your fault, Bre. My god, if you had been there… I would have lost you both, her father managed, through his own thick emotion.

Garrett stayed there a moment longer. A moment to get past the worst of it. Then he looked at Paul's wet eyes. The man pressed his lips tight and nodded a silent *thank you.*

Garrett let go of Bre's hand and with it the connection the four of them had shared. He had been there for her through the hard part. Now it was time to give them some time as a family.

Garrett found Lenny and the others on the back side of the barn staring at Governess, who stood facing away from them. Garrett almost didn't recognize her with her hood down, revealing long auburn hair spilling all the way down her back in twisting locks. He couldn't help but wonder why she'd chosen this moment to display her hair. It wasn't like she had hidden the red hair under her hood because the hood wasn't really a hood. When Governess changed any part of her appearance, she wasn't simply pulling a hood on or off; she was shifting into the change. So it begged the question: Why? But this was a question that would have to wait. The woman was staring toward the pasture with her feet spread apart and her hands beginning to glow.

What's this about?

Just watch, Lenny said, pointing.

Governess's emerald hands grew even brighter as the ground beneath them trembled. Roots as thick as the fat end of a baseball bat burst from the ground and snaked their way toward the sky. One after another, the thick vines shot up like a row of bean sprouts. From the vines grew long thorn spikes, each longer than Garrett's hand from wrist to fingertip.

Governess started forward as she continued to wave her green, glowing hands. The vines followed her path, bursting from each vacant footstep just after her foot lifted. One after another, after the next, until she had walked all the way around the large barn. The tall vines tipped inward over the barn's roof, finding one another and tangling into a solid shell of thorn and wood. Outside the vines, several trees pressed into the pasture from the surrounding jungle. Inside, the vines sprouted various fruits. In one corner, the vine roots pulled away from the dirt, creating a shallow pool.

When she finished, the tree-woman looked at the others with satisfaction. *This shall offer some protection from the creatures Apep has enhanced. The fruit and water will sustain these people for a time, and the trees beyond will hide this place with their foliage.*

Garrett leaned over and whispered to Lenny, "How the heck did you talk her into doing this?"

Lenny nodded toward Pete. "Why don't you ask lover boy over there."

Pete was grinning ear to ear. *This is perfect! Thank you.*

Governess nodded and looked at Garrett. *Continue to keep your promise to save my people, Garrett Turek, and perhaps I will not be forced to kill yours after all.*

Wow, that hurt a little on the inside, Gov, Garrett said, smiling. *Why don't you admit you have a heart in that woody chest of yours? You don't want to see these people in danger any more than we do.*

The petite tree woman pulled a face like she'd just gotten a whiff of David's feet. *Nonsense. I simply grow tired of hearing this one beg,* she said, pointing a finger toward Pete.

Pete's grin was stupid, and Garrett couldn't help but grin too. *Well, thank you. This should keep them safe until Apep and his armies leave.*

Governess nodded again.

For the first time, Garrett saw a way for humans to share the planet with trees that he hadn't seen before. If the trees kept their abilities, they could work together with humans, providing a sustainable way for both groups to live in harmony.

Soon, Breanne and Paul joined them, and they said their goodbyes to Juan and the others.

"Wait! There is something else," Juan said.

"What is it?" Breanne asked.

"We have been talking and, well… the protection you have created for us and the healing your blessed one has performed on my people… Like I said, we have been talking and… do you remember the woman David healed with the injured foot? The foot she was sure to lose if not for your friend?"

Garrett exchanged looks with Lenny. He remembered the woman. She had been sick with fever from her infection and would likely have died without David to heal her.

Breanne nodded curiously. "Yes, I remember."

Juan looked back at the group gathered behind him as a familiar woman shuffled shyly forward, a cloth-wrapped bundle in her arms. Her foot was good as new, but there was a sadness in her eyes. "Your David saved my foot, and you and your friends saved us all from an unspeakable horror. But did you know that before you came, my brother, Arturo, also saved us?"

Breanne frowned, shaking her head.

"When one of the dragons lunged forward to eat me, Arturo took its eye. And while he was fast enough to save his little sister, he wasn't fast enough to save himself. The dragon…" The young woman paused, steeling herself, determined to press on – to finish what she'd started and say it aloud, no matter her pain. "The dragon ate him."

Immediately Garrett flashed back to the one-eyed dragon frozen in a moment of time he had slowed. The dragon that had breathed fire on him and boiled the water he'd been standing in. The dragon with the oozing eye socket.

"Oh, I'm so sorry," Breanne said, reaching for the woman.

"No. Don't be sorry. What you all did… you saved us, and you made Arturo's sacrifice meaningful." She looked at all of them now. "I have something for you."

She held out the bundle and nodded to Breanne.

Breanne gently pulled back the cloth to reveal a sword.

"This sabre has been in my family for over five hundred years. It was passed down from one generation to the next. Arturo had planned to give it to his first-born son. But I think he would want one of you to have it. I see this one carries a sword," she said, nodding toward Garrett. "Can anyone else in your group wield a sword?"

Careful to use mind speak so only Breanne and the other sages could hear, Garrett said, *Lenny can use a sword almost as well as me. Maybe he could trade up his staff for the sword?*

Um… no way! I would stand a better chance of taking you out with this staff than with a sword. I'll stick with this baby. Besides, I already gave it a nickname, Lenny said, raising an eyebrow.

Garrett didn't bite. *Well, I'm not sure what kind of sword this is, but—*

It's likely a Spanish conquistador's sword. It's approximately three feet long, sharpened on both sides, and has a pommel and guard reminiscent of a Toledo-crafted sword. The age fits too. If you don't mind, Garrett, I will be wielding "this baby" myself, Breanne said, bowing her head to the woman as she accepted the sword. "May I?"

The woman nodded. "Please."

Breanne stepped back, falling into en-garde position.

Garrett exchanged a curious look with Lenny.

The corners of Breanne's mouth curled deviously as she whipped the sword into a figure eight, slicing the air with a buzz, then she stepped forward and lunged.

The woman beamed as her eyes filled with tears. "This brings my heart joy. Please, wield this sword in the name of Arturo, kill those foul beasts, and save your friend!" A sob broke from the woman as she covered her mouth and turned away, retreating behind the thorn-filled wall of vines.

"I will! Um, thank you!" Breanne called after her.

Garrett stood blinking at Breanne. The technique was odd, but it was clearly technique. And the way the sword fell into her hand like a familiar tool was evident. Then he watched as she slid her feet back to attention.

I didn't know you could use a sword, Bre, Garrett said in disbelief.

I told you – I attended Culver Military Academy back home in Indiana.

And they teach swordsmanship at your high school? Lenny said, his own shock equaling Garrett's. *Garrett, we've been attending the wrong school!*

Breanne laughed. *Competitive fencing, Lenny. I was the youngest on the team and the captain four years straight.*

Garrett was a little disappointed that all the time they'd spent talking, she hadn't told him about this. *I still don't understand. We could have been practicing together.*

I was busy learning how to knife fight, remember? Besides, I've watched you and Lenny bang sticks together, and it's my professional assessment that you two need all the practice you can get. Did you know that, combat-wise, sabre is the fastest sport in the world? You would have to slow time just to keep up with my flying lunge. Honestly, you boys are just far too slow, she said, giving him a wink as she sheathed the sword and slung it over her shoulder.

Lenny put a fist to his mouth. *Oh burn!*

Garrett couldn't help but smile back at the beautiful girl. *Well played,* he said, noticing that all around the barn's vine-covered perimeter, trees were crowding in, quickly transforming the farm into a dense jungle right before his eyes. *I think that's our cue, guys.* Garrett turned to David. *You ready to give us a refresh?* he asked.

Yeah, but can we go out to the road? I get nervous enough with you guys watching me, he said, looking at the crowd still gathered to see them off.

You got it, Garrett said, slapping David on the shoulder.

They made their way down the drive and onto the road while Juan and the others stood outside the vines, waving at them. It reminded Garrett of leaving his grandparents' house after Christmas dinner. They lived just far enough away that his family only visited once a year. So, when they left, Grandma and Grandpa would stand on the steps waving at them until they were completely out of sight.

Once they'd rounded the corner, Garrett turned to David. *Okay, you're up.*

Right, David said, holding out his hands, palms up. He sat down on the road, legs crossed, and said, *Everyone sit down in a circle and join hands.*

Garrett took David's hand in his right and Breanne's in his left. As David's hand began to glow, the first thing Garrett noticed was warmth filling his hand. The warm sensation spread through his arm and then his chest and within a couple seconds his whole body tingled with the strange feeling. Then he could feel it moving through him and into Breanne. As the warmth passed through his body, it took away all the aches and pain.

Stay with us, David. You're doing great, Garrett said, looking into his friend's eyes. David's pupils grew bigger and bigger as golden light radiated from them. As the light faded, David's eyelids fluttered, his pupils returning to normal before his eyes rolled back into his head.

Lenny let go of David's other hand and placed it behind David's back to keep him from hitting his head as he tipped backward. *And there he goes, folks. Off to la-la land. Sleep tight, David, ya douche licker. God! What I wouldn't give for a dragon's ball-sack right now.*

Breanne rolled her eyes.

Beside them, Governess shifted into something resembling a grizzly bear. It was wide-backed and stocky, with a head full of sharp canine teeth. *Place David Leigh onto my back,* Governess said.

With help from Paul, Garrett and Lenny heaved David onto the furry brown creature. Garrett secured his sword, adjusted his pack straps, and then helped Lenny secure his guitar.

You're really taking that guitar with you, Len? Garrett asked.

You damn right I'm taking it! We're going to another world, bro! What if there are no guitars on Karelia? Can you even imagine how bad that would totally blow?

Alright! Garrett laughed, holding his hands up. *But what about your staff?*

I'll carry it. That way I am always at the ready and besides, it makes a good walking stick.

The sun is rising. Let us make haste, Governess said, lumbering forward.

Pete smiled as he jogged a few steps to catch up with her. *That's my girl.*

21

Zerri the Chosen

Saturday, May 7 – God Stones Day 31
Rural Chiapas State, Mexico

Even from her hiding place beneath the vehicle, Gabi could sense the change in the air. It smelled like rain. As she peeked out from beneath the upside-down utility truck, the first drops splatted fat against the ashy ground. In the distance, a low rumble built as if the Earth itself began to growl.

Gabi's heart pounded. She didn't have to worry the sun would cook her beneath this metal box. But she did need to worry that she was trapped beneath a truck in the lowest part of a valley. Valleys were a terrible place to be during monsoons, and if this was to be a rain like she and Breanne had experienced on their way to Violeta's – this could be really bad. *Why couldn't it have been snow like before?* That was the first time in her whole life she had seen snow and, boy, how she wished for it now. Snow wouldn't drown her.

Outside, lightning flashed, and a new fear jolted her into near panic. She was under a metal truck in a barren valley. The perfect target for lightning. *¡María Purísima!* She might be electrocuted before she even had a chance to drown! And just when things couldn't get worse, she heard the thunder again. No, not thunder. This time, what she heard was an actual growl.

The grey snout of a dragon pressed into the opening at the rear of the truck. Gabi scrambled back away from the opening, and this time she wasted no time using mind control. The dragon resisted at first and a brief battle of wills ensued, but in only seconds, Gabi was able to force herself through the doorway and into the mind of the dragon. Immediately, she had a strange feeling – something was peculiar about this dragon.

Easy, friend. You don't want to hurt me. You want to protect me. Your queen wants you to protect me, Gabi said soothingly, trying to control her own fear and, with it, the dragon's mind. But it wasn't until the dragon answered that Gabi understood exactly what was different.

You speak to me? How is this you can speak to me, human? My queen is dead. You killed her! Cerberus the Mighty orders her avenged!

You're… you're a girl?

The dragon's head weaseled and squirmed its way forward like a pig's snout through mud until it was far enough under the truck Gabi could see its magenta eyes. Another flash outside, and the beast's eyes lit up as if charged by the lightning itself.

Female, yes, but you won't live to tell. I am going to eat you, little killer. I am going to avenge my mother and wash my mouth in your blood!

Gabi scrambled back, crawling onto the toolbox positioned behind the cab – the farthest point she could maneuver from the tailgate. The space between the bed of the truck above her and the toolbox below her was narrow, but she was a small girl, and unless the dragon lifted the whole rear end of the truck, she would remain just out of reach. Distance was her last line of defense.

The truck began to lift as the dragon forced its head farther inside.

Gabi's heart rattled in her chest like that of a rabbit cornered by a dog. Her defense was going to fail. She needed offense, but careful offense. As much as she wanted to scream that she had killed the dragon's queen and then force it to go kill itself, she knew that wouldn't get her out of this mess. Even if the dragon simply left, she would still be trapped. The weather would force her to make a run for it, or wait here and drown – or be struck by lightning. No. What she needed was knowledge – knowledge and allies. What she needed wasn't to destroy this dragon's mind, but to own it.

The bed of the truck groaned as the dragon inched ever forward, its jaws snapping at her.

No! Gabi shouted. *Cerberus lies to you! He killed her! He and that human, Jack. They want to rule you all. After they killed Mivras, I heard Jack say he and Cerberus were replacing the queen. That there was no one left to oppose them.*

The dragon stopped fighting forward. *Cerberus killed my mother?* the dragon asked.

Yes. Cerberus, Jack, and Apep, they are plotting against your people, but you are too smart. You are young, but you are no fool. Settle down and tell me why you keep the fact you are a girl secret?

Only the dragon's eyes blinked as it remained otherwise perfectly still.

Good. Gabi was in the dragon's mind fully now. If she wanted out of this, she would not only need to hold the psychic bond – she needed to strengthen it. But just as important, she needed to lie, and lie convincingly. *Yes, they killed your mother just like they killed Mivras the Blue.*

The dragon's nostrils flared, and Gabi could feel it becoming angry, but the anger wasn't for her. It was for Jack and Cerberus. It was working. Her power over the dragon's mind was working. Still, she could feel its will fighting her own for control, and she knew her hold was fragile.

Start slowly, Gabi told herself. Simple questions first. *What is your name?* she asked.

Outside, raindrops thumped in a slow rhythm against the metal truck. It wasn't raining hard – not yet.

Zerri, the dragon answered. *And I am hungry.*

Gabi swallowed, opting to ignore that last bit. She knew from her time with Ogliosh that all dragons eventually earned full names, but usually only after some special act they had performed in their youth. *Zerri, is this your full name?*

The dragon hesitated.

Tell me, Gabi urged.

My mother called me Zerri the Chosen.

And you are a female dragon? You keep this secret from the others. Why?

My mother said I am special. I am to keep my identity secret until we return to Karelia and finish the war. No others can know what I am.

Do you know why? Gabi asked.

I am the first female born of Azazel, the Queen of Queens.

Gabi didn't understand. *Why does this matter?*

You would need to know our ways to understand. Should other factions find out I exist, I would be in danger.

Other factions? *Zerri, pull your head out from this space. Check to make sure you are safe to stay here with me and then explain to me how you being a girl puts you in danger.*

The dragon stared at Gabi for a long moment, but she didn't move. A battle was raging in the dragon's mind. Follow her orders to find and kill Gabi, or believe Cerberus the Mighty and his human killed her mother.

Gabi focused, pressing her will on the dragon. *I'm a girl too, Zerri, and I lost my mom and dad because of… because of Apep, Ogliosh… and Cerberus.* It wasn't a complete lie, more like a lie sprinkled in truth.

Cerberus killed your mother too? Zerri asked.

No, not outright, but he had a part. Zerri, listen to me. Apep will betray you and your people. He is planning it as we speak. I can help you. I came here to tell your mother of their betrayal, but I never had the chance. More lies. And strangely, the lies made her feel… guilty. Why in the hell was she feeling bad about lying to a dragon she would rather kill outright than share words with? This wasn't the time for self-reflection. Killing this dragon would be killing herself, and she knew it. If she wanted to live, she had to be smart. *Your mother would want me to help you, and she would want you to listen to me. Now, remove your head from this space before you give away that I am in here, and then we can talk more.*

Zerri withdrew her head.

Gabi blew out a relieved sigh. *Are we safe?* she asked.

For a moment there was no answer, and Gabi worried that she'd broken her psychic bond the moment she could no longer look the dragon in the eyes.

But then Zerri spoke. *Dawn is here, and several dragons roam the area. Cerberus is searching for you several miles to the north, where the larger trees gather.*

At the mention of the larger trees, hope sprang up in Gabi's mind, and what followed was the makings of a plan. It was insane, and she wasn't even sure it would work, but it was something. She needed to keep the dragon near her a few minutes longer. She wanted a strong psychic link with her for what came next. *Zerri, can you stay and talk to me without drawing suspicion?*

Zerri hesitated. *I think so, yes.*

Good, now please, go on. Tell me about these other factions.

On Karelia, there are many queens. Each queen has a hive, but one dragon, the Queen of Queens, rules all hives. I am the only female born directly of Azazel, the Queen of Queens. The other queens were born long ago from other queens, and when the last Queen of Queens died, my mother battled and won the right to become the Queen of Queens. If the other queens found out I exist, they would want me dead so that they could compete for a chance to ascend to the ultimate throne. Killing me now, while I am young, would be easy for them. My mother wanted us to go home, finish this business with Apep, free the enslaved dragons, and return to the safety of our queendom before my existence was to be revealed.

So, wait. Would you automatically become the next Queen of Queens? Is that why they would kill you? Gabi asked.

Yes, Zerri admitted. *When a Queen of Queens bears no female children, upon her death, the other queens can compete for the right to the throne, but when a Queen of Queens has a female child, that child ascends automatically.*

And with you alive, the other queens would not a get a chance to be the Queen of Queens.

Correct, Zerri said. *My people are at war. My mother wanted only to free her people from enslavement to the dökkálfar. She knew that until this war was over, she couldn't protect me. Should my identity become known, other queens would offer great rewards for my demise.*

Gabi didn't understand it fully, but she understood enough. *Your secret is safe with me. But you must help me escape. You owe me this.*

Owe you? Zerri asked curiously.

Yes, you owe me! You owe me for trying to save your mother and sharing that Cerberus the Mighty plans to take over.

A dragon king, she scoffed. *The legends say there was a dragon king long ago and that he, too, bore three heads. They say he was the son of our god Typhon. They say his name, too, was Cerberus. Some of the others are even whispering this Cerberus is the God Son reborn, and now you say he has killed my mother.* Zerri's voice choked. *Cerberus and the human must not be allowed to rule!*

Gabi could feel her pain and sorrow buried under a layer of rage that was reaching a boil. This dragon's emotions matched Gabi's, and she hated it. She hated that she understood her. She knew exactly how Zerri felt, and it made her feel… sorry. María Purísima, she hated that she felt bad! Juro por Dios, if I get out of this, I will personally kill this dragon myself! *Zerri, you are right! They must not, but first you must help me, because you owe me, but even more, because I can help you get your revenge!*

What is your name? Zerri asked.

Gabi.

Is that your entire name? the dragon asked.

No. My full name is Gabi De Leon.

Tell me, Gabi the Lion, what is it I must do?

Outside, the rain picked up. Inside, Gabi still lay atop the toolbox, but below her water leached in beneath the truck bed, moistening the ground near the edges.

Go, Zerri. Go and bring me another dragon.

For the next two hours, Zerri brought dragon after dragon to the upside-down truck. Each time, Zerri pretended to investigate the other destroyed vehicles, asking the dragon to check around the truck.

Each time a dragon snout appeared beneath the tailgate of the upside-down truck, Gabi attacked the dragon's mind. Of course, all the dragons Zerri brought to her were boys, as Zerri was the only girl dragon on the entire planet. Gabi quickly realized that boys' minds were far easier to crack than Zerri's had been. She wasn't sure if it was because girl dragons had stronger minds or if she was just getting better, but she suspected it was a bit of both.

Each time, she entered their minds with ease and said, *You want to protect me. Your Cerberus is a traitor. We must avenge your queen. Mivras the Blue knew this. Mivras was trying to avenge his queen, and Jack and his pet killed him for his trouble, just like they killed your queen!*

Yes, just like they killed my queen!

I am going to help you avenge your queen, and together we will make the usurpers pay! Now tell me your name!

The dragons would state their name, and presto – she had them. Next, she would order the dragons to wander around the area nearby and be ready when called upon.

By the twelfth dragon, the ground had three inches of standing water. Gabi was dry, but she was going to have to climb down off the toolbox and through the standing water to get out. God, she wanted out of this cramped place – she wanted out so badly.

She had twelve male dragons, plus Zerri. Thirteen dragons. *Lucky thirteen,* she thought. She hoped it would be enough. Now it was time to call a friend.

El Tule? El Tule, can you hear me?

Little Lion, El Tule hears you.

22

Signs

Saturday, May 7 – God Stones Day 31
Southern Mexico, near Chiapas

Never had James been so happy for rain clouds to settle over him and let loose. He and the Keepers had been stuck for three hours, pinned in a heavily wooded valley. Now, despite the strange lightning and heavy rains, they were moving once more. With the added cover of cloud and storm, maybe – just maybe – the dragons wouldn't find them.

Not that James couldn't touch the Sentheye and cover his Keepers in a magical veil. He could and he would if he had to. But it wasn't easy, and it wasn't something he could just hold on to. God, if only he could. If only he could shield them while they moved. At the thought, guilt washed over him like the hard rain. How dare he wish more from god? How dare he not simply be thankful for the gifts Turek had already given? He tugged gently at Shadow's reins and trotted alongside Elaine's wagon.

"How is he doing?" James asked, nodding toward the back of the covered wagon.

"He's been quiet," she whispered. "This is the longest he's gone without speaking in twenty days. Clearly, he's hurting, James, and I just feel awful for him. He loved Sarah and before this happened, he'd been thinking of asking her to marry him. They had reconciled over the last year and half and were falling back in love. It is… it is so sad Garrett and the others were too late."

"It sounds as though you've forgiven Garrett for going off on his own without telling you. Has your rage subsided?" James asked.

"Has my rage subsided?" Elaine asked with a snort. "When you talk like that, you sound your age, old man."

James flushed and smiled, wiping water from his face.

"But no, I'm not angry. I was never angry. Well, maybe I hid my hurt with anger, but I trust god has a plan. I have faith, James – faith Garrett followed his heart and with it, god's will." Her face twisted into a frown. "Here," she said, reaching behind the seat and retrieving his raincoat. "Now put this on before you catch your death." She snorted again. "Has my rage subsided? I like it better when you sound like my son."

James waved off the coat. "Thanks, but it's a warm rain, for now anyway." He knew Elaine didn't mean them to, but her words cut. His face became serious. "I'm still your son, you know, and you'll always be my mom."

Elaine smiled, her face suddenly looking ten years younger. "And you'll always be that picky kid whose potatoes couldn't touch his peas, whose peas couldn't touch his porkchop, whose porkchop couldn't touch… Oh, it just drove your father—" She stopped short, her voice hitching as the youth slipped from her visage like a mask pulled away to reveal all the loss, tragedy, and pain she'd suffered these past weeks. A moment passed between them before she looked at him once more, her smile returning but not fully, not like before. There was heartbreak in it now. She nodded toward him. "You'll always be my son, James – always. I love you."

The canvas flapped open. "What's happing?" Dr. Moore asked, his eyes flashing to the sky. "Oh, my word. That's quite a storm building to the south."

Unable to find words, James pressed his lips into a thin line and held Elaine's gaze a moment longer.

Dr. Moore looked from Elaine to James, his brows knitting. "I'm sorry, did I interrupt something?"

"Dr. Moore, we were just talking about the rain," James said, pointing. "It seems the storm—"

"I've told you how many times, James? It's just Charles."

James tipped his head forward, a stream of water running off the bill of his ball cap.

"We were talking about how James should put on this rain jacket," Elaine said, frowning from under the canvas awning rigged to cover the cab of the wagon.

"I'm fine, Mother," James said wryly.

"Oh, you know I hate it when you call me that! This isn't *Mommie Dearest*, and I'm not Joan! It's just Mom."

"It would appear naming conventions are my weakness," James admitted with a grin.

Elaine narrowed her eyes to a glare, then turned her attention to Dr. Moore, her expression softening. "How are you holding up?"

He shook his head, his bloodshot eyes welling anew. "I… I still can't believe she's gone."

When Breanne had told her father of Sarah's death, James had heard the pained moan escape the man and thought sure something was killing him. James had drawn his sword, ready to face the unseen attacker in the back of the wagon. As a second moan broke from the man, Elaine had thrown back the flap. Dr. Moore was sitting up, face in hands, sobbing. "Not my Sarah," he'd said, and instantly James had known he'd been right. Something was killing the man, but he wouldn't be able to save him from the cause of this pain, for death itself could not be slayed.

"I'm sorry, Charles," James said.

"I know, and I know those kids did all they could. It's a hell of position they've put themselves in," he said, pulling a hand over his bewhiskered face and shifting his gaze skyward. "That storm. It looks like we're heading right into it."

"Yes, it seems so. That's what I wanted to ask you about, Dr. Moore… um, Charles. According to our map, we're on track and should cross into Chiapas State soon. Care to take an educated guess at when we will arrive? Bear in mind, the terrain is only going to get worse – dirt roads mostly, and I'm not sure how direct we can travel. We equipped our wagons with all-terrain tires, but muddy roads won't be easy no matter how well-equipped we are."

"Could be Arkansas all over again," Dr. Moore said.

Elaine opened the map, handing one side to Dr. Moore as he looked over her shoulder from behind the seat. "We are about right here," she said, dragging her finger across the map, then tapping.

Dr. Moore nodded sagely. "Yes, I see. It's hard to gauge, and if this rain continues…" He looked back up at the ever-darkening clouds. "I think, even at half the speed we've been traveling, we can expect to be within sight of the pyramid by late tonight or early tomorrow, as long as we stay on course. The key will be finding it once we get close. It's hidden in the back of a rather deep jungle valley."

Thunder rumbled deep from the south.

Shadow neighed, rearing her head back, her nostrils flaring.

"Easy, Shadow, easy girl. It's okay," James said, rubbing his steed's neck assuredly.

"That thunderhead." Dr. Moore pointed. "Beyond those mountains, near the heart of the storm – by god, I think that's about right where the pyramid should be."

"Maybe the storm will have passed before we get there," Elaine said, hopefully.

To the south, a ring of orange lightning cracked across the heavy sky, followed by a dozen simultaneous lightning strikes.

"Good lord!" Charles said. "I've never seen anything like that!"

"The God Stones," James breathed. "Now I'm one hundred percent sure that's the *X* that marks the spot. That's our destination."

"That's where our kids will be!" Dr. Moore said, climbing over the back of the seat.

"Let's move!" James said, but as he turned Shadow toward the south, three riders approached.

"Commander!" a young woman shouted as she galloped forward on a formidable armored horse.

"Report. Did you find a passage, Annie?" James asked. Annie was one of his best riders, a show jumper with fiery red hair and a face covered in freckles that stood out against her milky complexion. She'd had hopes of going to college on a scholarship – but that was before the prophecy came to pass and the world as they knew it ended. Annie had proven herself good with an arming sword and quick on her feet.

James had learned that, when war came, people typically reacted in one of three ways. They ran, they fought, or worst of all, they froze up. Though she hadn't been battle-tested, the day Jack attacked Undertown, Annie hadn't frozen up like some others had. Not even when they died right behind the door – right beside her. She didn't run away, and when ordered back, she listened. *Good lord,* James thought, feeling awful. She hadn't even graduated high school, and he was thinking how well she would fare in battle. But these were the times they lived in – at least for now… at least until he could get these people to safety.

Annie halted her horse next to James. "The road just ends in a solid jungle, but—"

"You found the other road?" Dr. Moore asked. "The map says there should be a road that breaks to the southeast *before* this one ends. It's right here on the map."

"Right. Sorry, Dr. Moore, but the road is gone," Annie said.

"Just Charles," Dr. Moore said, waving off the formality. "Now what do you mean 'gone'? Washed out? Already?"

"No, it's like it never existed. You can see where it turns but now it… it… well, it just ends as if the trees swallowed it."

"You said 'but' a moment ago," James said. "The road ends, but what?"

Annie gave a sharp nod. "But then, on the other side of the road the… well, the trees parted. Honest to god, Commander. We watched it happen. The trees parted wide enough for our riders to pass. It was like they wanted us to see it," Annie said, her own apparent shock still fresh.

James exchanged looks with Elaine and Dr. Moore. "Show me."

23

Three Shells and a Pea

Saturday, May 7 – God Stones Day 31
Rural Chiapas State, Mexico

Rain fell steadily as the sky lit up in strange orange rings of flashing light. Jack had never seen anything like this. It started with a flash, then a bolt of lightning. But the lightning didn't crackle down toward the ground, not at first. Instead, it streaked the sky, forming a perfect circle. When the circle connected, there was a concussive boom, and what followed must have been a dozen simultaneous lightning strikes all coming from the circle toward the ground. Then came another boom and another ring of strange light, followed by yet another series of the wicked lightning. The bigger the circle, the more lightning bolts shot toward the earth. And it just went on and on.

Cerb, this lightning is crazy as shit. Be careful! Jack said telepathically.

Don't worry about me, Taker. Lightning doesn't strike dragons in flight.

Really?

I'm pretty sure, Cerb answered.

Well, that wasn't reassuring, Jack thought as he turned to Apep. "What's happening?!" he shouted over the roaring and cracking of the strange storm.

Apep stared out over the valley, then answered with a reassuring calm in Jack's mind. *It's the God Stones.*

Suddenly, Jack felt stupid for yelling when he could have just used his telepathy, like he did with Cerb.

This is what happens when a dökkálfar fails to follow the advice of the ancient nephilbock. It was Ogliosh who spoke, sounding both worried and annoyed.

Like the massive giant, Jack stood far enough inside the temple entrance that he wouldn't become a victim of the strange storm. But not Apep, who stepped forward into the rain and spoke in their minds. *I am impervious to this storm, for I am the storm.* He held out his arms wide as if daring the lightning to strike him.

If you are the storm, then make it stop, Apep. My nephilbock army has entered Mexico and will arrive within the hour. If they walk into this storm, it could mean their deaths, Ogliosh said.

Apep put his arms down and turned to Ogliosh. *This one will pass quickly enough. But there will be others. The sooner we leave this place, the better.*

Jack concentrated and thought his words. *My hordes are complaining they are starving. With the nephilbock safely in Mexico, Ahi has already moved his horde across the gulf and into the southern states of America to feed on larger cities.*

My nephilbock will also be hungry and in need of rest, Ogliosh said.

America? Apep nodded approvingly. *Fine. As long as the trees stay put, I will allow my armies two days to feed and rest. Jack, you lead the dragons now – order Ahi and his horde to return with talons loaded. Two humans per dragon. Order them to do no harm to the trees, but they are free to burn cities at will.*

Now we care about the trees? Jack asked.

No, Jack. Use what little intelligence you have. Once our army is here and safe, there is no reason to provoke the trees into attacking. They are waiting. I want to keep it that way. Their queen is plotting something – perhaps getting her own forces in place. The goal is to open the portal and leave with our armies intact. The only war that matters awaits us in Karelia.

Perhaps that is all the trees want, Apep. Perhaps they just want us to leave, Ogliosh speculated.

No. That queen bitch wants my power! How could any being not want to be a god? You are alone in your naiveté, Ogliosh, but it is of no matter. You have me to think for you. Now, whatever the reason – she is waiting. As long as she waits, we have no reason to provoke her into action. Finish your final preparations. You have three days. Fewer if the tree queen attacks. Do not mistake my intention in this – if the trees attack us, I will open the portal whether or not the pyramid is ready, whether or not either of your armies are rested or fed. Nothing will stop what is to come. Do you both understand?

Jack nodded. *Yeah, I get it.*

Yes, Apep, Ogliosh answered. *Now I must go. We've work to finish, and my nephilbock approach. Their long walk is almost over.*

Yes, I should like to greet them as well – to lay eyes on the army that will bring the kingdom of Osonian to its knees. Besides, it's time they see the true god they serve. Give me a few moments with Jack, and I will join you on the other side of the pyramid.

Ogliosh pulled a strange face. Jack was sure it was anger, but since the giant was so god-awful ugly to begin with, who knew? Angry or not, the giant king said nothing as he turned and lumbered away down the long corridor.

Now I have a question for you, Jack, Apep said, shifting his gaze back over the valley. He raised his finger and pointed. *Why is it I have watched at least ten different dragons stick their heads under that upside-down truck in the last two hours? Why then do they meander around like confused pups?*

Jack followed Apep's gaze far below, to the soggy valley floor. The sun was up fully now, for what little good it did blanketed by a God Stone storm. But some light pierced the veil, and even through the rain he could see the truck and several dragons meandering lazily around the area. They acted as if they were searching, but as Jack watched, it was clear they were only searching the area another had just searched. There were a couple hundred dragons around the pyramid now and more coming and going constantly, but the burned radius extended for at least ten miles in all directions. With all this area to search, these few dragons chose to check beneath the same truck and then wander around the same tiny area with seemingly no purpose? This made no sense. Something was off.

Then, as Jack and Apep watched, two more dragons flew down to the truck and, while a small, unimpressive grey dragon waited, the other poked its head beneath the overturned vehicle. *What the hell?* A moment later, it withdrew its head and joined the others.

Now that is interesting, Apep said, pursing his lips.

What is? Jack asked.

Each time before, that one – Apep pointed at the plain-looking grey dragon – *flew away, returning moments later with another dragon. Now it is waiting. But waiting for what?*

Jack zipped his leather jacket and popped his collar up to cover his ears. *Something isn't right. I'll go down and check it out,* he said, walking toward the pyramid stairs.

Hold, Apep said sharply, narrowing his darkened eyes. *Did you ever play the game cups and balls, Jack?*

What? I… I'm not sure. Why was the elf choosing this moment to talk about games?

Dear boy, it's a game as old as time. I knew it as three shells and a pea. Do not go down there – instead call Cerberus back and have him roll that vehicle over. Apep smiled. *If I'm right, I wager we may find our missing pea.*

24

A Familiar Feeling

Saturday, May 7 – God Stones Day 31
Rural Chiapas State, Mexico

Rain beat down on Breanne and the others as spheres of lightning cracked the sky. She slipped, her feet going out from under her as she reflexively thrust her hands out to catch herself. *Shit!*

Bre, you okay? Garrett asked, pulling her to her feet.

Yeah, I'm fine, she said, wiping her hands on her pants. She was more embarrassed than hurt.

A shout startled her from behind as Pete slipped too.

Breanne turned in time to see him lying face down, sliding backward down the slope.

Son of a…

Dig your toes in, Pete! Lenny laughed.

This is turning into a goddamned mud fest, Paul shouted over the rain.

A bright orange flash of lightning crackled above them, finishing in a sonic crack, chased by a threatening roar of thunder. Everyone ducked their heads, waiting for the bolts of lightning that followed.

I saw six that time! And one was close! Too close! David said. Turning to Breanne, he spoke aloud, voice cracking, "I'm scared shitless of lightning, Bre! And this" – he pointed at the sky – "this is fucking nuts!"

"It's okay, David. We're in the trees. I don't think lightning will find us so far beneath the canopy." As she said the words, though, she wasn't sure if they were even true.

"Yeah, well, why couldn't I have just slept through this part?!"

She suspected David was speaking out loud to keep the others, specifically Lenny, from hearing him freak out. But he was too panicked to do it quietly.

David, you chickenshit, Lenny said. *Add lightning to the long list of things that David is scared of. Let's see, we got rats, bats, rivers, giants, dragons… What am I missing?* he asked, ticking off fingers.

A lot, Lenny, you dick, but that's beside the point! We're going to die out here! David whined.

Fear not, little humans, Governess began. Now that David was awake, she had shifted from the strange bear back into her familiar teenage girl form. *My people will sacrifice their canopies for your safety. The forest shall shelter you from this danger, as we have sheltered you from a thousand other dangers since first your kind came into existence. Now please, go on about your lives in utter ignorance of anything other than your own self-interest – we have you covered.*

David mumbled something Breanne didn't catch, and the moment slipped into an awkward silence. She suspected no one wanted to engage in a debate with Governess about the sore subject of the trees' sacrifice for humankind. At least she knew she didn't. As far as she was concerned, the trees had a right to be angry. Not wipe-out-humanity angry, but certainly the right to be a little jaded.

Finally, Pete broke the silence. *Bre, you really walked all that way with Gabi – in this?*

Actually, it was raining much harder on Gabi and me. We could hardly even breathe through it, but yeah, we had no trees to protect us out on the road, and the lightning was worse too – more frequent. It's best to just keep moving and push through.

She watched as Paul and the others looked at the sky, mesmerized by the strange lightning.

Sis, I want you to know I'm proud of you. Getting Gabi from the cenote to the village in weather worse than this? That's pretty damn impressive.

Thanks, Paul. She smiled, but her thoughts were on Gabi. She worried that if the storm worsened, the others might vote to stop and hunker down. *Gabi? Can you hear me?* Every so often she tried to reach her, but so far nothing. She was worried sick, and she had no idea how they were going to find her once they got to the pyramid. She just had to keep concentrating and hope Gabi would answer once they were close enough.

As they continued, Pete and Governess carried on a verbal conversation that only the two of them could hear in the rain, while Lenny continued to give David shit in mind speak regarding his mustache and how god must have made a mistake when passing out facial hair because Lenny knew of seven-year-olds more deserving of whiskery badassness.

Gabi, please? Please tell me where you are. I'm trying to find you. I want to be there with you, but you have to tell me where you are! Gabi, please! Breanne slipped again. This time, as she hit the ground, the voices of the others faded into the background and her vision blurred. She felt a familiar feeling, although she didn't understand it – not at first.

Breanne blinked suddenly in a dark, cramped place, lying on cool stone. A cave? Had she fallen in a hole? She looked up to find there was no opening, only a low ceiling. She pressed her hands to the ceiling to find it was metal. But the metal above her was uneven, like a corrugated tin roof. Not a cave. She placed a hand on the floor to find it too was metal, but smooth, and she was close to an edge. When she looked to her right, she could see an area of standing water reflecting what must have been lightning flashes. The flashes were coming through a rectangular opening on the opposite side, only feet away. What the hell was happening?

"Breanne?" Gabi's voice whispered. "Breanne, are you really here? But how?"

Breanne turned to find Gabi lying prone behind her on the same narrow space of metal. The young girl was speaking to her, and not in her mind but out loud! "Gabi!"

"I don't know if you're really here or if I'm hallucinating," Gabi said, reaching out and touching Breanne's arm. "You *are* real!" Gabi announced, throwing her arm around her in a big hug. "Oh, Bre! I thought I might never see you again! Come, we have to go – right now!" Gabi motioned toward the tiny opening.

Breanne frowned. "Where are we?"

"Go, Bre! Hurry!"

Not understanding where she was or even *how* she was, Breanne rolled down off the metal and into the shallow water. It was cold, sludgy, and smelled like a wet campfire. She made her way across the thick, sooty mud to the opening and looked back at Gabi. The little girl nodded. Breanne lay down on her stomach and prepared to squeeze through.

Suddenly, the ground shook, and she heard a roar. Not one roar but many roars, all roaring in unison.

Gabi! she cried, looking back.

Gabi's eyes went wide as saucers, and she gasped.

With a sudden force, the metal above their heads tore away, flying into the air and tumbling into the distance as if sucked skyward by a tornado. Breanne realized only now that she had been beneath a vehicle. She looked up and found the source of the deafening roar. Above them stood a massive dragon with three giant heads, each the size of the truck they'd been hiding under, and all six red eyes were staring at her.

As Breanne stared certain death in the face and the pain pieced her eardrums, her thoughts flashed to Garrett, her brother, and the others. *I'm sorry, Garrett! I'm sorry!* She screamed, and her world blurred again.

Breanne heard shouting in her mind, but over the buzz of her eardrums, she couldn't make anything out. Her brother and the others were running toward her, faces blurred as they approached, lips moving.

She shook her head, blinking rapidly, until finally the buzzing faded and she heard Garrett's familiar voice.

Bre! "Breanne!"

Then her brother's.

"Sis! Sis, Jesus Christ!" Paul was beside her now, shaking her shoulders.

Breanne looked around frantically, but the world was spinning, and she thought she might fall off. She couldn't make sense of it. *Gabi! Gabi! Where are you!* "Gabi!" she screamed.

Gabi isn't here, Bre. Take a breath and tell us what just happened, Garrett urged, kneeling down opposite Paul.

I was with her! I was just with her! Oh, dear god. We were hiding under a truck. We were talking. I touched her! It was real! Without warning, her stomach seized into a cramp and forced out its contents.

Ew! Pete said.

David gagged, pulled a face, and looked instantly green.

Don't you do it! Lenny warned.

Under normal circumstances, it might have embarrassed Breanne to hurl in front of her friends, especially Garrett, but not now – not in this moment. She felt Garrett's hand slip beneath her braids and begin rubbing her back.

Just breathe. Here, do you need a drink? Garrett offered, holding out his water flask.

Breanne nodded and wiped her mouth on her sleeve. She swished some water around and spit it on the ground. Her eyes raced back and forth, searching her mind for understanding as she tried to regain her bearings. *Gabi said we had to go, and then… and then the three-headed dragon was there standing over us and… Oh my god! I left her there!* Breanne shot to her feet. The world spun again, and she fell to her hands and knees. She didn't let her lack of equilibrium stop her as she began scrambling forward up the slope. She had to get to her feet and run. She had to get back there before it was too late!

Stop, Bre! Garrett begged. *Slow down. We're still several miles away from the pyramid. You can't run there – not in this! You'll never make it, and even if you did, it would take hours. Now what do you mean you were with her? Not like a vision – not like before?*

Breanne got to her feet and steadied herself, but before she could try to run again, she felt Garrett's hand on her wrist.

Bre, please, talk to me. Not like a vision you had before?

No, not like before. I was really there! she said, looking around and still not understanding. *I know what this sounds like, but it's true. I was thinking about Gabi. I slipped, and… and I think I hit my head, maybe? Then I was there… I was with Gabi!*

For a few moments, we lost you, Paul said.

We were looking all around, but it was like you just vanished, Garrett said, his voice still laced with worry.

I told you guys! She vanished, David said. *I saw it with my own eyes. She teleported!*

Teleported? Breanne said, tasting the word. She knew this whole thing had felt familiar, and now she knew why.

Look at her! David said, pointing. *What is that?* He leaned in and sniffed her.

Hey! she said, flinching back.

I'm not trying to be weird, Bre, but—

But your mustache says otherwise? Lenny interjected.

David scowled at Lenny then turned back to Bre. *BUT… you're covered in soot and you smell like a fireplace. You teleported, Bre! That's the only explanation.*

She nodded. *Yes! David's right. Like when Apep teleported me to Mexico! That's it, you guys! Gabi's in trouble, but maybe if I focus, I can go back!* Breanne said, throwing herself into a seated position on the muddy ground. She closed her eyes and began thinking about Gabi. *Take me to Gabi. Take me to Gabi!*

That might not be such a good idea, Bre, Pete said. *You said yourself that the last thing you remember seeing was Jack's three-headed dragon standing over the top of you, roaring and about to breathe fire.*

She felt Garrett's hand take hers, and she cracked an eye.

Unless you can teleport us all, there's no way we can let you go – not by yourself, Garrett said.

I want to save Gabi too, but I vote no way to teleporting within fire range of a dragon, David said. *Even if we could all teleport, we might show up dizzy and puking! It could get us all killed!*

Her brother took her other hand. *They're right, sis.*

Part of her wanted to argue, wanted to say, "The hell I can't go back!" But the truth was, she didn't even know how she'd transported herself the first time. Was taking others with her even possible? If she did, would she just get them all killed? As much as she hated it, she knew their best bet was to continue on. She couldn't risk their lives for Gabi's. *Oh Gabi, please, please, please be okay.* She nodded her surrender to the others.

Okay, let's go, Garrett said, nodding to Governess.

As they got moving again, David ran up alongside her, a huge grin plastered across his face. *Hey, it's still epic that you teleported, Bre! You have multi powers! You can see the future and teleport!*

Lenny pretended to be as excited as David as he hooked a fist and said, *And you don't have any weird facial hair. And you don't even pass out after using your power! And you aren't scared of—*

F-you, Lenny! David shouted, throwing up the bird.

Do not underestimate the power of the God Stones, hairy-faced one, Governess said, tipping her back to consider the sky.

Was that a joke? Did you just make a freaking joke, Gov?! Lenny asked. He began laughing hysterically. *It… it wasn't all that funny, but I'm seriously beginning to think if you can get over wishing all humans dead, there may be hope for you!*

Governess didn't laugh, and Breanne couldn't find humor in much of anything until she was sure Gabi was okay. Abruptly, she had an idea. *Governess, I think I know where I was specifically. There was only one part of the pyramid that had vehicles on it. It was in our base camp. Can you root and check the north side of the pyramid and tell me what you see?*

Know this, Breanne Moore. I feel all efforts to locate this one human only serve to further hinder our journey and delay our arrival. Do you still wish to stop? Governess asked, her voice taking a tone of warning.

Kind of ominous even for you, Gov, Garrett said, looking to Breanne.

Breanne nodded. *It's Gabi, Garrett. I have to know,* she pleaded, giving Garrett what her dad always called "the look."

Garrett turned back to Governess. *It's Gabi! Of course we wish it.*

Breanne forced a smile, but her gratitude was sincere. She hadn't been sure the look she'd used on her dad would work on Garrett, but she was glad it did.

Governess rooted to the ground. A few moments went by before she uprooted and looked to Garrett and the others.

Well, did you find her? Breanne asked hopefully.

Not exactly. It appears the Little Lion has been busy.

What's that mean? Garrett asked.

No time. While rooted, I discovered the nephilbock army is arriving at the pyramid.

And they have Gabi? Breanne asked.

The primary concern is no longer your lost friend, Breanne Moore.

Wait, what do you mean? she asked.

The pyramid is due east of this location. However, the nephilbock were hugging the coast to the west and have now cut over in a northeasterly direction. They have cleared the forest to the southeast, but some are roaming in the trees. The immediate concern is that more than a dozen nephilbock will intercept our position directly from the southwest, she said, pointing.

Breanne and the others spun their heads to match Governess's gaze, but she didn't see anything.

How long? Paul asked.

Two minutes.

Two minutes?! David repeated, swallowing. *Why would they be in the trees? I thought the dragons burned a path? Shouldn't we be safe?*

These are only a few compared to the larger mass. They are likely scouts, looking for small towns, farms, or stray humans. If they find a large enough population of humans to eat, they will signal the others.

Oh my god! To eat! David said.

Be quiet, David, Garrett said. *Do we have any other options besides running or fighting?* Garrett asked.

Perhaps I can dissuade them from coming this way. But we will need to double back and circle. If we are careful, we may pick our path through without running into more. Be warned, the nephilbock have a superb sense of smell when it comes to humans.

Great! Just send David running that way and we can all go this way – problem solved. Lenny smiled, pointing his staff in the opposite direction.

David ignored his friend, but his panic was growing. *Can't the trees just kill them?*

No. After the nephilbock entered Mexico, Queen Pando ordered my people to cease their efforts against Apep's armies. My people are gathering around the perimeter of the area Apep burned. Should Apep try to leave the portal open any longer than he needs to, my queen will order the pyramid attacked. Governess began waving her open hands, palms down. "Akoki Doe okimuezae oz ray ff doe! Doe oz rayray doeray muezae, flahak zae doe rahshi, doerayoki flah zaeokirah ray doe rahray ak doe shi!" A green glow appeared and brightened as a row of thorny hedges sprouted and grew, stretching to the east until it vanished into the wet forest.

Come, we must backtrack, Governess said.

Breanne and the others followed the hedge growing along their southward side as they ran. The new barrier reminded her of hedgerows along the cornfields in Indiana, but this one was denser than any she had seen. And taller too – fifteen to twenty feet, with thorns as long as her own palms.

They climbed down a steep embankment before Governess said, *Halt. This may suffice. I will root to ensure that upon reaching the wall, they go east. If, however, they turn west or breach the wall, I will uproot the surrounding trees and force them to fall on the giants and in between us and them. These actions should ensure they are not an issue.*

No, Garrett said adamantly.

No, Garrett Turek? Governess asked.

Garrett shook his head. *No. Everyone be prepared to fight. Governess, I appreciate what you're doing to protect us, but I can't let you order trees to die.*

Um, Garrett, you sure that's such a good idea? David asked.

It's one thing to not know the pain and turmoil humans were causing trees. But it's a whole different thing to know and still ask them to die. I can't… I won't do that. If they come, we fight.

Governess held Garrett's gaze for a long three-count, nodded, and buried her roots into the soaked ground. *As you wish, Garrett Turek.*

Breanne couldn't be sure, but it appeared something unspoken had passed between Garrett and Governess. And in that moment, something happened to her as well. Despite it all – Gabi, the giants, and the unknowns – she had just slipped deeper in love with this boy. Irrespective of their dire situation and the fact that love should be the furthest thing from her mind, there it was, flittering in her chest. This wasn't the smashing of her heart against her chest bones she had grown used to over the last few weeks. No, this was a different quickening of her pulse.

The nephilbock have reached the briar wall. If the disgusting beasts have any sense of direction, they should navigate to the right.

Breanne and the others stood completely still – completely silent.

In the distance, they heard a loud shout, and then the sound of wood being chopped.

David backed into Lenny. *What is it that?! Gov! Oh, come on! Tell me that's not what I think it is!*

The nephilbock have picked up your scents and are chopping through the wall. My plan did not work.

25

Catch Me If You Can

Saturday, May 7 – God Stones Day 31
Rural Chiapas State, Mexico

Zerri, now! Gabi shouted, staring up at the three-headed beast. *Breanne! Get ready!* she yelled back over her shoulder, but when she looked at where Breanne had just been, she was gone. *Bre! Breanne!*

Cerberus roared from above, its long, forked tongues flapping and its jowls shaking with rage. Dragon saliva rained down over Gabi's face. With sudden speed, one of the thing's giant heads lunged down toward her, its ruby-red eyes burning with anger as they grew closer and closer, bigger and bigger.

Gabi stumbled back, falling onto her bottom. *Zerri!* she shouted again through her mental bond.

From a dozen directions, dragons threw themselves onto Cerberus. The giant dragon fell off balance, staggering to the side and spinning. It was like watching a pack of hyenas take down an elephant.

A thirteenth dragon swooped down, landing between her and Cerberus.

Hurry, Zerri said, lying down on her belly.

Gabi scrambled to her feet and ran toward the dragon, but even as she approached the prone beast, she couldn't jump up high enough to mount it.

My tail! Climb my tail, quick, Zerri urged.

Gabi did, and in seconds she was atop the dragon.

Beside them, Cerberus shook like a wet dog, tossing loose the young dragons.

Gabi looked around for Bre once more, but she saw nothing. *Go, Zerri! Fly as fast as you can!*

Zerri leapt from the ground and flapped her wings. It was all Gabi could do to hold on to the small bones that protruded from the back of the young dragon's neck.

Zerri laughed.

María Purísima, why are you laughing?! He almost killed me! Gabi shouted in mind speak as the wind practically stole her breath.

No way! He wouldn't kill you. Apep wants you alive, Zerri said, climbing even higher into the stormy sky.

I still don't see how that's funny! Gabi said, wanting to look down but afraid to. Instead, she pressed her face to the dragon's neck, clenching the bone spurs with all she had.

That's because you didn't see the look on Cerberus's faces when the others attacked him, Zerri said, leveling off. *Now, which way?*

Go north toward the tallest trees. I have a friend waiting there, Gabi said.

A great roar sounded from somewhere behind them.

I hope your friend is formidable, because the big guy is right behind us.

Gabi channeled her psychic bond to communicate with the other dragons. *Don't let Cerberus catch us! Protect Zerri at all costs!*

The others answered the call as Gabi's mind filled with acknowledgments.

Attacking! a squeaking voice said.

Pursuing, answered another in a gravelly voice that sounded a bit like Gabi's Uncle Diego.

I've got the head on the left! said another, deadpan serious.

Which left? Left from behind or left from the front?

I've got his tail! said another.

His tail? Is that you, Bethos, you coward? Tails don't bite back! I think we will call you Bethos the Tail Biter.

As Gabi's head filled with snickering laughter, it wasn't lost on her that this mind control – or psychic brainwashing, or whatever the proper term – was working better than she could ever have hoped. All the voices talking at once were almost too much though, and she did her best to tune them out. Gabi lifted her head, daring to peek around the dragon's neck. Never had she moved so fast or been so high off the ground. It was terrifying and somehow exhilarating at the same time. *Just fly faster than you ever have, Zerri! Fly until you reach the trees. We have to beat him to the trees!*

I may be small, but there is only one of me on this whole planet!

A girl dragon? Gabi guessed.

Zerri laughed again. *Yes! That too!*

Then what else?!

Gabi the Lion, there is only one fastest dragon, and you are riding her!

High atop the pyramid, Jack watched through the rain in dismay as a dozen of *his* juvenile dragons attacked Cerb. Of course, Cerb the Mighty shook them off like fleas, but somehow the girl had mounted one of *his* dragons and fled! *His* dragon! Cerb gave chase, but now Jack's own dragons were chasing Cerberus! Jack wanted to call Cerberus back so he could help, but by then, the girl would have escaped. Jesus, the little bitch had been right there at the base of the pyramid this whole time.

Apep? Apep, can you hear me? We have a problem! A big problem!

What is it now? Apep snapped.

Apep had gone to the opposite side of the pyramid to greet the nephilbock army as they arrived. Which, honestly, was some bullshit. Jack should be there too. They didn't know who in the hell Apep was, but they sure as shit knew Jack the God Killer. They were writing songs about him, not about some elf they'd never even heard of! *You just better get over here. Some of my dragons are attacking Cerberus and the girl is fleeing – on a dragon!*

What? Apep shouted. *And you didn't stop her?*

Of course Jack had thought of that, and he'd tried, but it happened so fast and before he could reach her with disease, she was out of range. Jack didn't know what his range was exactly, but he'd just found out that a distance greater than a football field was too damn far. *You wanted me to stay up here, remember? Well, I couldn't reach her from up here! What was I supposed to do, chase them on foot?*

No. Lucky for you, I kept you out of her reach. If she's controlling dragons, she would have made short work of your weak mind, Apep said, appearing next to Jack, causing him to flinch. He hated it when Apep did that. *It appears they're heading north toward the taller trees,* Apep said.

Yeah. Cerberus said he's already had to kill half the group of juveniles that are trying to stop him from catching the girl.

Jack, listen to me very carefully. Tell Cerberus to stop that dragon before it reaches the trees. But no matter what, do not – I repeat, do not – chase them into the trees!

But I don't—

Tell him!

Okay! Jack frowned. *You don't need to get all freaked out about it.* He turned his thoughts to Cerb. *Cerb, you have to stop the dragon before it gets into the trees. Kill the dragon, but try not to kill the girl. She's no good to us dead.*

I'm closing in, Jack! Cerberus answered.

Jack focused, allowing Cerb's eyes to become his own. Suddenly, the tree line rushed forward. In front of him, a small grey dragon raced toward the trees, pumping its wings with all its might. A small brown dragon hit Cerb from the side like a cop car, trying to throw him into a spin. Cerb's left head turned and bit down on the neck of the offending dragon, crushing bones. The eyes of Cerb's left head watched as the small brown dragon spun limply toward the ground below. Jack's vision blurred as his view switched to the center head, the one focused on the little grey dragon. Jack found he could toggle from the eyes of one head to another as easily as switching channels on a television. Cerb was gaining on the little dragon, but the forest was close now.

I could kill them both with fire, Jack!

No. Don't do it! Jack said, focusing his own will on the small grey dragon. *Listen to me, you little shit! I am in command of this horde. The human you carry is controlling your mind! Stop now and turn back! Do it right now, and I will let you live!*

The dragon didn't answer.

Jack, we are closing on the trees! What do you want me to do? I can kill them, but I must act now!

Jack watched through Cerb's eyes as the final two pursuing dragons tried attacking simultaneously from opposite sides. Cerb's outer heads belched fire, making quick work of the dragons without the need to take his center head off the prize.

As the burning dragons tumbled toward the earth, Cerb shouted, *You're mine, little one! You have no one left to protect you!*

Apep's voice filled Jack's mind. *Back him off, Jack! He's too close. If your Cerberus provokes the trees into attacking, it will force us to leave this planet with both armies unrested and unfed! Back. Him. Off!*

Cerb! You're too close. Give it up and return to the pyramid!

Another voice filled Jack's mind. This one, he'd never heard. *Hey, Cerberus, you giant human-loving piece of nephilbock dung! You couldn't catch me if you had a head start!* The voice was small, feminine, and accented with a slight hiss.

The voice sounded as if it belonged to a teenage girl. At first, Jack thought the voice taunting Cerb must be the little Mexican girl, but he quickly realized that made no sense. He'd heard the girl's voice, and this voice sounded way different. And why would she call Cerb a human lover? Suddenly he understood. The voice wasn't the girl at all! It was the dragon!

Catch me if you can! she taunted.

Cerberus roared.

Cerb, no! It's a trap!

What's happening? Apep demanded.

The dragon is a… it's… Jack hesitated. If he had learned nothing else about playing at this level, he'd learned there were two things that mattered most: action and information. He had no problem with action, and now he had information Apep didn't have. Important information too. He didn't know how to use the information, not yet, but a girl dragon? That was something.

The dragon is what, Jack? Apep asked, interrupting his thoughts.

Fast. He's a fast one.

Well, stop him, Jack! Before he starts a bloody war!

As they closed in less than a mile from the tree line, the trees came alive as giant sequoias parted to create an opening. The small dragon dove, and Cerberus dove with it.

I've got her, Taker!

No! Turn away! Jack pleaded.

The small grey dragon vanished into the forest opening.

I can still get them, Cerberus shouted.

Jack watched through his dragon's eyes as the forest attacked, throwing boulders and smaller trees. *Stop, Cerb!*

Cerberus roared.

26

Come Out of the Rain

Saturday, May 7 – God Stones Day 31
Rural Chiapas State, Mexico

"You actually saw the trees move?" James asked, galloping alongside Annie.

Annie nodded. "We were stopped, trying to find the road. I was staring into the woods, and I heard someone whisper through the rain. They said, 'This way.' I spun, thinking it was one of the others, but they were both on my opposite side. There was no one to my right. That's when I saw them! The trees just started moving! There!" She pointed. "It's just up ahead."

James and Annie followed the road over a steep rise that flattened off, where it ended abruptly.

"See! Right there." Annie pointed to an opening in the jungle to the right.

Cautiously, James approached the opening. As far as he could see through the pouring rain, the trees had cleared. Not only had they cleared themselves, but they must have cleared any large stones, as the path ahead seemed too flat and smooth to have occurred naturally.

"Why would the trees be helping us?" Annie asked.

"I don't know," James answered, studying the opening. Only a few of his Keepers knew of Garrett's promise to Pando to find an item of magical power that would allow the trees to remain unbound. James, Elaine, and Dr. Moore had agreed it wasn't wise to tell the others of something that didn't exactly fit the prophecy. Not until they were through the portal and safe on Karelia. But James wasn't lying to Annie either. He really didn't know why the trees were helping them. Perhaps some influence of Turek, helping to make sure they reached the portal on time. "This must be the work of Turek, Annie. Come, let us gather the others. This is our path."

Dr. Moore climbed down from the wagon.

"Charles? Are you okay?" Elaine asked.

No, he wasn't okay. Of course, he wasn't okay. The world was ending, Sarah was dead, and his children were somewhere out there, in danger. He was anything but okay. He wanted to scream at this woman. This woman who could intentionally put her own child in danger, who could send her own child and the other kids into a temple with a giant and a maniacal elf. All while knowing at least one of them would die – her own son, for god's sake. But Charles didn't yell. He knew Elaine too had lost friends, lost her husband, and her son was also out there somewhere close to the eye of that impossible storm to the south. The difference was, she didn't seem to be a wreck about it.

"How do you do it, Elaine?" he asked, looking up at her from the ground as he pulled up his hood.

"How do I do what, Charles?" she asked, cocking her head sideways.

"How do you keep it together? How do you stay so goddamned poised through all of this? My little girl isn't the only one out there on her own, facing god knows what."

Elaine nodded, readying herself to speak.

Somehow Charles knew what she would say before she said it and felt himself becoming pissed off. Despite his rising anger, the answer would come, and it would cut him deep and true and to the bone.

"In a word – faith, Charles," Elaine said, but she wasn't gloating. She said it carefully, almost sadly.

Maybe she said it like that because she knew how he would respond before he even spoke. Maybe because she knew he didn't have faith. His wife had died in a car accident six years ago. But he had been given a second chance with a wonderful woman he didn't deserve, and he'd blown it, only to be given yet another chance. Over the past year, he had been working to make it right with Sarah. Now she was dead. What kind of god would do this to him? What kind of god would take away good people? What kind of god would let Ed be held hostage and allow trees to threaten humanity?

"Charles, you know, ever since I was a little girl, I was told I was special. I was told I was the last female born to my bloodline – to Turek's bloodline. I was told I was to serve a noble purpose and that someday I would have a son and that this son and his chosen few would lead humanity from the darkness into the light. In time, I was shown the prophecy, written in Turek's own hand."

Elaine's face lit with a warm smile. "It fascinated me. Turek wrote it in such a way that we didn't know what was literal and what was metaphorical. I studied Turek's words daily my whole life. Now I am seeing the prophecy come to pass. Some of it, I guessed right, while some, like Garrett running off to save your daughter, has, I admit, thrown me for a loop. But what I know is this," she said, her lips becoming a hard line. "This prophecy has driven men mad, including my first husband, Garrett's biological father. It has claimed the lives of many more, all good men and women who held the faith. My second husband, Phillip, died, John died, and many others dear to me lost their lives. Do not mistake my faith for weakness or callousness for I, too, mourn, but I must hold to my faith. We have over a thousand behind us, Charles. It is my duty to those I loved who've passed and those who follow us still, to see this through."

Thunder boomed and lightning crackled across the sky.

When the thunder quieted and the sky calmed, Charles and Elaine found each other's eyes once again. "I see the worry in your eyes. Come out of the rain, Charles. Come sit with me and know your daughter is in the best place she can be, with the people who will protect her, die for her, for she is with her sages. And know too, Turek has a plan, and we are all part of his plan. Soon we will be on Karelia! Soon we will be home!"

Rain speckled Dr. Moore's face as tears pooled and spilled down his cheeks, hidden by the rain. He had a feeling too, but his was sinking. He wanted to feel like she did – like there was a greater plan. And he wanted to feel like god was good, and he would protect them, and take care of them and all would be well. But that was bullshit. It was all bullshit!

How could Turek or god or whatever this writer of prophecy was let Charles's wife die in a car accident? How could god give him a second chance to be happy and then let him blow it? Okay, that wasn't fair… He'd blown it with Sarah the first time – that was on him. But how could this Turek let Sarah die? How could anything bold enough to call itself a god let good people die? Trees were holding humanity hostage for something no one was sure even existed. And maybe he shouldn't feel this way, but dammit to hell with humanity. The trees had Ed. They had his boy! What kind of god let trees hold the world for ransom? If good people dying and trees wrecking the world was okay with god, who was to say taking his kids away from him wasn't okay with god too?

Tears spilled freely now, and he was thankful for the hard rain splattering his face. It took a great deal of will not to let a sob break from his chest, but he spoke evenly. "Thank you, but I need a moment, Elaine. Just some time to clear my head."

Elaine nodded sagely. "Of course. Take all the time you need."

Most Keepers were taking this time to get as much sleep as they could, so the road was quiet. But as Dr. Moore passed a row of wagons, he noticed Emily tending to a group of horses. He moved to the opposite side of the path, hoping to go unnoticed.

"Easy, girl, you've been working so hard. Let me make you feel better." The raven-haired woman ran her hand softly down the horse's mane as a soft white glow emanated from her palm.

Charles stopped, drawn to the glow like a moth to a porch light. It only lasted a couple seconds, but he found himself wondering: Was he supposed to see this magic in his moment of greatest doubt? Was this supposed to make him a believer? Some sign to comfort him, to see there was magic in the world? If there was magic, then Turek must be real. But a god? No, not a god. He'd seen him in his dream, and he'd seen him in death at the bottom of Oak Island. Turek might be something, but he wasn't a god. And maybe that was for the best, because if he were a god, then that would make him responsible, and Charles didn't think he'd ever forgive him for any of this.

The horse neighed approvingly.

"That's right. Much better, huh? Well, you're very welcome," Emily said.

The momentary trance that pulled him to a stop dissipated with the glow. Dr. Moore found his feet once more and began to move.

"Dr. Moore?" Emily called.

He spun back toward her, clearing his throat. "Just Charles."

"Charles, I… I heard about your loss. I wanted to tell you I'm sorry. How are you holding up?" Emily asked.

This was the most he'd heard from the middle-aged woman with the tall boots and the raven hair this entire trip. He'd heard of her own loss a couple weeks earlier, and again he thought of Elaine's words of faith. Once more, rather than lift, his heart sank. Another example of a good person taken too soon. "I'm hanging in there. You?"

"It hurts. And I have a feeling it's going to keep hurting for a long time to come, but Turek blessed me with a gift to help the Keepers," she said, smiling at another horse as she brushed her glowing hand down its neck.

Dr. Moore could see through the smile. It was the shield she was using to mask the pain, and he knew without asking that she would trade that gift for her husband in a heartbeat. He forced a smile of his own, and it was fake and all wrong, yet somehow necessary. The bad feeling in his chest got worse, and his heart sank deeper into the pit of his stomach.

27

Now We Should Run

Saturday, May 7 – God Stones Day 31
Rural Chiapas State, Mexico

Garrett wiped water from his face, clenched his jaw, and drew the long curved sword Phillip had given him weeks earlier. As he gripped the ivory handle in both hands, he nodded at Lenny, who nodded back. From over the steep embankment, he heard grunts and the sounds of a monster smashing through the magically enhanced hedgerow of thorn-covered vines.

David, stay back and be ready to heal us, Garrett said, pressing his lips into a tight line. He looked at Bre. *Ready?*

Ready, she said, drawing her sword.

A sudden and angry cry rang out.

Poisonous thorns, Governess said evenly. She rooted and then quickly uprooted. *They are through and splitting up. Two are dying from the poison, half went east, the other five are coming this way,* she said, waving her hands at the wall of vines next to them. "Rayoz doe oki zae shi," she whispered. The vines unwound, creating an opening. *Do not be in such a hurry to fight, young lord. A battle avoided is also a battle won. Come! Let us cross back through.*

A small opening appeared, just large enough for them to pass through without getting stabbed by poisonous thorns. *Go! Go! Go!* he urged the others, as they passed through single file. He kept his eyes on the hill in front of him. When it was his turn, he ducked low, preparing to go, when movement caught his eye. Garrett took one last look up the embankment. A giant now stood staring dead at him. He had seen, and even fought, an Old One in the pyramid back in Petersburg, and he had seen these part-human, part-nephilbock through the eyes of trees when he thought the kraken had killed Jack. But standing here only twenty yards from a monster from the center of the Earth sent Garrett's heart into his throat. His butt cheeks clenched in fear and, for a second, he froze.

The beast was every bit of twelve feet tall and built like an oversized strongman. It had a barrel chest and big belly, but you could tell the thing was stacked with muscle. It stared at Garrett with two hate-filled eyes set close together. The nephilbock held its left fist in the air, unmoving.

Clearly this was a warrior, obvious from the scars on its face, its arms, and its legs. It wore a strange black-stained chest plate. The biggest giveaway that this was indeed a warrior was what it held in its right hand. Six fingers wrapped around the hilt of a black metal sword as long as Garrett was tall. He couldn't imagine fighting this thing.

Garrett! Garrett, you okay?! Pete asked from the other side of the hedge.

The giant spoke, and as it stepped forward, its fist dropped.

Four more giants appeared from beyond the embankment. Garrett gasped, his own eyes bulging. Without a moment more hesitation, he pulled his gum-glued feet free of his curiosity and rushed through the opening.

Okay, what now? David asked.

Governess waved a hand, and the small opening closed. *Now, we should run.*

They ran. Behind them, the sounds of chopping and grunting echoed once again.

As Garrett and the others moved quickly but quietly through the jungle, the soggy foliage helped to mask the noise of their movement.

The only sounds were of thunder, lightning strikes, and their heavy breathing – except for Governess. Garrett was pretty sure she didn't breathe at all.

They're going to track us, and we won't be able to stay ahead of them for long, Garrett said. It wasn't a question. If there was one thing he knew, it was tracking – a subject Phillip had drilled him in all the time. But Phillip had not only taught him how to track, he'd taught him how to cover his own tracks. Right now, it was raining and raining hard, so they had that going for them. If what Governess said was true, the nephilbock had an enhanced ability to smell humans. Again, the rain would help, but only if they had distance between themselves and the giants, which he was pretty sure they didn't. *Governess, is there standing water near here? A stream or river?*

Keep running. I will catch up, the tree woman said, rooting to the ground.

Garrett and the others continued through the jungle for what felt like another half a mile. Thankfully, their current trajectory toward the pyramid was down a gradual slope. However, the downhill run didn't seem to be enough for David.

God, guys, this has to stop soon, David pleaded.

David, dammit! Unless you want to be eaten, you keep your ass moving! Lenny warned.

A moment later, Governess caught them. *We need to continue downward and to the left. Once we reach the bottom, there is an overflowing stream moving southward.*

Okay, guys, that's what we need! If we can push ourselves to get to the stream, we can get in and the nephilbock should lose our scent! Garrett shouted.

They ran, scrambling downward over loose dirt and rocky terrain laced with a zigzag of exposed roots. Near the bottom of the steep slope, they found themselves standing atop a retaining wall of ancient, stacked stone. The wall seemed to stretch out endlessly in both directions, until it was finally swallowed beneath jungle ivy and fan palms.

Likely Mayan, Breanne announced.

Not pausing for inspection, Garrett took her hand and jumped from the waist-high wall. They kept their feet and went right on running, pushing their way between skinny saplings and jungle plants as the ground before them leveled off.

From somewhere behind them, rusty shouts broke the rhythm of their panting breaths. The leader was giving orders, Garrett thought, and they weren't that far behind either… shit.

This way, young lord, Governess said, pointing to their left. *We must make haste.*

They pushed on, and soon Garrett knew they were closing in on the stream. He still couldn't see it, but he could hear the roar of crashing water calling out a warning to stay away… double shit.

The stream was only about thirty feet wide, but it was moving faster than Garrett would have liked. They were just going to have to go for it. *Alright, jump in and swim to the other side. Heck, it might not even be that deep. Make sure you let it take you a ways down so they can't track our smell.*

I don't know, Garrett, it's moving awf—

David, I don't want to hear it! If you drown, it will be a hell of a lot better than being eaten. For god's sake, they might be here any second, and if they see us, they won't need to smell us. Now go! Get your ass in that water and swim! Garrett shouted, pointing at the stream. Of course, he didn't want his friend to drown, but there was just no time for a long, drawn-out debate over how afraid David was of rivers and streams.

Lenny ran forward and jumped into the stream. The current took him, and he swam hard for the other side, disappearing around a bend before making it to shore.

Paul, Pete, and Breanne all jumped next.

Go, David! I won't go until I know you're in, Garrett ordered.

Okay, Garrett. Okay. David pinched his nose shut with one hand and jumped.

Governess?

I will be right behind you, Garrett Turek, she said.

It wasn't until Garrett's feet left the ground he remembered the Mississippi and how Governess hadn't chased them out into the water. Oh no! She couldn't swim! There was nothing he could do about that now, though. As the water swept him downstream, he swam for all he had. He reached the other side just ahead of David and helped the coughing boy onto the bank.

Jesus, I thought I was a goner! David said, spitting a mouth full of muddy water onto the bank.

Garrett's attention was back upstream, the direction they had come. *Do you guys see her?*

Who?

Governess! Governess, where are you? Pete shouted in mind speak. *She didn't cross! Why didn't she cross?*

I… I don't think she can swim! Garrett said.

But… why didn't she tell us? We could have found another way, Breanne said.

Paul pointed upstream. *Look! Twelve o'clock!*

Across the stream, Governess rounded the bend in a full-on run, her autumn hair flowing behind her as her emerald eyes burned bright. When she was directly across from them, she raised her right hand in the air. Her fingers stretched, lashing out like long snakes, before changing into ropy, brown vines. Her five vine fingers stretched and stretched, reaching high above the stream, braiding together as they went along while her other hand, circled in green Sentheye, extended outward.

On Garrett's side of the stream, a tree groaned. They all spun and looked to find a thick branch bending outward over the water. Governess's vines wrapped around the branch, and she jumped. Swinging out over the stream, she let go, dropping and landing in front of Garrett and the others, one knee bent to the ground. Her vine fingers retracted back into her human form as she stood.

You mean to tell me you could have just carried us across the water one by one? David asked, hands on his hips in an accusatory pose.

Perhaps, David Leigh, but I fear the tree may have fractured under your weight, Governess said, her lips hinting at a grin. *Besides, there was simply no time to transport you across one by one.*

I'm just glad you're okay. I worried I lost you, Pete said.

Peter Ashwood, I am fine. Now, let us make haste. She pointed into the jungle. *The pyramid is this way.*

There was something in the way she'd answered Pete that Garrett couldn't quite put his finger on. If he didn't know better, he'd say her voice almost had a tone of appreciation in it. Or maybe he was just imagining it. Garrett looked at Lenny, who raised an eyebrow and shared a knowing look. Maybe he wasn't imagining it after all.

As the group continued onward, they used the same technique of moving with a careful urgency while pausing frequently to allow Governess to root and search for any nearby dangers through the surrounding trees. This careful strategy allowed them to make their way toward the pyramid while avoiding monsters.

Be right back, Garrett, Breanne said, picking up her pace to jog alongside Governess. *Governess? You remember earlier when you said—*

I remember everything, Breanne Moore. Which earlier are you referring to? the tree woman asked.

Breanne looked back over her shoulder at Garrett and rolled her eyes. It made him smile and want her even more, as if that were possible. Everything he was learning about her over these last several days – from all her funny quirks to her incredible intelligence – made him want to know everything about her. Every day he spent with her just made it worse. Worse because the timing was awful, but more, he wasn't sure she felt the same, and he couldn't talk to her about it until this was over. God, what if she didn't feel the same, and that was the real reason she wanted to wait? His stomach sank. *Stop it,* he thought, knowing his focus should be on not dying and not letting his sages get hurt… or worse.

Riiiiight, the earlier I'm asking about is when you said Gabi had been busy. What did you mean by that? Breanne asked.

When I searched the area for Gabi, she was not cowering beneath a dragon, Breanne Moore. She was riding one.

28

The Fall of Hyperion

Saturday, May 7 – God Stones Day 31
Rural Chiapas State, Mexico

Gabi felt her stomach drop as Zerri dove down, down, down into the trees. She forced her eyes to open as she peeked over the dipped head of the dragon and watched the ground race toward her.

A harbinger of flame announced itself with an angry roar somewhere behind them. *Zer—ri!* Gabi screamed as trees raced by on both sides, flashing past in foliage-green and bark-brown streaks. She clenched her jaw and squeezed her eyes shut again, anticipating the searing flame, but it only warmed Gabi's back. She stole a glance back to find the trees had closed in, sealing off their passage – protecting them. But their salvation had come at a cost. The forest behind them burned.

Finally, after creating distance from the flames, Zerri threw her head back, her body becoming vertical as her wings caught the air rather than sliced through it. Gabi grabbed the bone spurs, practically hanging from them.

Thankfully, with a few flaps of Zerri's wings, they settled onto the forest floor and Gabi could loosen her death grip on the dragon. *I thought I was going to fall! I was sure of it!*

Zerri laughed as she turned around, facing back the way they'd come. *I told you I was the fastest!*

A great groaning and creaking surged forth like windswept timber under a heavy gust, but there was no wind, only an angry flailing of limb and root as the forest of giant redwoods closed in around them, obscuring the burning forest beyond. Gabi could see smoke filling the sky beyond, but she saw no dragons – no Cerberus.

From another direction, two redwoods parted enough to let another tree come forward. The familiar cypress tree was shorter than the redwoods, but bigger around than any other. A smile lit Gabi's face.

El Tule! Gabi said, sliding down Zerri's scales and running toward the big tree. When she reached El Tule, she opened her arms as wide as they would go and laid her cheek against El Tule's barked trunk. *Thank you!* she said.

Gabi, it is good to see you again. Now, please, stand back. Hyperion, kill the dragon!

Roots from a redwood tree, wider and taller than any tree Gabi could have ever imagined, burst from the ground, filling the small clearing where Zerri stood with flailing tendrils. Gabi remembered reading about redwoods and how their roots only went five to six feet below the surface, but they could reach out over a hundred feet in all directions. The roots wrapped the dragon before it could lift off the ground. Zerri managed one frightened shriek before the thick woody vines constricted her neck, head, and face, tightening around her snout, cinching her mouth tight.

Now that Gabi was safely inside the forest, the dragon had outlived its usefulness. This was it – the moment Gabi had known would come, only Gabi had thought she would be the one to kill the dragon.

Zerri screamed in Gabi's mind, *Gabi! Make them stop! What are they doing?* The roots were too powerful for the small dragon. Slowly, the tendrils tightened even more. The forest filled with the sounds of straining wood fibers as they dragged Zerri beneath the forest floor.

Gabi looked on as half the dragon's body was swallowed and the other half sank deeper and deeper. Zerri's mother had killed Gabi's parents and her closest friends. Dragons were good for nothing but killing and eating humans. They would as soon eat her as look at her. Even Zerri would have eaten her if Gabi hadn't used her mind control first. They had burned forests by the acre, killing millions of trees just in the last few days alone. None of them deserved to live… None! All dragons needed to die!

So why then did Gabi's heart ache for Zerri? Why did tears well in her eyes and threaten to spill over? Why did she care? Why? Watching as the dragon slipped even deeper, Gabi became angry with herself. ¡María Purísima! Stupid girl!

El Tule! El Tule! Stop! Don't kill this dragon! Gabi screamed.

I do not understand. Why would you spare this wretched beast?

Please! I have it under mind control! I still have plans for this one! Please, El Tule.

Zerri's voice echoed in her mind again. *Gabi, why? It's killing me! Make them stop!* Zerri begged. Her open wings twisted backward, folding impossibly against the joints and threatening to snap at any moment.

I am sorry, Little Lion. We do not show mercy to this ilk, El Tule said with disdain.

Zerri's eyes bulged in desperation as her head thrashed against the wet earth swallowing her.

No, you can't kill it! You just can't. I need it, El Tule! It has valuable information only I can retrieve! Information that will help us on our mission to get your people a God Stone! she pleaded. As panicked as she was, she had enough sense not to reveal the dragon was a girl. It was hard to say if El Tule and the redwoods would know how valuable a girl dragon born of the Queen of Queens was to her people.

Information that may serve our cause. Hmm, the big cypress groaned. *This is why you – you who have as much right to hate dragons as any – wish to spare this one?*

Yes! she admitted, unable to hide the desperation in her voice.

Hyperion! Halt! Release the dragon! If it so much as breathes smoke, kill it! El Tule ordered.

Very well, the mighty Hyperion drawled out, its words measured, as if time had no meaning for the giant tree – as if life weren't hanging in the balance.

It's okay, Zerri. You're okay now, Gabi said, directing her mind speak only to Zerri, which was easy enough now that they had the psychic bond. The pathway she used to speak to Zerri felt different from the one she spoke to El Tule through. Neither was difficult for Gabi, yet both were distinct. Instinctively, she knew it was because the structure of a dragon's mind differed from that of a human, and both differed from that of a tree.

Free of the tangle of roots, Zerri crawled out from the dirt and shook her scales out like a wet dog shaking its coat. Fixing her eyes on the massive tree, Hyperion, she let out a long, sinister hiss.

Zerri, don't. If you attack, they WILL kill you. They were scared, Zerri, that's all. I told them you wouldn't hurt them.

The dragon approached Gabi and sat down. *Thank you for saving me. I will refrain from burning them,* Zerri said. *For now.*

Gabi felt a pang of guilt wash through her. She hadn't wanted to save the dragon. She had wanted to watch it die. Just like she had watched Zerri's mother die. Of course, Zerri didn't know that, and maybe that's what made this whole thing worse. She couldn't think about it right now. Right now, she needed to reach Breanne. She needed to tell her—

Another roar filled the forest as a gout of dragon fire burst through the trees from the direction they had come.

Gabi! Get down! Zerri shouted.

Gabi ducked low, staring up as strange flames lit the forest above them. Cerberus was back!

Hyperion! El Tule shouted.

Despite the dampness of the forest and the redwood's resistance to fire, none of it mattered. It was as if the sun itself had spilled out its own insides and dumped them onto the forest. Gabi looked up to find the giant redwood covered in red flame. Burning debris rained down from above.

Gabi, climb upon me! We must go! Zerri shouted in her mind as a large burning tree branch dropped between them.

Flames rose from the burning branch and the forest floor, blocking Gabi's path to Zerri. *Zerri! I… I can't see you!*

Her mind lit up again as El Tule ordered the forest forward. *We are under attack! Forward to the pyramid!*

All the surrounding trees began to move, but not Hyperion. Once the tallest tree on Earth, the giant moved forward no more. Instead, the magnificent wonder of the world stood for only a moment more, a wreck of flames and crackling timber, before it listed to one side – and fell.

There was so much fire and smoke that Gabi couldn't see which way it was falling, but she could hear it crashing through the other trees, a skyscraper falling and building speed as it went.

El Tule! Gabi shouted.

Run, Little Lion. Run as fast as your feet will carry you! The war is upon us! The world's end has begun!

"I told you to pull him back!" Apep seethed. His sunken eyes were wild now as he looked from Jack to the burning forest. He wasn't even speaking to him in his mind now. The elf wizard was so angry it was like he wanted to hear himself yelling.

Jack's lip twitched as he instinctively doubled up his haymaker. He didn't raise the fist – not yet. Instead, he left it balled and squeezed, white-knuckle tight at his side. *Cerberus! No! What have you done?*

I'm sorry, Jack! But the little bastard was taunting me. I couldn't allow it to escape. Besides, we've already killed so many trees. What are a few more? Cerberus asked.

"You've no idea what you have done!" Apep spat.

Heavy footfalls from inside the corridor announced the arrival of Ogliosh and his five nephilbock generals.

"The last of my children are gathering behind the pyramid," Ogliosh said, his fat eye flexing wide as it followed Apep's gaze to the valley beyond. "What's this? What's happened?" Ogliosh asked.

Eroch, the lankiest but tallest of the nephilbock generals, stepped forward and raised his stone hammer. "Look, my king. The trees are moving onto the charred ground! There are flames at the northern end!"

"Bring the nephilbock around the pyramid and order them to the perimeter," Apep commanded. "Jack, how long before you can get the other half of your dragons back here?"

"Well, for the hordes Ahi took into America, I don't know – two days," Jack answered.

"Unacceptable! How many will we lose if we open the portal tomorrow?"

"I… I don't know. None have gone as far as Canada, but some have gone as far northeast as New York."

"Remedy your failure, Jack! Order Ahi to bring them back, now! The portal opens at sunrise!"

"Apep! The nephilbock will not be properly rested or fed! The final preparations for the portal aren't even complete!" Ogliosh protested.

"Do you see what's coming, Ogliosh?" Apep asked, pointing. "Do you see it? I do! I can feel it! I can feel her!"

Jack shook his head. "Apep, we can hold them off while the nephilbock rest. Me and Cerb have been fighting trees for—"

Apep's face twisted. "Cerb? Cerberus is the reason we are in this mess! I ordered you not to let him attack, and you failed me!"

"But we can hold—"

"Silence! Silence, or so help me, I will kill you here and now! I don't need worthless human children! I need subjects who follow orders! The nephilbock are here! More than half the dragons are here! Tell your hordes to bring as many humans as their wings will lift. Tell them not to come back here with talons empty, Jack! Do you understand?"

Jack nodded slowly. The reality was that Apep was a paranoid dick, but right now, and as long as the Sound Eye sat upon his head, he was in charge. But the fact was, some of his dragons were going to be left behind. The only question was how many wouldn't make it back in time – a thousand, four thousand? Jack supposed some dragons left here on this planet might not be such a bad thing. Plenty for them to hunt and eat. Maybe they could keep this place from returning to the big shithole of humanity that it had been.

Apep spoke again, but his attention was on the giant king now. “The nephilbock will make do with what food we provide. It will hold them until we reach Karelia and the last war begins.”

“And you will allow us to eat the dökkálfar we slay, Apep?” The giant’s question was full of skepticism.

Apep let the question hang as he walked forward, but not toward Ogliosh or Jack. Instead, he walked down the long corridor. The others followed. When they were deep inside the pyramid, the corridor split in three directions. Straight ahead went deeper inside, leading to the mechanics of the pyramid. To the left and the right were two sets of stone stairs, both of which led to the same place. Apep turned, taking the stairs on the left. Jack and the others followed. Fifty steps later, they reached the top, ascending up through the floor of the pyramid’s temple. This was the highest point, and Jack felt like he could reach up and touch the clouds. The problem was they were in the middle of a God Stone storm. The sky was lit with strange lightning circles, flashing as bolts speared the ashen valley floor and surrounding forest. As badass as it was to be here on top of this skyscraper of a pyramid, all Jack could think was that this was some dumb shit.

Apep turned back to them, shouting above the thunder. “You ask if I will allow your nephilbock to feast upon dead dökkálfar! The dökkálfar you are about to slay are not my brethren, Ogliosh! Until the unconditional surrender of Osonian, I say, to the victor go the spoils! Kill and be fed!”

Ogliosh turned his one enormous eye to the sky. “Apep, we should not be up here in this storm. And you should not be up here with the Sound Eye until we are ready to open the portal.”

Apep stepped past a large stone altar, the place Jack imagined the elf would place the Sound Eye when the time came to open the portal. Stepping close to the edge of the flat roof, Apep looked down into the valley below. Ogliosh and his generals fell in next to the elf. From below, Jack heard shields banging as a spontaneous cheer erupted.

“Come! Join us, Jack – for tomorrow we leave this world behind!”

Cerberus came into view, circling once overhead before descending and landing on the temple behind him. The cheers below continued.

Jack popped the collar on his leather jacket and walked through the rain toward the edge – toward the cheering mass below. But when the more than twenty thousand nephilbock filling the valley below saw him, all the cheering stopped. There was no silence in the thunder and rain, but had there been silence – had there been a perfect windless day – Jack would have heard the anticipation of what was to come. Instead, he heard a slow, rhythmic beat of sword, ax, and hammer pounding shield as it became faster and louder. But then came something else. A chant erupted from below, and as Jack stared over the side, he watched as thousands and thousands of nephilbock dropped to one knee. Jack had no idea what they were saying, but when the chanting changed to song, he knew – they were singing for him!

Apep, Ogliosh, and his five generals turned and looked at him. Jack ignored them all as he looked down on the crowd of nephilbock. He had never felt more important than in this moment. He was the kid no one cared about. The kid from Petersburg nowhere Illinois. But now they saw him. Now this world saw him, and the next would see him soon enough. *If you are out there, Garrett, I hope you're watching. Goddammit, I hope you're watching, because I am bringing all this down on you. In this world or the next, I will watch you die.*

Above Jack, the rain stopped, the sky parted, and sunshine filled the valley once more. Somehow, he knew, this too was for him. Jack's father had never been good for much, aside from being a dick and slapping Jack around, but something he used to say on those rare occasions when a thing went right came to mind in this moment: Son, even the sun shines on a dog's ass now and then. *Well, old man, if you're watching from that hell I sent you to, the sun sure is shining on mine!*

Jack threw his fist in the air. Below him, thousands of weapons lifted skyward as a chorus of cheers erupted.

29

Prelude to War

Saturday, May 7 – God Stones Day 31
Rural Chiapas State, Mexico

The rain had finally relented when Breanne and the others caught their first glimpse of old-growth trees. Straight ahead and reaching far up into the sky stood a whole grove of massive alerce trees that had traveled to Mexico from South America. Breanne certainly was not an authority on South American trees, but she recognized these because they were among the largest in the world. According to Governess, they were close to the burnt ground, which meant they were within only a few miles from the pyramid itself. But up ahead, something strange was happening.

Guys, it looks like those trees are moving, Pete said, pointing.

The group stopped and squinted to see what Pete saw with his super-vision. At first, Breanne thought she was only seeing wind blowing through the trees. But then she realized Pete was right. The trees were swaying gently back and forth, but it wasn't the wind doing it. It was the motion created as the trees pulled themselves forward, away from them.

Come! Governess said, breaking into a run.

They followed Governess forward, careful to give the trees a wide berth so they didn't get tangled in the roots. The trees' tendrils reached, grabbed, and pulled, and the last thing Breanne wanted was to have her feet yanked out from under her.

When they reached the front of the grove, Governess found the tree she was looking for. The tree woman yelled in the language of the trees, and thanks to the Eyra of Tunga, they all understood.

"Fitz! By the order of the queen, halt!" Governess shouted.

The lead tree stopped, and the rest of the grove followed suit.

"What is… the meaning… of this, Governess… Larrea? I am… under strict… orders from… Queen Pando… herself." Fitz's words were slow and measured, just as Breanne imagined an ancient tree would speak, but with a twist of profound annoyance at being ordered to halt.

"Fitz, are you saying the queen has ordered you to advance on the pyramid?" Governess asked.

"No… she ordered… us forward… to close… the gap," Fitz said.

Governess rooted.

Moments went by, and the forest stayed quiet and unmoving.

As they waited for Governess to do… well, whatever it was she was doing, Breanne and the others sat down, happy for some rest. After hearing Gabi had somehow taken control of a dragon and escaped after killing Queen Azazel, Breanne wanted to talk to her more than ever. But she still didn't understand how she had teleported, and everyone agreed she shouldn't try it again until Gabi reached out to her and told her she was safe. Breanne didn't like the decision, but she couldn't argue with it. They couldn't risk Breanne being unwittingly teleported right into a den of dragons – or worse, the hands of Apep.

They sat in a circle now, all within earshot of one another, and it was Paul who spoke out loud first. "Anyone want to take a guess at why the trees are moving?"

There was something about seeing Paul speak aloud that was… she didn't know, kind of nice. It was nice to see her brother's mouth moving as he talked. Mind speak, while incredibly cool, could also feel distant somehow. For one thing, when people spoke with their minds, their hands didn't move, and their facial expression didn't necessarily match the emotion they were conveying either. Maybe everyone else thought so too because suddenly they were all doing it – talking out loud.

"I don't know, but I'm getting a sick feeling about it," Garrett said, looking at Breanne.

"What's up?" she asked.

"The Keepers. They could still be another day or two away, and now Apep's armies are here, and the trees are moving on the pyramid? I just don't understand what comes next. How can we still have days before the portal opens?" Garrett said, worry streaking his face as he poked absently at the ground with a stick.

"War," Paul said. "War is what comes next. And if the portal really won't open until the Keepers get here, then we could be looking at a couple days of fighting."

Lenny held the acoustic guitar in his hands, walking his fingers across the frets like Beethoven moving his fingers across piano keys. Lenny wasn't strumming the guitar, but it still made a small musical sound as his fingers tapped the strings. "Look, it's like you said, right? Whatever it is, it is. The portal will open when it's supposed to, whenever that is. When the time comes, you will be in position and lead everyone through to Karelia." Lenny's fingers reached the top of the neck before returning toward the bottom. His eyebrow rose as he twisted his mouth. "God, I want to go crazy on this thing!"

"Well, don't!" Pete said, looking past him toward Governess. "You might bring a whole battalion of those giants right to us."

"Shit, Pete, what's got you so sour?" Lenny asked. Then, giving Pete a wink, he followed up with, "Old Gov giving you the cold canopy? Let me guess, she decided she wants to put down roots and you're not ready to commit? Oh, wait! This isn't because she was expecting an oak branch and found out you were only packing a twig—"

"Lenny! Really?" Breanne said.

Lenny shrugged. "Sorry?"

Breanne gave him a glare.

"I mean… sorry," Lenny said, giving it a more sincere effort as he threw his hands up in surrender.

Pete shook his head. "No. For your information! We're actually talking a lot. The vastness of her knowledge is incredible."

"Yeah, the vastness of her knowledge… sounds hot."

"Yeah, Len, it is! So what?"

Lenny pulled a face and shook his head.

Pete laughed. "Make all the faces you want, Lenny. She's way smarter than you could ever hope to be."

"She is a tree, bro! She isn't even a she! You realize that, right? In fact, in the plant world, isn't the king clone a male species of a bush or some shit?" Lenny asked pleadingly.

Pete sighed and took a deep breath. "I can't believe you're still hung up on this. Listen up, because I'm only going to say this to you once, Lenny. I don't care how she identifies today or tomorrow. It doesn't matter to me if she identifies as a he or a she or if she is nonbinary. I do not care. I repeat – I do not care. What I do care about is that you are my friend and you support me no matter whoever or whatever I decide to be romantically involved with. But that's it, Len. You're my friend, and right now my friend needs to mind his own business."

Lenny nodded thoughtfully, his fingers continuing to work their way up and down the guitar. Finally he lifted his eyes to meet Pete's. "Okay."

"That it?" Pete asked.

Lenny nodded again. "Yep."

Now Pete scrunched his brows. "No more wisecracks?"

"No. I'm still going to make wisecracks because that's what I do. But you obviously know what you're doing and, as your friend, I know when to back off. Besides, you shared a whole lot more than you had to. So instead, I am going to shift my worry from your romantic involvement with Governess to worrying how she will kill all of us if we don't get the trees what they want. You're part of my plan now, Pete. See, the way I see it, you're the closest to her, so she'll kill you first. That should distract her long enough to give the rest of us a chance."

"You're such a dick. You know that?" Pete smiled.

Lenny smiled back.

Pete cut a glance toward the rooted tree woman. "I'm just worried. What the hell is taking so long?"

"Yeah, I'm ready to get moving and get this over with," David said. "And if you ask me, it's good the trees are moving forward. How the hell else are we supposed to get to the pyramid? We can't just walk through Apep's army, can we? Excuse me, Mr. Nephilbock. Pardon me, dragon, sir, can we get past please? I mean, come on! Have you guys even thought about how ridiculous it sounds to walk to the pyramid across open ground full of dragons and nephilbock?"

To Breanne it did sound ridiculous. And, judging from the plunging faces around the group, it sounded downright impossible to everyone else too.

"Look, guys, the fact is we don't know how this is going to work, but we just have to believe it will. We have to…" Garrett trailed off as Governess rejoined the group. "What's happening?"

"Garrett Turek. It seems Cerberus has attacked the area where El Tule is located. The dragon killed several older redwoods, including General Hyperion."

"What? Why did Cerberus attack now?" Garrett asked, pushing himself to his feet. Breanne and the others did the same, standing and brushing themselves off for what little good it did.

"It seems he was pursuing Gabi De Leon and the dragon she was riding," Governess said.

"Gabi! Is she okay?" Breanne asked.

"Indeed, Breanne Moore. Gabi De Leon and this dragon she has… acquired are in the woods to the northwest of our location. I have given El Tule our coordinates and asked that she return to us."

"Oh my god! That's fantastic!" Breanne said, feeling the first genuine sense of relief since, well, since she didn't know when. She also didn't plan what happened next, but in a moment of spontaneity she ran forward and threw her arms around Governess. "Thank you!" As her arms embraced the beautiful redheaded girl, who wasn't really a girl at all, Breanne moved past her excitement about Gabi and registered the other piece of news – the part about trees being killed in the attack. "Oh, Governess. I am so sorry. I'm… I'm sorry you lost people. Sorry you lost Hyperion." She hugged the woman close to her. Oddly, she didn't feel like a tree at all. If she didn't know better, she would think she was hugging a human. And as Breanne's own chin rested on Governess's shoulder, she noticed something else. Governess's hair smelled like jasmine. Had she always smelled so… good?

"This is unnecessary, Breanne Moore," Governess said, not returning the hug.

Breanne didn't really expect her to, but then she didn't know what she expected because she'd had no idea she was going to do this. Breanne supposed that not being thrown into some kind of wrist flip and slammed to the ground was a win. She released Governess, stepped back, and wiped tears from her eyes.

"Why do you weep?" Governess asked.

"I… I feel bad. I'm sorry."

"We're all sorry," Garrett said, stepping forward.

"Listen to me. All of you. This is war. I am here for the survival of my people – of my species. Do not weep for Hyperion, as I will not weep for any of you should you fall in battle," she said flatly.

Garrett shook his head. "That may be fine for you, Governess, but it isn't fine for us. Look, I don't know if you feel love or what, but you seem to feel hate pretty darn good, and I guess you can hate us for what happened to you and yours in the past, but we know better now, and we can be better. We will be better. But that goes both ways."

Governess looked at Garrett as if measuring him with her eyes. Her face was stone, but Breanne saw something there in the woman's eyes, a tell, but she couldn't be sure what it meant. Finally, the tree woman spoke. "Words mean as little as promises where humans are concerned. Now, you should be aware the queen has ordered my people forward. Right now, we are only closing the distance, but if attacked again, we will counterattack until Apep opens the gate, and we will not stop until he and his army have evacuated the planet."

The trees began to move forward once again.

"But if you all close in, won't that force an attack?" Pete asked.

"Perhaps, Peter Ashwood. If this is to be the will of Druesha, so be it."

"What about us?" David asked.

Governess looked to Garrett. "We can move forward with my

people until the attack begins or the gate opens, unless you have some other plan, young lord?"

"No," Garrett said, pursing his lips in thought. "But first, we need rest. We are wiped out and the war could come at any moment." As he said the words, his eyes fell on David.

David nodded, all serious. "Good call, Garrett. We've been moving all day. We got to hunker down to get some sleep."

"Yeah, except with all the trees moving, we can't build a camp here," Paul said.

Pete sighed. "And we can't have the trees carry us. What if dragons attack while we're up there? We would get smoked."

"Sounds like a shit sandwich without the bread," Paul said.

David nodded. "Yeah, a sandwich sounds good, but no thanks to that shit."

Everyone was looking at David, and by now Breanne had caught on too. "We need some kind of way to refresh that doesn't require us to actually make camp."

"Well, I don't see how… Wait a minute! Aw, come on!" David said, kicking at an uprooted fern.

Lenny, quickly losing patience with the game, secured his guitar to his pack and pulled a strap over one shoulder, then the other. "Just do it, David, you little Nacho Libre–looking freak! If you don't want to sleep for the next four hours, don't freaking pass out!"

David pointed up at Lenny. "Dude, one day you're going to turn into an elf and when that day comes, it is going to be the best day of my life!"

Lenny stepped closer, a big grin on his face. "Oh, you got jokes now, David?"

"You bet I do!" David said, tapping a finger against his head. "I been thinking 'em up this whole trip, Len! You hear me?"

Breanne stepped between the two boys. "David. Please? We need you."

David backed off, and she could see all the mad leaving him. "Okay, Bre, but only because you asked. Because you're nice. Lenny, though – Lenny's a dick!"

"Oh, come on, David. You know I love you. You're my furry little man! You're like a little emperor tamarin monkey!"

"I don't even know what that is!"

"Look it up, bro! If only that 'stache was white, you'd be a spitting image!" He laughed.

"Just shut up and let me do this," David said, motioning everyone to sit. "Gov, can you make sure trees don't walk over us while I do this, please?"

Governess gave a single nod. "Proceed, David Leigh."

They all returned to their small circle as David sat, legs criss-crossed, the back of his hands resting on his knees, eyes closed.

"See you when you wake up, my little mustached Buddha." Lenny smiled, holding out his hand.

David grumbled something and began to glow. As Breanne watched, a golden glow enveloped David. The boy reached out his golden hand and took hers. The warmth flooded through her as she took Garrett's hand, and he in turn he took Paul's, who took Pete's. When the glow became too bright to see, Breanne heard David speak, which was unusual considering David had never spoken during a healing, at least not that she could remember.

Then, just as the glow started to fade, she heard Lenny say, "Hey, don't forget me, David, I don't feel anything."

When she turned, expecting to see David passed out, he was holding Lenny's hand in his with the biggest smile plastered on his face. Lenny, however, was out cold, lying on his side, snoring loudly.

"David! But how?" Garrett asked.

David's eyes were wide in his excitement. "Not sure! But I feel great!"

"David?" Paul asked, lifting Lenny's arm and then releasing it. The arm dropped limply to the forest floor. "What did you say when you were glowing? I heard you mumbling something."

David frowned. "Oh, that's it, isn't it? I said something like, why don't you see how it feels for once, Len? Why don't you use all your energy to make me feel better and see if you pass out? Then I took hold of Len's hand and…" David squinted as if reliving the moment.

"Then I felt my whole body fill with warmth, and my chap-ass was suddenly gone."

"First of all, ew to your mud butt," Pete said, scrunching his face like he smelled something bad, "but second, that's awesome, David!"

"So, you pulled his, what? Energy to replenish yourself?" Garrett asked.

"I don't know, maybe something like that – but it comes from somewhere else too."

"It comes from the God Stones, David Leigh. One should not underestimate their power," Governess said.

"Yeah, I feel like you said that before. Now, how about we get moving, gang?" Paul said.

I would also recommend we return to thought transference should we require further communication. Nephilbock may still be in the area. Governess pointed at Lenny. *Now, I suppose I am to carry this one, young lord?*

Breanne raised an eyebrow at Garrett, exchanging an amused look at Governess's annoyance.

Garrett smiled. *Please?*

Governess rolled her eyes dramatically. *Very well, at least this one is less… robust.* She eyeballed David as she transformed, this time into what appeared to be a flat wooden cart. But rather than wheels, it had eight segmented stick legs, and a head just like a spider.

David said, *Hey! I heard that!* But, seeing what Governess had transformed into, his eyes went wide as he backpedaled.

Give me a hand, Garrett said, grabbing one of Lenny's limp arms.

Paul grabbed the other, and they laid Lenny on his side, careful not to smash his guitar.

After two more hours of walking with the trees, there was still no sign of Gabi. What was taking her so long? Was she in trouble? Could she not find them? Below their feet, all the vegetation was gone, the jungle completely burnt away, save for the trees now crossing the charred ground. They had been climbing up the side of a mountain for what seemed like forever, and now finally it seemed the ground was becoming less steep. Soon they stopped altogether.

What's happening? Breanne asked.

Ahead, Governess's eight legs ceased their forward locomotion, rooting to the ground. She spoke a moment later. *Our army has cut the distance to the pyramid in half, squeezing the nephilbock and dragons into a condensed area.*

And? What are the dragons and nephilbock doing?

As if in answer, a roar broke the quiet as an orange flame glowed through the canopies from somewhere beyond the ridge. There was an awful cracking that sounded like a tree being broken in two, and the late evening sky filled with inhuman screams.

Garrett Turek, beyond the next ridge, the war has begun. We have gone as far as we can safely. What are your orders?

While everyone stared at Garrett, the boy stood with a look of pure intensity as he contemplated their next move. The trees were moving again, now slowly making their way past them toward the battle ahead. *The portal isn't open yet. If we cross into that, we will die. We have to wait for the portal to open. Then we go. No matter what is ahead of us… we go.*

Paul said, *It could be days before the portal opens and a day or more before the Keepers get here.*

Breanne, can you try to reach your dad? We need to know where they are.

I can try… but what if I accidentally teleport? Breanne asked.

Shit. Sorry, I forgot about that. Garrett frowned, then both eyebrows shot up. *Wait a minute.* He reached into his cargo pocket and pulled out the Zippo James had given him.

This is no time for a signal fire, Garrett, David said.

I'm not lighting a fire, David. I'm calling James, Garrett said.

A large tree moved toward them, and this one didn't go around. *Look out,* Breanne said, pulling Garrett toward her by the sleeve as she and the others backpedaled over the churned ground, allowing the tree to pass.

Look, I'm going to need to concentrate. Gov, please don't let the trees run over me.

Governess transformed back to her human form, depositing a still-sleeping Lenny on the ground, and nodded. She rooted to the ground, and immediately the trees began giving the group a wider berth.

Garrett sat down. *Okay, Bre, can you talk me through this?*

I'll try, but I wish Gabi were here. She is better at explaining this than me. Just focus on James, on the lighter he gave you, and the last time he held it. Open your mind and talk to him.

Seconds went by, turning quickly into minutes. Garrett's face stayed fixed with intense concentration.

Just relax, Garrett. Relax and focus. She wanted to put her hand on his, but she didn't dare. He had to do this on his own. Then a horrible thought occurred to her. What if he teleported? What if Turek pulled him over to wherever the Keepers were right now, so that he could lead them the rest of the way? What the hell would they do then?

Garrett's face went slack, then his eyes opened to reveal two glassed-over orbs with constricted pupils. More minutes went by, and Breanne became so sure that Garrett was going to vanish at any moment that her heart began to race and her palms started to sweat.

Finally, Garrett's eyes fluttered and blinked. He looked at Governess. *Can you have the trees pull back, Governess?* Garrett asked urgently.

Why, Garrett? What happened? Did you talk to them? Breanne asked.

Yes, I talked to James like he was sitting right next to me!

That's amazing! How's everybody holding up? David asked.

What? Never mind that, David. Garrett frowned. *The Keepers are still miles away! At least another day, maybe longer! And even worse, they're coming in from the opposite side of the valley! How will they ever get past thousands of dragons and nephilbock in the middle of war? Even if I wanted to meet them, how could I get to them? Can you do it, Gov? Can you stop this? Can you back them off?*

No, young lord. My queen has spoken. She will pressure Apep to open the gate or lose his army by the thousands.

You really think a bunch of big trees can stop Apep and his armies? Pete asked.

Breanne nodded. *Right, and what about what happened in the Amazon? They killed your people by the millions.*

Ah, Breanne Moore, this is true, but now we have something we did not have in the Amazon.

They waited. For a second, Breanne thought maybe Pete's inherent ability to drag out the dramatic reveal was rubbing off on the tree woman.

Well? Garrett asked, finally unable to stand the suspense.

See for yourself, young lord. But do be cautious. If you are seen by what is on the other side of the summit, you may well bring the war to us.

Breanne looked at Garrett, and he nodded, taking her hand. Together, she and the others crept forward.

Following Governess's advice to be careful, Paul motioned for them to get down as they drew close to the summit. On hands and knees, they crawled up to the edge.

Breanne gasped, unable to breathe in or out as her eyes grew wider and wider, taking it all in.

You see now! You see why Apep has no choice but to flee this place!

Garrett was the first to find words. *She's here! Queen Pando is here!*

30

The Squadron

Saturday, May 7 – God Stones Day 31
Rural Chiapas State, Mexico

"Keepers! On me!" James shouted, holding a fist high in the air. "We have a path! Turek has moved the trees for our passage! Those who can hear, pass the message back to the others! Turek has made a way. Time to move!" James dropped his fist and pointed forward, and they followed. Despite the hard rain, for the next several miles the Keepers moved at a decent rate over relatively smooth forest floor.

The Keepers of the Light hadn't known where in the world the portal would open. They only knew they had a little better than a fourteen percent chance it would be the Petersburg pyramid. It could have just as easily been one of the pyramids hidden in Russia, Africa, or any of the other four scattered pyramids. But despite not knowing which of the seven pyramids would serve to open the portal, they had known travel would be likely. And knowing the God Stones would likely change the magnetic fields of the Earth had led James's father, Phillip, to design the wagons for travel in a world where cars might not function and roads might not be passable. With reinforced aluminum frames and off-road motocross tires, the wagons were lightweight and easy for the horses to pull.

When they realized the pyramid in Mexico was the one Apep would use to open the portal, James felt at least some relief they wouldn't have to sail any of the boats the Keepers had strategically placed along the Atlantic and Pacific coasts. At least they only needed to cross two countries housed on a single continent. Thank you, Turek.

Shadow neighed. It was a suspicious cry; not quite a warning, but she was definitely making sure he knew she didn't like this – she didn't like this at all. "Easy, girl. We're alright."

James! A distant voice called to him. James jumped, his hand reaching for the hilt of his sword. The voice sounded like *Garrett?* Instinctively he scanned the area. But around him the caravan moved forward unconcerned, while to his right Elaine and Charles seemed deep in conversation. No others heard the call.

James, can you hear me!? the voice called again.

Garrett, is that you?

It's me, James! Where are you? How close?

James's eyebrows knitted together. A dozen questions sprang up, but something in Garrett's voice was distressed. *What is it, what's wrong?*

Where are you!?

A full day away – maybe two.

James, this is super important. Which way will you be coming from?

The northeast side. What's this about, Garrett? James pled.

The war, James! You have to hurry. The war is here!

Another voice broke in, this one closer. "Um, Commander? Commander, are you… okay?"

James blinked. Garrett's voice washed away into the echoes of fading thought. *The war is here!*

"Commander?" Annie said again, her voice becoming worried. She must have approached from the rear, galloping alongside James without his even noticing.

"Report," James ordered.

"Commander, everyone is moving well. There are no gaps in the line, but…"

"But what? What's wrong?" James asked, sensing something.

"The trees are closing off the road behind us."

"Closing off the road?"

Annie nodded.

No going back now. James rubbed a hand across the patchy whiskers of his scarred face. *The war is here.* Maybe the trees were protecting them, ensuring they were guarded from the rear. Yes, that had to be it. Annie was staring at him, and she looked worried. Something niggled at James. Something was not quite right, but they had no choice but to press on.

Ahead, the narrow passage through the trees opened into a clearing large enough for his entire cavalcade to clear the trail and congregate. When the last of the Keepers cleared the trail, trees crowded in, sealing the road off as if it had never existed.

"James, do you see an opening on the other side?" Elaine asked.

James held up the binoculars, searching the tree line on the other side for the opening that would lead them the rest of the way. In the distance beyond, dark clouds loomed large and ominous. James felt a sudden urgency compelling him to hurry. He could feel it in his people, too. They all just wanted, no *needed*, to get to the portal – now.

Across the clearing, the trees at the southeast end seemed almost as out of place as the clearing itself. He recognized the massive trees as a mix of alerce and redwood, neither of which should have been here in this part of the world. Why were they here, and what were they doing crowded up at that end of the clearing, the end in the direction of the pyramid?

"I don't like this," Dr. Moore said.

"It's okay. Just let me find an opening. It's here. It has to be," James said. He scanned the far side twice but saw nothing save the massive trees at one end and an impassable mountain directly across. The steep terrain stretched on and on toward the west until it finally curved back north, out of the sight and in the wrong direction.

Panning back across the clearing once more, something caught

James's eye, and his breath hitched in a gasp. Directly across from them, a head poked up from the tall foliage. But it wasn't a human head. It looked like… like what? He twisted the zoom of the binoculars with his left hand while thumbing the central focusing wheel with his right. What came into focus was a small dragon head. James's mouth went dry.

"What is it, James? What do you see?" Dr. Moore asked, standing from the bench seat.

James didn't answer.

"James?" Dr. Moore urged.

The dragon rose up from the foliage enough that James could now see a long row of spikes running down the length of its black-and-white scales. But it was what James didn't see that told him this was no dragon. He squinted one eye, absently running his fingers over his scarred cheek. Even a small dragon would have wings, but this thing had none. Not that he'd seen a lot of dragons, but this thing's color and its face were all wrong. There were no horns protruding from its head, its eyes weren't right, and its snout was too blunt.

"James? Please, what do you see?"

"Just an iguana," James said.

Dr. Moore let out a relieved breath.

"Do you see a way out of this clearing?" Elaine asked.

James held up a hand. "More than one iguana," he said, his lips moving in a silent count. "Maybe a dozen." Now he noticed a scattering of dirt piles along the far side near the base of the rock outcropping, which rose steeply into the mountainous jungle beyond.

Dr. Moore pointed into the distance beyond the clearing. "James, no offense, but why in the hell are you worrying about iguanas? Shouldn't we keep moving?"

"Because theses iguanas are the size of our horses," James said, pulling the binoculars away from his face.

"But that's…"

"Impossible?" James finished, then pointed. "On the other side of this clearing is a huge mess of iguanas. There are piles of dirt over there, and that likely means they're nesting. Maybe they're protecting eggs. These things already know we're here, and I don't think they like it. And yes, they're big as hell. Look for yourself." James stretched his arm out to pass Dr. Moore the binoculars.

Dr. Moore pressed the binoculars to his face. "Jesus H. Christ! I see them. Their heads are up, tongues out, tasting the air. They know we're here alright."

James looked toward the eye of the storm, still several miles beyond. Then he looked back the way they had come, now completely sealed off with trees. A hard realization struck James. This hadn't been the work of Turek, and the trees weren't helping them get to the pyramid faster. They were slowing them down. "Dr. Moore, it seems I have led us into a trap."

"A trap? You think the trees are… trying to kill us?" Elaine asked.

"I don't know," James said.

"But didn't Breanne tell you Garrett made a deal, and they weren't to harm us?" she asked, looking to Dr. Moore.

Dr. Moore swallowed dryly and cleared his throat. "That's what my baby girl said alright. She also told me all about Apep sending creatures after her and Gabi. I knew we were at risk of crossing one of these foul things, but a nest? Please – tell me you have a plan, James?" he asked, pulling the binoculars away from his face.

"It will be okay," Elaine said. "James has a plan. Don't you?"

James scratched at his cheek absently and nodded. "I do, but you won't like it."

Dr. Moore dabbed a handkerchief across his forehead and situated his leather fedora. "Well, let's hear it, son."

Son? James was eight hundred years older than Dr. Moore, and yet in appearance, James looked to be in his twenties. *Son* actually felt right, but he hadn't heard anyone call him that since Phillip died. "Back in the day when the Templars were called to fight, we were almost always outnumbered. I often led what we called a squadron charge. This would include gathering a small group of knights along with their heavily armored warhorses into a tight unit and galloping full speed into enemy lines. We had a suicidal reputation, and we made it clear we would die for our cause rather than fall back. Often, the effect would break a hole in the enemy lines and send men fleeing in fear for their lives."

"James, you're not suggesting we charge those iguanas – are you?" Dr. Moore asked.

"No, of course not."

"Thank God… that would be—"

"Not us. Me and my squad." James twisted in his saddle. "Annie!" he shouted, then turned back, lifting the binoculars once more.

"You're just going to charge them? That's insane!" Dr. Moore said. "These aren't people, son! There's no telling how they will react. Don't you have a sniper rifle or something?"

James nodded. "Sure, but after the first shot, they're going to charge us. The way they're acting, I'm surprised they haven't already. Now I count twelve, but there are likely just as many I can't see. I can't risk these things attacking our people. Best I take the fight to them. Besides, the best way to back down a charging bear is to act bigger than the bear," he said, not taking his eyes off the iguanas gathered on the other side of the massive clearing.

Annie approached. "Commander, have you spotted our path?"

"I think our path is southeast into those trees," James said, pointing. "But first I need you to gather my Squadron Charge. Tell them to say their goodbyes quickly and join me here."

Annie's face creased with worry, but she nodded sharply and galloped off.

"Now hold on, son," Dr. Moore said. "You said most of the time the enemy lines broke. What happened when they didn't? What happened the times when the enemy didn't turn and flee?"

James's face turned grave. "A train wreck of sword and shield… and blood."

Dr. Moore shook his head. "And if this works? What then? We still don't have a path wide enough to get our wagons out of this clearing."

James nodded, studying the trees to the southeast. "We don't have a path wide enough for the wagons, but we can continue single file into the trees with our horses and bikes. It isn't that much farther."

"What about your provisions? What about the goods you had planned to take to the new world? Seeds, dried goods, clothes?" Dr. Moore asked.

"Turek has a plan for us, Charles," Elaine said. "And if his plan has us crossing through to Karelia with nothing but the clothes on our backs, or for that matter no clothes at all, then so be it."

James could see Dr. Moore trying to hide his concern and doing a poor job of it. "Dr. Moore, I see you are struggling with this decision, and I don't blame you for it, but we must put our trust in Turek, even if it means leaving this world in the same condition as we entered it."

Dr. Moore raised his hands in surrender. "I don't see where I have much of a choice, and I'll just say this, James, then I'll shut up. Despite whatever my gut is trying to warn me about, I'll put my trust in you. But even if this works out, I don't get the warm-and-fuzzies about heading into those trees. Especially without our gear and provisions." He pressed his lips tight and scratched at his cheek. "Well now, let's get on with it."

James smiled. He liked Dr. Moore. He liked him a hell of a lot. There was something to be said for a man who couldn't mask the visage of truth and who wasn't afraid to speak it plain. In James's centuries of experience, he'd learned a man like Dr. Moore was most often a trustworthy man. He was a man to keep close, a man who would be the first to call you fool and the last to abandon you.

Six other riders approached, accompanied by Annie.

"Commander!" a man with a curly brown beard shouted as he rode up.

"Mr. Bloomer! Everyone! On me!" James shouted.

The bearded man, Mr. Bloomer, and his five companions drew rifles and shotguns.

Annie drew her Desert Eagle forty-five–caliber handgun.

"Just the eight of you?" Dr. Moore asked skeptically.

"No. Just the seven. Annie, put that away," James said.

"But, Commander! I'm ready for this," she argued.

Of course, she wasn't ready. None of them were ready. He handed her his binoculars. "I know, but I need you here. I need you to lead everyone across when I give the signal."

Annie frowned, her freckled face dropping as she reached for the binoculars, clearly disappointed, but she acknowledged the order with a slight nod.

"Get the Keepers across safely, and if anything happens to us, I need you to lead everyone the rest of the way to the portal. You are the only one I would trust with this. Can you do that for me, Annie?"

Annie brightened, her somber nod changing to a determined one. In truth, Annie was more than capable of leading the Keepers the rest of the way should he fall, but James knew that was only part of it. By the end of this, plenty of his Keepers might not make it to the other side of that portal. But Annie was only seventeen, and he wasn't about to let her take part in a suicide charge.

Three men lined up on one side of James; two women and the crazily bearded Mr. Bloomer lined up on the other side. "What are we dealing with, Commander?"

"Overgrown iguanas, a dozen or more," James said in a deadpan voice so serious it left no question.

"Okay." Mr. Bloomer breathed out in what sounded strangely like relief. "Overgrown iguanas. I suppose it could be worse."

James raised an eyebrow and nodded. "Glass half full. I like it, Mr. Bloomer. I suppose you're right. It could have been a dozen dragons."

Mr. Bloomer shook his head. "Well, yeah, that would have been worse, but actually I was thinking spiders." His whole body shivered. "If it were spiders… Turek save us," he muttered. "I think I would die right here and now."

James frowned. "You would rather face a dozen dragons than a dozen overgrown spiders?"

"I would rather face a dozen of anything than a dozen spiders – overgrown or not."

James snorted at that. "Well then, Keeper, I suppose it's your lucky day!" He looked at the others, drew his sword, and gave a hollow laugh as he pulled back on Shadow's reins. "Let's do this!"

Shadow stood on her hind legs and neighed.

"James, go with god, my son!" Elaine called.

"Squadron Charge! Attack!" James shouted, dropping his sword as he spurred Shadow forward.

31

Say the Words

Saturday, May 7 – God Stones Day 31
Rural Chiapas State, Mexico

The cheering and rhythmic beating of steel on shield didn't stop when Jack turned his back on the thousands of nephilbock below only to find Apep and Ogliosh exchanging words out loud. The racket might have drowned out their words, but Jack wasn't an idiot. Apep had already told him the importance of speaking out loud when he wished for their conversation to be private. What did Apep think he was – stupid? It was obvious they were talking about him. Jack smiled to himself. If they were talking in secret about him, there could only be one reason – they were scared.

Noticing Jack staring at him, Apep went silent. Instead, the sickly-looking elf held his stare, eyeing him with a different look – a new look. And not just because everything looked different through Jack's red eyes, either – though it did. No. This was something else. This was the look of worry. *What's the matter, Apep?* Jack thought to himself, his smile deepening. *I thought gods didn't worry about anything.*

Apep stared down the bridge of his sharp blue nose for another moment before finally speaking. *Well, Jack, it seems you are full of surprises.*

Jack ignored him, instead looking up past the elf to Ogliosh, who stood still as a stone statue, quietly watching him. Jack held the gaze of the one-eyed monster fearlessly while keeping Apep in his peripheral vision. He wanted to tell the elf just how screwed he was. He wanted to say, *You've no idea how smart I am and how bad this is going to go for you.* Jack wondered now, *How many steps ahead are you, Apep? Two? Three? So then I need to be one step ahead of that.* Jack narrowed his eyes, careful to guard his mind as he thought, *You're mine, Ogliosh. You're mine or you're dead, and you don't even know it.*

Abruptly, the giant broke eye contact with Jack, turning his gaze away.

For a moment, Jack thought he had failed to guard his mind as Ogliosh had shown him. Shit, had the giant just read his thoughts?

Jack's relief came when the giant spoke into his mind. *King Helreginn approaches,* Ogliosh said, his eye fixed far down the pyramid stairs.

Apep stepped forward, lifting his chin. *Excellent! It is time he meets the one he serves.*

King? I thought you were a king, Ogliosh, Jack said, watching as Helreginn and two others climbed the stairs.

To my people in Karelia, I am indeed a king. He lifted a hand and pointed one of his six fingers toward the valley. *To our half-blood children, we are their gods!* He nodded toward the other five giants who stood spread across the uppermost tier of the pyramid.

After several minutes and hell if Jack knew how many stairs later, Helreginn and two of his bodyguards, or warriors, or whatever they were called, made their way onto the top of the pyramid. They vanished into the temple corridor only to reappear a few moments later after ascending onto the temple roof.

King Helreginn stepped forward, stopping in front of Jack and Ogliosh.

Now that the giant was closer, Jack recognized Helreginn from when they'd first met at the ocean's edge in Panama. The other two nephilbock towered over their king by a couple feet. The biggest of the three also looked familiar, but it wasn't the creature's face Jack remembered because they were all ugly as hell. No, he remembered this one from what it wore around its neck. Jack's eyes were pulled to a red Converse All Star, laced halfway up. The remaining laces tangled into a knot of other connecting shoes, forming the strange charm necklace. Protruding several inches from the top of the shoe was a jagged bone, gnarled and sucked clean of flesh. Jack couldn't help pulling a face as he realized the giant had been gnawing on the end of the broken leg bone, sucking the marrow from it. This was the same giant he'd seen back in Panama, alright, old candy necklace himself – nasty bastard.

The three nephilbock dropped to their knees and laid their foreheads down on the stone floor.

Ogliosh said something Jack didn't understand, and Helreginn and the other two rose. After another exchange of words, Ogliosh looked at Jack. *King Helreginn has something he wishes to say to you. Do you wish to hear it?*

Sure, but I can't understand them for shit. It just sounds like they're clearing their throats of some nasty snot when they talk, Jack said.

Step forward, Ogliosh said.

Ogliosh bent and placed his massive hands on both sides of Jack's head. The giant's hands glowed slightly, emitting a sort of blueish-grey light, and a sensation washed over him, like warm water filling his mind.

Ogliosh stepped back and dipped his head. Then he made a face Jack thought was a smile as his lips drew back to reveal a slightly parted mouth overflowing with shark teeth. Ogliosh spoke words Jack now understood. *Helreginn of Agartha – rise, noble king, you have done well! You have made your gods proud on this day. Not only have you lived and multiplied, but you have returned when called upon, bringing your people home to their gods.*

Thank you, Father. I am glad you are pleased, said the king. *The journey here would not have been possible without this…* He looked down at Jack, right into his ruby-red eyes, swallowing hard.

Jack smiled, not dumbly though. No. What Jack flashed was the best sinister smile he could muster.

Without this god you sent to us, the king continued, his dark eyes still locked on Jack. *The one who poses as a human.*

I do not pose as anything, King Helreginn, Jack said. *I was human once, but now I'm more.*

I am sorry, great one! Helreginn said, the fear thick in his voice.

You have nothing to fear from me, Helreginn. We've been in the shit… I mean, we've already been in battle together, and far as I'm concerned, you've proved yourself a friend.

Tell us, Apep commanded, his voice impatient and filled with annoyance. *What did Jack do that was so magnificent?*

Helreginn looked at his men and then back at Apep. *He and the three-headed god dragon slayed millions of the magical trees. Without their protection, my nephilbock would have never made it out of the Amazon. The trees would have slaughtered us all. Later, we were attacked again, this time by Hafgufa, the sea goddess, while crossing the great river. Hafgufa ate this… this Jack, and that's when I was sure you sent a god. For nothing can consume a god. Jack destroyed the sea goddess from within, consuming Hafgufa's power and releasing it into the forest, clearing a path, and allowing my people to escape the ocean and the trees.*

Yes, I see. Well, we are glad you are with us, Apep said idly. *Now, you see the crown upon my head, Helreginn? This is the key home. It's the power of the universe. The power handed down from gods of gods. I possess it. Your gods have agreed to help me fight the king of my people back on Karelia in exchange for—*

We know of our purpose, Helreginn interrupted. *My father told me the stories, long before I was sent to Agartha to grow the army that would someday be called upon. In exchange for winning your war, you will return our God Stone to the nephilbock and honor a peace treaty between our people.*

Apep looked like he might strike the nephilbock king dead on the spot for interrupting him, but even he had to know how stupid that would be. Jack readied himself to choose sides in whatever split second he might have.

Apep's lip twitched, but he didn't attack. *Good. Then I see no need to waste time. Tomorrow we will open the portal home, and the war will begin.*

Our journey was long. My nephilbock are in need of food and rest.

The dragons are bringing you what they can gather quickly. Once we are safely on Karelia, I will offer you rest before the war, but for now go, prepare your people. We can no longer stay on this… Apep trailed off, his attention drawn back to the valley.

Jack frowned, following Apep's gaze far across the valley to the north, where Cerb had attacked the trees earlier in the evening. The trees were moving forward. Now, as the sun sank into dusk, the ten-mile radius of charred ground around the pyramid had shrunk. The trees were pushing slowly inward. Per Apep's orders, no other attacks from the dragons had taken place, and the fires Cerb had caused were nothing more than smoldering white smoke. Still, the trees were moving, but now Jack saw something else, a glowing from across the battlefield. It definitely wasn't dragon fire, for this glow wasn't fire. Even through his red-tinted vision, he could tell the green light was obviously not coming from one of his dragons. Jack knew there were trees over there as tall as the Statue of Liberty, maybe taller, but then he watched as something rose from the redwoods. It grew taller and taller still. Jack was too far away to see what it was very clearly. It just looked like a brown mass climbing up and up, fifty feet above the tallest tree, then fifty more. Now, far to the north, stood the figure of a woman. She appeared to be a Black woman with black hair. Even from here, five miles away, maybe more, Jack could see her emerald eyes staring right at him. Right into his soul.

Pando! Apep gasped. *She has come for the God Stones!*

Send me and Cerb to handle her! Jack exclaimed.

Apep ignored him, spinning toward Ogliosh. *Order your nephilbock away from the forest edge and tell them to advance through the portal when they see it open! Jack, order the dragons to burn the perimeter! Do not cease until they stop their advance, or the portal opens!*

Jack sent the order, and the dragons obeyed.

From high above the temple, Jack and the others had a three-hundred-and-sixty-degree view of the jungle encircling them. Jack pointed as he noticed a green glow emanating not just from Pando, but also from other trees on the front line. Only these things no longer looked like trees. They were shapeshifters! None were as big as Pando, but they had transformed into humanoid shapes with long woody legs, arms, and hands – hands that were weaving through the air, casting a green glow! *She's doing something!* Jack announced. *They're doing something!*

Fire burst from his dragons as they swooped within range of the forest's front line, but the forest didn't burn. Instead, the flames met a magical shield that flashed green as the flames made contact.

No! No you don't! Apep said, stepping forward toward the edge of the temple roof. The dark elf extended his hands toward the west side of the valley. "Oz ray ff doe! Rayflah oki, rahshiak! Zae flah rayokioz doe okiozflah!" Apep's burnt fingers splayed wide as he continued to chant, "Oz ray ff doe! Rayflah oki, rahshiak! Rayflah oki, Ozflahoki!"

Ribbons of grey shadow poured from Apep's hands and darted out across the valley. In the distance, Jack saw two dragons fall from the sky. Wrong place, wrong time. Then a moment later, the forest edge lit up in a green glow as Apep's Sentheye smashed into the shield. An explosion of green and then orange lit an area of forest as wide as a football field. Behind the shield, trees burst into splinters. *You crushed it!* Jack shouted.

Apep smiled. *Time to teach a tree not to pick fights with a god!*

Unwise, dökkálfar, Ogliosh said, pointing.

The smile slipped from Apep's face as trees poured through the opening he had created.

These trees were much smaller than the massive redwoods. Stupid trees, Jack thought. Why would you send your smaller trees in first? As he watched, it quickly became clear these trees were changing shape. *Are those… rhinos?*

Before anyone could answer, a herd of rhinoceroses collided with the nephilbock with such force Jack could hear the echo of shields folding and bones cracking all the way across the valley.

Jack turned to find Apep staring at the scene, a look of absolute horror plastered across his crazy face.

Ogliosh! The time is upon us! We must open the portal now!

Ogliosh nodded. *Eroch, take the others and make any final preparations!*

Apep shook his head. *No time! We must depart this world now, before we've no army to take! Now, are you sure no time will have passed since last I opened the portal?*

I am sure. The portal will open on the same moon ring in which last it closed, Ogliosh said.

Jack watched as Apep's horror turned to something else. The elf's thin lips drew back to show teeth, and his boney fingers clenched into fists, as if he were psyching himself up. *Very good. My father will be ill prepared for what is about to befall his kingdom.*

Apep! What if Pando plans to follow you through the portal? She could be drawing close to try and enter! Ogliosh said, his eye focused on the giant tree monster still advancing across the shrinking valley.

Jack, instruct the dragons to continue firing flame on her shield! Once my nephilbock army is safely on the other side, I will signal you to break off your attack and order the dragons back. You're their leader, Jack. Make sure as many get through as you can before you follow.

You… you want us to go last? Jack asked incredulously.

After your dragons cross over, we will step through together, shutting it down before she can interfere, but we must act now! Apep flexed his hands, reached up, and grabbed the Sound Eye crown with both hands. His knuckles went white as he lifted, and his lips opened in a scream.

Jack watched as the crown tore free of Apep's head, taking bits of blue skin and hair with it. Dark purplish blood ran down the dark elf's face, filling his already crazy-ass eyes.

Apep blinked away the blood and walked toward the altar, hesitated, and turned back toward Jack. *Now go, Jack. Ogliosh, say the words!* Apep commanded, placing the bloody crown onto the altar.

Jack moved toward Cerberus, keeping his eyes on the altar.

Ogliosh reached down and repositioned the crown. Jack heard a loud click, but he wasn't sure if it came from the crown snapping into place or the crown itself.

The massive giant stepped back and spoke the words. "Ray ray

Shiokidoe! Flahshi ff raydoe! Flah Ray Ozzaeoki shioki zaedoeoki. Flah oz zaeoz oki okieshoki!"

The stone beneath Jack's feet shook.

Climb on! Cerb said.

The Sound Eye crown rattled on the altar, tipped up onto its side, and began to spin. Jack stopped, his eyes transfixed by the spinning crown. Faster and faster it spun, until it was spinning so fast it appeared to transform into a solid silver sphere. Below the altar, a recess in the stone filled with water that percolated upward, drawn to the sphere as if by some magnetic force. As the water filled the strange sphere, it changed from silver to a sort of milky color. Jack knew there was a better word for it, but he couldn't think of it as he stood there hypnotized by the smoky ball, still spinning – spinning and growing. And as it grew, it seemed to become unstable, wobbling crazily as if it might fly apart. With no warning, lightning from a cloudless sky struck the sphere. Once, then again, and then again and again. Jack stumbled back, throwing his hands in front of his face. A great ripping sound, louder than thunder, deafened his ears. Then, quick as a finger snap, the sound was gone. The smoke inside the sphere cleared, and Jack saw inside. He saw another world!

From beyond the ever-growing opening, wind billowed, carrying with it large flakes of weird purplish-colored snow. Jack held out a hand, shielding his face from the bright light and cold flakes as he squinted, desperately trying to see more.

"Yes! The time is upon us! Retribution is at hand! Your son is coming home a god!" Apep shouted into the still-growing sphere.

Jack! Let's go! Cerb shouted again.

The sphere was six feet tall now and still stretching upward, slowly expanding across the rooftop of the temple. Jack pulled his gaze from the strange snowstorm beyond to the portal itself. Below the altar, golden light reflected through the water. Watching it for a moment, he realized it wasn't light at all – it was gold itself. As the liquid gold crept in from somewhere below and upward into the portal, it hit the wobbly sphere and leached outward toward the sides. Snow continued to blow through in heavy gusts, melting as it made contact with the warm Mexican air.

The lightning really came on now, repeatedly jabbing the golden frame of the growing window.

Jack blinked. The strange sensation of every hair on his body standing up pulled his attention away from the portal. Being struck by lightning suddenly felt like a very real possibility. He looked around and no longer saw Apep, Ogliosh, or the other giants.

Jack! Are you trying to find out if you're immune to lightning strikes? Cerb shouted.

Jack ran up Cerberus's tail and leapt onto his back, gripping the dragon's neck bones. *Go!*

Cerb twisted and fell from the side of the temple roof, opening his wings and diving low into the valley below.

Jack looked back at the pyramid. The lightning ceased, the sphere stabilized, and the entire top of the temple was now a gateway to another world.

The portal was open!

PART II

VIE FOR THE PORTAL

32

Hallowed Halls

On Earth – God Stones Day 30, before the portal opens
On Karelia – Moon Ring 1
The Creators' Mountain, Karelia

Turek's footfalls echoed off the corridor's stark white walls of polished stone. How long had it been since he'd stepped foot in these hallowed halls? He stopped and straightened. So long he'd forgotten. Wait, sixty thousand… no, seventy? Yes, seventy thousand Earth years. He started walking again, taking comfort in the knowledge that time was but a moment consumed in a specific place.

The Creators' Path was a long passage set at a steep incline rising up and up, appearing to have no end. Turek grinned to himself. It was actually a lot more fun to slide down than climb up. But fun wasn't in the cards – not today.

Far ahead, the bright white of stone gleamed so brilliantly it gave the feeling one was walking into a white star, or perhaps heaven itself. He and the others had designed this path so that only the worthiest of mortals could find their way to the gods. Anyone who traveled the Creators' Path would only know they were nearing its end when a small black dot appeared in the distance far above. Obviously not heaven then. With every step, the dot would grow and grow until finally the traveler arrived at the Great Hall.

Turek didn't have to walk, but today he felt like walking. Phillip, John, and so many others who had sacrificed themselves in his name for the prophecy he had set forth weighed heavy on his mind. He wanted to mourn them all, and he would – in time. Right now, he needed to gather his thoughts and organize his mind for the conversation to come. And though he knew he would say it all, he wanted to feel like he had a choice. He wanted to feel like he could hold something back if it all went horribly wrong, more likely *when* it all went wrong. But maybe there was another reason he wanted to walk. Perhaps he was intentionally postponing the inevitable.

After seventy thousand years, what was a walk? Even one as far as this. What was the hurry? Other than the fact that the portal was about to open. Oh, yes – that.

Ahead, the small black dot appeared, signaling he was drawing close. They would know he was here, but this too was by intention. This single entrance to the top of the mountain ensured the creators would never be surprised by intruders. Turek rubbed his hands together nervously, quickening his pace.

The hall before him opened into an expanse of polished floors containing precious gems, bisected by a crystal river that held slow-moving water – water so clean and pure it was invisible, so that everything it held was seemingly suspended, floating in space. The mountaintop high above was supported by towering stone columns as large as redwood trees back on Earth, while in contrast, the walls of the Great Hall were roughhewn from the mountain itself, except on one side.

On this one side, the wall fell away, and the bejeweled floor extended outward onto an enormous terrace. Atop the terrace sat seven thrones of various sizes and, upon them, the seven creators minus one – minus himself. The center throne sat empty.

Turek crossed the Great Hall, his brothers and sisters facing away from him as they were no doubt performing the work of creation. Slowly, the thrones turned as all eyes cleared of their haze and fell to him. The creators were all here now, both in mind and body.

"So, you have decided to return? Bringing your self-banishment to a conclusion so soon? Why now, brother?" The voice, unmistakably Typhon's snide tone, was full of contempt.

Well, nothing like getting right to it then, he thought. But as he opened his mouth to speak, his eyes found Ereshkigal's, like a moth finds the flame. His heart fluttered and his voice stalled – he couldn't speak. She was still stunning. Eternally beautiful in any form. Be it her present dökkálfar form or in her true form of a light, it made no matter. She was simply perfect. She was also the reason he had left in the first place… mostly. He swallowed, finding his voice. "Brothers and sisters, the time has come for my return."

"And here you are," Typhon said.

Druesha, the creator of all plant life, bent her trunk forward. "You think you can simply say what you said and do what you did and… what? Beg of us the place you cast away? You? You who turned his back on his brethren?"

Turek appraised the creators – his family. As far as he knew, these were the only other beings like him in this entire universe or, for that matter, any other. His eyes drifted from one to the next. Had nothing changed since last he'd seen them? Ereshkigal, creator of dökkálfar, Durin, creator of dwarves, and Aurgelmir, creator of nephilbock, still held, as they had always held, the form similar to the design of humans – two legs, two arms, and one head. Their forms were much like their true form. The form they held as beings of light. The form the Great Mother had created them in. But this was not so with Druesha, creator of plant life, Typhon, creator of dragons, or Rán, creator of sea creatures. These brethren had taken the forms of their favorites too. Only their favorites differed greatly from their own true form.

Occupying the largest of the thrones towered a one-hundred-headed dragon, each head unique in shape and color, like a hundred faces. "Go back to your puny planet, brother. We are fine creating without you," Typhon said. His brother always had thought bigger was better. And though his chosen were the dragons, no dragon could have as many heads as their creator. To have a second head was a blessing and to have three would be a miracle, but only one had a hundred, and his name was Typhon.

"Typhon, please," Ereshkigal said evenly, then turned back to Turek. "You speak of time, brother – tell us of this time that has come."

Great Mother, Eresh was radiant. He didn't mind when the others called him *brother*. The Great Mother had created them and, in this way, they were brother and sister, but when Ereshkigal called him *brother*, it panged his heart. He didn't want to be thought of as a brother, not by her.

"I have been gone epochs. For you, maybe my absence was only days, years—"

"Days? Years?" Aurgelmir interjected. His strained voice raked curiously as the giant's massive single eye stared unblinking. "What is a day year?"

"Surely you remember Earth time, Aurgy? It passes differently. Passing days eventually equal years," Turek explained.

"Do not mock me as ignorant with your new nomenclature. I, like my nephilbock, never forget, and I have no history of days that equal years. I remember a small blue planet circling a sun in short cycles. And it is of no matter – we are not on Earth, Turek. We are in the Karelian dimension, where all things center around Karelia, including time. Or is it you who fails to remember time?" Aurgelmir asked.

Turek smiled at the big giant. "No, Aurgy. I've not forgotten. Nor have I forgotten your dry logic. Oh, how I have missed you, brother."

The giant smiled then; all his teeth were murder sharp, but there was no menace there. "I have missed you too, little one."

Little one. Turek knew the title wasn't regarding his size. It was the fact he was the youngest of the seven creators. He was the last creator born, true, but only by seconds. It was semantical really. And whether it was or wasn't, Turek took it as a term of affection.

Typhon's heads sighed impatiently, warming the air all around him. "Speak of your purpose, brother. I am nearing the end of creating a clever species of dragon. This creature can swim through sand like a fish. Instead of breathing fire, it inhales sand and exhales molten glass at will. The abstract landscapes of colored glass are unlike anything Karelia has ever seen."

"It had better only swim in sand and be more dragon than fish, Typhon," Rán warned, her voice soft. "The ocean is my domain."

Rán, too, was stunning. A fair-skinned beauty from the waist up, and all fish and scales from the waist down. Turek smiled. "Rán. Sister. Do you know that on Earth there are legends of you? They call your favorites mermaids. And you, Typhon. You are a legend on Earth too. We have become the origins of their mythology. It was interesting to see them take a bit of fact, embellish it, and create their own stories and religions."

"They? They who, brother?" Rán asked, her deep sea-blue eyes boring into him.

"That is what I have come to talk to you all about. My humans on Earth have reached nearly eight billion. What I have learned living among them is—"

"Eight billion? A throng so dense on a planet so tiny?" Typhon laughed. "Humans are tiny themselves, but how could so many live there without destroying the planet?"

"Humans cannot destroy the planet, Typhon. But it can become uninhabitable, which is what has been happening."

"Ah, now we get to the crux of it! Let me guess, you want to bring them all here because you have run out of room? That's why you have come back now?" Druesha asked, looking quite majestic planted atop a throne in the form of an emerald tree with golden leaves.

Turek's eyes glistened as he swallowed down his emotion. "No. By now, most of the inhabitants have already died. I would wager only a couple million remain and, as I stand here before you, the number continues to shrink."

Durin stood in the seat of his throne and pointed a hammer at Turek, speaking in his heavily accented voice. "Wager to what end, brother? Trouble ourselves with your human ilk for what?"

Hearing Durin's voice after seventy thousand years made Turek realize two things. He had missed his brother even more than he knew, and whether or not he wanted to admit to it, creating the accents of old Norse had been based solely on his longing to hear Durin's voice again. "Durin, I don't expect you to care about my creations any more than I care about yours. Which is to say… greatly. But I am not here to beg a home for my humans, and yes, I said home because this planet is as much their home as it is the home of any being here."

"Then speak your truth, Brother Turek," Ereshkigal said.

There was that word again – *brother*. It pricked him like a needle, annoying but tolerable. "I am here to win an old argument. I am here because you, Eresh, you became angry with my humans simply because one fell in love with your dökkálfar. They had a baby, and you had that baby killed."

"So, we are to be subjected to a historical lesson?" Rán asked.

Ereshkigal held up her hand. "The decision to terminate the child was all of ours. We all agreed the creation of a new species was only to be performed by creators. This decree was the law then and is the law to this very day."

"Terminate? No, Eresh! It was murder! You murdered the child! And we didn't all agree, Eresh! I didn't agree!" Turek said, raising his voice. He'd told himself he wouldn't let her do this; he wouldn't let her anger him. Yet already he was yelling. He sucked in a calming breath.

"And so you fled, like a child in the throes of a fit. Stomping off and taking your humans with you. Well, most of them anyway," Ereshkigal said.

"I left because you interfered. It wasn't enough for you to kill the child – you betrayed my creations! You stole their God Stone, Eresh! You were going to let your dökkálfar enslave them!"

"You said you came here with a purpose!" Ereshkigal snapped.

"He's come to us as a beggar, nothing more." Typhon snorted.

The others looked on silently, watching him – judging him.

Turek took another calming breath. "You all agreed my greatest creation was not worthy. You stole their God Stone, and you sentenced them to death or slavery. You did this all because you believe only you should have the ability to create. And because I didn't agree with you, I was forced to take action." Turek held out empty hands. "I've come to beg nothing of you. I am here with a message, my brethren. You were wrong then, and you are wrong now. Great Mother gave us the ability to create beings with a full spectrum of emotions that mirror our own." Turek looked directly at Ereshkigal. "If our Great Mother did not want creation to take place without help from us, why would it be possible? How do we know this isn't our Great Mother's will?"

Ereshkigal pointed an accusing finger toward him. "No, Turek. You are wrong. This is an old argument, brother, exhausted in its labor. Tired in its—"

"Silence, sister. I have not finished, and I am nowhere near tired. If I am wrong, all of your favorites are guilty of the same or perhaps something far worse."

"Preposterous," Ereshkigal said. "It happened only once, and we slew the woman along with—"

Turek's smile turned sinister, cutting the elven creator's words to silence without a sound, and then he spoke. "No, Eresh, not only once. Apep has a half-human daughter. Well, he had a daughter, but a dragon slew her."

"Apep! The banished prince? Don't be absurd. He hates your humans. Besides, he hasn't even been gone three full moon cycles!" Ereshkigal scoffed.

"It matters not how long he was gone from Karelia! It matters how long he was on Earth. You have all been to Earth."

"I forget time passes so differently in that tiny dimension," Rán said.

"Yes, sister, it does, but that's not what I'm referring to. The rules of poking a hole between dimensions apply no matter who is doing it." Turek's face took on a visage of grim determination. "When Apep returns, it will be on the same day the portal last closed."

"Syldan only left this morning," Ereshkigal whispered.

Turek nodded sagely. "Yes, and despite Apep having been gone over twelve thousand Earth years, very little time has passed here," he said, suddenly remembering Aurgelmir's unfamiliarity with the term *day*. "The point is this. Apep will arrive on the same moon ring his brother departed Karelia for Earth."

The dökkálfar creator pulled a face as if she'd taken a spoonful of salt. "That means—"

"That means he will arrive this moon, Eresh."

Ereshkigal straightened. "It matters not. Apep stole the God Stones and opened the portal not once, but twice. Whether you are right or wrong, this moon ring or the next, King Vulmon waits with all the might of Osonian at the ready. Should Apep return, the king will put an end to this disobedient would-be prince once and for all. That is assuming Prince Syldan doesn't complete his mission and kill his brother first."

"For Syldan, over ten thousand Earth years have passed, Eresh."

Ereshkigal shook her head in irritation. "Time is still time, even in the tiny dimension of Earth. If what you are saying is true, they should both be long dead! How did they even live this long? My dökkálfar don't have life spans eternal!"

"The God Stones were not meant to exist on Earth. Their power changed everything it touched," Turek said. "Apep and Syldan became immortal. Even some of my own humans lived well beyond the limits I had set for them."

"Regardless. Syldan will retrieve his brother and the God Stones, then return home. If Apep arrives here alive, his father will deal with him. If he somehow survives, and what you say can be proven true, I will correct the issue myself."

Turek nodded. "I see. Tell me, Eresh, and what of Syldan? Will you kill him as well?"

"So strange your question. Of course not. I already told you, Syldan is on an important quest to retrieve the stones and either kill Apep or return with him. Once he succeeds, he will return the stones to King Vulmon, where their fate shall be determined. But not your stone. Yours is and will always be the dökkálfar's God Stone. Yours is a lost people, Turek. They have no place among the favorites."

The other creators shifted uncomfortably, but it was Durin who spoke. "What Ereshkigal means to say is the God Stones shall be returned to their rightful favorites – except yours, which was taken by the dökkálfar fairly."

Of course, this wasn't true. Eresh had interfered when the humans' God Stone was taken, but Turek was past that. And despite knowing Ereshkigal was the strongest opponent to self-creation, Turek knew she was lying and would not make her chosen return the God Stones to the others' favorites – not for free. And if the others trusted her to do so, they were more fool than he thought. All his instincts told him she had assisted Apep in getting all seven God Stones and in building his backdoor alliances with both the dragons and the giants. "Syldan has also fathered a half-human child. A child that still lives."

Ereshkigal stood from her throne with a jolt. "You lie!"

"Eresh, is that what you think? You think I have come to you with a false tongue?"

The others turned to Ereshkigal expectantly.

The elvish goddess swallowed and composed herself. "If this is true, I will put both brothers to death myself, and then I will personally go to Earth, find the child, and destroy it! This does nothing to support your argument, as I will do what I have always done when the rules of creation are broken."

This he believed. This he knew was the one moral she held on high, no matter what other lies she told. This was her truth, and it guided her whole heart. This single disagreement had grown until it was a chasm between them, so deep and so wide it seemed impossible to cross. Yet that was exactly what he'd come here to do. He had to cross the gulf between them and find her again. "Oh, my dear Eresh, I'm just getting started." Turek's smile turned melancholy beneath his grey beard as he turned an accusing gaze upon the others. "Aurgy, your own nephilbock king and six others accompanied Apep to Earth. Were you aware of this?"

The cyclops turned his gaze down upon Ereshkigal and narrowed his big eye. His voice came dry and strained, as if speaking at all was an effort. "I have come to suspect one of my brothers or sisters knew the fate of Ogliosh, though none have admitted it. I suspected Ogliosh and his men were killed somewhere on Karelia, likely by Apep, their own God Stone stolen. Now you tell me they have joined with this elvish ilk?" He paused for a long moment. "I'm forced to deduce it was you, Ereshkigal. You helped bond their alliance and hide their departure. Why?"

Ereshkigal crossed her arms, looking peeved, but she didn't deny it.

Aurgy nodded regretfully. "Ah, now it seems obvious. Apep needed them. But my nephilbock wouldn't have assembled the God Stones into the Sound Eye even if it meant their deaths. Unless… unless they entered into some kind of promise or deal."

"Hold that thought, Aurgy," Turek said, turning next to Typhon. "And you are missing your Queen of Queens, Azazel. Can I assume you too were unaware of her departure, or are you in a secret alliance with Eresh?"

Typhon's heads roared in unison. For a moment, brief as a thunderclap, all the inhabitants of Karelia stopped and froze in fear.

Turek did not flinch. "So, you knew. Tell me, big brother, what was in it for you?"

Typhon settled a hundred stretched jaws and chose his centermost head to do the speaking. It was suddenly the largest of the hundred heads, all horns and teeth, and black as a starless night sky void of moons and suns and hope. The dragon's red eyes burned into Turek's, but Turek held his brother's stare. Beneath the charade of his false exterior, his brother was a being of light just as he was – a creator, just as he was. Special only in the task the Great Mother had given him, just as Turek himself was.

"I learned of the alliance Apep had made with Azazel and the handful of followers she had planned to take, and I allowed it. Should she succeed, Apep has promised to free dragons from the dökkálfar slavery."

Turek narrowed his eyes at Eresh. "So, the truth is you have no allegiance to Syldan nor his father, King Vulmon."

"So what?" she snapped.

The whole idea of favorites was that each be given a God Stone to balance the power among them. But it also was the responsibility of the favorites to protect their God Stones. The creators were not supposed to interfere with the affairs of their favorites. To interfere would lead to fighting among the creators, and if that happened, Karelia and all the good work they had done could be destroyed. But Turek knew Ereshkigal had not followed their agreement. The elven creator had helped her favorites steal the God Stone from the humans when she learned one of her dökkálfar had made a human woman pregnant. She interfered, killing the dökkálfar, the woman, and the child – in doing so she had broken Turek's heart. This revelation that Typhon had known Apep left with the God Stones did not surprise him. He'd been too blind to see it then, but now it was obvious his siblings had always meddled in the affairs of mortals – not just Eresh, all of them.

"You knew what Apep planned? To return with an army of his own?" Turek asked.

"For Azazel, laying and growing eggs takes time," Typhon said, unconcerned. "As you already pointed out, time works differently in Earth's dimension. Growing an army in only a few Karelian moon rings would be unheard of. But by going to Earth, Apep could return with a small army of dragons. Within a few moon rings, he could amass an army large enough to overthrow his father and free dragons from slavery."

"This is disgraceful!" Druesha said, her golden leaves trembling with rage. "You have been conspiring behind our backs? Plotting and planning?"

"A horde of dragons released into this world could be deadly to the balance, Typhon! What were you thinking?" Rán said.

"It would only be a small horde, hundreds at most. They grow slowly and hatch with a high failure rate. It would be nothing this planet couldn't handle."

"Unfortunately, that's where you are wrong, brother. And I am afraid that's where this story becomes far graver than any of you could imagine. Apep will open the portal at the doorstep of Osonian, this moon ring. Accompanying him are not hundreds of dragons but thousands."

"Thousands!" Durin shouted.

"Thousands?" Druesha said in disbelief. "That many will surely destroy Osonian, but worse, they will destroy Metsavana, the Forest Father."

Metsavana was one of the creators' most magnificent creations – a single tree larger than any other. Trees were the favorite of Druesha, but the creation of the Forest Father had required the assistance of all of the creators. The elven city of Osonian was built on and around the great tree, rising up beneath its canopy in towering stone works, while below and around its massive branches were smaller villages and cities, all lit by magical light from deep within the canopy of the tree itself. Turek smiled fondly at the memory of the challenges he'd faced creating Metsavana's light source. Like a sun, it shone brightly during the day, fading to darkness at night. Oh, how very much he'd like to see the marvel of Karelia again. The combination of creations was a beautiful example of how the creators could work together to complement one another when they were at their best. But he wasn't there to talk about his brethren at their best – he was there to reveal them at their worst.

"Thousands! But that can't be possible!" Typhon scoffed, but Turek could see his brother was only feigning worry. Beneath his surprise, he calculated the possibilities of a Karelia where his favorites could dominate.

"You told me it wouldn't be that many!" Ereshkigal said, leveling her eyes at Typhon.

"You have only yourself to blame," Turek said evenly. "On Earth, Apep has stolen the God Stones away from Ogliosh and forced the nephilbock to assemble them. He now possesses the Sound Eye, donning it upon his head like a crown and proclaiming himself a god. Your dökkálfar has been using the Sentheye to do in only seconds what should have taken years. He hatched and grew over ten thousand dragon eggs into fire-breathing juveniles."

"Apep is proclaiming himself a god?" Ereshkigal asked, her face creasing in worry.

"Eresh," Turek said, and this time the word left his lips with even more sympathy than he meant it to. "What did you think would happen if one of our favorites ever possessed all the God Stones. Or worse, one like Apep?" He looked at his brothers and sisters. "What were any of us thinking?"

"This is all the work of your favorite, Ereshkigal!" Aurgelmir the giant bellowed, pointing an accusing finger.

"She doesn't carry the burden alone, Aurgy. Accompanying Apep and his army of dragons are over twenty thousand nephilbock."

The giant's eye went so wide Turek thought it might pop. Aurgelmir launched upright from his throne and stomped down the dais. The mountain shook with each step, and when he reached Turek he stopped, giant toe to little toe. "Now I know you are lying to us, brother! But what I don't understand is why! Why the game? Why the charade?"

Surprised at the sudden accusation, Turek shook his head. "I speak no lies, brother."

"Then tell me – tell me how seven nephilbock, all male, go missing, and from them an army of twenty thousand are born? The math doesn't work, Turek! What you claim is an impossibility."

"No," Turek said, sad for his brother's narrow-mindedness. He was disappointed Aurgy hadn't put it together on his own, because to put it together on his own would at least show him capable of realizing the possibility and all it carried with it. Instead, Turek must pull back the veil. "It was actually twenty-five thousand, brother, but war against the trees and the sea monster of Earth has taken its toll. Aurgy, your nephilbock have bred with the human women of Earth and created an army that is half human and half nephilbock. They all serve Apep."

The giant's enormous eye stared unblinking until finally he dropped to one knee. "No," he rasped, "the greatest sin by my favorite of favorites? Please tell me this isn't…"

Druesha whispered, "And the trees of Earth? That must mean… Pando? Oh, dear Great Mother. The Sentheye has animated them, and they are… are warring?"

Rán splashed water from the pool atop her throne and blurted out, "Hafgufa, the first sea monster I ever created, she too battles on Earth?"

"She did, yes. But a boy and his dragon have slain her," Turek said.

"Oh, my beloved little Hafgufa! Slain by a human boy and a single dragon?"

"A boy! What boy? Boys don't have dragons!" Typhon shouted.

"A three-headed dragon has been born of a human boy's ability to wield the Sentheye. Worse still, Azazel allowed them to blood-bond, and now… Well, now, I don't know what he is, exactly. Other than to say he is no longer mine or yours, Typhon."

Aurgelmir's hand clenched into a six-fingered fist, his sorrow turning to rage. "We must be at the portal when it opens! We must take the God Stones back and erase this mess!"

Ereshkigal pressed her perfect lips into a tight line. "Yes, and then we should close the portal immediately thereafter. Let them all kill each other on Earth. It will be the cleanest way to rectify this."

Durin pulled at his beard, also nodding. "I agree – with no Senth-eye, it will only be a matter of time before the little world of Earth cleanses itself."

"Then it is decided," Rán said.

Turek held up a hand for silence. "I still have much to tell you. Sit with me and let me give you a full understanding, and perhaps you will see why this course of action would be… unwise."

"What other choice is there?" Aurgelmir asked.

Ereshkigal folded her hands. "I suppose we could go to Earth and fix this properly. Cleanse the world ourselves. After some time, we could put some lesser creatures there, like before."

"This is easy for you to say. You don't have thousands of species of plant life sustaining the planet's atmosphere. You want to… what? Wipe it out? Make it a barren world?" Druesha twisted her emerald trunk as if to gaze upon Ereshkigal.

"If you cared about any of them, why haven't you been back to visit them? All these billions of humans have probably chopped most of them down by now."

Druesha frowned. "I've been consumed doing the Great Mother's work."

"The Great Mother! The Great Mother has given us only her back since our creation!" Typhon sneered.

"Turek was there on Earth for the last seven moon rings!" Durin the dwarf said in an accusing tone, all spit and bile, but it carried an edge too.

It was an edge that flayed Turek's heart. Back when Turek had opposed the killing of his human for becoming pregnant by the dökkálfar, Durin had been on the fence, as had Aurgelmir. Ultimately, they sided with the others, but he knew it had hurt them to do so. Now, it seemed Durin was ready to blame him for it all. "What are you saying, Durin?"

The dwarf stroked one of his beaded beard braids. "What I'm saying is, maybe the question we should ask is why *you* allowed this to go on. You were there all this time. You could have intervened! Instead, you wanted to be right!"

Turek held up his hand again. "Enough of this! For a moment, stop blaming each other and stop blaming me. Sit with me and let me tell you all of it from the beginning to the end. Let me tell you how each of your creations play into this and what I fear is about to happen."

"What difference will it make? Even if all our favorites have blasphemed in some way? It will only further our resolve to cleanse this madness," Durin said, then raised his war hammer and looked to the sky. "It is what the Great Mother would expect!"

"I can assure you it is not. I already know what our Great Mother wants."

Ereshkigal stepped down off her dais, the train of her white gown sliding silently across the jeweled floor. "How… how could you know this?"

Turek met her eyes. Eyes as dark blue as a Karelian sky. Eyes frozen and icy. Oh, how he had missed those eyes – eyes he knew were capable of warmth, capable of looking upon him with love.

"Yes, tell us, Turek. How can you claim to know what the Great Mother wants?" Rán asked.

Turek blinked, breaking eye contact, and with it the trance Eresh held over him. He drew in a breath and steeled himself for the next part. "Because, you see," he said, smiling, "our Great Mother has shown me."

33

Choosing Battles

Saturday, May 7 – God Stones Day 31
Rural Chiapas State, Mexico

Jungle foliage slapped James's legs as he raced across the clearing, the other Keepers a horse's length behind his own. This clearing wasn't a natural occurrence. Obviously, the trees moving off to the sides had created the sporadic strips of churned-up earth. James's lip curled on one side, one eye squinting. The trees had planned this – planned to trap them here and let iguanas kill them. It was true that iguanas were mostly vegetarian, but the males were also as territorial as wolves. The sudden realization of the trees' betrayal pissed him off. He sheathed the sword on his hip, reached over his shoulder, and drew his M97 Trench Shotgun from its scabbard.

As they neared the other side of the clearing, James spotted the first iguana with his naked eye. It was big. Bigger than he'd expected. At least the size of his horse, but longer. He jerked the forestock of the trench gun with his left hand while holding Shadow's reins with his right. A shell racked into the chamber with the magical sound of a pump action.

James carried this specific gun for a very specific reason. Built for close-quarters combat situations during times of trench warfare, the true beauty of this pump action was the fact that as long as he kept the trigger depressed, he could fire as fast as he could pump the forestock and, for James, that was damn fast.

He closed on the iguana and leveled the barrel, letting go of the reins altogether as he squeezed his thighs tight against the saddle. Supporting the gun against his shoulder, he took aim, and at ten yards, he fired. *BOOM!* The blast rocked him back in the saddle. Shadow didn't miss a beat as she charged forward, undaunted by the blast. But then, she was trained for this and a whole lot more.

James twisted left in the saddle, searching for the iguana, the trigger still depressed on the M97. He was sure he'd gotten a piece of it.

To the right, someone screamed as gunshots erupted.

James spun back around in time to see two more iguanas go down, but there was only one rider! The other two were gone, lost in the jungle foliage, or worse. The riders' fallen horses kicked from their backs as more iguanas attacked them. He eased back on the reins, turning Shadow toward the chaos. Mr. Bloomer and the other two riders on his left turned to converge on the downed riders.

Someone's scream cut through the storm, but he wasn't sure whose.

Before James could reach them, a black-scaled iguana leapt from its cover in the foliage directly in front of James.

Shadow stood on her hind legs, her front legs stomping down on the iguana's head.

James shouted in surprise as he slipped from the saddle, falling into the foliage. *Dammit!* That was on him. He should have reacted faster – should have had his legs locked in. He was on his feet quickly though, his trench gun still in hand and finger still depressing the trigger.

Gunfire rang out, but he couldn't see anyone now, only Shadow. He made for the horse.

A wave of rumbling thunder faded as something between a sneeze and a hiss pulled James's attention to the churned-up trail left by the trees. Between him and Shadow stood the black-scaled iguana.

The iguana hissed again as two more iguanas came into the clearing, both beasts a mix of patchy black and white.

James clenched his jaw. "Come on then!"

The iguanas were close, and as long as he pointed the gun in the right direction, he couldn't miss. Shooting from the hip, James pumped the gun three times in rapid succession. *BOOM, BOOM, BOOM,* each round of double-aught buckshot finding home, exploding soft iguana flesh into glorious bits and pieces and dropping all three of the bastards dead. *They don't call this a trench sweeper for nothing,* James thought, letting out a relieved breath.

James let off the trigger and pumped the shotgun, readying the final round. He pulled three more shells out of his bandolier just as he caught movement from the corner of his eye. James spun in time to take the full force of the iguana's charging head directly to his gut. His arms flew up as he went backward, lifting off the loose trail and into the jungle foliage. The gun fired harmlessly into the air, but the force of the blast ripped the weapon violently from James's hand, possibly breaking his trigger finger in the process. He hit the ground hard.

The iguana wasted no time bounding into the foliage and landing atop him, all claws and jaws.

Quickly, James realized it wasn't so much the iguana's bite he needed to worry about, although that was likely to be pretty damn bad. It was the thing's claws. He flailed for his sword, but he couldn't draw it.

The iguana pressed its claws painfully into his chest and lunged forward to bite. If not for the leather ammunition bandolier crossing James's chest, those claws might have already opened him up.

Behind the iguana, Shadow neighed as hooves came down on the lizard's back. The iguana turned in time to take a kick from Shadow's rear leg.

The iguana's ribs crunched as it twisted, freeing James of its claws. He scooted backward through the fan palms, trying to get to his feet as Shadow spun back around to face the wounded iguana.

Shadow neighed again, but her cry was even angrier than before and her eyes were wide with rage. She bared her teeth as she lunged forward and bit the iguana on the neck.

The iguana's tail thrashed at Shadow as it tried to turn and attack.

"Good girl, Shadow!" James shouted, drawing his arming sword as he ran forward, worried the injured iguana would bite back or use those deadly claws on his horse. James shoved the sword into the thing's throat, ending the battle quickly.

"Good girl!" he repeated, ripping his sword free. He quickly scanned the area for his trench gun, but he didn't see it, and there was no time for a thorough search. The others needed him.

James mounted Shadow once more, sword in hand.

Galloping down a strip of churned ground toward the screams of his men, an ancient rage built inside him. The iguanas were overwhelming his people.

"To me!" James ordered.

His men obeyed, bolting toward him. Five iguanas – no, six – gave chase. It was hard to tell how many as they kept disappearing into and out of the jungle as they pursued the group of Keepers.

Mr. Bloomer, Ms. Holly, and Ms. Shrader galloped past James, but he didn't see the others.

Mr. Bloomer's voice came in a panicked rasp. "The other three are down, Commander! Those bastards pulled them into the jungle!"

The man didn't suggest it, but James understood the question hidden in Bloomer's panic. Should they pull back? With his men behind him, he and Shadow were the only thing standing between the iguanas and his people.

At the sight of James turning to face them, the lizards slowed their pursuit. Stalking forward, they prepared to pounce.

James squinted one eye and sneered. "Hold this line, Mr. Bloomer. No one retreats. Protect the Keepers! Kill whatever gets past Shadow and me!"

"But, Commander!" Bloomer shouted.

These vile creatures had just killed three of his Keepers – three of his people! Anger swelled in James as he and Shadow swept through a half-dozen more iguanas like the hand of god come to cleanse the world of sin. Yet the lizards continued to come, as if from nowhere. *Let them come!* James thought. For the three Keepers who watched, he would show them the fury of an ancient man and the love he held for the people he led.

As the iguanas charged, James never looked back and never ordered his people to help. But he didn't have to. For a few brief moments, his Keepers obeyed. They watched, and they witnessed, until they could witness no more – until they could no longer simply hold the line, just in case. As James slayed one territorial iguana after another, it inspired his Keepers anew.

The sound of battle cries as sword met bone rang out behind him.

James's patchy beard, speckled in blood, lifted with his face as he smiled. The others had seen everything James hoped they would.

James dealt another death blow, and when he turned, rather than finding only more iguanas bearing down, he found three Keepers surrounding him. They had dismounted their own horses, drawn their own swords, and attacked with a fearlessness that brought tears to his eyes. It was easy to order a man into battle. It was quite different for men to choose battle from the safety of the saddle. These Keepers had chosen to fight with him even in the face of death.

Mr. Bloomer bellowed as he threw his lance, skewering a charging iguana. The lizard slid forward, stopping at Bloomer's feet. Drawing his sword, he finished the beast, only pulling his sword free in time to spin and cut down a second that seemed to come from nowhere.

But the final blow of the battle came from Ms. Holly when, after burying her own arming sword into the white belly of a massive male iguana, it twisted, turning on her. Spinning not away from the beast but toward it, Ms. Holly freed her war hammer from its hanger at her waist and planted the spiked end in the left eye of the iguana as if she were mining for gold.

When it was over, James's wrist throbbed from dealing death blow after death blow, he was covered in battle blood, and he was sure Shadow, who had fought every bit as hard as he had, was as exhausted as he was. But that was of no matter. Three of his brethren had fallen, and only three remained. James said a prayer for his dead Keepers, hugged Ms. Shrader and Ms. Holly, and placed a hand on Mr. Bloomer's shoulder, looking at each of them in turn. "We will celebrate them as heroes when we reach the new world, just as all of you will be celebrated as heroes." James bowed his head in a silent prayer. The others followed their commander's lead, bowing their heads too.

When James lifted his head, he nodded toward Ms. Shrader. "It's customary for the commander to give soldiers who've proven themselves in battle a war name." James placed a foot in one of Shadow's stirrups. He paused there as if in thought.

Ms. Shrader, a petite woman with a round, flat face and short black hair, sheathed the two short swords she had artfully wielded in the battle and looked up anxiously. The woman was ambidextrous and known for her ability to handle both swords with simultaneous ease. Had there ever been a question of her effectiveness with two swords in an actual battle, there would never be again.

"Shredder," James said. "That's what I'm calling you now. Lady Shredder."

Lady Shredder beamed a bright smile.

"And you," James said to Ms. Holly, saddle leather creaking as he threw a leg over Shadow and raised his sword to the sky.

Ms. Holly, a tall, thickly built woman with broad shoulders, sucked in a sharp breath and held it in anticipation. She had long, sandy-blond hair bound in a braid that stretched down her back. The thick rope of hair seemed substantial enough to moor a ship to a wharf. Ms. Holly was thirty-two, and before this, she worked at a greenhouse and designed residential landscaping. James looked to her hip and the bloody war hammer hanging from it. He remembered the day she'd chosen to learn how to wield the war hammer. It was during one of the Keepers' secret meetings after his father, Phillip, had told the story of a battle Turek had shared with him long ago. A story of fighting giants – a story of a woman wielding a war hammer. James smiled at the memory. "Holly the Hammer," he announced with an assured nod. "Or Lady Hammer for short."

Ms. Holly blushed, and red blotches formed on the fair skin of her blood-speckled neck. She smiled shyly and whispered, "Lady Hammer. Thank you, Commander!"

Across the clearing, the Keepers started moving toward them.

"Mr. Bloomer," James said, "your war name is Sir Bloomer the Spider, but I'll just call you Sir Spider."

The blood drained from Sir Spider's face.

"You don't like your name, Sir Spider?" James asked.

Sir Spider looked as though he'd seen an actual spider crawling on him in that very moment. "Commander, I…"

James gave him a hard look. "You fought like a man who feared nothing, so I am giving you the name of the only thing you fear. I know your worth, Sir Spider. I have fought beside you, and even if you do not know, I do! They do!" he said, pointing at the others. "Now, let your name be a reminder. Use it. Use it to inspire fear in others because it is you whom all should fear!"

Sir Bloomer the Spider smiled then, showing all his teeth, but his smile was wicked. As James held his gaze, the Spider's curly beard suddenly looked more like a tangle of arachnid legs.

A few minutes later, Elaine, Annie, and Dr. Moore reached them, the head of a procession of travel-worn Keepers.

"Are you injured?" Elaine asked.

"I'm okay, but I lost three," James said grimly.

"Dear god, I'm so sorry, James," Elaine said, looking at the others. "Jason, Riley, and… and Michael," she said sadly. "We will celebrate them on the other side."

In all the commotion of battle, James hadn't realized the rain had stopped. Above them, the clouds began to break apart.

"Look!" Annie shouted, a finger pointed to the sky.

Between the breaks in the clouds, dozens, maybe hundreds of dragons were flying past at full speed, making for the pyramid to the south. Making for the eye of the storm. James looked toward the south as a hum, low at first but then growing louder and louder, drew toward a crescendo until finally a sudden breaking sound shook the Earth like a volcano exploding. It only lasted a second, like the sonic boom of a plane breaking the speed of sound – only louder. Then it was gone. The distant sky glowed as lightning struck, then again and again and again. They were too far to see more than flashes as the bolts of electricity struck down seemingly in the same spot over and over. A moment passed before James realized what he was seeing.

In the distance, what must have been fifteen miles away, something grew taller and taller, stretching into the sky. James gasped, "The portal is opening! We must hurry!"

They pushed on, ignoring the dragons above as they in turn ignored James and the Keepers. They had one mission now: make haste – get to the portal.

As they approached the trees on the north side of the clearing, the last of the day's sun, already hidden behind building clouds, sank out of sight, replaced by a green glow filling the sky beyond. James's pulse quickened as bursts of dragon fire exploded all around the portal. Whatever was happening, it had to be some kind of battle. An innate need to be there, fighting alongside Garrett and the others, helping to get these people through the portal, pulled at James. They were so close now, only a handful of miles!

Pulling his attention from the sky was the massive forest standing before him. Their only way forward was through this forest. James stood before his Keepers, staring up at the mighty trees, and he swore he could feel their restlessness. The air seemed electrified with a tension so conspicuous he could taste it thick on his tongue. James swallowed hard. The iguanas hadn't killed all of his Keepers, but would the forest allow them to pass? And if not, what then?

34

The Valley of Ash

Saturday, May 7 – God Stones Day 31
Rural Chiapas State, Mexico

The last of the day's sun was fading as Garrett and the others looked down into a valley of impossibility. His mind was quiet. Like him, his friends must have been unable to find words. Hell, they might not have even been breathing! He sure wasn't – couldn't. The valley below was full of nephilbock, while what must have been hundreds if not thousands of dragons circled above. In the center of it all stood a pyramid the size of a mountain, and poised atop it was a box-shaped temple. It was unlike anything he had seen in pictures. It didn't have the tiers of Maya or Aztec pyramids. Instead, it appeared more like what he had seen in photos of the Egyptian pyramids, but that wasn't right either. This one had stairs straight up the center on all sides, but the stone was otherwise smooth and dark, and he didn't think any of the Egyptian ones had a big boxy structure on top, either. *Bre? Have you ever seen a pyramid like this?*

No, she whispered in mind speak, her voice full of the same awe he was feeling. *No, nothing like this. I mean, when Apep brought me here, it was still partially covered, and I was sick and… no. No, not like this,* she said, shaking her head.

Pete whistled. *I've seen about every pyramid there is to see – not in person, but in books I mean – and I've never seen anything like this either.*

Garrett thought he could see others standing atop the temple. From this distance, they had to be giants. Giants like the one he'd fought in the temple back in Petersburg. There was something else too – a massive dragon.

Following his gaze across the few miles of charred ground, Pete confirmed Garrett's worst fear. *That's Jack's dragon alright, some big-ass giants, and Apep and Jack too.*

Pulling his eyes from the temple, he looked around the forest perimeter. Giant tree people stood, evenly placed, maybe a hundred yards apart, but it was hard to gauge from this angle. The strange tree people were waving their hands back and forth as green Sentheye spread down the line of trees from the ground to the top of the tallest redwood, all the way back to… to Pando. Garrett craned his head up and stared in wonder. He didn't need Pete's eyesight to see the Trembling Giant was living up to her name now, as she stood what had to be five hundred feet tall.

With a sudden bright flash, the dragons attacked, breathing fire into the front line of trees just above their position.

"No!" David wailed, throwing himself onto the ground behind Garrett and the others.

Garrett ducked down instinctively, but the flames dissipated against the green glow of Sentheye. When he lifted his head and peered back through the green shield, he could see the dragons were attacking all across the valley.

Look! Pete pointed.

From high atop the pyramid temple, a plume of grey shadow, reminding Garrett of a massive swarm of angry hornets, launched toward him, crossing several miles in only seconds. The mass of grey shadow struck somewhere to their left.

With a great ripping sound, the invisible force field protecting the trees tore apart.

The nephilbock closest to the east wall of the pyramid turned and rushed the wall as dragons swooped low. But then something came from within the wall of trees.

What on earth? Breanne asked.

A herd of rhinos rushed forward through the opening in a full stampede, colliding with the nephilbock before the dragons could react. In a moment of confusion, the dragons did nothing. Then they refocused their efforts at the opening in the tree wall, apparently deciding they couldn't help the nephilbock without killing them too.

Garrett stared, mouth agape. There were no words for what he was seeing. No words for the insanity—

"Balls!" Lenny shouted. "What in the big fat scaly dragon nutsack is happening?!"

Garrett turned to find his friend had crawled up alongside him. "Glad you're awake." Garrett smiled, feeling better already just knowing Lenny was there beside him.

"Someone want to tell me where we are and what the hell is happening?" Lenny shouted.

Please! Allow me! Pete said from Lenny's opposite side while pointing at his head to signal mind speak.

Lenny nodded. *I hear you.*

You passed out when David healed us and, um, well, David didn't. Gov carried you here, to the edge of the forest. We just found out Pando is here, and her army is pressing forward. She is apparently trying to force Apep to open the portal or fight her and her entire army. She and some massive shapeshifters that look like what I would expect proper Tolkien Ents to look like are casting some insane emerald magic that is acting as a force field. Additionally, she is utilizing some smaller shifters that seem to be taking on the form of rhinos. Oh, and finally, your ears are pointed, and your skin is purple. There you go. Now you're all caught up, Pete finished, slapping a hand on Lenny's shoulder.

Lenny looked horror stricken. His hands shot out in front of him. He flipped them back and forth, checking their color. Still confused, he grabbed for his ears as his eyes did the impossible and went even wider. *Oh, holy shit!* he exhaled.

Pete practically fell over, laughing and pointing. *God, I had you so good! And you fell for it hook, line, and sinker!*

Lenny raised a fist.

Don't even think about it, Len, Pete said, still laughing. *After the temple back in Petersburg, you know you had that coming.*

The memory of the underground temple beneath Lake Petersburg brought with it a spine-tingling chill only a near-death experience can bring. *Petersburg. Man, that was a hundred years ago,* Garrett thought. After David had healed Pete's gut wound, Lenny had taken an exuberant amount of pleasure in sharing that Dagrun was Eugene's brother, Eugene was actually Apep, and neither of them were human. Then he'd dropped the bombshell on Pete, explaining with delight that Pete's new love interest was the one who'd just run a knife into his gut and was really Apep's daughter, a half-elf who was also pretending to be Eugene's old lady wife, Lilith. Then with classic Lenny style, he wrapped it all up by stating that if they lived through this, he would never let Pete live it down.

Hey, Len? If we don't die, I'm never letting you live this down! Pete said, finally containing himself.

Beneath Garrett, the ground trembled. He looked back at the pyramid just as lightning struck the top. *What's happening?!*

Governess's face stretched into a contorted smile. *My queen's plan has worked. Apep has opened the portal! It has begun, Garrett Turek. We are at the world's end!*

No! No, wait! This can't be right! Garrett said, jumping to his feet. But even as he said the words, beyond the shield, nephilbock abandoned the battle and began making their way toward the pyramid stairs. *The Keepers won't be here for another day! What is she doing?*

She is creating an opportunity, young lord. One that you would be wise not to waste.

This isn't right! This can't be right! he argued.

If your Keepers are meant to pass through the gate, they had better show up soon, Garrett Turek, Governess said.

No shit, Captain Obvious! Garrett said, a sick feeling twisting his stomach. Something was wrong. Something had to be wrong! Maybe James and the others didn't realize how close they were. Perhaps they were just beyond the trees on the other side. That could be it, couldn't it?

Young lord, we are past formal titles. Captain is unnecessary when addressing me, nor is it an accurate title for my position.

Garrett opened his mouth, but then stopped. There was a twinkle of amusement in her eyes. He'd almost missed it, but damn if it wasn't there. She was messing with him!

Governess cocked her head in what Garrett was sure was bogus bemusement. Then, pointing toward the pyramid, she said, *The portal is opening. I propose we make haste, cross the valley of ash, and make our way to the top of the pyramid without undue delay. My queen will ensure Apep does not leave the portal open any longer than necessary.*

They all stood looking at Garrett.

Gabi still isn't here, Garrett! We can't leave her! Breanne said pleadingly.

Garrett pressed his lips into a tight, determined line. *She will be here when she is supposed to be, Bre. She has to be. Because the truth is, Governess is right – we can't wait.*

Whatever happens, Garrett, I won't leave this planet without her, Breanne said, and Garrett knew she meant it.

None of us will, Bre, he promised. *The sages stick together. But we have to go. If she hasn't caught up by the time we cross, call to her.* He knew it was risky. For all he knew, calling to Gabi might pull Breanne to her, and he could lose them both. He wanted to sound sure of his plan, but in truth, he wasn't sure at all.

David swallowed hard, finally finding some words. *Gosh, I don't know, you guys – that looks worse than crossing into Mordor!*

Garrett looked at each of his terrified friends and then down the steep slope leading to the valley below. Trees continued past them, lumbering awkwardly forward as they descended the slope and, in doing so, pushed the already constricting valley border ever forward.

The look on his friends' faces told him they were scared absolutely shitless, and he was too. *Listen, guys, Frodo and Sam didn't have what we have.*

Yeah, well, what's that? David asked shakily.

They didn't have us. Garrett smiled.

Let's do this! Paul said.

What about the Keepers? Peter asked.

Just like Gabi, they will show up when the time is right, and we'll help them through when they get here, Garrett said, with a confidence he didn't feel.

Breanne pressed her lips together and nodded sharply.

Garrett nodded back, fighting to control his own nerves as he took her hand in his. *Now let's go!*

They stepped over the edge onto the slope, the steep grade and slippery rock forcing them onto their butts.

This is such a bad idea. So bad – so f-ing bad – so f-ing bad, David chanted as they slid down and down across rocky ash and mud.

Finally they reached the valley below and, with it, the front line of the forest.

On the other side of the green-tinted shield, Garrett saw nephilbock everywhere. Most were moving toward the pyramid, but high above, the dragons were still attacking, lighting the shield in flames. It felt comparatively safe behind the shield, but they couldn't stay there – they had to get to the top of that pyramid. *Governess, can we pass through?*

She stepped in front of him, her hand changing into a long sword. *Give the order, young lord!*

Guys, wait. Can we talk about this? David pleaded.

Lenny spun his staff.

Pete switched off the safety on his rifle.

Breanne drew her Toledo sword.

Paul cracked his knuckles. *Just remember what we practiced! Stay together! Move in formation!*

Garrett turned back to his friends. *When we are out there, listen to Paul! And stay on me! Pete, use your eyes! Only fire guns as a last resort! That goes for everyone. Gunshots will draw their attention for sure. Oh, and move fast! We have several miles to cover.*

Garrett turned forward again to Governess and gave her a nod. She smiled at him – maybe for the first time. And he was sure it was an actual smile, as genuine as the emerald twinkle in the tree woman's eyes. She nodded in return as she waved her hand.

The green shield in front of them dissipated like a wind-blown fog. Then came the sound. It hadn't been quiet with the groaning of the trees and dragon roars, but the sounds had seemed distant, muffled. Now sound crashed through the opening, a combination of cracking lightning and dragon screams, but mostly it was the sound of the God Stones punching a hole through space that assaulted them with a deafening force.

Behind him, David begged again, *Please! Please, guys!*

Their new reality assaulting him, Garrett gave him a look that was both empathetic and determined as he fixed his jaw tight.

Aw, dammit! Dammit, dammit, dammit! David chanted, bouncing on his toes.

Garrett turned away from David and the others as he looked back through the opening in the shield and into the chaos.

Steeling himself, he nodded to Governess and charged.

Garrett jogged forward, Lenny on one side, Breanne on the other, Paul on the other side of her. Pete and Governess were side by side and right behind him. David was bringing up the rear. In practice, Gabi would have been next to David. Above him, a dragon screeched. *Pete! It's diving!*

I got it! I might need to stop, though, Pete said, looking up.

No! There is a nephilbock to the right, Governess said. *Take my hand and let me be your eyes, Peter Ashwood.*

Okay, Pete said.

Garrett glanced over at Lenny, who just shook his head. When Garrett looked back up, the dragon lurched sideways, one wing twisted awkwardly. The dragon dropped from the sky, flailing and crashing into the ground with the force of a jet plane.

Nice, Pete! Garrett said, glancing back at Pete.

Um, thanks, Garrett, Pete answered, looking surprised that his own ability had been so effective.

They ran on, with the nephilbock thankfully focused forward on the temple and unaware of their presence, but Garrett knew that would only last as long as they were bringing up the rear. Above them, dragons flew past in the opposite direction, consumed by the encroaching forest.

As they drew closer to the pyramid, Garrett could see the nephilbock flooding the steps and surrounding the north face of the pyramid. *I wonder why they're mostly going to the north side?*

I think it's because there's probably only one opening in the temple above, and it faces the north side, Breanne said.

Makes sense. It's the path of least resistance. Straight up and in through the front door, Paul agreed.

Are we sure there isn't a back door we could use? Pete asked.

My people have confirmed there is only one door, Peter Ashwood, Governess said.

Garrett pushed down another stab of panic at the thought of trying to force themselves through a doorway full of nephilbock.

Well, lucky for us, the pyramid temple might only have one door, but it has a wide row of stairs on all sides. We can choose to climb any side we want, Breanne said.

They were approaching from the west, which was the less-occupied of the two sides Garrett had been able to observe. They could try to go at it from the back, but that would make their jog around the mountain-sized pyramid much longer. This made the west side their best bet. Best to just get up the stairs and then worry about how to get through the door and onto the temple roof when they got there. *No time to go around. We'll climb this side,* Garrett said.

The others agreed, and over the next several minutes they traversed nearly a mile without drawing the attention of dragons or nephilbock. But soon they drew closer to the crowds, all trying to get to the base of the pyramid.

It wasn't long before the sages drew unavoidably close to a company of five nephilbock walking some distance behind a much larger group. The giants were facing away from Garrett and his friends, affording them the choice to either slow down and stay behind the giants, hoping not to be noticed, or to continue to push the pace by giving them a wide berth. The choice was simple. They needed to keep pushing.

Above the pyramid, the small sphere was growing larger and larger, louder and louder, as lightning angrily struck again and again. Then, without warning, the sound was suddenly gone. It was like someone had pressed the mute button on the TV remote.

The sudden quiet pulled Garrett's attention up to the ever-growing sphere, and through it he saw… another world.

He frowned, trying to understand what he was seeing. The entire sphere was filled with strange violet… What? Snow? The whole thing looked like a giant snow globe that had just been shaken, but the color was wrong. Through the snow and perhaps a thin layer of clouds, Garrett could make out the shape of two suns, each shining with a different kind of light. The alien light sparkled through the crystal snow, giving it the appearance of amethyst, blowing like precious gems made impossibly feather-light.

Beyond the otherworldly snow, Garrett could see shapes, mountains maybe, but something else too – something moving inside the lavender blizzard. His eyes strained – desperate to see more, desperate to see what the hell was moving – but the edges of the sphere sucked in, flattening to a thin golden line that stretched high into the sky. On one side of the golden line, the strange snow blew into their world, swirling and gusting, while on the other side there was nothing. He frowned, realizing he was viewing the portal from the side, not the front. The golden line was the frame of the window.

Garrett stumbled, nearly falling, as new sounds filled his ears. Lowered voices, marveling to one another at what they had just witnessed high above the pyramid, mingled with heavy breaths and a particularly loud wheezing sound coming from David. He looked over at the giants, suddenly worried about the noise. *Guys, go wide. It's dark enough that maybe they won't see us.*

Garrett, we got to slow down soon. I can't hold this pace, David rasped.

Garrett slowed. The pyramid was still a few miles ahead, but thankfully at a mostly downhill slope. If not for the dragons, nephilbock, and the fact his friends would get dropped, he and Lenny could be there in twenty minutes tops, but it would take twice that at a fast walk.

The five nephilbock started shouting in a language Garrett didn't understand.

They see us! They're coming! David shouted, and Garrett remembered David was still holding the Eyra of Tunga.

What did they say?

Food! Humans! Kill them! David said, walking backward as his face drained of blood.

The nephilbock closed the distance in a few long strides.

Garrett grabbed for the running trails of his mind and with them his focus, slowing the two nephilbock closest to him to a near stop. He tried to catch a third one, but the giant stopped and turned its attention to Lenny before stepping into Garrett's area of effect. The massive beast had a thick red beard and was bald other than a tuft of hair stretching down its back in a long red braid. It stomped forward, baring its teeth like a grinning shark as it swung a spiked hammer the size of a steel anvil at Lenny's face.

Lenny juked the swing, and the hammer stuck into the ground with a quiet *thunk*. Before the giant could pull it loose, Lenny stepped onto the hammer, took two more steps up the handle, and leapt, striking the giant across the face with a full swing from his staff. The nephilbock stumbled sideways, its nose a spray of blood. In only seconds, Lenny had done serious damage and positioned himself on the beast's back. The next strike landed across the back of the giant's neck.

As Lenny's nephilbock fell, Garrett's attention was pulled away by Breanne shouting, "I don't think so!"

Garrett looked over his shoulder in time to see Breanne parry the swipe from a broadsword, dart in, and run her own sword deep into the belly of large-bellied nephilbock. Paul was also in motion, grappling with a solid nephilbock with no neck. Paul caught the muscular giant's massive fist in his own hands and squeezed. The giant let out a cry and dropped to his knees, the bones in his hand fracturing under Paul's crushing strength.

Directly behind Garrett, Governess was dealing with the fifth and final giant. He didn't need to look to know they must have been standing practically back-to-back because even over the chaos, he could hear her chanting in an even but firm voice. Strangely, he drew comfort from knowing she was there, and all five giants were accounted for. He just needed to deal with his two.

Garrett ran forward at full speed and leapt up, driving his sword from overhead and into one giant's chest. It took all he had to get the height combined with the striking power he'd need to penetrate the giant's chest, but the sword sank deep. The nephilbock's strange eyes rolled back, taking the beast with them.

From his left came the sounds of bones breaking as Paul finished his off with his bare hands. *Breanne!* Garrett heard her brother shout.

But Garrett couldn't look. He still held both nephilbock in slowed time. As the dead nephilbock fell back in slow motion, Garrett yanked his sword free and started forward for the other nephilbock, which was taller and thinner. But before he could get to it, he heard a bone-breaking noise come from the giant. Garrett released time, and both nephilbock dropped – dead before they hit the ground.

Pete stood next to him. *I think I'm getting the hang of this! The trick is to focus specifically on the bone you want to break! You got to really get in there and visualize the exact—*

Later, Pete! I mean, thank you! But later! Garrett turned to find Breanne still locked in a sword fight with the fat nephilbock. The giant was swinging a sword as long as Garrett was tall, like he was trying to hit a home run.

Breanne ducked. The blade swooshed over her head. She jumped up, her front leg lunging so far forward Garrett thought she might do the splits, but instead her lead foot planted as she thrust the sword, piercing the giant again, this time deep through its knee joint. She pulled the sword free as she stepped back and dodged the thing's massive fist.

Lenny and the others, having all finished with their own fights, now stood and watched.

Garrett started forward. *Why aren't you helping her, Paul?*

Does she look like she needs help? Paul asked.

As Garrett assessed the bleeding nephilbock, he realized Paul was right. This thing had more holes in it than a showerhead.

It's best if we just keep a lookout and let her finish this. That thing's all but done. Sis! Flunge! I want to see a flunge!

Flunge? Garrett asked.

It was her signature move at State!

No sooner did Paul say it than Bre executed it, parrying the nephilbock's sword and then leaping through the air in a flying forward lunge. The giant, slow and bleeding, didn't stand a chance as the narrow blade struck home.

This time, Breanne let go of the pommel, instinctively knowing it was done. She turned away before the beast hit the ground, finding Garrett, her brother, and the others. Garrett could see that she found no joy in slaying the creature. There was no cheering, only a shared understanding they had all done what needed to be done.

Everyone okay? Garrett asked.

They nodded.

Governess stepped forward, her own wooden sword coated and dripping from battle. *We should press on, young lord.*

They made their way southeast for thirty more minutes, still intent on taking the west stairs and praying that they could get there before the dragons gave up the fight with the trees and turned to the portal.

The combination of nephilbock pushing toward the portal, dragons blasting the trees' magical shield, and the cover of darkness seemed to be enough to keep the group from being noticed by more than the occasional single nephilbock and, on one other occasion, another small group of four. They handled all of these without injury to themselves and no need for David's healing powers.

Once they were close, they crouched behind a rock outcropping and studied a steeply rutted bank of dirt sloping away from the pyramid. *We'll need to climb up that steep dirt mound to get to the stairs,* Garrett said.

Breanne pointed. *That's where they piled the dirt they uncovered from the pyramid. The rains have eroded deep fissures. If we can get to the embankment, we can climb up inside of one of those fissures and stay pretty well hidden.*

But what then? Paul said, pointing to the stairs above. *They're mostly climbing up the pyramid's front, but then they're spreading out climbing the stairs on all sides as it narrows to the top. I don't think we can fight all of them! There are dozens, maybe even a hundred! There won't be anywhere to hide once we reach the stairs.*

They couldn't simply wait for everything to cross through – not from here, anyway. If they did that, who was to say Apep wouldn't close it before they got up there? No, Garrett knew no matter how bad it got, they had to keep pushing forward. They had to get to the top of the pyramid.

Look, guys, we have to get closer. We have to make it to the stairs and up them if we can. We can't miss the portal! Maybe they will clear off… or, like Bre said, we can hide in the fissures until they thin out. Garrett shook his head in frustration.

What if they don't clear off? David asked.

They have to go through the portal sometime, right? We just have to be close when they do, Garrett reasoned.

Yeah, and when they do, those thousands of dragons blasting the trees are going to be next in line for the portal! Pete said, his voice all worry and doubt.

If we wait for the dragons to clear, the portal may close before we enter. Look, I'm not saying I'm right about this, but I feel like we need to go. I feel… I don't know… I feel something pulling at me to get there now! Garrett said, looking pleadingly at Breanne.

She nodded slowly, as if searching for something within herself. *He's right. Garrett's right. We need to go now.*

Did you see something, sis? Paul asked.

No, I just feel it too. She looked at Garrett, and he saw the trust in her eyes.

He nodded. *Thank you, Bre.*

Breanne forced a smile as she held Garrett's stare. *Don't thank me. Just be right.*

35

A Sky of Fire

Saturday, May 7 – God Stones Day 31
Rural Chiapas State, Mexico

Gabi ran between moving trees and over churning ground through a walking forest lit by fire. Ash and burning debris rained down from above as the sound of trees crashing into trees, twisting wood, and snapping fibers filled her ears.

The forest was under attack.

She hadn't thought Cerberus would actually do this. She hadn't thought the dragon would really attack the trees. This was her fault! It was her escape that had prompted this; her running to the trees started a war! She fell hard as the ground rolled beneath her, flipping her onto her back.

Gabi gasped – there was no sky above her, only fire. She tried to roll back over, but the roots of a tree slapped over her like reins over a horse's back. The roots weren't looking to strike – they were reaching for a hold. Gabi yelped as the roots grabbed at her. They gripped, wrapped, and pulled, but she wasn't the ground, and she wasn't attached to anything! Instead, the roots dragged her under the earth as the tree pulled forward.

"No!" she screamed again, clawing at the loose earth, but her cries were blotted out by the sound of other trees crashing and pulling and burning. Her screams went unanswered. No one cared about a little girl in the way of giants – a little girl somewhere she shouldn't be.

All eyes were on the great fall of Hyperion.

Gabi didn't know if she'd die before the colossal tree landed on the ground or after, but she was sure she was going to die. As she slipped beneath the ground, she realized it would be right in this very moment. She kicked and clawed feebly at the earth as it swallowed her.

Sucking in a deep breath, Gabi squeezed her eyes tight, preparing for the inevitable crushing of dirt, when she felt the ground tremble. The noises around her changed from crackling fire and roaring dragons to a concussive collision of massive tree meeting immovable earth. A powerful sonic wave of exploding tree filled her world even below the ground.

Gabi's eyes, still slammed shut, did not dare to open against the rolling earth. She felt her body lift and tumble, quickly losing track of which way was up. She wanted to scream! María Purísima, she wanted to, but all she could do was squeeze her eyes tight and hold her breath. This was all there was – her last defense against certain death. When her chest began to burn, she felt something grip her hard around the waist. Oh, no! Another root wrapping her to pull her deeper still!

Her lungs were afire when finally she let out her last breath and sucked in dirt, expecting the pain of being yanked in two. But instead of being ripped down, she was lifted. The dirt fell away. Her body was no longer in the earth nor on the ground. If it wasn't roots wrapped around her waist – then what was it?

It is okay. I've got you! Zerri said, flapping her wings.

Gabi choked and spat dirt from her mouth, unable to speak even in her mind. She blinked, pawing at her dirt-filled eyes with her wrists. She was alive.

Wings pumping, Zerri darted between trees at incredible speed, the ground beneath Gabi racing by too close. Not crashing into a tree would be nearly impossible if the forest were standing still in the light of day, but this forest wasn't standing still, and the sun had already set.

Zerri! Gabi screamed, finally able to form words. *Pull up above the trees!*

I cannot! If I do, the dragons will see us for sure. Trust me, Gabi. I've got this! Zerri said, twisting onto her side as she narrowly dodged the trunk of a huge sequoia.

Trust her? Trust the daughter of her parents' murderer? How could she? No, Gabi, trust the dragon who saved you from certain death, she told herself. And despite everything, she did somehow trust her. *Which direction are we going?*

Does it matter? Away from fire and falling trees! Zerri said, and this time she pulled Gabi tight to her chest, tucked her wings, and spun in a full three-hundred-sixty-degree twist. The ground flashed by in a blur before becoming a streak of bark, then smoky sky, then bark again, her dizzying view finally settling back to the ground.

As the forest moved forward, Gabi tried to get her bearings, which was impossible flying this fast and low to the ground. The smoke-filled forest wasn't helping either. *What is that?* she asked, noticing a green glow to the left.

Zerri must have looked too because she answered, *I have no idea. Some kind of magic—*

Zerri's words were cut short as her whole body rocked to the side.

The ground came fast – too fast. Gabi screamed, *Breanne!* She was unsure why she screamed for her. There was nothing Breanne could do for her now.

As the ground closed in, Zerri twisted onto her back, crashing into the forest floor at full speed. Gabi heard all the air evacuate the dragon's lungs in a guttural exhale. Zerri's grip on Gabi went slack as they slid through foliage, dirt, and rock, but Gabi didn't dare let go. She held on to one talon, gripping it desperately with both hands, trying not to fall off.

Finally, the dragon slowed and stopped.

Around them, trees pressed forward, sure to swallow her again if it wasn't for the larger dragon lying in their path. But beneath her, the dragon wasn't moving. Gabi placed her hands palm down and pressed on the dragon's scales. *Zerri! Please, Zerri? Please wake up! Please! Please be okay!*

In her mind, Gabi heard a voice, but the voice wasn't Zerri's.

Gabi, can you hear me!? Breanne asked.

Hearing Breanne's voice was overwhelming. Enough to nearly break her. She shook the dragon again. *Zerri, please!* Then she changed her focus. *Bre! Bre, Santa María, I'm here! Where are you?* the girl asked.

We're on the west side of the pyramid, Gabi! Still at the bottom, but we're climbing now! You have to get here! There was a brief moment of silence and then, *Gabi, do you hear me?! Can you get here?*

Gabi lay down and pressed her ear to the dragon's chest, trying to listen for something – a breath, a heartbeat, something. Did a dragon have a heartbeat? Was that a breath she heard now? There was too much noise! The trees bending and moving as they marched, dragons screaming in the distance. She couldn't hear anything! She couldn't be sure! But she knew if she couldn't get Zerri to wake up, she had no chance.

Gabi, are you there?! You have to come now! Breanne's voice cracked.

Gabi's own throat shut up tight as her dirt-crusted eyes welled and blurred. *I will find a way.*

You have to, Gabi! I won't leave this world without you!

36

Serenade

Saturday, May 7 – God Stones Day 31
Rural Chiapas State, Mexico

I *think I see our opening, guys – look.* Garrett pointed as a group of nephilbock passed in front of the rutted wall of dirt. They paused briefly, looking up like they might start climbing, but for whatever reason, they moved on toward the front.

When Breanne had said she felt something too, she hadn't been lying, necessarily. She was having a feeling – not a vision. This feeling came from her gut and it was telling her she should trust Garrett Turek. Of course, she had been trusting him. After all, by ditching a prophecy to cross a continent during an apocalypse and save her from an evil elvish wizard, he had done the most romantic thing any boy had ever done in the history of romantic things. Never mind that she'd ended up saving him; it was the intention that counted. No, trust wasn't an issue, but in this moment, what she felt almost seemed beyond trust – almost… otherworldly. Then another thought occurred to her. She sure hoped love didn't feel otherworldly.

Well, just for the record, I don't feel shit except my ass trying to hold back the load I'm going to drop in my pants if we get attacked by all those giants on the stairs! David exclaimed in what was as close to panic as she had seen in boy's wild eyes. Maybe not as bad as the time the bat landed on his back and he almost fell into a pit of rats, but close.

It will be okay, David, she said.

Okay? Look at those things! How is this going to be okay?

That's our shot, Garrett said, nodding towards the now-vacant wall. *But we have to go now and go like hell, before more come this way. Now it's only sixty yards tops, but David, you are going to have to haul ass! And I mean haul!*

Lenny slapped the boy on the shoulder and offered words of encouragement in his most serious voice. *I need you to dig deep into that mustache, bro. That's where your power lives! It's all in the 'stache! You can do this!*

You are such a dick! You know I'm the slowest! What if I get dropped and a giant… David trailed off, looking sick as he rubbed his palms across his knees.

Lenny smiled. *I will be right beside you the whole way.*

David nodded slowly. *You promise, Len? Don't mess with me! You know I can't fight one of those things by myself!*

Promise, Lenny said, slapping David on the back.

Count of three, Paul said, holding up a finger. *One!* Then another. *Two!* And finally, another. *Three!*

They ran.

To Breanne, it felt like when she was a kid, running through the night with her brothers, playing midnight tag. She had the same feeling that a monster hiding in the shadows would grab her from behind. She pushed harder and harder, burning battle adrenaline like gasoline. Finally, she slammed into the dirt wall. Gasping for breath, she realized it was much taller and steeper than she had thought. Garrett and Paul were already there as Pete and Governess came sliding in, slapping palms to the dirt just after her.

She turned to find Lenny twenty yards back, pulling David to his feet. He must have fallen but, even worse, several nephilbock had appeared from the darkness to their right and were running toward them.

Run, you guys! Run! she shouted into their minds. Someone was pulling on her arm. *Garrett! They're going to get caught!*

Climb, Bre! he said, pushing her into a crevice. The dark void was narrow and only a couple of feet deep. She found a foothold and pushed herself up, but when she reached for the next, there was nothing to grab. *I… I can't find anything to grab, and it's too steep!*

Below Breanne came a soft, urgent chant. "Flahak doe okidoe! Eshoki oz oz akshi flah zae. Flahak raydoemue! Flahak ozzae!"

A glow enveloped Breanne as dirt rained down on her from above. She squinted her eyes and glanced up to find vines stitching their way back and forth across the rear of the crevice and up into the darkness above.

Climb, Breanne Moore! Climb! Governess urged from below.

She scaled the crevice up into the darkness as fast as she could – not knowing where the others were, not knowing if they were safe. Breanne kept reaching blindly, grabbing for the next hold and the next.

Two things happened in her desperation, neither having to do with the other, nor her current situation. First, she heard a voice – a familiar voice, but it came as a frightened scream.

Breanne!

Breanne's heart leapt to her throat. *Gabi!* But before she could answer, a second thing happened. Breanne's eyes went cloudy as a not-too-distant future came into view, and as it did, Breanne lost herself along with her grip on the vines. She felt the sensation of falling as she tipped backward from the crevice.

As she fell back, her foot slipped into the vines, tangling. In that split second of time, music filled her ears. Not the horrible Christmas music that had once haunted her nightmares – something else. Her vision cleared, but not to the present. She knew she was seeing the future – a fleeting glimpse of something important, a clue. But only in the form of a confusing flash, like a pile of puzzle pieces spread across a table. Then, her body slammed into the wall of the crevice along with the back of her head and the future was gone, jolted away from her.

Breanne Moore, you must climb! Governess's voice pleaded from below.

She felt the tree woman's hand pushing her up, lifting her as she reached for the vines once more. *Where are the others?* she asked, blinking back the pain from the impact to the back of her head. Thankfully, the embankment was soft, and she hadn't hit anything substantial enough to split her head open, but damn if it didn't hurt.

No time! We must hurry! Governess said. *Do not stop and do not look down, Breanne Moore!*

But she did look down, and as she did, Governess transformed, her arms and legs growing longer as she stretched her body out from the wall. *Come! Everyone, pass beneath me quickly!*

In the darkness below, she saw Pete and the shadow of someone behind him climbing through the hole that Governess had created. Then she remembered the voice she'd heard before she fell. *Gabi, can you hear me?* she asked, knowing the risk of answering could teleport her directly to the girl like last time, but frankly, she didn't care. Time was running out!

Bre! Bre, Santa María, I'm here! Where are you? the girl asked.

We're on the west side of the pyramid, Gabi! Still at the bottom, but we're climbing now! You have to get here! Breanne reached, pulled, climbed, and reached again. *Gabi, do you hear me? Can you get here?* Unbearable silence stretched between them as Breanne reached up again and then again until finally she couldn't stand it. *Gabi, are you there?! You have to come now!*

I will find a way, the young girl said, but she didn't sound confident.

You have to, Gabi! I won't leave this world without you! Breanne said, tears filling her eyes. No matter what; no matter if she was the only one who stayed. No matter if Garrett, her brother, and her father all made it through the portal, she would stay behind. For Gabi, she would stay. She couldn't leave her alone in this world.

She was at the top of the crevice, but if she climbed out, the giants would see her immediately. *Guys! What do I do?*

Pete crawled up next to her. With the two of them side by side, there wasn't even a foot of space between them. Pete peered up the stairs. *Jesus, there must be a hundred of them on the stairs!*

What do we do? she asked.

The others are right behind us, Pete said.

Guys! Don't stop! There's one right behind me! It's going to get me! David screamed, his voice pitched high in hysteria.

David Leigh, calm yourself. Pass beneath me. The nephilbock shall come no farther, Governess said, and then she was speaking in the language of the gods in words even the Eyra of Tunga could not decipher. "Flahak rahshi doe zae! Rahoki ozokioz ray eshray akray oz doe! Ak flah zaeokirah ray rayrayoki rahray oz shioki okidoe oz doe doeeshshiray flah akray raydoe ray!"

The walls shook as below them the vines stretched and grew. A moment later, Breanne heard a nephilbock's scream. *What did you do?* Breanne asked.

The vines below us have become deadly daggers of poison. As I said, none of the foul beasts shall find their way up this crevice. But be warned, in time, they could simply double back and choose another path up. I have only bought us a few fleeting moments.

Guys, what's the plan here? Pete asked, looking as pale as David had. *As soon as we climb out, the nephilbock are going to see us! We can't fight all these things. Do we just wait them out?*

I… I'm thinking, Garrett said.

Well, think fast, bro! Lenny urged. *There are more nephilbock down there, and they're not climbing this crevice! They're going around!*

At the sound of Lenny's voice, Breanne thought about the glimpse of the future she'd seen earlier. She still wasn't sure exactly how, but it was important, and it had to do with Lenny. *Lenny, can you climb up here, please?*

What? Yeah sure, but why? Lenny asked.

Just trust me. I need you to climb up. Guys, help Lenny pass.

Bre? her brother called. *What's this about? It's a long way down, and if the fall doesn't kill him, deadly thorns or the nephilbock will. Can you at least tell us what's so—*

Actually, I'm good, Lenny said. *Pete, climb down.*

My pleasure! I'm a whole lot closer to those things than I want to be. Pete retreated back down the crevice below Breanne.

A moment later, Lenny climbed up next to her. *Sorry, this is kind of tight with my guitar on my back.*

Yeah, um, about that. Lenny, I need you to turn so I can help you unstrap that guitar, she said.

Lenny frowned. *It's okay,* he said absently as his attention drifted up past the landing to the stairs where dozens of nephilbock stood sentinel. *Jesus, there are so many of them! You guys, the giants aren't climbing the stairs, they're just standing there. I think Apep has them standing guard until the entire army makes its way up the front stairs! Balls! I bet he's got a bunch on the other sets of steps too!*

Lenny, turn and take that guitar off… please? she asked again.

Bre, I don't understand your problem with my guitar. I'm not crowding you that much. I'll climb back down if you want. Hey, you never said why you wanted me up here—

Lenny, she interrupted. *I called you up here to take off that guitar. Can you trust me?*

Lenny hesitated, giving Breanne a hard look. *Of course, I trust you, but I need this guitar, Bre. If we…* He stopped himself. *WHEN we make it through that portal, I have to have this with me. They probably won't have guitars on Karelia, and I just don't think I want to be part of a world where guitars don't exist!*

Lenny! I'm not trying to make you give up your guitar, she said carefully, knowing how her next words were going to sound.

Then what? he asked, his forehead crinkling in confusion.

I need you to play it.

Play it? Now? Why on earth would I play it? Lenny asked.

I need you to trust me, Lenny. I need you to climb up there and start playing.

Climb up there? With them? And… and play my guitar? You know how crazy that sounds, right? Why? Why would I do that?

I saw something, Lenny… A… a vision.

A vision?

Yes, a vision. We were all up there and there was music. Acoustic guitar music.

Lenny's face went full lemon as he stared back at her. *You're serious! So, what then? What happens when I climb up there? Do they become instant Lenny fans and start a mosh pit, and then what, we crowd-surf all the way up to the portal?*

Breanne frowned. *No, I don't think so. I think—*

What you mean, you don't think so! Do you even know what's going to happen?

Hold on a sec, Garrett said. *I'll go first.*

No. Unless you can slow about a hundred nephilbock? Breanne asked, hesitating. When no response came, she continued. *It has to be Lenny.*

Well, I'll be right behind you, Len, Garrett said.

Breanne watched as Lenny pulled himself carefully upward, peeking out over the edge of landing.

Jesus, they're right there! I won't get three strums in before they kill me, Bre!

Lenny's voice was suddenly shaky, and Breanne realized the boy was frightened to death. Despite all his bravado, he was truly scared. Until this very moment, she'd seen Lenny as a carefree spirit along for the adventure, along because he was Garrett's best friend – his best friend until the end. Ready to face down anything. But not now – not this. What the hell did she expect? Could she blame him?

He lowered himself back down, his face less than a foot from hers. In the low light of distant dragon fire and otherworldly color cast by the God Stone portal, Lenny's eyes glistened pleadingly as he leveled his gaze like an errant hammer blow to her soul. A sudden wave of guilt washed over her. What gave her the right to ask him to do this when she couldn't even tell him what would happen? What gave her the right to send a boy to face a hundred monsters with nothing more than a guitar? All she knew for sure was that this was the way – the only way. She opened her mouth, knowing what she had to do. She couldn't ask Lenny to go this alone. "Lenny," she whispered aloud. "Lenny, I will—"

What's happening?! David shouted into her mind, causing her to startle and nearly lose her footing once more.

Lenny! Wait! Don't you go! David shouted.

Lenny's forehead stayed creased, but for a different reason now. *What's wrong with you?*

I'm coming up. Sorry, Paul! Look out, Garrett. Hold on, Lenny – just you hold on!

Ouch! You're crushing my shoulder! Pete complained as David shoved past him.

David, what are you doing? Garrett asked.

I'm going with him! That's what! I'm the healer and I'm going! David said, with a determination Breanne had never before heard in the boy's tone.

Can we all just take a second here? I appreciate it, David, I really do, but I still have to climb up first, and I'm telling you—

Nope, I will go first, David said, wedging his way upward.

David, I don't know what has gotten into you, but knock it off. We can't all three fit in this space! Lenny said.

David stopped climbing. *Listen to me, Len. I know how you feel! I feel it all the time and when I do, you're always there. Sure, you give me crap about my amazing 'stache, but I know it's only because you aren't capable of growing your own awesomeness. But I also know I'm going to be okay, Lenny! I know because you got my back! You always got my back! I'm just saying I... I know you're scared, but don't you worry, Len! I got your back!*

Lenny closed his eyes, and for a minute she thought sure he was going to unload a barrage of insults at David. Instead, the boy took a deep breath, opened his eyes, and said, *Bre, are you sure?*

She nodded and forced a smile. *And I promise, I will be right behind you.*

Right behind me because I will be right behind him! David said.

What song am I supposed to play? Lenny asked.

I... don't remember, she said, but then she wasn't sure she ever really knew.

Well, don't you think that's kind of important?! he asked.

Outside the crevice, they heard a grunting sound that was so deep it sounded like a lion growling.

Breanne Moore, we are out of time. The nephilbock have made their way around my trap and are nearly to the top, Governess said.

Just play whatever comes to mind – whatever you feel, Breanne said in her best encouraging voice.

Right. Great. Perfect, Lenny said, passing his staff downward toward David. *Here, take this.*

Seriously? David asked.

If you're backing me up, you need something other than that noisy rifle unless you want to draw the attention of a hundred giants.

David reached up for the staff. *No thanks. Apparently, that's your job.*

I hate you, Lenny said, cracking his neck from one side to the other. *Well, here goes everything,* he said, reaching up.

Oh, Lenny? One more thing. You need to focus while you play. Focus on the nephilbock.

Riiiiight… that's helpful… thanks, Lenny said sarcastically.

Breanne shrugged apologetically.

Lenny vanished over the side as David climbed up past her as quick as he could with one hand holding the staff.

Breanne climbed over the edge right behind David to find a half dozen nephilbock bounding down the stairs with a dozen more on their heels. To her left, three more giants were climbing over the edge of the dirt embankment and onto the landing.

Lenny shot a pleading look back to Bre.

Play, Lenny! she shouted.

Lenny set his jaw and looked back toward the charging nephilbock. Then, holding the guitar by the neck in his left hand, he raised his hand high in the air and brought it down on the strings as he stepped back into a fighting stance. Or maybe that was his rocker stance – she wasn't sure.

Is that… Is he playing "Sweet Child O' Mine"? Paul asked.

He's totally playing "Sweet Child O' Mine," Garrett answered. *I would know that guitar riff anywhere!*

Lenny's panicked voice exploded in Breanne's mind. *Guys! If this was supposed to piss them off, it's working perfectly!*

Lenny continued to play Slash's famous chords as Garrett and the others began appearing beside her. Something was wrong. This wasn't working at all. Oh, dear god, what had she done? Her thoughts flashed back to the vision. She had seen them climbing the stairs; she had heard the music… The nephilbock were… what? Dead. She remembered seeing them lying on the stairs. Weren't they dead?

This isn't working! Lenny shouted again, running past them along the landing away from the first of the advancing nephilbock to reach the bottom step.

From the opposite side of her, Paul intercepted the first giant that had climbed up the embankment. The giant stomped down at Paul, but Paul was too fast, knocking the other leg out from under it. What was she missing? What the hell was she missing? They were dead in the vision. There was music playing, and the giants were dead. Wait! She'd heard something else! That's it! *Sing, Lenny! Sing the lyrics!*

Oh, come on! I don't sing! I shred!

Just do it! Breanne shouted into his mind.

Lenny sang halfheartedly, his voice breaking, "Whoa, oh, oh, sweet child o' mi – yine."

The giants kept coming.

Still not working! If you were hoping to kill them with my voice, it isn't happening! Lenny shouted.

Breanne threw herself back onto her butt as another giant appeared over the dirt wall and lunged for her, its massive six-fingered hand swiping just over her head. She raised her pistol and took aim, but just before she squeezed the trigger, the giant slowed to a near stop. Then two more slowed as they appeared from over the side. *Garrett!* Breanne said with relief.

I can't hold all three of them for long, Bre.

Breanne scrambled backward and turned back to the stairs.

David stepped in front of Lenny, placing himself between the boy and a hundred charging nephilbock. He cocked the staff over his shoulder like a baseball bat. *Oh! No… You… Don't!* he shouted at the closest giant.

Behind them both, Pete took aim with the rifle.

Lenny was right, she thought, they weren't dying. What had she missed? What had she done? An old panic crept up, one that used to freeze her in place just like the time-frozen giants Garrett was struggling with. It wasn't slowed time that held her hostage – it was debilitating fear. But Breanne wasn't that girl anymore. She could do this! She could solve this! In the vision, she was on the stairs surrounded by dead nephilbock, the guitar was playing, and Lenny was singing. She knew that had to be right! Think! She was moving up stairs, careful not to… Not to what? Not to wake them up! They weren't dead in the vision! They were… they were sleeping! *Lenny! Sing to them and focus on putting them to sleep! Focus, Lenny! Put them to sleep!*

A burly giant covered in a carpet of red chest hair drew back its sword as David swung the staff.

Oh, for shit's sake, we're going to die! Lenny said, turning back toward the stairs and screaming at the top of his lungs, "Whoa, oh, oh, sweet child o' mi – yine!"

Lenny's voice cracked again, but this time something happened. His voice changed and magnified. As if infused by magic, Lenny's voice transformed into perfect pitch, emanating up the stairs as if blasted from a bullhorn by Axl Rose himself.

Simultaneously, the hairy giant's sword collided with David's borrowed staff, and the sound of fracturing steel pierced the night sky. The colossal length of gleaming metal blew apart in an explosion of golden energy and steel shards.

David stumbled back, nearly colliding with Lenny before landing hard on his ass.

Breanne gasped wide-eyed at David, who sat staring in wonder at the staff now lying across his lap. *I knew it! This thing is magic!*

When she looked back to the stairs, she found Lenny standing on the bottom step, his fingers still playing the chords, but the guitar didn't sound acoustic anymore. It sounded like an electric guitar… No. No, not exactly. It was strange, somehow more. Like Lenny's voice, it sounded magical. Above Lenny, the giants slowly lowered themselves to the ground, sitting, then lying down, then closing their eyes and going perfectly still.

She turned to find Garrett lowering his hands. The three giants he held in time were all lying prone, still as the dead.

My god, Lenny! You did it! You did it! Breanne laughed.

Only thanks to you, Bre… and David, Lenny said, offering David a hand and pulling the smaller boy to his feet. *You and that pornstache of yours came through, you fearless little shit!*

David beamed, all teeth and whiskers. *This staff is magical, Len – did you see what it did?!* he said excitedly, offering the staff back to Lenny.

David, whatever that was, there was no way you could have known that would work. Listen to me because I am only going to say this once. Lenny smiled, placing a hand on David's shoulder. *Don't never, never ever EVER, shave that 'stache! No matter what anyone says, even me.*

Does this mean you're going to stop giving me smack about my 'stache? David asked in a voice full of hope as he extended Lenny's staff toward him.

Lenny waved off the staff and laughed. *Keep the staff, David, you earned it. But hell no, of course I'm going to keep making fun of you! That thing looks like a ferret crawled onto your face and died there!*

Guys, this is touching, but we need to move! Garrett said, pointing up the stairs.

He's right. Her brother nodded. *We need to get up there before more of these things come.*

Or worse, before the dragons head for the portal! Pete said.

Breanne stepped around a now-snoring giant and up the first few steps. *Be careful not to bump them and wake them up.*

I suspect the magic Lenny cast will have these vile creatures sleeping until the spell dissipates, despite any accidental nudging, Breanne Moore, Governess said, stepping next to her, but Breanne noticed she was also walking with care.

Really? Are you sure enough to test your theory by giving this ugly one a kick to the head? Garrett asked.

They are all ugly ones, young lord, she responded, as if tasting something foul. *But your point is well taken. The power of the God Stones is mysterious indeed.*

It felt like it took forever to climb what must have been close to a thousand steps as they made their way cautiously toward the top. The entire way up, Breanne's heart racked her chest. Whether caused by the hundred sleeping giants, the distant roars of a thousand angry dragons, or the color beyond color cast by the portal above, she wasn't sure. But when she felt a gust of wind hit her back and heard the familiar voice, she was sure why her breath hitched suddenly and her pounding heart stopped cold.

"Garrett Turek! I've been waiting for you to show your coward-ass face!"

37

An Unlikely Alliance

Saturday, May 7 – God Stones Day 31
Rural Chiapas State, Mexico

C*erb, do you see that nephilbock there?* Jack pointed toward King Helreginn, standing at the base of the pyramid near the front staircase. Helreginn and a few of his larger nephilbock were overseeing the army as they ascended the pyramid toward the portal – toward home.

I see them, Taker.

Take me to him.

Shouldn't we be protecting the nephilbock from Pando's army?

Cerb, no one commands us. Our queen is dead, and we lead the dragons now.

What about Apep? the dragon asked.

Apep? Apep thinks he's using us, but he has another thing coming.

Cerberus laughed. *Very well, Taker! Very well!*

Cerb landed behind the king and his men. The first one to turn and notice him was the biggest of the King's guards, tennis shoe necklace guy, and damned if he wasn't gnawing on that ankle like a dog with a bone. At the sight of Cerberus, the red Converse All Star dropped from his mouth to hang back in formation. He licked his lips and grunted.

The king and the others turned.

Jack slid from Cerb's back and approached the king.

The king dropped to one knee, and his men did the same. Even down on their knees, they still towered over Jack. "King Helreginn, we need to talk," Jack said, making sure to speak aloud in case Apep or anyone else was listening.

"How may I serve you, Taker?" Helreginn asked.

"There is something you should know, and I don't know how you will like hearing it, but it has to be said. Oh, you guys can stand up," Jack said, motioning them to stand.

The king and his men stood, all eyes staring down at him expectantly.

"You are half nephilbock," Jack announced.

The giants looked at one another, then back at him.

"You think we don't know what we are?" Helreginn asked, but there was no shitty attitude in it.

Jack was glad he understood their language now. It would make this so much easier. "No, great king, what I want you to understand is what you are not."

"What we… are not?" The king frowned, exchanging confused looks with his men.

"You aren't nephilbock any more or less than you are human," Jack said.

The king narrowed his eyes, as if he'd been insulted. The other three giants shifted uncomfortably.

"It's alright. I don't say it to piss you off. I don't care for humans either, and I'm at least half one myself. But that's not all I am, King. I'm way more than that," Jack said, thumbing his chest. "Not that I give two shits, but humans will never accept me as one of them… not now. But see, dragon blood runs through my body too, yet I'm not a dragon neither, not all of me anyway." Jack let that statement hang there for a second. The next part was going to be tricky.

"I think we're a lot alike, you and me. You see, we'll never be accepted by humans, not that you want to be. But I'm here to tell you these gods you worship on top of that pyramid and that elf who wants you to fight his war – they won't ever accept you either. Not fully, not once this is over. They're using you. And when it's done, and you have no more use, they will discard you and whatever's left of your people because you aren't nephilbock either. Maybe they'll find you a deep hole like the one you just crawled out of and tell you to go there where you can live out the rest of your days, or maybe your fate will be even worse. I can't say for sure. But I know what ain't going to happen. They ain't going welcome a bunch of half-humans into their kingdom unless it's to serve them their dinner… or be dinner."

The posture of the men changed, and for a split second Jack thought the king's men might actually attack him. But the king held up his hand. "What is your point? Why have you come to me with this? What do you want, Taker?"

He was pretending – pretending what Jack told him either wasn't true or wasn't news. "My point is that I accept you, brother. And the difference between my relationship with the dragons and yours with the nephilbock is that I rule my other half and you worship yours. If you want to be accepted by the nephilbock, you need to overthrow your gods and make them bow down to you. Or you can join me and the dragons, where you and yours will find acceptance… brother."

The king stared down at Jack for a long moment and then said, "You dare to blaspheme against our gods, little one!"

"If you're talking about Ogliosh and the others, they fear me. So, I ask you, who is the god?" Jack spat. "You might also want to remember who protected you – who saved you from the forest and who slayed the sea demon."

Beside Helreginn, his men drew weapons.

Jack stared right back up at them. *Be ready, Cerb.*

Cerb stood with three heads fixed, one on each guard.

Jack let his own eyes bore into the king's as he focused on the Sentheye, ready to rip the nephilbock's life away at the slightest hint of attack. But no attack came.

The king looked over his shoulder, then back to Jack. The king knelt down, whispering so only Jack could hear. "Neither I nor my people will ever forget what you have done, little god," the king said, showing his teeth. "You became the ruler of your betters to find acceptance. I will not allow my people to become slaves or be discarded by anyone – not that insane dökkálfar, not your dragons… and not even our gods. We have waited too long and come too far to be betrayed. Yet, there have been no promises broken."

Jack frowned, trying to puzzle out what all that meant. When he thought he'd understood, the corner of his mouth twisted up, he raised an eyebrow, and he whispered back, "No, not yet, King, but once they're done using you for what they want, you'll see what's up. Come find me then."

Helreginn's scarred face was somber as he nodded ever so slightly. He stood and looked back down at Jack.

"Cerb, we're finished here. Carry on, King Helreginn, but hurry up and get your army through. My dragons can only protect your people from what's coming for so long."

As Jack flew Cerb toward Pando, a thought occurred to him. Apep couldn't care less whether Jack lived to make it through the portal or not, so long as they protected his army until they were safely on the other side. "Defend my army until everyone is through, Jack." That's what Apep had said. *Oh, don't worry, you crazy elf son of a bitch, I'll do your job, and we'll just see how long the nephilbock follow you when I'm the one that has been out here in the thick of it protecting YOUR army while you sit up there on your pyramid looking down at the rest of us.*

As Jack looked toward the towering tree queen – who actually looked less like a tree and more like a giant human chick with an ugly-ass Afro – he realized the truth of it. Apep was afraid. He called himself a god but was nothing more than a chickenshit. Not Jack, though. If there was one problem Jack didn't have, it was standing his ground even when he should have thought better of it. Even when it meant a broken nose or busted teeth. Jack wasn't a coward.

What's the plan, Jack? Cerb asked.

You just fly grizzly-dick straight toward that oversized stick and we light her up like a stack of kindling! Jack ordered.

Cerb obeyed, and when they got close to the green shield, Jack reached for Pando with all the disease he could muster. As he did, he smiled. He had already killed thousands of trees, an ancient dragon, and a sea kraken. Now he would add giant tree queen to the list!

But as he reached for Pando, the smile fell from his face.

Through the green fog, Jack watched as the tree woman's own face screwed into an evil grin and his power stalled. He couldn't penetrate her shield! *Light her up, Cerb.*

Fire blasted from all three heads at once, hitting the shield with a blinding shower of orange, red, and blue flame. But the dragon's breath was Cerb's and Cerb's alone. Jack hadn't added anything to it, and though Cerb was the most badass of all the dragons, Jack could see it wasn't enough. It just plain wasn't enough. The shield absorbed Cerb's fire just like it had from all the other dragons attacking.

Behind the haze of green, Pando's grin twisted into a sneer as she held up a hand and then dropped it.

Get away from her, Cerb! Go! Go! Go! Jack shouted.

Cerb banked hard to his left.

Jack stole a glance over his shoulder in time to see the night sky fill with objects flying out from behind the green shield. Whatever they were, they were coming toward them fast. As the first one closed in, Jack shouted, *Boulders, Cerb! Boulders! Go faster!*

Cerb's scales rumbled beneath Jack as the great beast let out a growl and pumped his wings.

Jack watched helplessly as dragons fell from the sky by the dozens behind them. Giant boulders smashed into them with such force most were dead before they hit the ground. Anger welled inside him. He looked ahead, toward the pyramid, then back to the line of trees. The trees were moving forward faster now, closing the distance between them and the pyramid. As they raced closer still, Jack could see most of the nephilbock were through the portal, and it would soon be time to order the dragons through. All that remained were the nephilbock already climbing the pyramid itself. The front stairs, and then the stairs on the other sides.

Shall we take another run at her, Jack? Cerb asked.

Something wasn't sitting right with Jack. Apep had known he'd have no chance against the tree queen and her army, and Jack was getting damn sick of being used. He wasn't a coward, but he needed to think smarter. He needed to think like Apep.

No, Cerb. Forget her. We need to focus on getting our army through the portal. We do that, and the tree queen doesn't matter anyway.

Dragons, hear me now! Jack thundered. *I have returned to you the slayer of the Sea Demon, Brother of the God Son, Nightshade the Taker! Your queen is dead! Mivras is dead! You follow me! The time has come to leave this place! The trees are no longer our fight! Our battle awaits us on Karelia! Turn to the portal now and prepare to fight something we can actually eat!*

Jack's mind filled with cheers as hordes of dragons abandoned their fight with the trees' shield and turned to the portal.

Cerberus roared until his roar turned to a laugh. *Well said, Taker! Well said indeed!*

Jack's face lit in a twisted smile. *Damn right it was!* Jack said as Cerberus sliced through the night air. *Damn right!*

Up ahead, Jack noticed something on the west side of the pyramid. *Cerb? Do you see that? Fly closer to the side of the pyramid.*

What is it?

The stairs, Cerb. It looks like something killed all the nephilbock on that side!

Cerb dove to get a closer look. *There are humans near the top!*

At the sight of the group on the stairs, an overwhelming pulse of hate coursed through Jack's veins. *It's Garrett Turek! Land behind them, Cerb!*

The massive dragon slowly flapped its wings and settled onto the stairs.

Jack felt his heart pound with rage as all the blood rushed to his red eyes. "Garrett Turek! I've been waiting for you to show your coward-ass face!"

38

Common Goodness

On Earth – God Stones Day 30, before the portal opens
On Karelia – Moon Ring 1
The Creators' Mountain, Karelia

Silence filled the terrace, as if all sound had lifted from the mountain in a gust of Karelian wind, but there was no breeze – only sharp gasps followed by a deafening hush. *There it was,* Turek thought, the impossibility of it spoken aloud. *Our Great Mother has shown me.* There, he'd said it! A weight heavy as the universe itself lifted from Turek's shoulders, and he knew with his whole heart this was right no matter what came next… This was the way.

Finally, it was Typhon who broke the shocked silence. "Liar! Why? Why would our Great Mother show herself to you? You, the youngest! You, who abandoned your duties!"

Turek smiled. *No turning back now,* he thought, and plunged forward. "Not just me, Typhon. I think she shows herself to all of us if only we bother to look. On Earth, my people reigned superior over every living thing. There were no dragons to oppose them. No elves. No giants. Well, not at first – but I will get to that," Turek said, clasping his hands behind his back as he began to pace in front of the creators' thrones. "I noticed it first when my humans began worshipping the stars, then the Earth, then soon they were worshipping the sun and the moon and the sea. They worshipped Norse gods, Greek gods, Hindu gods, and after some time they began worshipping one called Buddha and later one called Jesus."

"So what? Your humans worshipped false gods! All our favorites stray. What does this have to do with the Great Mother?" Rán asked.

"False gods? I thought so too, at first. But I watched, and I listened. You see, with no elves or giants to war with, my humans found reasons to war with one another. Whether it be for land, race, or religion, they found reasons. But then, when I met this one called Buddha and later the one called Jesus, I suspected something greater at work. There was a thread, a common" – he paused, searching for the word, then brightened – "goodness… yes. There was a common goodness to their teachings. I began to suspect the Great Mother might be working through them."

"Through these humans?" Druesha laughed.

"Yes," Turek answered, no hint of humor in his voice. "Them and many, many more. Who they were made little difference, as it was the fundamental message of goodness that drew my suspicion. But you see, my suspicions were all anecdotal. I chalked it up to my longing for you, my brothers and sisters. But later, it became clear there was much more to it."

Turek's fellow creators stayed quiet now, listening.

"I want to tell you the story of Garrett Turek, the first son born of a prophecy I made up. I want to tell you how each of your creations played into the prophecy coming true. A prophecy I had only minimal influence over executing. For I chose to live as one of my humans – not just appear as one. I actually took a wife, made love, bore a child."

The Great Hall exploded in shouting, each trying to be heard over the other.

Finally, Ereshkigal held up a hand, silencing the hall. "You fell in love with your creation and bred with her? You bore a child?"

"I did," Turek said simply. "Each of you should have the experience of living at least one lifetime as your creation. I lived many. I experienced both life and death as a human many times." He couldn't tell if the look Eresh wore now was one of disgust or hurt, and though he didn't want to hurt her, he hoped it was the latter. "Now, if I may continue?"

Typhon shifted uncomfortably and nodded a hundred heads.

"After my daughter was born, I wrote a prophecy as a sort of test – a test to see if my suspicion that our Great Mother was not only paying attention but influencing, and perhaps even more. Soon, as I prophesied, Apep escaped his dungeon prison with no help from me. Soon after, I allowed Apep to kill me. Then I stood back, giving the test my full attention as I observed. And as I had written, nine more women were born in my bloodline, and then a male named Garrett Turek."

"Convenient coincidence!" Aurgelmir grumbled. "Apep's escape isn't enough to convince me, nor is a lucky guess at your blasphemous lineage!"

"Silence, Aurgy. I have a feeling he is just getting started," Rán said.

"Thank you, Rán. Indeed I am. Indeed I am." Turek launched into the entire story. A story of facts too impossible without godly intervention. Eventually he told of Lenny Wade, Prince Syldan's own son, and how he ended up adopted and sent to the tiny town of Petersburg, becoming the closest friend to Garrett and his number one sage. He told of how Syldan followed the trail of his long-lost son and ended up in Petersburg himself – just in time to play a role in the sage's destiny. Turek explained how Syldan faced Apep at a critical time and provided special guidance along with the Eyra of Tunga, a magical item that had already proven critically important in their journey. He told of Breanne Moore and how her family found the God Stones in the first place, and how she too became one of Garrett's sages, although admittedly he had helped with that.

"So, you admit, you interfered after all?" Typhon accused.

"I told you, brother, I would speak truth – all of it. I dreamed of her and Garrett. And in my dreams I provided them guidance to find one another," Turek said, knowing how it sounded.

"You… you say you dreamed of them? What else do you dream, brother?" Durin asked.

"Yes, do tell us of your dreams," Druesha mused.

"You find it so hard to believe I dream?" Turek asked.

"No. I dream too… of my creations… of my work," Ereshkigal said. "I used to believe it was our Great Mother providing me with creativity."

"But not anymore?" Turek asked.

"I… I don't know what I believe," she said quietly.

"Don't you see? The dreams I had on Earth were real. They were real for me and for Garrett, and the Moores. But know this. I did not instigate them and, if not me, then who but our Great Mother herself?" Turek swallowed. "You may believe nothing I tell you. You may choose to believe I manipulated this whole thing, but if you believe one thing, you must believe this. In the last dream I had of Garrett, he had just drowned in the river, as I prophesied. As he lay dead on the banks of the river, I met him in a dream. During the dream, he felt the presence of his father and a few others he had held close in life but whom had sadly passed on."

Durin broke in, "How do you know what he felt?"

"Because, Durin, I felt them too – not only felt them, but saw them. They were there in the dream – in the distance. I told Garrett I was proud of him. I told him he was dragon-marked and reborn of dragon blood and fire. Then he asked me if I was god and I told him no, but that I was one of seven creators and the one who created humankind."

"I don't see the point in—"

"Wait, Durin," Ereshkigal said, holding up her hand again. "And what did the boy say?"

Turek smiled. "He asked, 'Then who is god? Who created you?' 'The mother,' I said. 'The one who clapped her hands and created something when there was nothing.'"

Frowns of confusion fixed on the faces of his fellow creators.

"Clapped her hands when there was nothing?" Turek repeated, but now it was a question. "Those aren't my words. Don't you see? And I would never have referred to our Great Mother as 'the mother.' But she would not refer to herself as 'great,' only 'mother.' Then it happened again with another human called James. I knew James in life. Now he is leading the Keepers to the portal. James dreamed of me when all my Keepers were about to be killed by a group of the dragons. We spoke in a dream, in which I said, 'Mother has given all the ability to touch her.' James woke from his dream and, for the first time, used the Sentheye to hide his people from the dragons. Again, my brethren, these were not my words."

"You're saying the Great Mother was speaking through you?" Druesha breathed.

"Yes. Yes, she had to be. And there is something else. I told Garrett he must set right what has long been wrong, and to do this he must follow his heart. He did follow his heart, and somehow against all odds he finds himself nearing the portal to Karelia."

Silence lingered for a long moment in the Great Hall. No doubt the heft of what Turek had shared, if it were believed, was weighty indeed. And if they were to believe, what did this mean for them – for creation and for Karelia?

"You have brought us a story, Turek," Typhon said, a long, spiked tail whipping upward and then slapping back down against the bejeweled floor.

Durin lifted his war hammer and pointed it like an angry finger. "I agree with Typhon, brother. As compelling as this is, it is still only that – a story. How are we to know any of this is true? You bring us words, but you bring us no evidence that our Great Mother has, for reasons unclear to us, chosen your banished humans to… to what?"

Druesha's leaves rattled softly. "I do not know what this could mean even if it were true, but with no proof…"

"With no proof, it means nothing," Typhon said flatly.

Turek nodded, unclasping his hands from behind his back. He stopped pacing and turned to face them straight on. "You are right, of course. Except for one thing," he said, holding up a finger.

"Go on," Aurgelmir urged.

Turek's eyes twinkled like twin stars. "I can prove it, brother."

39

I Won't Be Him

Saturday, May 7 – God Stones Day 31
Rural Chiapas State, Mexico

With only a handful of steps ahead of him, Garrett spun at the sound of his name. There, a hundred feet below, sat Jack atop a black-scaled dragon with glowing red eyes and three massive heads. The three dragon heads roared in unison, and Garrett noticed the dragon's eyes weren't the only eyes glowing red.

What… the… hell? Lenny said slowly.

Garrett reached for time, splaying his fingers. *Take him, Pete!* It was only right Pete should deal with Jack after what he did to his mom. *Everyone else go! I'll hold the dragon!*

We're not leaving you, Breanne said.

Yeah, no way, Lenny said.

Cerberus roared again, but the roar came slow and wrong, like a slow-motion yawn. Garrett had him, but it was all he could do to hold the massive creature in the envelope of time. *Hurry, Pete!*

"What's the matter, Garrett? You got nothing to say?" Jack asked, his own voice just fine as he slid off Cerberus and onto the stone stairs.

Garrett aimed every bit of his focus at the dragon, creating a pocket of time, a prison to hold Cerberus in. But, he realized with sudden dread, it hadn't included Jack.

Jack continued upward, climbing one step, then another. "You got nothing to say about what you did to Danny?"

Four more stairs, and Garrett could see the red stripes on black leather that seemed to complement those inhuman eyes. What the hell had happened to him?

Jack stopped and looked to his left, spit, and then kicked one of the sleeping giants in the face.

The giant's eyes popped open, and Jack spoke strange words, pointed at Garrett, and then shouted the same incomprehensible sounds again.

How in the hell did he learn to speak giant? Paul asked.

The giant sat up drunkenly.

Garrett strained to hold Cerberus. Beside him, Pete shook uncontrollably. *Anytime, Pete! Anytime!*

I can't do it! If I do it, I'll… I'll kill him! Pete said, but the words came as an affirmation to himself.

I fail to see the problem with that, Paul said, reaching down and grabbing hold of a sleeping nephilbock by the leg.

Below, Jack kicked another nephilbock, stirring it from Lenny's sleep spell.

Paul closed his eyes, focusing, as Garrett's control on the massive dragon slipped.

Taking two steps back down the pyramid stairs, Paul twisted his torso and let fly the giant.

Jack dove to the side, but the flying nephilbock crashed into two of its brethren, just woken by Jack. The force knocked all of them back like bowling pins into Cerberus. As the great beast regained time, fire bellowed from all three angry heads.

Cerberus held his ground well enough, but the impact was enough to knock the dragon's heads to the side, throwing the flaming death into the temple wall far to the right of Garrett and the others.

Behind Garrett, Pete was screaming, *I can't be like him! I can't become what he is! If I kill him, that's what I am, Garrett! I won't be him! I won't let him make me like him!*

It's okay, Pete. But for god's sake, either give someone the death stare or run! Garrett shouted.

Behind Jack and Cerberus, thousands of dragons filled the sky, all heading for the portal. All heading straight for Garrett and the others.

Below them, Cerberus stomped up the stairs, all talons and menace. Stone scraped and chipped as the dragon's neck built toward another burst of flame.

Jack reached out, fingers splayed.

Everyone! Go!

In only a few steps, they reached the landing. But as Garrett looked back, he saw one dragon head appear, then another, and still another. Six red eyes and three mouths open and full of molten iron set to pour! The wall to the roof was fifty feet up if it was an inch, and the distance to the corner was another sixty or seventy feet.

FUBAR! Paul shouted.

Garrett's skin flamed with the hot itch of dragon runes as he spun, turning back toward the dragon and praying he could somehow block the dragon fire and save the others, but there was no way – no way he could block it all – no way this would work! *Turek, if you can hear me, please! Don't let them die!*

"Kill them, Cerb! Kill them all!" Jack shouted.

40

We Are So Close

Saturday, May 7 – God Stones Day 31
Rural Chiapas State, Mexico

James led his Keepers by hoof, pedal, and foot to the northeast end of the clearing. "Halt!" he shouted, bringing everyone to a stop just short of the tree line, where alerce, redwood, and oaks rose high into the evening sky. The old giants stood sentinel, statue still, as if guarding secrets hidden in the darkness beneath their canopies. Darkness that looked like it could swallow James and devour all the men and women he led. Yet beyond the many trees and the secrets only they knew, and the shadows thick and black, was the way – the only way.

James dismounted Shadow and walked toward the trees. "I don't know why you brought us to this clearing, but if you were going to kill us, wouldn't you have just done it yourself?" he asked, looking up the trunk of a medium-sized alerce tree.

The tree didn't answer.

James frowned. Did he expect it to answer? Maybe, he thought. Maybe he did. He knew the trees could hear him. He was well aware of Garrett and his sages' agreement with the trees. "Will you let us pass then?"

James looked past the tree and into the forest beyond, steeling himself. If they didn't part, he couldn't get the wagons between them. Was this another trap? He'd no way of knowing, no time, and no choice. He could only see the terrain beyond the trees rise up gradually before darkness claimed it all.

The giant statues of wood remained quiet and still. James stole a glance back over his shoulder, but only a glance. His eyes flicked back to the trees as he spoke. "Annie, tell the others to unhitch the wagons and take only what they can carry comfortably. Pack the horses with what food and water we have. We're going in single file."

From somewhere deep within the shadowed obscurities, James heard a loud scream. He startled at the silence broken, then frowned. He'd heard this strange scream before.

Annie looked grave.

"It's okay, Annie, it's only a howler monkey," James said.

James helped Elaine and Dr. Moore unhitch their wagon and saddle the horses. "Do you think the trees are going to let us pass?" Dr. Moore asked.

James nodded. "I do. I think they have to."

"Have to? Why?" Dr. Moore asked.

"Because we have to be at that portal before it closes. That's the prophecy," James said, as if there was no other answer.

"Just look at it, Charles! Look at the portal! I know at this angle and from this distance it's hard to tell, but it's true, there's a whole new world only steps away! In a few miles, we will walk into Karelia, and Turek will be there, waiting to greet us! I just know he will."

Dr. Moore nodded absently, and James could see the worry he was trying to hide. "Dr. Moore. It will be alright. We will keep you safe."

"It's not me I'm worried about, son. I just want to get to my kids. The sooner the better."

"I know, and we will. You still have plenty of rounds for that pistol?" James asked, nodding toward the man's shoulder holster.

Dr. Moore drew the forty-five and ejected the magazine. He checked the load, then slid it back in and thumbed the safety. Grabbing nervously at his pants pocket, he nodded again. "Three magazines."

James nodded back, buckling the girth strap of one of the horses. He walked around to the front of the horse, lifting each leg to ensure the saddle settled. "Good, you will be riding Fred. If you need to shoot, Fred won't spook."

Dr. Moore cleared his throat, looking a little more at ease. "Old Fred and I are well acquainted, aren't we, boy?" Dr. Moore said, climbing onto Fred.

"Probably has something to do with all those treats you've been feeding him, Charles." Elaine smiled.

Fred neighed approvingly.

As the Keepers moved into the trees, a heavy uneasiness swelled inside James. He felt as though at any minute the forest might animate and attack them – crush them. And if they did attack, there was nothing James could do to save his people. He had no idea how to fight a force of trees, not with his limited numbers and armory. Neither guns nor swords would offer any practical defense against a giant oak tree, let alone the massive redwoods and alerce trees. These out-of-place trees must have traveled a great distance to be here, but to what end, James wasn't sure. For now, the trees were still, as if waiting for a signal.

The deeper into the forest James led the Keepers, the more he realized they were winding through a narrow pass between two mountains. When finally, they reached the end of the narrow pass, the Keepers found themselves standing on the shore of a wide stream. On the opposite side of the stream, the forest was alive.

James held up a fist, bringing the Keepers to a stop. This was the first time he, or his Keepers, had seen a forest moving en masse. Roots burst from the earth, flung themselves forward, and plunged down, piercing the ground as they flexed taut to pull back up through the earth. Rhythmically, the trees swayed as they shambled upstream, their waterlogged canopies hunched like the weary shoulders of battle-worn soldiers long on the march.

"Good god! Can you believe this?" Dr. Moore asked, his thick eyebrows knitted up and mouth seeming not to know whether to smile or draw back in terror.

"The magic of the God Stones is powerful indeed," Elaine said, her face sharing none of the confusion or concern of Dr. Moore's, but James wondered if it should.

"Well, now we know why the trees aren't moving behind us."

Dr. Moore nodded. "They're waiting for the trees ahead to clear out. The question is, where are they going and why?"

"Look," James said, pointing downstream. Fire and strange light illuminated the sky beyond. James pulled binoculars from his saddlebag and assessed the distance. The stream gave him his first unobstructed view at any real distance since entering the forest. "No, Dr. Moore, the question is, will they care if we join them?" He pointed downstream. "Because I'm afraid their path is our own."

"What do you see?" Dr. Moore asked.

"I see fire. I see… I see some kind of green… green magic. War, Dr. Moore… I see war."

Elaine smiled. "Be not afraid. We will pass through it, Charles."

Dr. Moore nodded, and when his next words came, they twisted at James's soul. "Those three men you lost back there – they probably thought the same thing."

James pulled the binoculars away from his eyes and cast his gaze on the ground. He swallowed dryly. The pain raked his soul like sandpaper.

"I'm sorry, James, I didn't mean to…"

"No. It's okay, Dr. Moore," James said, but he offered no explanation for why it was okay, because he honestly didn't have one. Why had Turek allowed three of his men to die? And although he knew the risk that even more could die was very real, he knew this was the way – had to be the way.

Maybe more would die. The fact was, the prophecy didn't say they were invincible, only that Garrett would lead them through the portal. They couldn't follow the stream on this side – sheer cliffs had seen to that. And they couldn't go back. There was no time to find another way, even if one existed. No, they had to cross the stream, which meant they had to enter the walking forest. This was the way.

A familiar scream startled James from his thoughts. It was only one at first, but soon the cries of the howler monkeys were unmistakable. Then James heard something else even less mistakable – the cries of his Keepers.

James twisted back in his saddle. “Annie! Get them across the stream!” James shouted, spinning Shadow toward the commotion.

Annie spurred her horse and shouted, “Keepers, on me!” She charged forward across the stream, others splashing into the stream behind her.

Dr. Moore drew his pistol.

Elaine nocked an arrow on her recurve bow.

James had no doubt of Elaine’s ability with the bow. He’d seen her hit a running squirrel at twenty-five yards more than once. She’d been a big part of the reason they’d often enjoyed fresh meat over the last few weeks. What James wasn’t as confident about was Dr. Moore’s ability to hit anything from horseback with that forty-five. “Cross, Dr. Moore! Whatever is coming, we will handle it!”

“No. I want to stay with you. I want to help, whatever it is!” Dr. Moore said in a tone that wasn’t a question.

As the screams and howls grew close, Keepers flooded out of the narrow forest passage in a mass panic as they plunged into the stream. James would have to wait for all the Keepers to exit the passage before he could do anything.

James spun a restless Shadow in a circle. She was raring for a fight. “It sounds like howler monkeys alright, but they rarely attack.”

When the last of the Keepers burst from the forest passage, James got his first look at what was attacking his people. “Dear god!”

“More of Apep’s work!” Elaine said, drawing her bow and loosing an arrow.

The arrow crossed the twenty yards, finding the first and largest howler monkey, striking it in the throat. The monkey, stretched up to its full height of eight feet, maybe more, fell back and thrashed. Three others screamed as they moved away, each one dragging a Keeper into the jungle by leg or wrist, while still more advanced.

“Cover me!” James shouted, drawing his arming sword from his hip. "Go, Shadow!" Shadow bolted forward, running through the advancing howlers as James cut one down from the saddle.

Dr. Moore opened fire, dropping two at thirty yards with the forty-five and, as James promised, Fred didn't spook.

Ahead, a woman screamed.

A familiar rage filled James's chest as he spotted one howler dragging a woman. Afraid the oversized monkey would kill the woman or vanish into the ever-darkening forest, James threw the sword, burying it in the beast's furry shoulder.

James leapt from the saddle and ran weaponless toward the beast. Now that he was off his horse, the thing seemed even bigger. As James closed the distance, he roared.

The monkey answered in kind.

James bared his teeth, fists clenched.

The monkey beat its chest.

At less than five yards, a loud crack echoed through the night. James pulled up short.

The howler monkey dropped its arms, fell back, and relaxed in death.

James turned to find Dr. Moore fifteen yards back. "That was fine shooting from the saddle, Dr. Moore!" James shouted, pulling his sword from the dead monkey's shoulder.

"You doubted me, son?" Dr. Moore smiled grimly.

Gunfire erupted again as Sir Spider, Lady Hammer, and Lady Shredder shot down several others as they advanced. The remaining howler monkeys must have quickly realized that, despite their size, they were no match for superior firepower, and they retreated back into the shadows of the forest.

James helped the woman up. Her arm hung wrong, likely dislocated or worse. "You three" – James pointed toward Spider, Hammer, and Shredder – "I want you covering our flanks until we are safe on Karelia. Expect anything! Expect everything! Dammit! I won't lose another Keeper between here and that portal! Am I clear?"

"Yes, Commander!" they shouted together.

"Good. Now let's get Ms. Clare to Doc Schafer and see if he can't get that arm back in place." James climbed back onto Shadow, set to make his way back up to the front of his Keepers.

"Son?" Dr. Moore said.

James turned. "Doctor."

"You did good. You saved that woman."

"No. I lost Keepers. I failed to keep my people safe."

Dr. Moore opened his mouth to speak, but James couldn't do this, not now. He turned Shadow away as quickly as he could, clucking his tongue.

The truth was, James had no idea who or even how many he had just lost, and there was no time to figure it out now. A sick feeling filled his stomach. Three weeks had passed since he'd led the Keepers away from Petersburg. Until today, he had only lost one – one who hadn't listened and had run out into the open when he shouldn't have. Now, in only one day, he had lost how many? Five for sure, but how many before they got here? Six more? A dozen? Their screams echoed in his mind. They'd trusted in him, in Turek. His stomach twisted. These people had been doing everything right. They had been following him, and he had failed to keep them safe, failed to keep the promise of leading them to the portal. He tipped his head back to consider the sky. *Turek, please, we are so close!*

James's eyes dropped to the path ahead. He had just sent his people into a walking forest on a path to a war. "Come on," he said to Shadow, "we have to get to the front of the line."

41

Find Your Moment in the Pain

Saturday, May 7 – God Stones Day 31
Rural Chiapas State, Mexico

Jack's voice echoed off the temple wall as Breanne ran harder than she'd ever run. "Kill them, Cerb! Kill them all!"

Too far, she thought, as goose bumps pricked her skin and her neck hair stood rigid. Maybe… just maybe she could make it to the corner of the temple before the flames came. Push, girl! Push with all you have! And she did, and dammit, there was a chance… there was a—

A giant stepped out from around the corner. Not a half giant. Not some mix of human and nephilbock from the center of the Earth, but a full-on, thirty-foot-tall, one-eyed monster of a creature. They were all going to die! Breanne's heart dropped into her stomach like a lump of concrete.

She slid to a stop and raised her sword, but it was like raising a needle to an elephant.

The giant raised its fist.

Tunnel vision obscured her periphery, giving Breanne the sense it was just her and the cyclops until a familiar voice chanted. Breanne blinked. *Governess!*

Behind her, she heard a roar that sounded strangely high-pitched. She half expected to feel flames and, in a desperate moment, considered jumping over the side of the pyramid. She would slide down the steep, smooth stone all the way to the bottom and then have to figure out how to climb back up without getting killed and without missing the portal altogether. But she hesitated. Something about that roar wasn't right. It wasn't just not right – it was all wrong. It didn't sound like Cerberus, and it was coming from the wrong direction.

When Breanne chanced a quick glance back over her shoulder, her eyes widened. A dragon, much smaller than Jack's three-headed Cerberus, dropped from the sky onto the three-headed beast's back. Its talons ripped at the larger dragon's center head, and it spit fire. But it wasn't the dragon that slacked Breanne's jaw in wonder – it was the girl sitting atop the dragon, holding on for dear life. It was Gabi!

Bre! Run! Gabi shouted.

Cerberus bucked and growled. One of his outer heads reached back and bit into the smaller dragon. The smaller dragon shrieked and hissed, fighting to free its shoulder from Cerberus's mouth.

Breanne turned back to find Governess had shifted into a tall tree Ent, like those who stood staggered along the perimeter casting the shield spell. She wasn't as tall as the thirty-foot cyclops, but she must have been fifteen feet or better. The tree woman threw her arms around the giant's waist, locking her hands together in a twist of wood as she lifted. For a second, Breanne thought she might actually lift and throw the behemoth. But despite her strength, the giant had the size, leverage, and power.

The giant spun, slamming Governess into the temple wall.

"No!" Breanne screamed, running forward and sinking her blade deep into the giant's knee.

The giant howled out a gravelly cry of agony, swiping a hand toward his knee as one might aim to bat down an angry wasp who'd just gotten a taste.

Breanne dodged, jumping back.

Garrett, Lenny, and the others were there now, Garrett slashing with his own sword as Paul grabbed the giant's ankle and twisted.

Behind them, Jack followed. "You're not getting away this time, Garrett!"

The giant dropped to a knee, its one enormous eye stretched wide in horror. It shouted something she didn't understand.

A voice answered from above them, on the roof of the temple. "You're too late, Garrett!"

Breanne felt bile surge up her throat.

"The portal is open! My army is all but through, and your Keepers…" Apep laughed. "Where are your Keepers, dear boy? I told them their prophecy was a farce! I told my brother, and all who would listen, yours was nothing more than a fool's errand perpetrated by a weak human wizard named Turek. Not a god! Not like me! Never like me!" Apep leaned out over the top of the temple roof. "Just look at what I have done! I've written my own prophecy!"

Garrett! Look out! Breanne shouted so only he could hear.

Garrett spun just in time to see Jack closing in.

His hand shot out, fingers spread, trying to put Jack in a time hold. Yet despite her warning, Garrett hadn't been fast enough. Jack had already cast his disease, evident as Pete buckled, dropping to the ground, his skin turning a jaundiced yellow. All Garrett could hope to do now was slow Jack's draining and diseasing of Pete.

"No!" David shouted, his own skin turning yellow, but with a golden glow. The younger boy pushed one hand out like Garrett had; he reached down and pressed his other hand against the bare shoulder of a sleeping nephilbock. Lemon-yellow light poured thick from his outstretched fingers into Pete's back. It was different from the other healings she'd seen David do. This wasn't only a glow. It was like… like dense smoke, but yellow, and bright as the sun.

The crunch of bone pulled Breanne's attention from Jack and David as overgrown Governess broke the giant's hand around her throat. With a groaning twist, she ran a sword through the giant's stomach.

Beside her, Paul yanked the giant's ankle out from under him, and together he and Governess wrestled the giant toward the edge of the pyramid, creating the opening she needed.

Apep, she thought, craning her neck up to find he was no longer there. Breanne clenched her jaw and bolted past Paul and Governess toward the corner of the temple. In her mind, she heard David begging Garrett to let Jack go.

He's still… draining Pete's… life…, Garrett, I… can't… keep… pouring… it on! David begged.

Dammit! Garrett shouted back. *Okay… but when I release him, put everything you got into Pete… and David, dammit, don't pass out! You make for the corner fast as you can!*

A slew of angry shouts and what must have been metal crashing into stone erupted behind her, but Breanne didn't slow, and she didn't look back. She rounded the corner, sliding on a thin layer of dirt as she ran toward the temple entrance. There were no nephilbock in sight. They must have all made the climb into the temple and through the portal by now.

She entered the corridor that led to the temple. She'd been here before, but her memory of it was fuzzy – she'd lain half dead after Apep had kidnapped her. God, it had only been a few weeks earlier, but it felt like a lifetime.

Several more yards down the corridor, light spilled in from openings on both sides. Straight ahead were stairs that descended in a spiral wrapped around a cylindrical stone shape. There was a time when knowing how this structure worked would have fascinated her archaeologist's mind. Right now, she couldn't give two shits. She wasn't going down – she was going up. Up to wherever Apep was. She took the stairs on the left and climbed.

When Breanne stepped onto the roof of the temple, she wasn't ready for what she saw. Across the roof stood the portal, edged in golden liquid. It stretched hundreds of feet into the air, and even though she'd seen it from below, now that she was standing before it, she knew it was like nothing she'd ever seen – nothing she could have ever imagined. Her lips parted and her sword drooped as she stared through it, and into… another world.

Only steps away, on the far side of the universe, a weak flurry of the curious purple flakes tumbled to the snow-covered ground. From the sky high above, magenta clouds parted to reveal the deepest blue Breanne had ever seen. Deep and dark, like she could swim in it. But it wasn't her sky, and it wasn't her sunshine punching peculiar rods of light between the clouds. And, as the clouds parted further, racing away as if late for something, she realized, there wasn't only one sun – there were two: one yellow, one white. Beyond those, she could see three moons, each partially eclipsing the one behind it. There was something else, another planet maybe? Or was it another moon? She wasn't sure, but it had rings – red rings. Breanne's eyes lowered from the ethereal sky to find it collided with mountains, but they looked all wrong… They looked, she didn't know… upside down, maybe. Wait, were they floating?

She had expected a wormhole or something. Some long psychedelic tunnel, maybe. But who was she to hold any expectation of something so profoundly impossible? Still, here it was, as real as she was, solid as the stone beneath her feet.

Movement caught Breanne's eye, and her gaze fell, drawn from the otherworldly landscape to the threshold beyond, where an army of nephilbock collided with men riding creatures that resembled horses but weren't horses. Her breath hitched as she tried to drink it all in with her eyes. The men weren't quite men either. Their skin was dark blue as the sky, with swooping *S*-shaped eyes matching Apep's own. How? she wondered. How was the army already there, waiting? She didn't see a city, only an open prairie of bizarre plants and tall reeds dusted in fine blue crystals, framed beyond by odd mountains in a world illuminated by the light of two contrasting suns.

On the outskirts of the chaos, high upon a hill, sun gleamed off golden plate armor as an elf skirted the madness of battle and rode toward the portal. Armored warriors flanked the shining elf on both sides. Breanne's eyes widened, fixed fast to the men, the sky, and the world beyond—

When the pain came, it came sudden and awful, lighting her mind in brilliant fireworks of instant agony. Reflexively, her hand went to her face as she dropped hard to the stone roof, her sword clanging away from her. Breanne's eyes rolled back into her head, clouding over, taking her away from this painful moment and to one happening elsewhere.

As if from a perch on a cloud, Breanne saw a huge chunk of California, Nevada, and Oregon fracture from the continent and sink slowly into the ocean. Before it completely disappeared, the image changed, and Breanne watched the United States split apart from the Great Lakes, across Illinois, Missouri, Arkansas, Mississippi, and Louisiana, tracing the line of the Mississippi River. The vision blurred and changed again. This time, she was in a place she'd seen before. Only now she was on the ground, standing in the very spot she'd first met Garrett and the last place she'd seen Turek. She was back in New York City, standing on a sidewalk in the ruins of Times Square. The city was in even worse shape than before, with most of the building destroyed by the trees or smoldering in the melted ruin of a dragon feeding frenzy. Even in her vision, her gorge rose at the sight of a street covered in human remains and dragon dung. *Why? Why are you showing me this now?!* she shouted. *Why!*

Find your moment in the pain, a majestic voice answered.

She somehow expected this voice to belong to Turek, but it couldn't have been. The tone belonged to a woman.

I don't understand! Breanne pleaded.

The voice spoke again. *Mother has given all the ability to touch her. Find your moment in the pain!*

Her eyes cleared, and she was back on the temple roof – Apep standing over her.

"The one who got away! Come back for what? Revenge? You won't find it here, girl. This is my moment!"

My moment, she remembered from the vision. Breanne squinted up at him, confused by his appearance. Patches of skin were missing across his forehead; his pointed ears were torn at the tips, and strange-colored blood crusted his face. But beyond his wounds, his eyes were sunken and black, his body reedy, like he'd lost a bunch of weight and aged a hundred years. He pointed down at her, his blackened fingers wafting a foul smell reminiscent of rotted flesh and ripe body odor.

"Well, young Moore, you're the budding archaeologist. You of all people should know Egyptian history, and therefore you no doubt know the stories of Apep from your studies? Even before this glorious day, I once ruled your kind. In Egypt, they feared me. They called me the god of chaos, the snake god, the nemesis of Ra. But thanks to your kind's incredibly brief memory, history is full of holes. My brother and Turek imprisoned me while humans told stories of chopping me up and destroying me. But I cannot be destroyed!" Apep reached down, snatching her up by a fistful of braids.

Breanne screamed as he jerked her to her feet. The pain pulled her right back into that place where Apep stole her and teleported her over and over until he nearly killed her. She flinched, too late, as a bony backhand struck her across the jaw. Pain shot through her face again as her bottom teeth pushed through her lower lip, filling her mouth with the tang of copper.

The insane elf spun her, twisting her arm behind her back as he yanked back on her braids. "Look, little Moore! Look at what is coming!"

To her right, thousands of dragons were closing in, filling the night sky as they raced toward her, toward the portal. Beyond the dragons, the tree line was lit in an ever-constricting green glow as Pando pressed forward, her army of trees pushing toward them faster than Breanne had seen them move before. For the first time, Breanne noticed four more nephilbock were standing across the roof near the edge of the portal, focused only on the portal itself.

They nodded toward Apep and stepped through.

Apep placed his mouth close to her ear, washing her face with his foul breath. "I would love to leave the portal open longer – long enough to ensure the complete destruction of this wretched planet – but you see there! The tree bitch is coming! But she will be too late! You are all too late!" He laughed then, but there was a note of disappointment amid the triumph. "I am sad I will not get to watch this place be destroyed. Ah well, if this planet somehow survives, they will go back to simply being trees," he said, nodding toward Pando. Then he jerked hard on Breanne's forearm, yanking it up between her shoulder blades.

She cried out.

"You, however, I still have time to kill." He spun her back toward himself and struck her again, a hard fist to the face that rattled her teeth and buckled her knees.

Breanne's body dropped involuntarily into a squat as she blinked back tears and spit blood. In her peripheral vision, a dragon head appeared over the side of the temple roof – then another and then another as voices echoed up from the stairwell.

Apep grabbed her by the throat and lifted her up off her feet to meet his eyes.

Help! Please! She couldn't breathe. Her neck was going to break! Her throat! She couldn't breathe!

Breanne's eyes bulged as a voice from the vision rang out in her mind. *Find your moment in the pain.* When she had transported to Gabi and then back, she hadn't understood how she did it, but now, in this moment of blinding pain, she realized the message *was* the answer. She had thought of wanting to be with Gabi just as she had fallen and hit her head. In that exact moment, she had teleported, appearing next to the girl. And when she returned to Garrett and the others, it was the roar of the dragon that had pained her ears to the point she thought they'd burst. Pain was the answer! *Find your moment in the pain!*

Apep twisted, dangling her over the edge of the pyramid.

Breanne found Apep's sunken black orbs and mouthed the words, "Thank you."

A confused frown creased the dark elf's distorted face, but quickly it turned into a sneer. He let go of Breanne's neck and dropped her, just like he had dropped her father's best friend, Jerry, into the Money Pit on Oak Island one month ago. He'd sent Jerry flailing to his death, and now he was sending her to meet the same fate. Breanne plummeted down, gravity making quick work of the fifty-foot drop to the stone stairs.

But Breanne had something poor Jerry hadn't had. She had the pain, the moment, and the answer. Unlike Jerry, Breanne didn't scream as she fell because she knew the stone below would not claim her.

When Breanne reappeared, she was standing directly behind Apep. Unlike the other times she'd teleported, this time she hadn't gone far, she wasn't dizzy, and she didn't need to orientate herself. Looking up at the tall elf's back, she still held her wits – and that wasn't all Breanne Moore held.

Her fingers wrapped tight around the hilt of the dagger, drawn from the sheath strapped to her lower calf when her knees had buckled. Breanne didn't hesitate for a single second as she lifted her clenched fist high above her head. Drawing back the blade, she thought of all the fear this evil creature had unleashed into the world. In a split-second flash, she thought of Gabi and what his bringing the God Stones to this planet had taken from the poor girl. Then she thought of her father, and how Apep had nearly killed him. Breanne roared out all the hate she held, thrusting the double-edged stiletto into Apep's back, driving it as deep as it would go.

The blade sank all the way to the hilt.

Apep spun toward her, his widened eyes a kaleidoscope of confusion and pain. He reached behind himself, futilely grabbing at the knife. The dark elf's sunken face twisted from rage to panic.

"Thanks for teaching me how to teleport!" Breanne said, stepping to the side as Apep staggered forward, swiping his bony hands out in a miserable effort to grab her.

Across the temple roof, Jack was sitting atop his dragon.

Garrett, Paul, and the others were there now, having climbed the stairs to the rooftop.

Gabi and a small dragon came up the stairs behind them.

For a moment, confusion held them all in a moment of inaction. Except for Apep. His terrified eyes ignored them all now, turning instead toward the portal. Toward what he had waited thousands of years to get back to. Toward his birthright. His kingdom. His heaven to rule.

As Apep approached the portal, still pawing at his back, he stole a glance back at Breanne as some realization lit his face. "It's hard to… to pat yourself on the back… when there's a knife sticking out of it." He groaned out a laugh, as if at some inside joke only he understood. "That's what she said. That's what that bitch, Azazel, said!" Bloody spittle flew from his mouth.

Across the threshold, an elf dismounted the horse-like creature.

He was old and grey-haired, clad in armor that outshone the half dozen soldiers flanking him on both sides. This was the one Breanne had seen riding toward the portal when she first climbed the stairs. The old elf stepped forward, blocking Apep's path as he stared through the portal, searching a world that must have seemed as strange to him as his world did to Breanne.

Behind the elves, down a rolling hill some distance away, a killing field of nephilbock and dökkálfar collided in the gore of war.

Finally, the elf's eyes settled on Apep. "What have you done?" he asked.

Breanne could no longer see Apep's face, but he'd stopped flailing. The knife was still stuck fast in his back, but now he was composed once more and… laughing?

"I'm glad you still live, Father – glad you could… could be here to see your kingdom destroyed!"

"Venom through the lips of a snake. I am no father to the monster you have become."

"Oh, old man, I'm neither snake nor monster. But a god! I left here an outcast, but I have come home your better, everyone's better! I have come home…" Apep tried to laugh again, but it got lost in the gasps of blood-filled lungs as he sucked for breath, one hand still behind his back, but not flailing in panic. No. Breanne watched, her brows knitted, her eyes fixed on the elf's fingers as they stretched with methodical deliberateness, searching to find purchase on the handle. "I have come home to rule," he managed.

"Where is Syldan, Apep? I sent him to retrieve the God Stones this very moon ring! Where is he?"

Apep coughed again, straightened, and stepped forward, one step from entering the portal. Face to face with his father and now – within reach. "For Syldan, it was over eleven thousand years ago!" he spat. "And in that time, he imprisoned me! You ask what happened to your precious favorite son! I'll tell you what happened, Father. He's already met his fate for… for what he's done to me, and now you… you and the rest of Karelia will meet yours," he said, finishing in a wheezing gasp.

Tears filled the old elf's eyes, and Breanne could see his cheeks clench and tremble.

"That's right, Father. I ran him through myself!" Apep coughed and spit blood at his father's feet.

Above them, the sky filled with the screams of dragon roars as thousands descended on the portal. The old man looked to the sky and stepped back, his face stricken by shock. "What have you done?"

"Done? I have only just started!" Apep shouted. Behind his back, Sentheye spilled from the tips of his burnt fingers, making up the distance his hand couldn't.

Breanne stared at Apep's smoke-circled hand, knowing his fingers would never reach the dagger, but as Sentheye swirled around the handle, she knew they wouldn't need to. She also knew with hundred-percent certainty what came next. Apep was going to use the Sentheye to rip that dagger from his own back and then shove it through the right eye socket of the old elf's head.

It wasn't a guess. It was a fact. Breanne had just watched it all play out from the corner of her eye.

As her vision cleared, the old elf straightened himself and stepped forward again. "I've brought the entire might of Osonian here to ensure you never set foot on this world again!" He reached for his sword, preparing to draw it.

Breanne already knew he would be too slow – too late. Everyone around Breanne, whether confused, afraid, or just plain waiting to see how it played out, stood fixed. But Breanne wasn't the girl crippled into inaction by her own fear – not anymore. That Breanne had been freed when her mother forgave her. No… when she forgave herself.

Standing here now, she knew the only one who could change the future was the only who knew what the future held.

The blade slowly withdrew from Apep's back. Sentheye was already penetrating the wound, healing it. "I have something for you, Father."

No! Breanne ran forward and slapped Apep's smoky hand away from the dagger's hilt. Sentheye dissipated like a breath-blown smoke ring as she reached up, grabbing the handle with both hands. But Breanne didn't pull the blade out. Instead, she gripped it as tight as she could, shoved it back in, and wrenched, twisting the knife with all she had. Bone, cartilage, and only god knew what else crunched from deep inside Apep's chest. Breanne hoped like hell that horrible sound was Apep's blackened heart breaking apart.

Apep let out a feral cry, pulling away from her and toward the portal and the old elf. But Apep's hands were empty of evil intent.

In an instant, the elf king's sword was drawn. He stepped forward, meeting Apep's momentum with a driving thrust of his own sword. "I should have killed you instead of showing you the mercy of banishment, and for this, I am truly sorry. But my apology is not for you. It is for your brother. The true prince of Osonian. Die, knowing I will erase you from our history! Die, knowing you shall be forgotten!"

High above, the first dragon raced through the portal, followed by more and still more.

Apep dropped to his knees on the threshold of the world he would never have. A dream forever unrealized. This moment would be the closest he would ever get to going home. He looked up at his father, the king, his voice a confused whisper Breanne could barely hear. "But… I'm a god."

The king placed his foot against Apep's chest and ripped the blade free. "You are a nameless nothing," he said, drawing the sword back, swinging, and cleaving Apep's head from his shoulders.

Apep's lifeless body tipped backward onto the temple roof.

All sound faded to the background except Breanne's own breath, in and out and in. Her eyes followed Apep's head as it tumbled, raven hair tangling. It crossed a few feet of stone, wobbled, and went still. She blinked. *Oh dear god!* She slammed her eyes closed. Apep was dead! He was really dead! She opened them again and tore her gaze from the gore. Sound came rushing back to her.

The old elf's eyes lifted from his dead son and met Breanne's own.

She saw pain and sadness oceans deep, but she firmed her resolve, refusing to look away.

The old elf looked from her to the dagger protruding from Apep's back and pressed his lips into a tight line. "The seer told me of the death I would meet at the hands of my eldest son."

The soldiers flanking the king pulled at his attention, and with it, his gaze.

She followed his eyes toward the sky. Dragons poured through the portal by the hundreds and onto the killing field beyond. Behind the king, fire blossomed and dökkálfar screamed. Still, the king held up a hand. "Did you see this? Did you see my fate and change it?"

Breanne nodded.

Beyond the king, the dragons had joined the nephilbock and were attacking.

"My king, please! We must close the portal!" a soldier urged, not taking his eyes off the dragon-filled sky.

The king returned a slow nod of his own. It didn't feel like a thank-you, more like a strange realization shared between two strangers. The king's eyes broke from Breanne and with them, his attention.

The king's eyes widened as he looked to the altar where sat spinning the key to closing the door between two worlds.

42

I'm Sorry, James

Saturday, May 7 – God Stones Day 31
Rural Chiapas State, Mexico

Garrett saw Bre step back, Apep drop to his knees, the knife still in his back, and then… then his head. Apep's head was right there, only ten steps in front of him, his dead eyes looking right at him. He was dead. Apep was dead!

Bre! That… was… amazeballs! Lenny shouted.

Sis! You did it! Paul shouted.

Garrett ran toward her, everyone talking in his mind all at once.

But their words fell away to shared confusion when beneath them the temple began to shake, as if at any moment the entire structure might crumble right out from under them.

Garrett spun, looking over the temple roof to find a tree climbing the stone stairs of the pyramid and nearing the top. And it wasn't just any tree.

El Tule! Gabi shouted.

Everyone was moving now, shaken loose of the portal's trance and Apep's death. Too many voices now, all shouting and screaming, everyone running, El Tule drawing close, his canopy already reaching above the temple roof. What the hell was happening? Apep was dead! Why was everyone freaking out? What was the…

Oh… Shit.

At that moment, Garrett realized he was an idiot. The God Stones! The God Stones were up for grabs.

The old elf king looked to the Sound Eye and stepped through the portal and onto Earth. Behind him, one of the giant cyclops had turned from the killing field back to the portal and appeared in the center of the king's royal guard. This was one of the big, big giants, like the one they'd just killed at the top of the pyramid stairs.

With surprising speed, the giant slapped three of the king's men from their horse things with a swooping backhand, while in the same motion, it turned to its other side, kicking the closest horse thing closest to him. The force sent the horse thing, along with the rider, careening into the others. By the time the king could turn to see what was happening, all six of his men were dead, and the giant had its big eye fixed on the God Stones.

The giant stepped toward the portal, its tongue slipping out between its shark teeth, wetting its lips with greedy intention.

El Tule was on top of the pyramid now, his long branches reaching for the God Stones.

Standing on the valley floor behind El Tule, Pando stomped forward.

Guys! The God Stones! Garrett shouted.

Balls! Lenny shouted, running forward.

But they were all too slow – too slow to beat the one person who had not been mesmerized by Apep's death. One person who'd had his eye on the prize and was close enough to act. It wouldn't be Garrett, Lenny, or any of his sages that got to the stones. It wouldn't be El Tule or Pando, nor would it be a giant or an elven king.

One person would beat them all.

Oh, no! Please, no! Garrett said to no one.

Twenty yards away, Jack reached for the Sound Eye crown – upturned and spinning on edge like a flicked penny.

"Jack! Wait!" Garrett shouted. He threw his hands forward, and the Sentheye answered instantly, slowing time. But not for Jack. At the same moment, Cerberus had charged forward, intercepting time itself.

Cerberus roared in slow motion, his neck a lantern being slowly turned up until fire emerged from his three throats. He was moving too fast – he was too angry, too big! He was too damn powerful!

A scream escaped the deepest part of Garrett as he tried with all he had to hold the massive monster in the pocket of time.

Still, Cerberus roared, and the dragon's fire came.

Finely etched runes glowed red beneath the skin of Garrett's arms and chest as dragon flame poured over him in a harmless warmth. Harmless for Garrett, but despite how badly he wanted to, nor how pure his focus, he couldn't stop the volcanic eruption of hell fire from overwhelming him. He couldn't prevent the fury of Cerberus's incinerating breath from roiling past him, bright, thick, and terrible, and sadly, he couldn't shield the one behind him from an inevitable death.

As a gut-wrenching scream pierced Garrett's mind, he closed his eyes, not needing to look back to see he'd failed.

El Tule! No… Please! No! Gabi screamed.

Cerberus's flames dissipated as a new warmth consumed Garrett, hotter than dragon fire, because, as Garrett instinctively understood, this new fire wasn't coming from a dragon.

Garrett opened his eyes to find his shadow stretched out on the roof before him, cast by firelight and accompanied by the sounds of crackling wood and the smells of burning cypress. An abrupt and engulfing wave of rage struck Garrett. Pain and anger and hate that didn't belong to him.

Garrett's eyes flashed to Gabi, still perched atop the small grey dragon. The girl's eyes glistened wet and full of pain, but her face was all rage as she screamed aloud. Her small dragon leapt forward like a runner at the sound of the starting pistol. The little dragon took instant flight, crossed the short distance of twenty yards, and collided with Cerberus for the second time, striking the enormous dragon in the side like a blast from a shotgun.

The force of the impact drove both dragons across the temple roof and through the portal – into Karelia.

Gabi, wait! Breanne shouted, but it was too late.

Behind them, El Tule fell backward, his canopy meeting the stone stairs with an exploding crash, reverberating through the temple roof.

Garrett, what do we do? Pete shouted.

"Face me, Jack! I'm here!" Garrett shouted.

Jack glanced up, his hand still hovering above the altar – above the God Stones.

Beside Garrett stood Pete, Lenny, David, and Governess. Behind them, an angry Pando looked on, her own path suddenly obstructed by the massive trunk of a burning El Tule. The elven king froze, still too far to strike at Jack and wise enough not to try.

The cyclops too stood on the portal's edge, hesitating.

Jack seemed to take it all in as he set his jaw in fixed determination. "You're not taking this from me like you took Danny! No way! This world… this world is wasted! But in the next world… in the next, I'll be the one who everyone fears! You can stay here and waste with it, or you can follow me to the other side! Either way, Garrett! Either way, you'll get what's coming!" Jack shouted, lowering his hand.

"Jack, humans can't touch the God Stones! You touch it and it will kill you!" Garrett yelled.

Jack narrowed his ruby-red eyes, as if building his nerve.

"Jack, don't!" Garrett warned.

Jack sneered at Garrett, lowered his hand onto the Sound Eye – and grinned. The crown of stones slowed beneath Jack's palm, teetered, and tipped before wobbling flat. "The power of the God Stones is mine!"

The sky far above fractured like shattered glass as lightning crackled across the sky.

He should have died, shouldn't he? This wasn't right! This wasn't the way it was supposed to be! Unless… unless Jack wasn't human… not completely… not anymore.

"The God Stones return to the one who possesses them. By their power, I command they return to me!" Jack shouted. "Guess you got a choice to make, Garrett! What's it going to be?" Jack lifted his hand from the crown, smiled wickedly, and ran through the portal.

The crown, now sitting upright on the altar, shone strangely bright as it began to slowly turn.

As soon as Jack set foot on the other side, there was a loud boom. The portal trembled and started shrinking.

Garrett! What do we do!? Your brother isn't here yet, David said.

Garrett looked back toward Pando and then down at the pyramid below them. The Keepers weren't there, and unless they magically appeared in the next couple of seconds, they weren't going to make it in time.

Garrett! It's closing! Lenny shouted.

What the hell was happening? Had he failed the prophecy? But what could he have done different? Was it because he didn't stop Pando from pressuring Apep? Was it because he made the deal with her in the first place? Or was it because he didn't stop Jack? No. Go back further, Garrett, you idiot. It was because you didn't listen in the first place! Because you didn't lead the keepers here from Petersburg. He had ruined it all the way back in the beginning, hadn't he? What if this was all for nothing? What if he'd doomed this whole thing from the very start? What was going to happen to the Keepers now? What was going to happen when they got here to find Garrett and the others gone and the portal closed?

Garrett!? I can't stay here! Gabi! Breanne pleaded.

He looked up to find all eyes on him. The portal was a quarter of the size it had been and closing like a slowly deflating balloon. He didn't want this. He didn't want all their lives in his hands. James, his mom, Breanne's dad! They were all supposed to be here! Jesus, he didn't want to fail the Keepers, humanity, or his friends. *Stop that! Stop whining!* he told himself. *You're not the kid in the hallway who stayed quiet, hoping the problem would go away.* Jack was on the other side, and soon he would have all the power of the universe. He wished Coach was here. He would tell Garrett what he needed to do. But he already knew what he needed to do, didn't he? He needed to suck it up and get it done. Because prophecy or no prophecy, Garrett and his sages had a bigger mission now, and it was to keep his deal with the tree queen and save humanity.

The portal grew smaller and smaller.

We're short of time here, Garrett! What's the play? Paul asked, his voice urgent.

If he didn't go right now, they would miss the opening. His sages were about to let him miss the opening. That's how much they trusted him. That's how much they believed in him. Dammit, he had to believe in himself. *Christ, suck it up and get it done!*

Breanne took a step closer to the portal. *I'm sorry, Garrett. I have to!*

Wait! he managed, plunging a hand into his pocket. He pulled out James's Zippo lighter and closed his eyes. *James, if you can hear me, keep them safe! Keep them safe, and I will be back. I promise! I'm sorry, James!*

Stuffing the lighter back into his pocket, Garrett didn't wait for an answer. The portal was now merely a man-sized door. Garrett glanced back as the others crowded in.

Lenny bounced on his toes, smiled, and nodded.

Breanne bit her lower lip and adjusted the grip on her sword.

Paul looked too serious as he racked the slide on his nine mil and gave a sharp nod.

Pete and Governess shared determined looks, clasped hands, and nodded at each other and then to Garrett.

David's eyes bulged and he looked like he might shit himself, but even through his fear he managed a slight nod.

There were no more seconds left for waiting. He drew his sword and met his friends' eyes. Sucking in a tense breath, Garrett tightened his jaw, took Bre's hand, and nodded. *Let's go!*

As Garrett darted across the threshold and into another world, his mind filled with Pando's voice. *Do not forget your promise, Garrett Turek. Six months from this day. Fail me, and humanity dies!*

43

Show Us the Proof

On Earth – God Stones Day 30, before the portal opens
On Karelia – Moon Ring 1
The Creators' Mountain, Karelia

Turek looked up at Typhon. This was it. Everything hinged on his eldest brother. The first born of the Great Mother. Perhaps only seconds separated them in an eternity of existence, but Turek understood, as did they all. Typhon's opinion mattered. Typhon the eldest. Typhon the biggest. Everything he created was colossal because he was colossal. Being the biggest and the oldest left him somehow feeling that he held sway over the others. If it were just in Typhon's mind, that would be one thing, but he believed it so fully that the others did too.

Not Turek though. No. For he was at the other end of it. The youngest. The least wise. Turek the ignorant. Turek the baby. Turek, who had a temper tantrum and ran away. That's how they saw him. All because of seconds. Only a handful. Seconds gave Typhon big-brother wisdom and Turek little-brother naiveté.

Typhon barked out a laugh. "Proof? I should like to see this proof."

"I was hoping you would say that… big brother," Turek said,

breaking eye contact with Typhon to look at the others. "Typhon has spoken. Do you all agree? Do you all agree to see my proof?"

It was Ereshkigal who spoke first. "Yes, Brother Turek. If you have proof our Great Mother is here with us, guiding our creations and speaking in dreams… Oh yes, I should very much like to see this proof as well."

"Thank you, Eresh. And what say the rest of you? Do you agree to see my proof?" Turek asked.

All at once, the others agreed.

A weight lifted from Turek's chest, and he wanted to let out a breath. He wanted to grin wide. He wanted to dance. Why didn't you see *this* coming, oh wise Typhon? he thought, but he didn't say it aloud.

But then Typhon's eyes flashed. "Wait! I never said I agreed to anything! I said I should like to see your proof, but I—"

"And I will show you, brother!" Turek said, cutting him off. "But whether or not you claim to have agreed, our brethren did agree, and as such I have majority and will be given my due."

"Then enough talk. What is this proof?" Druesha asked.

"The portal will open at any moment… Yes, I feel it even now, do you all feel—"

"Then show us! We have to be there to stop these blasphemous abominations from crossing over," Durin said, hefting his war hammer and pointing it over the terrace.

"Easy, brother. You need not hurry. The proof I wish to show you requires we do nothing."

Ereshkigal clucked her tongue. "Nothing?"

"This will be my proof. We shall let this play out, and if I am right, our Great Mother will show us where this ends."

"And if you are wrong?" Rán asked.

Aurgelmir looked grave. "If he is wrong, the balance will be broken, Karelia could be destroyed, and all the work we have put into creating this – the most complex, largest, and indeed most magical place in the entire dimension – will be for naught."

"Aurgy, 'tis honest air you breathe, but I ask you, brother, have you no faith?"

"Faith!" Typhon said, a hundred mouths of teeth bared as if set to bite. "You preach faith to us!"

"Yes, faith. So what if I'm wrong? So what if it upsets the balance? We will do what we have done since the moment of our own creation! We will take up the task of creating!"

"*We* never stopped!" Ereshkigal shot back, steel in her voice.

Turek hardened his face with determination. "No. No, you haven't, but maybe you should. Maybe there is something else the Great Mother wants of us."

"Something else? What else? There is nothing else!" Typhon chuffed. "We were born of her to do her work! She clapped her hands when there was nothing, and then there was everything. Then there was us! Her clap echoes in my mind – in my sleep. Yet you accuse us! You seek to challenge our purpose as if you know the desires of the Great Mother better than us. Well, know this, youngest of seven, outcast by your own making, deserter of your duties – nothing can change the sound of an echo."

"I'm not asking to change anything, Typhon. I'm just asking for time and a little faith. Do you feel it? The portal is opening even as we speak. The time has come to choose. Keep your agreement with me or betray me once again."

"Betray you!" Typhon chortled.

"Enough," Aurgelmir said. "We've no more time for old wounds. Already the abominations are flooding through the gates and attacking the elves."

Ereshkigal frowned, her eyes going somewhere else. "Yes. There are so many. So powerful! If we deem it wise to put an end to this, we must act with haste."

Typhon's eyes rolled white. "Dragon hordes! So many and already so large!"

Durin stood. "We must go now before the damage is done and the balance is destroyed!"

All eyes fell to Turek, but he held their scrutiny with a patient stare, as if the inevitable destruction of Karelia weren't knocking at the door. The choice was before them.

"You truly believe the Great Mother spoke to you through your dream?" Ereshkigal asked, her voice no longer unbending. She was asking now – truly asking.

Turek hated the tears that sprang to his eyes. This human form was human in all it held. The others held their favorites as false phantasmagorias, but he and he alone took on the human form in all its flesh and bone, emotion, and frailty. He alone lived in his body fully. Finally, he swallowed dryly. This was it. This was the moment.

"You think me a fool? What, if not faith, would give me reason to want to let it play out? What if not for belief? For certainly, without faith, a fool I would be. I'm not asking to swarm this world with my favorites. I'm not even trying to stop the flooding of this world with yours. All I'm asking is to let my son and his companions cross through. I am asking for us, all of us, to stay here – not interfere and simply watch."

"Let this happen?" Aurgelmir asked, looking at the at the others as if expecting outrage. "The God Stones are coming back here in the form of the Sound Eye, and you want to let it happen? No one being should ever have so much power. Apep alone could destroy the planet. Worse, what if he turns the power of the Sound Eye upon us?"

Durin waved off the concern. "Turned on us? We would simply smite him!"

But they didn't know that to be true, did they? They didn't know if they could survive an attack from a mortal wielding the Sound Eye. They were immortal – but were they invincible? Could the Sound Eye threaten their own lives? The Sound Eye was, after all, their creation. Hence, it was the Great Mother's own essence. The truth was, Turek didn't have any of those answers, but he had faith – and faith alone was compelling him to take a chance. Aurgy was wise to worry, and if the others were as wise, they would latch on to this and would fear being destroyed by their own creations over all other fears. But were they as wise as Aurgelmir? Turek quickly got his answer.

"You are suggesting a truce and that none shall interfere?" Rán asked.

"We simply watch?" Druesha asked.

Typhon's heads nodded as he spoke. "I see little risk to my chosen. A truce then? With no interference unless it be the will of the collective." All his former bile was gone now, but Turek knew it had only been quenched by the sweet vision of dragon hordes flooding Karelia en masse. *Have your favorites, Typhon, just so long as you get them to all go along,* he thought.

The others nodded, albeit uneasily, agreeing to just go along too.

Whether ignorant or foolhardy brave, with the exception of Aurgy, the others saw no risk to themselves. Oh, but it terrified Turek, excited him, and he'd never felt so alive! He let out a long-held breath as a giant smile pushed crow's feet to the corners of his own wise eyes. "Yes, a truce!" he said, laughing unrestrainedly. "I've not come begging anything other than you all do nothing. Just come and sit with me, and together we will watch and talk. I want to hear about your creations, the good and the bad and all I've missed! That's all I ask. Oh, how I have missed you!"

Ereshkigal smiled, and it warmed him, though he wasn't sure her smile was for him or the fact that the God Stones were coming back and the one who held all the power was one of her chosen. "How do you propose we ensure everyone obeys the rules?" Ereshkigal asked.

"Return now to your true forms and join me in the center of the Great Hall. We will stay together in light," Turek said, spinning on a heel. By the time his back was to his brethren, he was no longer human. His body fell limp and lifeless to the floor. The form Turek held now was the form the Great Mother had created. The same general expression of shape he'd created his own favorites in. Two arms, two legs, hands and feet, a torso and head, but what swirled within his form was Sentheye pure, a color that existed nowhere else in the universe.

The hundred-headed dragon, Typhon, faded away, replaced by a form nearly identical to Turek's own. Rán followed next, shedding her mermaid form and returning to light as she floated down from the pool on her throne. And so went the rest. The giant nephilbock cyclops, Aurgelmir. The bejeweled tree, Druesha. The dwarf, Durin. The beautiful dökkálfar, Ereshkigal. They all shed the mirages of their favorites, though none left corpses behind as Turek had, as none lived as their favorite as he had.

With all the creators returned to the light of their true forms, they sat in a circle at the center of the Great Hall.

Turek spoke. "Reach, join me, and remain joined until we have seen this through to the end."

"Yes, but how will we know when we've reached the end, little brother?" Aurgelmir asked.

Turek smiled gravely. "When all the inhabitants of Karelia are destroyed, or our Great Mother's wrong has been made right."

44

Helpless

Saturday, May 7 – God Stones Day 31
Rural Chiapas State, Mexico

The forest was alive with the sound of swaying trees as they creaked along, dragging themselves toward the pyramid. As if autumn had come early, leaves fell all around them, liberated prematurely in the violent gesticulation of an animated forest.

With his lantern held out before him, James led Elaine and Dr. Moore between the moving trees as they worked to get to the head of the line. Just as James had hoped, the trees ignored them, but ignoring them meant the trees didn't stop for them either, making it vital the Keepers stay out of their path. Staying clear of the trees proper wasn't so hard, but their roots stretched out both above and beneath the ground, often tripping up an unsuspecting horse, spooking it and causing the rider to be thrown. Most of his Keepers with bikes ditched them, having given up trying to pedal through the ever-churning soil. A few pushed theirs along, hoping for a chance to ride again as they drew close, or maybe they were hoping to take their bicycles into the new world.

Not only were the trees seemingly no longer a threat, but James could no longer hear dragons roaring, nor could he see the soft glow of the green magic up ahead. There was something though, a glow of light between trees. Like sunlight cast through an open door – a really big door. The light had to be coming from the portal. Oh, how he wished he could see it clearly, but it was impossible with so many trees in the way, blotting out the sky. Since crossing the stream, James had only caught glimpses of the portal between the constantly shifting trees. Still, his eyes constantly searched ahead, begging for a closer glimpse of their new world.

James found Annie riding alongside Emily at the head of the group. Some time before, they'd descended gradually into a valley where the scorched ground had turned to muddy ash. The only signs a forest had once rooted here were charred husks of tree stumps.

With no forewarning, the trees stopped moving, and the forest went deathly still.

James held up a fist. "All stop."

"What is it? What's happening?" Dr. Moore asked.

James stared ahead; his eyes bunched up as he looked up toward the unnatural glow seeping through the forest canopy. The last of the leaves dislodged from their movement ticked softly against the forest floor. In the new silence, James heard his own heart thump against his chest, and a new urgency gripped him.

"Come on! We must be close. Let's move! We need to push forward!" James could feel it now. At any moment, the pyramid would show itself.

Exhausted as they were, the Keepers found voice to cheer. James knew the cheer wasn't for him. It was for Turek. It was for the portal and all the hope it held! They were going home! They were going to another world! James looked at Dr. Moore, then to Emily, Annie, and finally Elaine, a smile stretching across his face. Through their discomfort and fear, they all smiled back, and it was true, and it was good. They smiled through the pain of saddle sores, exhausted muscles, and blistered feet. They smiled through the pain of tragedies suffered, loved ones lost, and broken hearts. They were going home! They were finally going home.

A pressure built in James's head as a voice filled his mind. He held Elaine's gaze as the smile faded from his face.

James, if you can hear me, keep them safe! Keep them safe, and I will be back. I promise! I'm sorry, James!

James's brows bunched. *Garrett! Garrett, what? What's happening?* But the pressure in his head was gone, and so was Garrett. Garrett was gone.

"James? James, what is it?" Elaine asked.

James didn't answer. He was replaying it in his mind over and over, every word. *James, if you can hear me, keep them safe! Keep them safe, and I will be back. I promise! I'm sorry, James!*

"James! Speak to me!" Elaine begged.

Ahead, the otherworldly light filtering through the now-stagnant trees faded, withdrawing from their canopy like a quickly dissolving sunset.

"Come on!" James shouted, prodding Shadow forward with the tap of his heel.

James led the Keepers another mile through still trees before breaking from the tree line. "No! No, no, no! This can't be right!"

"What's happened! Where is the portal!" Elaine asked.

A hundred yards ahead sat a pyramid of magnificent proportions. Stone stairs littered with dragon bits, dead nephilbock, and smoldering tree branches climbed skyward toward a large temple. To the side of the stairs lay the husk of a massive smoldering tree trunk. Above the pyramid's temple, the night sky was clear and full of stars. But it was what he didn't see that wrenched his guts.

The portal was gone.

Elaine rode past James, shouting, "We can't see it because we're too close! Because we're right under it! We have to climb the stairs and we will see! You will all see!"

James's heart broke because Elaine hadn't heard what he had. *James, if you can hear me, keep them safe! Keep them safe, and I will be back. I promise! I'm sorry, James!* James's heart broke because he knew what they would find atop the temple. Still, he urged Shadow to the base of the pyramid, tears streaming down his face. They would all have to see for themselves.

When he reached the top of the temple, he found Elaine collapsed at the stone altar, sobbing. "I don't understand! What did we do wrong? How could we have missed it?!"

More Keepers were making their way up the stairs now. "Get up, Elaine. Don't let the others see you like this."

"See me like this! We failed, James! Garrett should have been here! He should have been leading us like the prophecy said, not traipsing off after some girl!"

"Some girl, Elaine?" Dr. Moore said from behind them. "That girl is my daughter!"

"I'm sorry, Charles! But none of it matters now!" Elaine said.

"You said it would be here!" Dr. Moore pointed accusingly at James. "You said to have faith, remember? You said we had nothing to worry about! It was all written!"

"It was until Garrett ran off—"

"Knock it off!" James shouted, turning his head toward the stairs.

"Who cares if they hear, James! They're going to know soon enough," Elaine said.

James held up his hand. "Do you hear that?" he asked, walking toward the edge of the stairs. "Someone is screaming."

Charles spun, following James toward the edge of the temple roof. They peered over at the pyramid stairs. "We're under attack!" James shouted, drawing his sword.

On the stairs below, four nephilbock were blocking the path of the Keepers trying to climb the stairs. Two more rounded the corner.

"Where are they coming from?" Charles shouted, running across the roof to peer over the other side. "Oh, dear god! James, there's more!"

James peered over the edge. All across the west stairs, several nephilbock were pushing themselves up into sitting positions and blinking. It was like they had been knocked out somehow but were waking up. "Shit!" James shouted, running down the stairs. He ran down the long corridor and out onto the landing toward the stairs. Below him, the nephilbock were killing… and, dear god, eating his people. James didn't slow as he reached the edge and leapt.

James propelled himself out over the stairs, raising his sword and driving it through the neck of the closest nephilbock.

The nephilbock fell forward, and as it did, James ripped his sword free, kicking backward off the giant and into a backflip, landing on the stone stairs in a crouch. Around him, Keepers screamed as the nephilbock fed.

James screamed in rage, meeting the next nephilbock head on, beheading the giant in three strikes. Gunfire broke out from below, and more of the nephilbock fell. Above him, Charles fired the forty-five into the face of a giant holding a dismembered arm. The giant fell, but another pressed forward.

James ran back up the stairs as Dr. Moore clambered to load a new magazine, dropping it to the stone stair. James knew he wasn't going to get to him in time.

From the opening to the temple, Elaine appeared, bow in hand.

The giant grabbed Dr. Moore, opening its mouth to bite as it swung the man around, lifting him off his feet.

James was fully behind the giant now, Dr. Moore obscured by the monster between them. But James heard the man scream and saw the great head of the giant as it lunged forward to bite.

James reached the last step, his eyes wide as he stared up at the back of the giant's head, too late to save Dr. Moore from its homicidal teeth.

When the arrow exited the giant's mouth through the back of its neck, dark blood splattered James's face, freezing him to the stone.

For the briefest of seconds, the giant went statue still.

James frowned, drawing back his sword, set to strike.

The beast's arms dropped, and its knees buckled, as if someone toggled the creature's power button. The dead nephilbock landed hard on its knees and tipped backward toward James.

James's breath hitched as he sucked in a gasp and dove out of the way.

The massive thing tumbled down the stairs, crashing through others not quick enough to avoid the falling giant.

The gunfire died down as the last nephilbock died some hundred feet below.

Dr. Moore stood, brushed himself off, and spun around to face Elaine.

Elaine lowered her bow, pressing her lips into a tight smile that said so much without saying anything. She was sorry for what she'd said earlier. She hoped he would forgive her. Then she found James next, and her eyes told him the same thing.

James nodded, his jaw tight as he turned away from her to the Keepers below. The pyramid stairs were strewn with the bodies of his people. The people he swore he would protect. How many had he lost? Below, some were moaning in physical pain, while others wailed the tragic cries of loss.

James clenched his jaw even tighter until he was biting down so hard his teeth threatened to crack. He made his way down the stairs, counting the bodies as he went. Midway down, he paused at the body of a woman lying face down. She was slender and young, with thick fire-red hair hiding the side of her face.

James fell to his knees, a moan that couldn't have come from him escaping his lips. As he blinked water-filled eyes, his heart turned to something horrible as it climbed into his throat and threatened to choke him to death. He swallowed down bile. "No," he choked. "No, dear god, no!" With a shaking hand, James bent and reached for the girl, hesitating before touching her hair. "Please!" he begged. "Please, no!"

James brushed the locks of red from Annie's face. She didn't look dead. She looked asleep, not dead. James shook her. "Annie! Annie please… please wake up! God please!" James croaked, collapsing to a seat as he pulled the dead girl onto his lap. Rocking back and forth, he pleaded, "Please! Turek! What have I done? Why? Why?!"

From farther below, James heard screams. "Annie! No! Oh god, no! Annie!" her mother shouted, running up the stairs, Annie's father in tow.

"Oh, please no!" her father begged, ripping her away from James. He began CPR, but James knew too much blood had pooled beneath. Annie was gone. She was gone, and she wasn't coming back.

Annie's mother slapped him hard in the face. "You did this! She wanted to be just like you! This is your fault, James!" An inhuman sob broke from the woman. "My baby is gone because of you!" She slapped him across the face again and again until her sob broke into a wretched moan full of anger and pain. She struck him again, harder now, as she cried Annie's name.

James took it. He didn't want it to stop. God, he wished it had been him! He would trade Annie's life for his own. *Take me, Turek! Why didn't you take me?*

Finally, more Keepers came, pulling Annie's mother away.

She was right. All was truly lost, and he was the cause. He'd failed. He'd failed Garrett, he'd failed his Keepers, and he'd failed this seventeen-year-old girl.

Below them, the forest stirred, opening to make way for something.

A woman in a flowing gown appeared from the trees and approached the stone stairs. She was a giant but clearly not a nephilbock. Fifteen feet tall with dark skin, she wore a flowing gown and had hair that looked like tiny twigs with small blooms of golden flowers. But it was her emerald eyes that froze James in place.

Around him, Keepers gasped and screamed as they clambered to get away from this new threat.

The giant woman ignored them all as she walked up the steps, until her jade eyes were even with James's own, which were swollen red and still spilling tears down his cheeks. Behind the woman, her long gown stretched all the way down to the dirt, where it writhed in the dirt, snakelike, as if alive. Her feet still several steps lower, she leaned forward, placing her face close to his. "Keeper James. The failure of the Keepers of the Light!" She drew back and laughed. "It seems you have arrived tardily for your departure." The giant looked around, appearing disgusted, before turning back to James. "Hmm. And, I am afraid, fatally."

James narrowed his eyes, but he didn't look away.

A buzz sliced the air, followed by a hollow *thunk*.

James recoiled, drawing himself back as he twisted to find Elaine standing atop the pyramid stairs, a sneer on her face, and an empty bow in hand. "Leave him alone!" she shouted.

The giant woman straightened and grew taller until, without

taking another step up, she reached Elaine. "Ah, the mother of Garrett Turek. Oh, how nice to make your acquaintance. I am Pando, the Trembling Giant."

James scrambled to his feet, climbing the temple stairs as fast as his burning thighs would carry him.

"Amusing," Pando said, pinching the arrow stuck fast in her overgrown forehead between thumb and forefinger, then plucking it as if pulling an annoying thorn.

James climbed past other Keepers who were caught on the stairs, afraid to go either up or down. Finally reaching the top, he stood panting next to Elaine.

Pando looked Elaine in the eyes. "Have you, inside your tiny human brain, somehow concluded yourself a threat to me?"

Elaine swallowed. "No," she said flatly.

"I can see the hate in your eyes, Elaine Turek. Let this arrow be a reminder to you. Let them all see." Pando reached out with a splayed hand. Her fingers twisted into five gnarled vines. They stretched and writhed toward a woman several steps down.

As the vines whipped wild and lashed out, Lady Shredder screamed, drawing both her bastard swords. As the vines closed in, Shredder swung and chopped at the vines, but they came to crazily and too fast.

"Stop! Stop this! We won't attack you!" James shouted.

But Pando didn't stop.

Ms. Shrader, now Lady Shredder, was snatched from the stairs, her petite frame dangling from the vines, both swords clanging to the ground. "We can no longer be killed by you or yours," Pando said, the arrow still pinched between her two fingers.

"No!" James screamed, finding Ms. Shrader's eyes. The eyes of the kind woman from Petersburg were round as her face. James held her gaze like a promise. A promise this would somehow be okay.

Pando shoved the arrow into the woman's head.

The pyramid stairs erupted in screams, but James couldn't hear any of them over his own.

Pando tossed the body onto the stone stairs as one might pitch litter into a ditch. Then the tree queen ascended the stairs once more, her body shrinking a little with every step. When she reached the top step, she was no taller than Elaine.

Pando smiled. "See what you made me do?"

Elaine's fists tightened until they shook.

"Ah, careful with your wrath, Elaine Turek." She looked at James and waved a finger. "You dallied, Commander. You took the long the way around, as you humans say. But really? Playing with iguanas and monkeys. It is no wonder you missed your ride."

"You tricked us. Delayed us! Half our people are dead, Pando! What happened to peace? What happened to the treaty you made with Garrett?"

Pando's playful smile fell away, replaced instead with a visage of hate to rival Elaine's own. "I agreed not to stop you and not to harm you on your way to the portal. I have done neither."

"You just killed one of my people yourself! And because of your trickery, half my people are dead!" James shouted.

"No. Your people are dead because of you. I killed one because you attacked me. That, Commander, is an eye for an eye. And really, did you think I would let the bloodline of Turek and mother of the chosen one off this planet? Why? Why, pray tell, would I do that? From what I can ascertain, my odds of acquiring a magical item that will allow my trees to remain unbound are as good as they could be. Acquiring the mother of Garrett Turek is a boon and one that I will gladly use to my advantage."

Dr. Moore climbed onto the landing and stood next to Elaine. "You have my son, Ed?"

"Ah, Dr. Charles Moore. I do have your son, and now I have you, Turek's mother, and the not-so-good commander here."

"What now, Pando?" James growled.

"What now? Yes, what? But before I tell you of your fate, I wish to share with you a story of a time long ago. Well, long for you, I suppose. Consider it context. Do you remember a particular campaign in Europe where you, James Paul, ordered your army to clear a forest? Do you remember? Do you remember the thousands of trees you personally ordered felled?"

James found himself not understanding and not getting a chance to answer if he did. Pando wasn't looking for an answer.

"Do you remember why, Commander? Because I remember it all. I remember all my trees pleading for help. Even across an ocean, through seaweed and sea moss, their screams carried to me. Cries that went unanswered because there was nothing – nothing – I could do to save them! Say it, James Paul! Say why you butchered my forest – my trees!"

James stared at the tree woman, saying nothing, though he did remember. He remembered having trees cleared for over five miles in every direction, and he remembered why.

A flash of grain radiated through Pando's brown skin. "Say it!" she shouted.

James gritted his teeth. "So we could see the enemy coming."

"So you could see!" Pando spat. "You killed thousands of my trees so you could see! Chopped them down, sharpened them into abatis and burnt what was left – so you could see! We were so insignificant that you would fell us for a better view. That is the way of the human. Take everything. Leave nothing! Do you know how many times I have heard the screams of my trees and been able to do nothing?" Pando leaned in close to James now, her eyes burning like green fire and her voice a guttural, hate-filled growl. "You want to know what now? I will tell you what now, James Paul. Now you are mine, my prisoners. Now you belong to me until the descendant brings me the God Stone he has promised."

James felt sick. "There are hundreds of us, Pando. We have no provisions! What would you have us do for food and shelter until he returns?"

"Oh, do not fear, Commander, you need not worry about your people. I only need the three of you."

From far below, the forest creaked and groaned as creatures emerged from the surrounding woods. Tall tree creatures, neither male nor female in appearance, but walking on two legs, swinging two arms. The creatures marched forward creakily, as if made of rusty metal, but their limbs were clad in bark. When they reached the stairs, their left arms turned into shields and their right to long swords. They began stomping up the pyramid's stairs.

Keepers caught on the stairs, too afraid to go forward or back, now climbed as if their lives depended on it.

"What is the meaning of this?" Elaine demanded.

"The meaning?" Pando asked contemptuously, her face again showing wood grain. "Have you not been listening? Your kind slay my trees by the millions, and you ask me of meaning?"

"But we didn't know better! And now we are working for peace!" James argued.

Pando clasped her hands behind her back and nodded thoughtfully. "That is not enough, Commander James Paul. Because Turek knew better. He knew better, and he has done nothing. Your race still owes me, Keeper. Your race owes me my pound of flesh!"

James's eyes went wide, his hand went to the hilt of his sword. "But you can't! You can't break the treaty! Even if Garrett somehow finds a way back, he won't help you stay unbound if you betray him!"

"I promised not to stop you from reaching the temple. I promised not to cause you harm on the way. Well, you are here! I have kept my word. The safety of your people expired when you arrived. I owe you nothing. I owe Garrett Turek nothing. If your little mage returns with what I seek, he will give it to me happily to save his mother, his brother, and the father and brother of the girl he loves." Pando's smile stretched wide, sinister and wrong.

Keepers ran past James, scrambling across the platform and into the temple's entrance.

Below, the forest of shape-shifting trees in humanoid form kept coming, pouring from the surrounding forest in a steady stream. The trees split into thirds, with a third coming up the stairs, another third wrapping left around the pyramid, and the final third wrapping right. Like an army of ants, they came and they came.

Pando's face went stone serious. "You asked what now, Commander. I will tell you." Pando leaned in so her lips were close to his ear, but she didn't whisper. Her voice came in a level, matter-of-fact tone that said this was simply the way it was and there was nothing he or anyone else could do to stop it. "You will listen as your people scream and die. You will learn what it is to be truly helpless."

"You can't," James begged.

"Oh, but I can. I am going to kill your people, James Paul. I am going to kill them all while you watch."

Epilogue: Jack

God Stones – Moon Ring 1
The killing field, outside of Osonian

Jack stepped through the portal, something crunching under his feet as he cut quickly to the left. Cold bit at his face and fingers. He looked down to find a thin layer of blueish-purple ice crystals coating the stone beneath his feet. After only a few steps, the flat stone ended, giving way to the world beyond.

The weird snow stuff seemed to be clinging to a field of grass, tall and thick. Most of the crystal-covered grass had been smashed flat from the hordes of nephilbock, but Jack had run off to the side, trying to get his bearings and figure where in the heck he was – where Cerb was.

Cerb! Can you hear me? he shouted telepathically. Before him, down a gentle slope, an absolute slaughter of war raged – weapons crashed, creatures screamed, and blood splashed.

Jack's first look behind him revealed the portal was shrinking fast. He also realized he hadn't entered this new world on top of a pyramid – he'd entered from within one… sorta. Four massive stone columns rose into the sky until finally tipping into one another, forming the skeleton of a pyramid. He figured he'd better not wander too far because he wasn't sure what would happen when the portal closed. A few days back, he'd overheard Apep telling Ogliosh the God Stones came back to the one who opened the portal once they stepped through. But Apep's dumb ass was dead, and so Jack figured if he touched them, well then… well, that might make them his, and it had worked. He was sure of it. He'd felt something. Yes, something, but he'd better stay close anyway.

Now that he was clear of the pyramid, he could see off to the side. In the distance, he saw mountains that appeared to float. And far to the right of the field, he saw a great wall, and on the other side, towering high above, was a tree. But not like any tree Jack had ever seen. This tree was impossibly big. From inside the tree, he saw light. He squinted, not believing his own eyes. It looked like there were chunks of land with entire cities hanging from its enormous branches. They reminded him of ornaments hanging from a Christmas tree. But not exactly. The tree wasn't like a pine tree. This tree had a canopy, and the cities hung underneath it. He couldn't see the trunk, or the ground below – not from here, not with the big-ass wall rising up and blocking his view.

I'm here, Jack! Cerberus shouted.

Where in the hell is here, Cerb?

Go left from the portal over the rise.

He could have stood another moment and taken in the mountains, the suns and the moons, the sky, and all this world held, but Jack knew better. He knew better than anyone, better than Garrett and his idiot friends. Better than Apep, that was for damn sure. Stand here to take it in and lose it all, or take a knife to the back. Jack stole another glance back through the quickly shrinking portal as he started up the hill to his left. Garrett and the others just stood there, unsure and looking dumb. Part of him struggled with letting Garrett live, but he was way too smart to let his revenge best him, not after what he'd seen happen to Apep. Besides, Jack was ninety-nine percent sure he'd have his shot. Why so sure? Easy. They weren't about to leave that little Mexican kid on this side with him. Too bad they'd be too late. That would make his revenge all the sweeter.

When Jack reached the top of the rise, he found Cerb and the small grey dragon circling each other.

That human is trying to mess with my head Jack! I can't… I can't keep her out!

The girl was sitting atop the small dragon. Her eyes narrowed at Cerb.

You killed El Tule! You killed him for nothing! I'm going to make your stupid mouths eat each other, Cerberus!

Get out of my head! Cerberus screamed.

Jack sneered, anger flushing his face. He'd had enough of this little shit. He raised his hands to disease her, but then dropped them. No, wait. Apep had told him his mind was too weak to take her on. Be smart, Jack. Be smart. If he attacked her with disease, she might turn it on him or force him to hurt Cerb.

The two dragons continued to circle as the girl strained to destroy Cerb's mind.

Jack! Jack! I need you! Cerb shouted.

There was another way, wasn't there? Jack nodded to himself and smiled. Oh, stupid little girl, you're going to pay in a big way, and all I got to do is tell the truth. *Little dragon! You hear me, little Zerri? Oh, I know you hear me! Do you know who really killed your mother? Because I do!*

Behind Jack, there was a sound different from the sound of battle. It was a change in the air, like someone closing a car door when you're inside. He heard the voices of Garrett and the others.

You killed my mother! the little dragon said.

Zerri, your mother made me what I am. She made me dragonkind! We did not kill our mother – our queen, Jack said, doing his best to look heartbroken.

Then who? Who killed my mother? the little grey dragon asked.

As the Sound Eye materialized atop Jack's head, a roguish smile stretched across his face. *Your mother's murderer… is sitting on your back.*

Glossary

Ancient Language of the Gods

Akoki Doe okimuezae oz ray ff doe! Doe oz rayray doeray muezae, flahak zae doe rahshi, doerayoki flah zaeokirah ray doe rahray ak doe shi!: Vines, I beckon you to my will! Fill your thorns with poison, grow long and sharp, pierce the flesh of any who try and pass!

drac: creatures who are half-human, half-dragon; called "lizard people" in ancient times.

Flahak doe okidoe! Eshoki oz oz akshi flah zae. Flahak raydoemue! Flahak ozzae!: Grow and climb! Weave your way toward the sky. Grow thick! Grow strong!

Flahak rahshi doe zae! Rahoki ozokioz ray eshray akray oz doe! Ak flah zaeokirah ray rayrayoki rahray oz shioki okidoe oz doe doeeshshiray flah akray raydoe ray!: Grow sharp and long! Ooze foulest of death from your tips! Find the flesh of those who would dare climb you and dispatch them from this world!

Oz ray ff doe! Rayflah oki, rahshiak! Rayflah oki, Ozflahoki!: Bend to my will! Obey me, shadows! Obey me, Sentheye!
Oz ray ff doe! Rayflah oki, rahshiak! Zae flah rayokioz doe okiozflah!: Bend to my will! Obey me, shadow! Seek the forest and destroy!

Ray ray Shiokidoe! Flahshi ff raydoe! Flah Ray Ozzaeoki shioki zaedoeoki. Flah oz zaeoz oki okieshoki!: Gods of Karelia! Hear my command! The God Stones are united. The way must be revealed!

Rayoz doe oki zae shi: Open and let us pass

Spanish

¡Acuéstate, por favor!: Lay back, please!

¡Ojos rojos! ¡Diablo rojo!: Red eyes! Red devil!

Por favor, déjame ayudarte: Please let me help

Juro por Dios: I swear to god

María Purísima: Holy Mary

Nahuatl

El Tule Ahuehuete: Old man of the water

Acknowledgments

Oh, dear wife. Once again you allowed me the time I need to create my crazy stories, and for this I thank you and appreciate you.

Mom – even today, many years after your untimely departure from this world, you still inspire me in my life and my work. I miss you.

I want to thank my editing team, specifically Kristen Tate at the Blue Garret. We did it again! And there is no one I would rather do this with. As always, you made editing fun and I learned even more through the process. Without you and your team there is no book… at least not a very good one.

A special thanks to the readers who took the time to not only read my work but also review it. Reviews are incredibly important to authors and I appreciate each and every one. It's like warm apple pie with just a little bit of ice cream on top… only better.

Finally, I want to thank my friends and colleagues who read the early drafts, for the conversations on the long Saturday trail runs and over lunch at work. Thank you for getting excited with me.

Otto Schafer, April 2022

About the Author

Otto Schafer grew up exploring the small historic town in central Illinois featured in the God Stones series. If you visit Petersburg, Illinois you may find locations familiar from the books. You may even discover, as Otto did, that history has left behind cleverly hidden traces of magic, whispered secrets, and untold treasures.

Currently, Otto is working on the fifth book in the God Stones series. He and his loving wife reside in a quiet log cabin tucked away in the woods. When Otto isn't writing you can often find him running the forest trails near his home, deep in a tangle of thoughts he'll need to rush home to put on paper.

Sign Up to Read More

Garrett and Breanne's adventure is well underway, but they've got a long journey ahead. If you want to see what happens next, please sign up here and I will be sure and keep you abreast on how the next book is progressing as well as other projects I am working on. Just click here to sign up or go to my website: www.ottoschafer.com.

If you enjoyed this book, I'd love to hear from you and hope that you could take some time to post a review on Amazon. Your feedback and support will help this author continue to create future works for your enjoyment. I want you, the reader, to know that your review is very important and so, if you'd like to leave a review, just go to my author page on Amazon. I wish you all the best and thanks again.

Check out my website and blog here: www.ottoschafer.com

Connect with me on social:

Instagram – www.instagram.com/ottoschaferwriter

Facebook – www.facebook.com/ottoschaferauthor

TikTok – www.tiktok.com/@ottoschaferauthor

www.ingramcontent.com/pod-product-compliance
Lightning Source LLC
Chambersburg PA
CBHW020605310726
48979CB00008B/1358/J

* 9 7 8 1 7 3 4 1 1 5 4 6 8 *